"Dark and clever fu... ...our blood, crawl under your skin, and haunt your dreams."
—Sherrilyn Kenyon, #1 *New York Times* bestselling author of the Dark-Hunter series

"The best debut I've read all year. *Nightshifted* is simply amazing!"
—Kat Richardson, bestselling author of the Greywalker series

"*Nightshifted*'s main character, Nurse Edie Spence, has a distinctive, appealing, and no-nonsense style that you won't quickly forget. Add to that a paranormal population that needs medical care for some very odd reasons, and you have a winner of a debut novel."
—Kate Elliott, author of the Cold Magic series

"Fresh, exciting, dark, and sexy, *Nightshifted* is excellent urban fantasy that grabs you by the throat and pulls you along for a wild ride. Cassie Alexander is an author to watch!"
—Diana Rowland, author of *Mark of the Demon*

"There's so much paranormal stuff out there that I often find myself longing for some true urban fantasy. *Night-shifted* is the one I was starving for. It's gritty and dark, its heroine jaded and tough, and both of them are studded with moments of humor and human frailty."
—Angie-ville.com

"Medical drama and vampire cold wars intersect in this solid urban fantasy debut. Alexander's zombies are particularly well designed, and the hospital environment adds an intriguing additional dimension. Edie's life is

"Dark and driven, full-moon insanity that will get into your blood, freeze-dry your skin, and haunt your dreams."

—Stephen King, *New York* bestselling author of the *Dark Tower* series

"The best debut I've read all year. *Abattoir* is simply amazing . . ."
—Kat Richardson, bestselling author of the *Greywalker* series

"An absorbing, often charming . . . . . . . . . *A. Science* has a narrative sophistication and an unobtrusive style that you won't usually find . . . fiction that a paranormal procedural . . . that adds punch . . . . . . to some . . . tired clichés . . . and you have a near classic debut novel."
—Kate Elliott, author of the *Cold Magic* series

"Fast, exciting, fun, a story so well-plotted it catches hold . . . from the first page that grabs you by the throat and pulls you along for a wild ride. *Classic* Alex Adams is a delight to watch."
—Diana Rowland, author of *Mark of the Demon*

"I like it very much and . . . . . . . . . . . . . I found myself . . . . lost in this . . . . . . . . . . . . . . . . . . . . it's the perfect mix . . . . . . it's . . . . . . to love, and character . . . I look forward to the second . . . . . . . . . with promises of funny, and horror, funny."
—Alyssa Day, the

"Richard Kadrey had vanished to add gory . . . . . . . . to this solid urban fantasy debut. Alexandra . . . Noir . . . . . are too tough . . . well-developed . . . and the hospital environment . . . adds an intriguing . . . . . . . dimension."

full of hard knocks . . . and her gradual development into a character who can allow others to care for her is satisfying."
—*Publishers Weekly*

"*Nightshifted* is like a dark and twisted version of *Grey's Anatomy* with vampires, zombies, and werewolves taking up residence in County Hospital's Y4 wing . . . The story moves at a similar pace to a hospital setting where there are small lulls in action with sudden, even frantic bursts of action. That sort of pacing made *Nightshifted* an exciting read as I was constantly on edge, waiting to see what was going to happen next."

—*All Things Urban Fantasy*

"I loved this book. What a breath of fresh air! A memorable scene with an STD-afflicted dragon (yup) had me on the edge of my seat, the budding romance with Ti (zombie firefighter!) is sweet and tender, and I just plain loved hanging out with Edie. *Nightshifted* is a very strong start to what promises to be a wonderful new series!"

—*My Bookish Ways*

# Also by Cassie Alexander

*Nightshifted*

*Moonshifted*

# SHAPESHIFTED

CASSIE ALEXANDER

St. Martin's Paperbacks

This is a work of fiction. All of the characters, organizations, and events portrayed in this novel are either products of the author's imagination or are used fictitiously.

SHAPESHIFTED

Copyright © 2013 by Erin Cashier.

For information address St. Martin's Press, 175 Fifth Avenue, New York, NY 10010.

ISBN: 978-0-312-55341-8

Printed in the United States of America

St. Martin's Paperbacks edition / June 2013

St. Martin's Paperbacks are published by St. Martin's Press, 175 Fifth Avenue, New York, NY 10010.

10  9  8  7  6  5  4  3  2  1

*To everyone who helped make the
Affordable Care Act a reality.*

# ACKNOWLEDGMENTS

I'd like to thank all the usual brilliant suspects—my editor, Rose Hilliard; my agent, Michelle Brower; my incomparable alpha reader, Daniel Starr; for the book you're holding in your hands. Aleta Rafton, my cover artist, and Laura Jorstad, my copy editor, and their counterparts in other countries translating me. My husband, Paul, for his perpetual support, and Rachel Swirsky and Barry Deutsch again, my late-night writing friends.

I'd also like to thank Jen Coreas and Kelsey Luoma for their Spanish help—although any mistakes that remain are definitely mine!

And my thanks to everyone who's read about Edie so far, especially to my fellow night-shift employees who e-mail me late at night. I hope I've made your shifts go by a little faster.

# CHAPTER ONE

I'd lost fifteen pounds in six months.

Being a nurse, I'd run through the worst-case scenarios first: cancer, diabetes, TB. When I'd checked my blood sugars and cleared myself of coughs and suspicious lumps, I was left with the much more likely diagnosis of depression. Which was why I was here, even though here was an awkward place to be.

"I can tell you anything, right?" I asked as I sat down across from the psychologist.

"Of course you can, Edie." She gave me a comforting smile, and adjusted her long skirt over her knees. "What do you feel like talking about today?"

I inhaled and exhaled a few times. There didn't seem to be any good way to launch into my story. *Hi, I used to work with vampire-exposed humans. Once upon a time, I dated a zombie and a werewolf. So, you know, the usual.* I snorted to myself, and admitted: "I'm not sure where to begin."

"Anything that feels comfortable for you is fine. Sometimes it takes a few sessions to rev up."

"Heh." Six months was a long time—I should be getting over things already. Things like being fired . . . well, shunned, which felt a lot like firing. Maybe I should have let them wipe my memory when I'd had the chance. Figured I would make the wrong decision. "I've just been through a rough time lately."

"How so?"

"I had this job that I really enjoyed. And I had to leave it. To go elsewhere. Ever since then, my life just feels . . . plain." I'd spent the end of winter up to now, July, working the full-time night shift in a sleep apnea clinic, monitoring patients while they slept. It was dull. My skin was paler than ever, and my social life was long gone.

There was a pause while she attempted to wait me out. When I didn't continue, she filled the gap. "Let's talk about what you used to enjoy. Maybe we can figure out what you enjoyed about it, and think how you can bring those qualities over into your current situation."

"Well. My co-workers were good people. And my job was exciting." I paused, chewing on the inside of my cheek.

"What was exciting about it?" she encouraged me.

I looked at her, at her nice office, nice couch, nice shelves with nice things. It must be *nice* to be a psychologist. I looked back at her. She smiled, and opportunity blossomed inside my heart. We, she and I, had patient–therapist privilege. As a registered nurse, I knew the boundaries. As long as I wasn't a danger to myself, or to anyone else, she'd have to keep what I told her quiet. It wasn't like she was going to believe me, besides.

I leaned forward, my elbows on my knees. "What do you think about vampires?"

The smile on her face tightened for just a fraction of a second. "It's more important that I know what you think, not the other way around. So, tell me, Edie. What do you think about vampires?"

"What if I told you they actually existed?" I said. Her smile appeared increasingly strained. "Here, I won't make it into a question. I'll tell you what I think. They do exist. There's quite a few of them out there, actually. They have human servants, some to do their dirty work, and others just to get blood from, like human cattle."

The words poured out. I knew I wasn't supposed to say anything, and I knew from looking at her that she didn't want to hear it—but it felt so good to finally talk about it. The dam had broken. I couldn't stop now.

"And there's werewolves too. There were two big packs, but now there's just one, and they race around on full moon nights in the parks outside of town, and then there's also zombies, and I dated this zombie for reals once—I knew he was a zombie going into things, and I still dated him. You know how I knew? He told me. I was his nurse one night. At the hospital where I used to work."

I sank back into the world's most comfortable couch and pressed a hand to my chest. "I cannot believe I just told you all that. That felt so good." Looking up, it was clear my confessions hadn't had the same effect on both of us.

She gave me a tight high smile. "Do the vampires tell you to hurt yourself?"

*Not lately!* was the wiseass answer that I wanted to give—but everything I told her was going into a file. If I was going to abuse her listening skills, the least I could do would be to take things seriously, and stay polite. "No. They don't. They're not in my head either."

She tried a different tack. "Do the vampires tell you to hurt other people?"

*Not anymore!* "No. They're not allowed to talk to me anymore."

I could see her measuring me, weighing my sanity. It was pull up now and laugh, like everything I'd said had been part of a prank or crazy joke, and wasn't I hilarious?

Or sink like a stone—which was the direction I was heading in. It could be said I lacked the gene for self-preservation that most people came installed with.

"There was this one vampire that I was really close to. She kicked me out to protect me, after I destroyed all the extra vampire blood in the county. I saved everyone . . . but I ruined everything too."

The therapist inhaled and exhaled deeply. "Edie, at twenty-five you're a little old to be having a schizophrenic break. But we need to do some reality testing here."

Reality testing. Like everything that'd happened to me this past winter wasn't real. I stared at the patterned carpeting beneath my feet. "That's the thing. It was all real. All of it. But I can't tell anyone about it. You know what'll happen to you when I leave this room? If you believe me?"

"No." Her face looked like she was sucking on an increasingly sour candy. "Why don't you tell me?"

"The Shadows will come out of the ground and erase your memory of everything I said. Maybe even of me." I nudged the carpet with my toe.

"Edie, how long have you been having these delusions?"

I didn't answer her.

"I know you're a nurse, and no one wants to put you on meds less than I do, but my co-worker next door—he's a psychiatrist. We can go together and check in with him. He could get you in as an emergency visit, and then you can go fill your prescription. Risperdal does wonders for people."

"Risperdal?" I startled and looked up. I was crazy . . . but I wasn't *crazy*. "No."

"Edie—" Her voice went low. I grabbed my bag and started walking toward the door. "You're not going to hurt yourself, are you?"

"Not if I don't stay here," I said as I shut the door behind me.

\* \* \*

In nursing school I'd done a psych rotation. The nurse I was following and I ate Risperdal-endorsed microwave popcorn out of a brand-new plastic bedpan. It was incongruous at the time, participating in even a small part of the pharmaceutical promotion machine, and eating out of bedpans like they were bowls for food. After that, I'd always made sure to bring my own Tupperware, and limited my brand endorsement to using whatever med-of-the-month-themed pens were lying around.

I didn't want to be on the med of the month, though. Even though I knew meds were helpful—vital, in some cases—for depression. It was just that . . . well, my problems felt situational. You would have thought that it was the stress of working with vampires and werecreatures that did me in, but no, my depression had come after that, with the onset of spring.

I drove home with the windows down, hoping that the fresh air flowing over my face would make me feel more alive. It did—until I thought about the fact that I had to work tonight. My stomach curdled, and I finally put two and two together. Working at the sleep clinic was killing my soul.

There're only so many nights you can watch someone sleep on a video monitor and stay sane. I had two years of intensive-care-level experience, and yet I'd spent the last six months watching people sleep, listening to them snore. It was like going from being a fighter pilot to a model-airplane captain—the joyless kind glued to the ceiling at a Toys "R" Us.

My phone rang. I saw the picture of my mom, and picked it up like you're not supposed to in the car. "Hey, Momma—"

"Hey, Edie! Can you come over?"

A lifetime of being my mother's child meant I could tell from her voice that something was wrong. "Um, sure. Why?"

She attempted to deflect me. "You're not on the phone in your car, are you?"

"No," I completely lied. "What's wrong?"

"Nothing—I just—" She hesitated. My mother was good at many things, but lying was not among them.

As I waited her out, my brain itemized every bad thing it could be. The list was shorter than it'd been six months ago, since the supernatural community was now shunning me—back then, if she'd called me up like this, I might have panicked and hung up to call the cops, for whatever good they could do.

Thank goodness she'd never known where I'd been working, who I'd been hanging out with, or what I'd been up to.

Now the first spot on my reasons-my-mother-could-call-me-in-the-middle-of-the-day list was occupied squarely by my brother. Jake had had a brief reprieve from his heroin addiction when I'd been working at the hospital. As long as I was employed there, the Shadows worked their weird magic to keep him immune to heroin's effects, no matter how much he shot up.

He'd been clean up until I'd gotten shunned, when his protection abruptly ended. And sure enough, Jake had been hooked again soon after. I tried not to think about him most times now. Thinking about him only made me sad.

I stopped at a red light as the awkward lull on the phone continued. "I just got some bad news is all," my mother finally went on. "You're pulled over, right?"

"Of course I am," I totally lied again. Whatever it was, it must be bad. I prepared myself for the worst. Jake, found facedown in some gutter. The image came too readily to mind, followed by sadness and shameful relief.

"Good. Well. I have cancer," she went on, matter-of-factly.

"What?" The car behind me started honking. I looked up. The light had changed. "What—where?"

"I was thinking maybe you could come over and join Peter and me for dinner? And then we could talk about things." The car behind me honked louder.

Talk about things. Sure. Wait until dinner? Oh, hell no. "I'm coming right over, Mom."

At least she didn't fight me. "Sounds good, honey. See you soon."

Throughout my entire life, my mother had been my rock. My childhood had been crazy, and while as a teen I'd resented that, now that I'd grown up I realized she was human, and she'd done the best she could. Knowing she was frail and sometimes fallible made me love her all the more. I couldn't lose her now. My heart was racing in my chest, and I felt like I'd been punched. I drove through the light and pulled to a stop on the next side street to gather myself.

I looked down, and my mom's picture was still up on my phone's screen. It was blurry—I smudged it with my thumb, then realized it wasn't sunscreen transferred from my face; I was crying. I inhaled deeply and swallowed it down. No. Not yet.

I needed to figure out how bad things were first. There were tons of different kinds of cancer. Thousands, really. There were all the chances in the world that this was an easy one, right? Tons of things that doctors could do. Chemo, radiation, or surgery. My mom was tough, she could get through it. She had a great support system: her church, her husband, me.

*But that might not be enough,* a small terrified voice whispered inside me. No one knows better than a nurse that sometimes, despite the best interventions and intentions, good people die.

I turned the screen off on my phone and carefully set it down on my passenger seat so I wouldn't be tempted to throw it out the window.

Up until recently, I'd known creatures that lived—barring holy water showers or tripping into wooden stakes—forever.

If I had to, I'd make them make my mom live forever too.

# CHAPTER TWO

I drove over to my mother's house on the side streets, avoiding the highway, where I'd only be tempted to speed dangerously and cut people off.

Still, each lurching stop seemed like a personal affront—as though everyone who was trying to get home during rush hour was intentionally blocking me. I rolled up my windows so people wouldn't hear me yelling obscenities.

By the time I got to my mother's house I was hoarse, but exhausted in a good way. I took a moment to compose myself in the car, picked up my phone and put it into my purse, and walked up to the front door.

Which was locked.

"For crying out loud—" I knocked on the door. They knew I was coming, Jesus—

Peter opened up the door. "Sorry. We called Jake too."

"Yeah, well, the bus system takes a lot longer to get here." If my brother even had bus fare. But I could understand Peter, my stepfather, wanting to assess Jake's condition before letting him in.

"Edie—dinner's not done yet," my mother apologized from the kitchen of her house. I dropped my purse on the floor, took off my shoes, and joined her.

"I'm not even hungry, Mom. Tell me about everything. Now."

"Well—" Her eyes darted to Peter first. It was so unlike anything I'd ever do, that look to him for permission, and it made me want to shake her. But that was who she was—she wasn't going to change now. "It's breast cancer. Stage four. I've known for a while now—"

"Are you kidding me?" I said, my voice rising in anger. Peter took a step forward, waving his hands at me to calm down. I'd seen her two or three times since Christmas—talked to her about once a week on the phone. She'd seemed down, but not sick. Or sick, but not cancer-sick. I'd assumed she was just depressed about Jake. "Why didn't you say anything?"

"You just seemed so depressed, Edie. I thought you were like me. Upset about Jake."

No, I'd written Jake off. It was an entirely different feeling than upset. "Mom—how bad is it?"

"Well, you know, the doctors have been trying very hard to get ahead of things. But it seems like they can't. We didn't find it early enough. The chemo's not working, it's on my liver too, and it's inoperable—I've got a couple of months, maybe a year, but—"

"You're wrong," I interrupted, and looked to Peter for confirmation of her words. He looked away. "Oh, no—no way. They're wrong." I ran back out to my purse, and returned with a notepad and a pen. "Okay, tell me what their names are. I'll ask around about them, find out if they're any good—which I can already tell you that they're not—and we'll find new doctors for you. Better ones. The best ones. Best ones ever."

"Edie—" My mother looked so harmless from behind the island of her kitchen, the light shining down from above, haloing what I now suspected was a very good wig. "It's not going to be like that."

"You're wrong." If there was a way I could go into her body myself and individually strangle cancer cells, I would do it.

"There's quality of life to be considered too, Edie—" she began.

"You're a nurse. You should know how that is," Peter said from the side. I turned on him. I didn't care what he had to say about things. For all I knew, it was sleeping with him that had given my mother cancer. Like HPV. Or all those winter trips to Florida he'd made them go on— maybe it'd gotten in through her skin.

I knew I was getting a little irrational, but it was better than the alternative.

"I want you to be on my side in this, Edie." She came out from behind the island, and I could see her fully now, the way her clothes didn't hang right. When had that happened? How had I been so blind? I was a nurse, for crying out loud. But she wasn't a patient. She was my mom.

"I want to be on the fighting side!" I pounded my chest with a fist.

"That was always your problem, dear." My mother smiled at me, sadly. "You never knew how not to fight."

I spent the rest of dinner determined to prove her wrong— as if somehow making it through until dessert without blowing up again would show her that she needed to change her damn mind. I ate with a vengeance, swallowing underchewed bites of food, feeling overcooked chicken scratch at my throat on its way down—all the while realizing that Mom wasn't eating as much as she ought to.

If it was any consolation—which it wasn't—at least I'd

be here when Jake got his effing act together enough to arrive. Maybe he would be on my side in this, and we could talk her out of giving up together. And maybe there were little green men living on the moon.

He'd probably hope she'd die, so he could get his inheritance, and then shoot it all up his arm. I stabbed another bite of chicken with a knife.

After dinner, we sat in the living room to talk. Turns out when cancer is the elephant in the room, there's not very much to talk about. Mom told me about her church's mission project, down in Mexico, and I listened without actually paying attention.

I didn't even feel like I could cry. Crying would be an admission that things were irredeemable. If I kept being strong, I could somehow force her to be strong too.

So at the end of the night, after Jake didn't show up, I took my dry-eyed leave.

"Really, Edie, we should hang out more," she said gently as I hugged her on her spot on the couch so she wouldn't have to stand. Trying not to notice how weak she was when she hugged me back.

"I'll come by tomorrow," I told her, as Peter escorted me to the door.

"She needs some rest, Edie," he said when we turned the corner to the front hall. I bent over to push on my shoes and grab my purse. "She's very tired these days."

He blocked the door with his hand, and looked pointedly at me. I knew what he was saying with his eyes.

I could think whatever I wanted to think, but he wanted me to keep it to myself.

Peter and I didn't always agree—but I had always thought I'd known, up until today at least, that he had my mother's best interests at heart. If he thought I was just going to take this lying down—

The shadows in my mother's face were mirrored in his too. I'd been busy pretending they weren't there so I could be mad at him. Now I wondered how many nights he'd spent up, kneeling beside her at the toilet, how many pillowcases he'd found beside him in the morning covered in her hair. I shoved my three-year-old self down into a box and found the grown-up nurse in me again. I stood a little straighter, and let her take charge.

"I'll visit every other day, so I don't wear her out. Let me know if you need to take a break too." I took a step forward, staring at him. "And this time, tell me if anything changes—or I'll never forgive myself, or you."

He grimly nodded, and then opened the door to let me out.

I drove off like a sane person. I didn't take out any mailboxes or lampposts on their street. But two streets over I almost hit a garbage can, so I pulled over again.

Now it was safe to cry. Huge sobs welled up, and I had no Kleenex in my car, so I was forced to daub at my teary-snotty face with the bottom of my shirt. I'm sure I looked charming, asphyxiating with sorrow and baring my pale stomach in turns. When I reached the end of my crying jag fifteen minutes later, exhausted, I knew I could safely drive.

A part of me that wasn't dissolving in pain started doing calculations. Things would be easier if I hadn't destroyed all the extra stored vampire blood in the county last December—the thing that had gotten me shun-fired. If I hadn't done that, and I were in this situation now, I could steal some vampire blood from work . . . or I could just stand outside the transfusion lab and waylay someone, karate chop them in the neck or some shit, and make them give me all their keys.

But I didn't know if the lab was still being used, since I'd ruined things so successfully seven months ago, over the holidays.

While I wasn't paying attention—or while that distant part of me was plotting—I took the exit to County Hospital again. I didn't fight myself, even as I pulled into the parking lot.

It took a while to find a spot, as seven o'clock was prime visiting time, which was good since it'd make it easier for me to get in. I knew from prior experience here that the intensive care units were on lockdown, and you'd need a badge to get inside.

But floor Y4, the one that cared for all the supernatural patients, had another barrier—and just one elevator. I wove back through the stairs and hallways until I found myself, feeling odd in civilian clothing, outside its orange doors.

First things first. I rummaged in my purse until I found my old badge. I'd kept carrying it, even though I didn't think it'd do me any good anymore. Chances were if I met an old "friend," I'd be dead, and not have time to wave an expired badge around. But old habits die hard.

I ran my badge in front of the elevator's lock. The lights didn't flash. I waved it, more slowly, again.

No such luck.

Second—I kicked the door. "Hey!"

My voice echoed in both directions down the hall. I didn't know what else was on this floor; I'd never looked around when I'd been working here. Now I wondered how far I was from a security guard. "Hey!" I shouted, with more force, and slammed my fist on the door.

Y4 didn't need guards, normally—because it had the Shadows. Creepy tar-like things that fed on the hospital's pain, they lived deep inside the ground underneath it.

They monitored guests at Y4 and kept an eye on the elevator door.

"Come on—" I looked up at the acoustic-tiled ceiling. There were plenty of cracks up there for them to hide in. "I know you can see me. And I know you know who I am."

The Shadows wiped the minds of anyone who saw anything they shouldn't. I'd had the option, when I'd left, to let them wipe me. "Please. It's important—" They were the ones that'd initially contacted me to work on Y4, in exchange for straightening out my brother. I knew they had similar bargains with the rest of Y4's crew.

Silence. Maybe they weren't even here anymore. Maybe they were being punished. They'd abandoned Y4 once before, to chase after an escaped prisoner of theirs. I'd destroyed the stored blood in their absence, rather than let it get stolen. There'd been a war on—it made sense at the time.

But if I'd known I'd be condemning my mom— I waved my badge across the reader again, angrily. "Let me in!"

"Why?" Darkness coalesced over my head like a tiny storm, bringing back bad memories.

"I want in. I want my old job back." I took a step back so they couldn't rain on me. I didn't want them to touch me—if they washed over me, they'd know my heart in an instant. And it was still in their power to erase parts of my mind.

"You have nothing we want anymore, human, and we're shunning you, besides." The darkness began to drift away, like blowing smoke.

"Come on—" I pleaded with the ceiling tiles. If I hadn't just come straight over after seeing my mom, I never would have said it, but— "Isn't there anything I can trade you?"

The remnants of the cloud stilled, looking like a thin membrane overhead. "You know who we were looking for?" The thing that embodied their presence thrummed in time with their speech, looking like gray lung tissue shuddering back and forth with unholy breath.

"No. Who?"

"Santa Muerte. She is still missing. Should you find her, then we may talk."

Done with talking, and done with me, the wisp of gray evaporated.

I didn't know how the hell I was going to be able to find something—or someone—that the Shadows couldn't even find. Them sending me off on some goose chase was not a feasible answer. Dammit to hell—

A crew of three people, none of whom I recognized as a former co-worker, were returning in scrubs from the taco truck. They were surprised to see me there, and one of them waved a badge in front of the door.

If I could just get downstairs—I might know someone who was on P.M. shift right now. If I explained what was going on with me, what had happened to my mom— everyone down there who was on staff was human. They all still had beating hearts.

As the elevator doors opened for them, I tried to step in alongside them. One of them blocked me. "I just want to go down—" I said by way of explanation, trying to sound innocent and kind.

The man who blocked me shook his head. "No you don't. Trust me."

"No, really, I do. You don't know me but—" I held the door open as his smile got tighter. "Please, it's just—"

"You're not authorized." The one nearest me gently

pried my hand off the door. I let him because I didn't know what else to do—fighting with them was not going to help my case.

Without my hand, the elevator doors closed, taking them away.

I looked up to the ceiling, where the Shadows had been. "This isn't the last of me," I told them.

But if I didn't think of things, fast, and make some miracles happen, it might be the end of my mom.

CHAPTER THREE

# CHAPTER THREE

What was I even talking about? Or thinking of?

I pulled my little Chevy into the parking lot of my new apartment "home." How could I explain things to her if my plan actually worked? *Yeah, Mom, just stay still while I inject you with this strange red stuff. And if you feel a little like eating raw meat afterward, I won't blame you.*

I'd met daytimers before, the servants of the vampires who had only gotten a drop of blood. They were mostly miserable people, scrabbling for their owner's favor to survive. I couldn't condemn my mother to that existence, even if I could get my hands on vampire blood.

This evening had been a fool's errand, just an excuse to keep the denial rolling, doing something, keeping up pretense, instead of giving up again.

I walked up the stairs to my place on the second floor and opened the door. Minnie, my Siamese, still loved me. She wound around my ankles as I stumbled to my couch.

Moving had been a top priority once I'd gotten a new job, so as to avoid any unwanted visitors in the middle of a full moon night. My new place was the upper right half of an older fourplex near the south side of the city.

The only decoration I had on the wall was a giant silver cross. The couch I sat on had most likely fallen off a werewolf's truck, and the mattress in my bedroom had been recently turned upside down to hide the stab wounds—stab wounds that had probably been meant for me, but I hadn't gotten to ask the stabber about them at the time. The world I'd been in had been a dangerous place. I'd barely gotten out alive. It was no place to send my mom, even if I could figure out how.

I pulled out my phone and called a few numbers, though—the denial train continued. I went through my address book and dialed old friends. Asher the shape-shifter had helped me out more than I deserved, and I called him first. I left a message on his voice mail. "Hey. I know I'm shunned. But I've got a problem—and, as usual, a stupid plan. Call me back."

Then I called Anna, the vampire who was partially alive, and the one who'd initiated my shunning for my own good. I got a high-pitched beeping, like a fax machine calling, from her old line. I dialed it again, hoping against hope that I'd misdialed and this time she'd pick up.

Nothing. Just more faxing beeps. I stared at the useless phone line. I guessed vampires didn't have to worry about early termination fees.

Lastly, I called Sike, the only daytimer I'd ever been fond of. I got the three rising beeps saying that her phone was disconnected—dead—which made sense because so was she.

I didn't know how to get ahold of anyone else without stalking Y4 directly, which I figured the Shadows would put an end to as soon as they realized I was camped out-side. And I didn't want to tempt them to wipe my memory.

I reluctantly pulled out my laptop. If the Shadows were going to offer me a needle-in-a-haystack's chance of help, well, I was stupid enough to try to take it. For now. But I knew that in my current state the Internet could be dangerous for me—I was only one bad search away from staying up all night going from WebMD to crank sites, and winding up at dawn trying to convince myself that my mom'd get better if only she drank her own pee.

I carefully typed in *Santa Muerte* and swore to myself I would have the strength to leave the rest of the Internet alone. I was surprised to be rewarded with a few hundred pages of hits.

Santa Muerte—the literal translation "Saint Death"—did exist. At least as much as the Easter Bunny and the Tooth Fairy. She looked a lot like the Virgin Mary, except for the fact that she was a skeleton inside of her voluminous robes, with a skull-head and bone-hands. Anyone could pray to her—and there were tons of people who felt neglected by the Catholic Church who did. She was the patron saint of the downtrodden. Prisoners, gunrunners, drug dealers, assassins, kidnappers—a saint for people who had to assume God was going to disapprove of their life choices, but who still felt a need to pray.

If disenfranchised people prayed to her for aid, she was my kind of deity. "If you're not too busy helping murderers, maybe you could get off your lazy Saint-ass and heal my mom," I told my computer screen while I clicked through to the next page.

While Santa Muerte was interesting conceptually, she didn't seem to be of any current help to me. I doubted the Shadows were chasing a nebulous concept. They'd been holding someone physically imprisoned who had then escaped, which implied an actual person, someone who probably liked the name. Being the Saint of Death sounded majestic and grim, no matter what language it was in.

Once I got away from abstractions, there were a thousand other things she could be. If she was even a she. I snorted. She could be anything. A person whom they'd trapped, an ancient vampire, or some unknown werecreature. A cryptid. I knew there were weird things in the world now, things I hadn't even imagined existing a year ago. Santa Muerte was just the final piece of strange straw on the were-camel's back.

I closed my laptop's lid and curled into a ball on my couch, and when Minnie came over to snuggle me, I didn't push her away. I must have fallen asleep there, because the next thing I knew my phone was ringing in my hand.

"Hello?" I mumbled. I hadn't looked at the incoming call on purpose. Then I could pretend it was someone who could help me, calling me back.

Instead I got the peeved voice of the receptionist at the sleep clinic that I'd left hanging for my night shift. "I don't suppose you're coming in to work tonight?"

"No," I told her, and hung up.

There was no way to get back to sleep after that. I couldn't believe that my mother had cancer. A couple of months. Less than a year. By this time next year, I'd be . . . without a mom.

It was too horrible to grasp. I tried to do things to distract myself, seeing as feeling bad for myself or her wasn't going to help. I read books without reading them, flipping pages at random. I tried to watch a comedy, but the whimsical acting felt like an insult to my current life.

As I wandered around my place, I wished I had someone to talk to about things. I didn't mean to be a loner, but that's just how it was. My zombie boyfriend had left town months ago, and I couldn't see the werewolf I'd briefly dated—one-night-standed—again, after the shun. Same thing for Asher. I was tempted to call him up again regardless, but leaving repeated messages on his voice mail would be too pathetic for words.

I just wasn't good at keeping track of people. The fact that no one ever seemed to keep track of me either was not lost on me. I'd never known how to relate to the real world, or myself; I'd just run from crisis to crisis trying to even things out. Fix my parents' divorce, fix my addict brother, fix my patients at work—with all the placating and atoning I was doing, in a previous life I must have been an asshole. I'd managed to maintain a vague sense of self via helping people, and in return it gave me a feeling that I had a semblance of control.

But losing my mom would send me reeling. I could feel it. Everything beginning to spin away.

I went back to my room and poured the Ambien out of my pill bottle. I popped two of them, drank a full glass of water, and surprise! It was eight A.M.

I woke up normal, only remembering that I'd been upset about something and what was it, when memories hit me in the stomach like a physical blow. I reached for the Ambien again and spilled them out to count them.

I could just stay in bed. They said that Elvis had a diet where he took sleeping pills so he wouldn't get up and eat. I wondered how long that'd work for me. Just because I'd lost fifteen pounds didn't mean I was thin—as long as I drank some water with my pills, I could probably keep going on stored fat for an easy week. I'd be like Sleeping Beauty, up until I got evicted.

If I remembered right, I'd sort of quit my job yesterday. It wasn't too late to call in and play the I-just-found-out-my-mom-got-cancer excuse. They were nice to me there, even if the work was slow.

I tried to imagine myself going in tonight, though. Sitting in the small video booth, listening to people snore, thinking about my mom, all alone.

That wasn't going to be healthy for me. Worse even than double-Ambiening it for a few day-nights.

I shoved myself to sitting and reached for my computer.

There were tons of nursing jobs on Craigslist, mostly wanting experience that I didn't have. I sent my résumé out anyway, scattershot, just to give me something to do. And then I cleaned my place—it was bigger than the old one, but funkier too, so my rent had stayed pretty much the same after I'd moved. The hardwood floors meant that Minnie's hair had collected in tufts in the corners of the living room. Suddenly hunting all of these down seemed monumentally important, and I set myself on the task industriously.

Anything to do something. Just not to think.

I was chasing down the last of these when my phone rang. I picked it up, dust covering my face. "Hello?"

It was one of the places I'd sent a résumé to earlier. The person on the far end of the line had a slight accent, and wondered if they could ask me some preliminary questions.

"Sure." I opened up my laptop and brought it back to life so that I could use it to cheat if need be. "Where are you guys located?" I asked, to buy myself some time.

She gave me an address, and I plunked it into my browser first off.

"Yes—two years of prior hospital experience. No, I don't speak Spanish." Some things weren't worth lying about when they could be easily disproved. My browser hopped into map mode and pulled up the street view of the Divisadero clinic. I saw it had a huge Santa Muerte mural painted in front of three elaborate crosses on its wall and a dramatically shadowed numeral seventeen. The woman on the phone began making polite excuses to get off the line with me.

"No, wait, please. I'm very interested in working there. Public health has always been a passion of mine." Completely not borne out by my résumé or working experience, but hey. I shrank the map program and saw just how much farther south Divisadero was, and made an assumption about how much of a pay cut it would be. There couldn't be that many other qualified nurses applying. I zoomed back in quickly. The mural on its side was huge, and her outstretched skeleton hand seemed to be beckoning me. "I can even interview today." I crossed fingers on both my hands. *Please, this time, just let me get what I want.*

She inhaled and exhaled loudly, and gave me a time two hours from now.

"Thank you—public transportation? I have a car—if you say so. Okay. See you then."

I hung up the phone with her and paused to really think. Despite the fact that I'd slept normal hours last night, I wasn't used to being up during the day. I was covered in dust and cat hair—and I'd just volunteered to be at an interview in two hours. But it was an idea. The mural seemed more stagnant than it had barely a minute ago; now that I wasn't deluding myself, her outstretched hand was more pointing up the street than calling out to me. But still. Nothing said I actually had to take the job. I might as well see, right? And two hours was long enough for a shower and coffee.

After my shower I blow-dried my hair and got dressed in a just-past-the-knee skirt and a blousy summer-weather-appropriate top, hoping it would say *interview* but not *mug me*, and walked to the train station in the pre-noon sun. Today would be as hot and humid as every other day this summer had been, the sun breathing over Port Cavell's shoulder like a stalker.

While I felt confident that no one actually wanted to steal a Chevy from last century, the Divisadero clinic was more than a little into what I'd been trained to think of as the bad side of town. No wonder she'd suggested I take public transportation.

The fourth leg of the train ride was the longest. As the train snaked aboveground to where the fifth and sixth stations were, the entire population of the train rotated through the car, everyone but me. When we reached the sixth station, I got out alone.

This was an open station, and just below it in the shelter the train platform provided was an open-air market of sorts. There were stands with fruit piled up, and ropes strung from side to side of the bottom of the pavilion, knotted off and lined with shirts. There was a cart with a grill and something good-smelling cooking on it. I took the next few steps down.

The platform above provided some shade, and maybe the trains created a passing breeze. There were women pulling small children behind them. Smoke from the grill caught a crosswind and made me cough nervously. Everyone around me was speaking Spanish.

People were looking at me, registering that I was there, that they didn't know me, and then looking away. I didn't feel I was in danger, but I did feel like an outsider. I got my bearings while trying not to turn my back completely on anyone. I'd been too paranoid for too long to let my guard down now. According to the map in my head, the clinic was two blocks up. I set off down the sidewalk while listening for footsteps behind me.

The road was lined by the walls of run-down businesses, a few painted fresh white over graffiti. Others were turquoise and pale pink. There were some cars parked outside, though none that would have shamed my Chevy. The road itself could only questionably be called such, full of potholes and patches of gravel. The sidewalk wasn't much better.

I looked back where I'd come from. Who knew there was this whole other world that I'd never been to before, or even seen? I thought back to the train. Had I taken that line before? Yes. It'd been a while, but I had—I'd just never gotten off at this one stop. It was like Europe—you were sure it was there, but you mostly only saw it on TV.

Kind of like cancer too.

A car pulled up beside me, and the music playing inside it turned off. I elbowed my purse a little closer to my chest.

"Need a ride, lady?" asked the man inside the car. I thought about ignoring him. I didn't want to be the type of person who thought poorly of anyone, but I also didn't want to wind up a sad morality tale that women told to other women on dark nights. Still, it was one P.M., and there wasn't anything in my purse worth stealing.

I leaned over. "I'm just walking to the clinic. It's up that way, right?"

"Yeah. Just up the street. Tell Hector I say hi." He nodded and turned his music back on, veering back into the center of the street and heading up to proposition another pedestrian.

Just a gypsy cab—a cabbie without a license. I relaxed a little but kept walking quickly. There were men standing on a corner, outside what looked like a liquor store, but that was farther down. I saw the clinic itself, its name at the top of one wall, the letters painted on where the original ones had fallen off. I realized I was facing the wall that had been on the street view—but that the mural was gone, replaced with off-white paint that hadn't been weather-beaten by an entire summer's sun. Santa Muerte was gone.

I wondered what that meant for me.

I stood for a moment, trying to compose myself. Just how much of a fool's errand this would be. An early-teens kid standing outside the clinic door walked over to me. He looked me up and down, eyes narrowed, judging me, and then he clucked, shaking his head. "You've got *susto* bad, lady. You won't find help for that in there. You need to come with me and see my grandfather."

My left eyebrow rose involuntarily. "I'm fine. Thanks."

"Are you sure? Only *farsantes* in there. My grandfather is a *curandero*—" He kept going, his patter confident. His pants were a little short, and the center of his shirt had the logo of a brand I didn't recognize.

"I'm sure. Thanks, though. I appreciate your concern." I squeezed around him and opened the door.

"Don't put that in your mouth, *mija!*" a mother told a child inside. An elderly woman coughed in a corner, running rosary beads through the fingers of one hand. A pregnant woman sat with one hand on her full belly, the other pushing a stroller back and forth with a sleeping occupant inside. And two men were having a discussion— one of them didn't have any teeth, and the other had a grotesquely swollen hand.

They may not have been my people, as I had come to understand it, when I was working with the vampires, daytimers, and sanctioned donors on Y4. But they were patients. And just like that, I knew where I was again. It was home.

Hard plastic chairs lined the waiting room walls; the bulk of the clinic itself was walled off by double-paned plastic. I presented myself at the nearest window, and a woman with short dark hair and copper skin told me to wait a minute for Dr. Tovar to see me.

# CHAPTER FOUR

"Miss Spence?" My name rang out from the side door. I stood and smiled, and went over to the woman in pink scrubs holding it open. She looked me up and down and snorted dismissively, but she still opened the door. "Dr. Tovar will see you now."

I followed her down a corridor with instructional posters in English and Spanish. I could count the Spanish words I knew on both hands. I knew *corazon* meant "heart," *sangre* meant "blood," *dolor* meant "pain." Other than that, I was pretty good at guessing, and quick to call the translation line at the hospital if need be. The woman I was following knocked on a closed door and, at an answer from the occupant, opened it for me.

Dr. Tovar held my résumé in his hands.

He was beautiful. Dark skin, black hair, a strong jaw, wide shoulders under a tweed coat—suddenly I wished I'd dressed up a little more for this, until I remembered he was a doctor.

Doctors were bad ideas, and off limits, for any nurse. You got into fights with doctors too often to think of them that way. At the hospital, it was like war. Nurses were on the front lines, and doctors were like distant generals who never believed you when you said you were running out of ammunition while they were yelling at you to march.

When he was done frowning at my résumé, he glanced up and looked surprised, for the briefest of moments, to see me. Regaining his composure, he gestured to the extra chair.

I sat down across from him. This room was a personal office with a simple desk and worn-down chairs, not a place for seeing patients. There were books in both Spanish and English behind him, thick medical dictionaries that looked out of date. If it were any smaller, my knees would have met his beneath the desk.

"And just why am I looking at your résumé?" He had a mild accent, the kind that said he'd grown up somewhere else but lived here a very long time.

"Lucky, I guess?" I tried halfheartedly to sound convincing.

He looked up at me with a grimace, and his eyes traveled up and down the length of me, much as the woman who'd walked me down the hall had. At a club or on a date, it might feel sexual, but here I felt like he was cataloging all my flaws. When he was done, he sighed. "You don't speak Spanish, do you?"

"I'm sorry, but no. I can play a mean game of charades, though."

He didn't crack a smile. "What do you know about serving diverse patient populations?"

I'd had to camouflage the second-to-last job on my résumé. No way to put *works well with vampires* down in the prior employment blank. "I worked at a county facility. We saw all kinds of patients there."

"Why did you leave?"

"I didn't like working night shift."

"And yet your next job was at a sleep clinic? Your . . . current job?" he said, after inspecting the dates more closely.

"I'd rather work days. And with patients that are awake."

He made a thoughtful noise. He wasn't that much older than me, early thirties, but he seemed older, like he was required to exude the aura of middle-aged wisdom here. I guessed as the doctor of a community health clinic, it was expected of him.

"So, um—what happened to the mural outside?" I asked, trying to make small talk.

He gave me a dark look over my résumé. "We painted over it. I don't want people praying to death on my watch." I swallowed and nodded as he went on, setting my résumé down. "Nothing personal, Miss Spence, but you're completely unqualified to work here. You don't speak Spanish, you've never done real clinic work with people who were awake, and you've never been out of a hospital setting. I don't think there's anything you can offer us. At all."

His tone wasn't rude; he was just being forthright about the facts. My instinct was to fight him—but with what? My mom was right. Just because fighting was the only tool in my tool belt didn't mean it was always the best one for the job. And why should I, now that the mural was gone? It'd been foolish to think I'd gotten some sort of a sign.

And being rejected here didn't mean I was condemned to work at the sleep center. I'd sent my résumé out to a ton of other places. At least now I knew I needed to come up with a better why-I-left-my-last-job lie.

I stood and reached out to shake his hand. "Ah, well. Sorry for wasting your time."

He took my hand and shook it. His hand was warm and strong, and he gave me a begrudging nod. "Not many people try to work down here."

"Is that supposed to make me feel better?"

"No." A quick smile crossed his face, and then he gestured to the door.

I saw myself out the short hallway. Strike one. But I probably had twenty-four hours' grace at the clinic—it'd take them that long to find my replacement, and I hadn't seen my current job up on Craigslist this morning. No way for them to know I was fishing for a new one. I should call them tonight, in case none of this went well. I tried to muster up some enthusiasm for going back there, and found myself hollow.

I let myself into the waiting area just as the far door to the outside world opened. Two men came in, one holding the other as he stumbled and bled. The mother sitting in the waiting room screamed, while her daughter stared innocently.

*"¡Médico!"* the standing one shouted, pulling the bleeding man another step into the room. The elderly woman with the rosary beads began to pray aloud.

I stepped through and let the door close quickly behind me to protect the staff. I could see into the plastic-windowed wall to my right where the receptionists had scurried off like rabbits. Hopefully to tell someone in charge there was a bleeding man out here.

"They tried to kidnap me!" The standing man pointed what I belatedly realized was a gun at me. Instantly I held up my hands. *"¿Quién eres?"* he asked me.

I didn't know what he was asking precisely, but the gun helped make it clear. *"La enfermera,"* I said, at least knowing the Spanish word for "nurse." I opened up my purse slowly and pulled a pair of gloves out. "Let me see your friend."

As an actual clinic employee had yet to be seen, the

gunman grunted assent. I moved closer to the bleeding man. He was shot in his upper arm. Behind us, with the men distracted and the gun pointed at me, the other patients filtered out, stepping over the wounded man's trail of blood.

"That's gotta hurt. Let's get you sitting down. How long ago was this? How much blood did he lose?" I kept asking questions, trying to distract them both from the mass exodus happening at the door. I inspected the rest of him visually and with both gloved hands—he'd slimed blood all over himself in getting dragged here. There could be a second, worse gunshot wound hidden somewhere else on him, easy. When I didn't find anything else, I tested a finger near his wound, and he yelped.

"Pray for me, Grandmother," he begged the elderly woman sitting behind us, the only waiting room occupant left inside.

The grandmother snorted, loudly. "I would sooner die than pray for you!"

I heard the back room door slam open behind me. "Goddammit, I told you all to call ahead. You all have our number." Dr. Tovar was at my side. He looked at me. "You go home. Now."

This wasn't my fight, my place, or my people. But I was here, and my hands were covered in an injured man's blood.

"I mean it! Go home!" Dr. Tovar yelled at me.

"I'm not some dog you can shoo away!" I yelled back. He closed his mouth and glared, but then he turned to our patient rather than continuing our fight.

The door to the outside world opened up again. I turned around to see. Two men stood in the doorway, sunlight pouring through from behind, casting them in deep shadow. They both held up guns. The man holding his friend dropped him to hold his gun up too.

"Not in here!" Dr. Tovar yelled. The standoff continued over our heads. I looked back at the floor, not wanting to gawk at the men holding guns. "We're off limits!" Dr. Tovar yelled again.

None of the men moved.

I closed my eyes and winced, waiting to hear a round, not knowing who or what it'd strike. The grandmother prayed louder, *"Santa Muerte, escucha la or ación de su hijo pobre."*

I opened my eyes in surprise and turned to look at her. The gunmen were closer now. I could make out their faces and see the beginnings of strange tattoos high on their necks.

"I said my clinic is off limits!" Tovar yelled.

"Your clinic, and your people. For now," the nearer of the gunmen said. "But Maldonado has unfinished business with him." He twitched his gun at the man bleeding on the floor.

I instinctively leaned in over the bleeding man to protect him—and found Dr. Tovar was already there. Our shoulders touched. If they were going to shoot the man, they'd have to be content with a leg shot—or shooting through one of us. The tweed of his coat rasped against my upper arm where my sleeve ended.

"The seventeenth is coming, Doctor. Did you tithe yet?" the gunman asked of Dr. Tovar, jerking his chin up slightly.

"You can't have him," Dr. Tovar stated again.

"That's not an answer."

"Your answer is tell Maldonado to go fuck himself," Dr. Tovar said, his voice frighteningly calm.

The first gunman started forward, and the second

swatted out a hand to hold him back. Their faces were as cold-blooded as any vampire as they contemplated shooting Dr. Tovar and me.

The second one released the first. "Come on. He'll come out eventually," he said.

"We'll shoot you in the street, like a dog," the first threatened, staring at Dr. Tovar, lowering his gun.

And then they retreated, the door closing behind them, taking the sunlight and shadows with them.

The grandmother went on a tirade. *"¡Rezo y rezo y sigue siendo lo mismo!"* Then she stood up and left the waiting room, clearly disgusted with all of us equally.

I wanted to run after her and ask her who she was talking about, how she knew anything about Santa Muerte—I didn't get to ask many questions back in December when I was being shunned out the door.

But I was helping Dr. Tovar. I looked over to him, and he nodded at me. "Let's get him up and into the back room."

We did so, with the help of the man he'd come in with. One of the receptionists held open the door.

# CHAPTER FIVE

I tried to make eye contact with Dr. Tovar while we were involved in the process of cleaning up our patient.

When the man's shirt came off, I could see that he was covered in grim prison-looking tattoos. He talked angrily to his friend, but mostly in Spanish, so it wasn't illuminating. And Tovar ignored any pointed looks I gave him.

What I was trying to say with my eyeballs was, *Are you going to report this?* I knew we were supposed to report all gunshot wounds that anyone received to the police. And keep the bullets too. But now wasn't the time, not in front of the patient, and this was not my place.

"Why don't you go to my office, Miss Spence," Tovar said when he was almost done. I inhaled to argue, and then remembered the wisdom of not doing so for once. I took off my gloves, washed my hands, and went outside.

I figured it was going to take him a while to clean up, and I owed it to myself to see if the elderly woman had come back. I went up to the hallway door, looked around at the waiting room through the thin pane of wire glass, and didn't see anyone out there but a janitor scrubbing at the bloodstain on the floor.

I tried the handle and stepped out, keeping the door open with my foot. I looked around the room until I was confident I'd seen it all and gave the janitor a shy wave for interrupting him.

The old woman was gone. Damn.

Was Santa Muerte an actual saint to that woman? Or a personal friend? A concept—or an entity? I wished she was still around to ask, or that the Shadows' request had been more specific. They could have at least given me a Wheel of Fortune clue. If finding Santa Muerte—the person, place, or thing—would make them heal my mom, then somehow I would. I quietly walked back down the hall to Dr. Tovar's office to wait for him.

It took an hour for him to finish up, which I used to confirm that the medical books on the shelves were actually old. Not spirits and humours old, but close. I hoped they weren't using them for modern medical advice.

I touched the skin on my shoulder where his coat had scratched against it. Hard to believe that the man who'd been dismissing me so analytically this morning was that passionate about saving his patients. And yet— There was a cough from the hallway outside that let me know I'd been caught snooping.

"Sorry. I'm naturally curious." I stepped back around the desk as Dr. Tovar came in. "What was all that about?" I asked, making guns with my thumbs and forefingers, and shooting them at the wall.

"Turf wars." He looked like he didn't know how to explain it to me. He was angry still, but holding it in. I could almost see it surge underneath his skin. If he'd been a were, I wouldn't have been surprised to see him change. He sat down, exterior calm, and I did the same. "It's an election year. The current mayor's cracking down on crime at the edges of our side of town. Less space, more pressure. It's like putting the lid on a boiling pot."

"Do people come here like that often?" I turned one of my imaginary handguns to shoot my own shoulder.

"Often enough."

"And you don't call for outside help?" Might as well be fearless about questions; I'd already been unhired for the day.

"There's a reason they don't call nine-one-one, you know." The anger in his face relaxed to make his dark eyes look weary instead.

"What if that'd been worse?"

"Then I'd call. We're a clinic, not an emergency department. I wouldn't let him die over his or my pride." He shrugged. "Do you bring gloves everywhere you go?"

I nodded. "Hand sanitizer too. The world's a disgusting place."

He agreed with a snort, and appeared to be studying the top of his desk, thinking hard.

"Who is Maldonado?" I asked him.

The question made him glance up at me. He began shaking his head, frowning deeply. "You saw things you shouldn't have today, Nurse Spence."

While I might not have heard that particular line before, boy, had I heard others just like it. I held my breath.

"I suppose you think I have to hire you now. Or you'll tell people how I run things down here."

While I might not have been above blackmail for a good reason, getting a job was not one of them. "No. I don't think that at all. I'm not judging you in the least." His eyes narrowed as I went on. "I've had to work at some . . . interesting places before. Ones I couldn't really put on my résumé."

His eyebrows rose. "Being a witness to attempted murder doesn't put you off?"

If he only *knew* the kinds of secrets I'd had to keep. "Without going into details—trust me. I've seen worse."

He tilted his head forward. "That's funny. You look like the kind of person who goes talking to police."

"I'm confused—do you want me to be incredibly honorable and report you to authorities and not get hired? Or do you want me to be useful, morally hazy, and gainfully employed? Because personally I like the one where I wind up with a job."

At my protest, his face had the smallest flicker of a smile. "You do seem to understand some of our natural expediencies, and actually have basic nursing skills. Those things might be more valuable to me than you speaking Spanish, the way our summer's going so far."

I squinted at him. "Are you offering to hire me?"

"Yes. If you want it, against my better judgment, the job's yours."

This was what I'd wanted, right? But now—like so many other times before—it wasn't how I'd wanted it. Still, this place was my only link to Santa Muerte, whoever or whatever she may be.

"Oh, so now you're wise enough to be scared?" he asked, sounding smug.

How could I even answer that? "I want the job."

"See you tomorrow then. At eight A.M.," he said, and pointed toward the door.

I nodded. I was halfway down the hall when I realized he'd never given me an answer about Maldonado.

The waiting room was still empty when I reached it, although the janitor was done. Maybe that woman would be back tomorrow. She'd called out to Santa Muerte like she knew her personally—in prayer, no less. Rosary and all.

Praying while using a rosary smacked of comfortable familiarity. If even one person knew of a Santa Muerte, no matter who or what that was, there were bound to be others. I'd just have to find them.

The same early-teens kid from before blocked my path. "Oh, lady, you still need a *limpieza*. Bad. I have the *don,* I can tell."

"How can I need that if I don't even know what that is?" There was drying blood on the ground outside too, slightly darker than the rest of the surrounding stains on the cement. I wondered if the janitor had even tried to clean it up out here.

"My grandfather, Don Pedrito, he can heal you." He patted his chest with authority.

"Look." He was thin, rail-thin, with wrists that my hands could wrap around, the fingers meeting and then some. "I don't have any money. But tomorrow I'll be here. I'll bring you a sandwich."

He pulled his head back as though he'd been hit. "I don't need your charity!"

"And I don't need your limp-pizza. Whatever the hell that is." I stepped around the blood on the ground.

"You'll need it eventually. You have a curse on you. You'll see."

"Maybe tomorrow. But not tonight."

He heaved a sigh and glared at me. I shrugged and walked around him, and then walked the two blocks back to the train station in the daylight. I wasn't scared in the crowd anymore. I felt alive.

And when I got home I called up the sleep clinic to officially quit.

# CHAPTER SIX

I felt substantially less alive at six thirty the next morning. I'd gone to sleep easily enough, thanks again to Ambien. But six thirty was early enough to make me feel frail. I got out of bed like the floor might roll away from me, then stumbled up to make coffee, take a shower, and head out the door. I remembered to make a sandwich for myself before I left, and an extra sandwich for that kid too. I could eat it later if I didn't see him again.

I was tempted to call my mom from the train, to make plans to see her tonight, but I didn't know what her sleep schedule was like. I made a mental note to call her later.

The ride felt different today. The train shook back and forth on the rails, the early-morning light strobing through the windows, looking like the beginning of an old-time film reel. I reached the right station at seven forty-five A.M. and descended the stairs.

"This phone's mine, move your damn blanket over!" This morning I noticed a row of pay phones, long since missing their earpieces, and surely free of dimes. They now provided the backbone for a cardboard shelter where two homeless people were arguing over the edges of their blankets.

There were more people milling, getting on and off the

train. It was windy today, thank goodness, creating a rare breeze. It sent pieces of trash scudding around on the ground, weaving in between people's feet, looking like they too were queuing up for the train.

I moved to the periphery and struck out for Divisadero. I walked past shit by the side of the road that looked, to my clinical eye, too big to be from a dog. I'd have to be more careful where I stepped today.

I looked behind me and wondered if the man I'd helped treat was somewhere in the crowd—or if those who'd come to get him were. I didn't think I saw anyone I recognized, but I did walk a little faster at the thought.

The same bloodstain was there on the stoop when I reached the clinic doors. Blood's really hard to get out of a lot of things, especially cement. I was pondering this when I heard a small moan from behind me.

I jumped and turned around. It didn't sound human, really, more like wind stroking past the end of an open glass bottle. I heard it again. I stood there on the sidewalk for a second, overly conscious of my attempts to avoid stepping on the stain from yesterday's altercation, trying to locate the source of the sound with my ears.

"Hey, lady."

The kid from yesterday walked up the block. "Hey," I said back.

"You still need a *limpieza*. I can tell."

"Yeah, that's still not gonna happen. I gotta get to work. First day on the job." I pointed with my thumb to the clinic behind me. He wagged his head in exaggerated disapproval at my playing for the other team. "I'm Edie. Who're you?"

"I'm Olympio."

"What do you do all day, Olympio?" It was summer now, otherwise I'd have asked him why he wasn't off at school.

He grinned, showing uneven teeth. "Try to stop people from going in there. You all can't do half the things my grandfather can."

"How so?"

"You all take months to figure out what's wrong with someone, and then pills for the rest of their lives. My grandfather, he can heal you in just one day."

As a nurse, I'd heard all sorts of holistic health bullshit. I'd seen patients who'd been burned by cupping, who had made themselves ill by eating mislabeled "remedy" pills contaminated with lead. "Yeah?" I said, my eyebrows rising.

"Yeah. You got something wrong with you, lady. I can tell. I don't know what it is, but my grandfather is a great *curandero,* he'd know."

"Well." I was quiet for a moment, trying to hear the sound again. There was a storm drain across the street—it could be wind going by its entrance. "Well—" I regrouped. "I disagree. No, wait. Actually, I do agree—there's something wrong with me." I was sure I looked worried about my mom. I'd seen it in the mirror this morning, in the corners of my eyes. "But it's not the kind of thing that other people can fix."

"My grandfather—"

"I'm late for work. I brought an extra sandwich, though. For lunch. Maybe I could trade you for it, and you could tell me more. At noontime."

He leaned back, casual, ready for wherever business took him. "Hey, I'll be here trying to rescue people from you all, all day."

I grinned at him. "Make sure you stand in the shade. I don't want to know what your grandfather does for heatstroke."

* * *

I went into the clinic. There were already three people waiting. The receptionist saw me and buzzed me in. I went through the door, and as it thunked shut Dr. Tovar stuck his head out of his office. "It's eight oh five. Are you always late?"

"Sorry."

"I know you didn't get lost, seeing as you were here yesterday," he went on, and then pointed down the hall. "Catrina will get you set up. Your first patient's a *tecato*, needs a dressing changed on an abscess." Then he slammed the door.

Another woman came to my side and rescued me from the hallway, pulling me into a short corridor lined with rooms.

"I'm Catrina. And he's not always a hard-ass. He just thought you quit was all." She wore much the same outfit as she had yesterday, a pink scrub top seamed in purple, with matching scrub pants. She had light brown skin and short cropped black hair. Her face's angular cheekbones gave her back the traditional femininity that the short hair took away. "Is it true you don't speak Spanish?"

"What's a *tecato*?" I asked in response.

She stuck out her lower lip and blew air up her face. "You're going to be useless here."

"I really want this job," I protested.

"Why?" She leaned in toward me. "Are you some sort of stupid do-gooder?"

"No. Yes. But no." I took a step away. I couldn't really say, *Hey, I'm looking for Santa Muerte so I can trade her in to get a favor for my mom, and I heard someone talk about her in your waiting room yesterday.*

She crossed her arms and squinted at me. I saw a strange tattoo on the back of one of her fingers, but now was not the time to ask about it. "You have a record?"

"What?" She'd startled me.

"Shoplifting. DUI. Something dumb," she guessed.

"No!" I protested. "I just hated my last job is all. I need to work here."

"I don't want to waste time training you if you're just going to leave."

That was a reasonable enough fear. I crossed my heart in a Catholic fashion. "I promise not to."

"Oh, well, now that you've crossed, I believe you for sure," she said, her voice dripping with irony. "Do you even have scrubs to wear?"

"Yes—I just—" It hadn't occurred to me to bring them. I wasn't used to wearing scrubs during the day. "I should have brought some in. I'll bring them in tomorrow."

"If I did not see you jump in to help that gangbanger yesterday—" She ran a hand through her short hair. "*Tecatos* are heroin addicts," she said, and watched to see if I'd flinch. "You're not going to get grossed out, are you?"

"No. I'm good with addicts, Spanish or not." At least here I'd get paid to deal with them, unlike all the times I'd tried to help out my brother. "Who else will I see? What else will I do?"

"Didn't you ask any questions?"

"I was busy not getting hired—until I got hired." I gave her a weak smile and she sighed again.

"Well." Her hands found her hips. "You'll be double-checking the work the medical assistants do—there's three of us. I've been here the longest, and I'm also a phlebotomist," she said, like I ought not to forget those facts. "Other than that, there's wound care, people with diabetes, missing toes, some ostomy checks, paperwork, more paperwork, oh, and when shit hits the fan, you'll be doing triage."

"How often does that happen?"

"Every few months. When the gangs go to war. The

ambulances come for the dead guys, and we get the live ones."

"When's the last time that happened?"

Her lips thinned into a line. "We're due. It's the heat outside or something. Makes people angry and dumb."

"Does Dr. Tovar report things?" I didn't want to straight-out ask about the bullet wound from yesterday.

Her face said she got my meaning, even as she chose not to answer me. "Depends on the thing."

I gave a one-shoulder shrug. "Okay." I wasn't a stickler for the rules, especially when I didn't know what they were.

She handed over a set of keys. "Anything that can be stolen is locked down, and everything can be stolen." I could see her mentally dismissing any prior hospital experience I had. "I'm not sure where you worked at before. Most people are nice, and even the bad ones need our help. But there's a reason we're separated from the outside world with bulletproof plastic."

I was quiet while she gave me the rest of the tour. There were three small rooms that they saw people in, in addition to Dr. Tovar's private office, and a slightly larger office in the center of the building with an attached break room. Then she put me into the first patient room and said, "Wait here."

I waited. I tried keys until I found the one that unlocked the cabinets, so I could figure out what was where. I was shoving boxes of gauze aside when the doors opened behind me and a man walked in.

"He's got a fever. His name is Frank," Catrina called from the hall behind him.

I knew hazing when I saw it—or smelled it. I stepped aside, and gestured for him to sit down on the table. He was Caucasian, but he'd been in a lot of sun. He stumbled over to the table, leaned against it for a bit like he might puke or fall to the floor, before remembering to turn around and sit down.

He had an odor like stale beer and pee and whatever else you smell like when you never take a bath and you've worn the same pants for a month.

"Hello, Frank. How can I help you?"

He looked me up and down—even his gaze was disgusting. Between my nurse radar and a lifetime of being female, I knew then that the next phrase out of his mouth was going to be inappropriate.

"You can give me a kiss," he said slowly, leaning dangerously forward.

I put a hand on one shoulder to press him back upright. "No, thank you. Why're you here?"

He laboriously rolled up one sleeve, revealing the scars of living down here. Divots of healed ulcers from skin popping, and some straight cuts over his wrists, maybe self-inflicted when he was sober. The price of hard living and infrequent access to medical or mental health care.

Not finding what he wanted on that arm, he rolled up the sleeve of the other, and I saw it. A wound dressing that was almost as grimy as he was, right in the bend of his arm. He'd punctured himself either with a dirty needle or into an unclean site, and pushed germs from the outside world inside his flesh where they could grow.

I knew from my own brother that there weren't any safe needle exchange sites in this town. I pulled on an extra set of gloves.

Unfortunately, looking at his wound required being in breathing range of him. I tugged at the tape, which had fused with his arm hair. He grunted in pain until I managed to rip it loose. When I did, the packing at the center of the abscess popped out. It smelled worse than he did, and I was surprised there weren't maggots inside waving hi.

"You wanted this changed?" I asked him. His whole arm was red and swollen, and I didn't need a thermometer—I could feel his fever through my gloves. He seemed stuporific. Was this his natural state? Pickled from alcohol? Or had the infection gone to his brain? It was hard to say when you didn't know someone's baseline. "Hang on."

I grabbed an entire box of alcohol wipes out of the cabinet, and started using them one by one to draw grime away from the wound, to find its margins. The surrounding area was puffy and tight, and the center gleamed with lymph and pus. Once I determined the edges of his infection—heated swollen skin down almost to his wrist and going up his upper arm, like the points of a flame—I made a face.

"You're going to need some antibiotics." From a hospital. I didn't envy whoever was going to have to start his IV. He muttered something; I didn't know if he was talking to himself or to me. "I'm gonna get the doctor, sir."

I took a step toward the door, then turned. "Hey," I said, and held up a hand to wave until his eyes tracked on me. He did live down here, after all. "Do you know anything about Santa Muerte?"

With his good hand, he tapped a cross over his chest. And then he passed out on me.

I stuck around to help watch him until the paramedics came. He woke up a few times and tried to get out of the room, until I redirected him. Luckily, he couldn't talk well enough to refuse medical care. Nothing was sadder than a patient who was lucid enough to say, "Leave me alone, the liquor store closes at nine." The paramedics navigated their gurney in through the narrow hall and out again like pros, lashing him down onto it with casual efficiency. Un-surprisingly, they already knew him by name.

Once they were done, Dr. Tovar came back from sign-ing papers and jerked his chin at me. "Cellulitis? Good catch."

Not really. Just looking at him, smelling him, you knew that he was going to have something. I'd bet money he was covered in MRSA. Good thing my immune system was already strong-like-bull from prior hospital time.

I couldn't not wonder how my brother was doing. If he even knew about Mom's cancer. If he even cared.

Frank had a mother too.

"You're not having second thoughts, are you?" Dr. Tovar asked, eyeing me. He seemed concerned.

I shook my head, and caught back up with reality. "No. Just not used to working days yet is all. But I will be, by the end of this week," I promised with a smile.

His gaze softened. Maybe he knew false bravado when he saw it. I bet he saw a lot of it down here. He exaggerat-edly looked at his watch. "Why don't you go to an early lunch then? There's a bench in the parking lot in the back. Or you can eat inside."

"Thanks."

He nodded at me as he closed his office door.

I got my lunch out of the small fridge in the break room. There was no one else taking a break yet. Dr. Tovar wan-dered by again, called by Catrina into another one of the smaller rooms. I found the bathroom, then took myself on a repeat tour. There was one door that Catrina hadn't opened. I tried the handle, and it gave. The men's bath-room perhaps? Dr. Tovar was the only man I'd seen so far here. I peeked inside and saw a storage room, with a sec-ond small fridge at the back of it.

Medical fridges were different from house fridges; they were all lockable and stainless steel. I felt the weight of the keys in my pocket and fished them out, looking for the shorter ones that would fit its smaller lock.

One clicked, and I opened the door.

There were three racks with tubes in them. I reached in and picked one up. The tube had a red top, which matched its contents. I tilted it back and forth. It looked like blood to me.

"What are you looking at?" Caught, I jumped, dropping the test tube to find Catrina standing behind me.

"Nothing," I said instinctively—even though I was. I regrouped and picked up the test tube on the ground. I held it out to her. "What are all of these for?" None of the tubes had a label.

"None of your business." She took the tube from my hand and wedged herself beside me to replace it inside. I shuffled back out of her way while she slammed the fridge's door and relocked it. Afterward she whirled on me. "I gave you the wrong set of keys." She snapped her fingers and held her hand out.

There was no good reason to collect or keep label-less blood. But I'd just gotten hired. I couldn't get fired before I managed to figure anything out. I frowned. Even if I gave her the keys back, I knew what I'd seen. Reluctantly, I dropped the key ring into her hand. "What's all that about?"

"None of your business is what," Catrina informed me, pocketing the keys, then glaring at me. "I don't know why he hired you. Don't be a brat."

I swallowed. There was no space in this small room for me to get away from her. "I'm just asking why. It's not like I'm going to tell anybody."

She squinted at me, and her lips puckered thoughtfully.

"I have you figured out now. You're here because you're a troublemaker."

Proving myself to people today was taking an exhausting turn. This wasn't an argument I could win—and if I was honest, she did have a point. "Obviously," I said, and made a show of looking at my watchless wrist. "But it looks like I'm a troublemaker still on lunch break," I said, and then I walked around her.

# CHAPTER SEVEN

I could only think of one reason why anyone would have unmarked labels of blood lying around—but I was biased, I had vampires on the brain. Hands clutched around my paper lunch bag, I went through the waiting room, heading outside. Maybe a walk would clear my mind.

Olympio stood there, leaning against the wall, hiding in a fractional amount of shade, still hoping to direct our clientele his grandfather's way. After the morning I'd had, I might just help him.

"Peanut butter and jelly?" I said, offering the extra sandwich I'd brought for him.

He made a face. "I don't need your sandwich, lady."

"Edie," I corrected him. I looked up and down the block. "How about a trade? A sandwich for a tour?"

"I don't know if that's a good idea," he said. He sounded a little unsure, but now he was looking at the sandwich.

"Just a block or two?" I held it out a little closer to him.

He shrugged. "Sure," he said, and grabbed the sandwich with practiced nonchalance from my hand.

We walked around the neighborhood. Brightly painted buildings fought with general decay. Signs were in Spanish first, and then English, if at all. Any storefront window had bars or chain link covering it, and the roads did not improve. I wondered if any public services got down here, excepting the clinic.

There were moments of hidden beauty. Old-school murals with block forms from the end of last century, and huge motifs, intentional rip-offs of traditional Mexican art. And graffiti, surprising in its vitality, bold streaks of color, with letters so distorted I could hardly read them. Olympio told me who worked where, short stories from his life. He began by not sharing too much, but when I started asking questions and seeming appreciative, he morphed into a tour guide. When we reached the end of the next block, he pulled up short.

"You see that?" He pointed at a mural with an elaborate triple cross. "That's where Three Crosses territory begins. That's how they mark their space."

I had seen others behind Santa Muerte on the clinic's wall online. "Like a warning sign?"

"Like we'd better turn back."

I stood on the street staring at the mural for a little longer. "Those were the guys from yesterday, right?"

"Yeah. The second ones."

"What are they fighting for?" I hadn't seen any gold mines along our way.

"Territory."

"Really? I heard them mention a tithe." I thought back to the moment. It was a little blurry, seeing as I'd been afraid I was going to get shot. "Yeah—they asked for a tithe, right before Dr. Tovar told them to fuck off."

Olympio bounced and laughed at this. "Ha!"

I furrowed my brow, trying to understand all the layers at play here. "But—I thought you didn't like him?"

"We have different business practices. But I never said I didn't *like* him," Olympio clarified.

"What's a gang need a tithe for, anyhow?"

"That's just the fancy term they're using for the bribes they're demanding. You give them money, they protect you from themselves, and then they get to build their fancy church to Santa Muerte. Like she needs a church, or even wants one." Olympio's bearing was one of extreme disgust.

I tried not to tense up or show any excitement. "Who is she?"

Olympio gave me an odd look. "She's one of us. She knows our hearts."

Person? Saint? Spare alien from *Star Trek*? Whatever. If she was what the Shadows were looking for, and I could trade her in to heal my mom, I needed to see. "Can you take me to her?"

Olympio's eyebrows rose, and he gave me a mystified look before shrugging one shoulder. "Sure."

Together we went down a side street, then came back on another block.

Was it really going to be this easy? No way. If it was, the Shadows would have done it themselves. But I couldn't help hoping as I followed him. I didn't know how I'd catch her, but I'd think of something. I'd flat-out lie. Anything to save my mom.

Olympio went into a wide alley. Partially hidden by a second-story overhang, one entire wall was covered with a bright mural. A woman stood in rings of primary colors, red, green, yellow on a wall of blue, like she was Venus stepping forward from the ocean inside a rainbow clamshell. She had purple robes down to the ground, which was painted with red roses the size of small cars. The only thing incongruent was that she had a skull for a face, and hands of bone. She held a globe in one hand as though she were weighing it.

There was writing over her head in thick red script, the same color as the roses. REINA DE LA NOCHE.

The rest of the blue wall around her image and the roses was covered in names. Names covering names, as though alternating groups were trying to claim her, and numerous solo names written in not by artists, but in pen and ink, or chipped into the stone of the wall.

Olympio stopped in front of the image, and as I realized what he meant, my stomach fell. "This is her, isn't it."

"Yeah. The Three Crosses act like they own her. This is the last of the murals that they haven't put their crosses on. And if they see you praying to one of the other ones, the ones that they control, they'll come by and try to collect one of their tithes."

"Tithe of what?"

"Whatever you've got on you. And if you fight them, they'll take you away and you're never seen again."

"Oh." I'd been a fool to think I could succeed where the Shadows had not. The Santa Muerte legend was just an excuse to shake people down.

He side-eyed me. "You're disappointed?"

"I sort of assumed she'd be a person."

Olympio laughed. "She's better than a person—she's a saint. She can see everything. She protects us. Life is hard down here. She understands that." He went up and put his hand on her dress. I could tell from the other stains on the paint that numerous other people had done that too.

"So—" I looked at all her imagery. "She's death?"

"She protects people who know they're going to die. Which is pretty much all of us. It happens faster down here than it does wherever you live. Faster to us than all the rich people on TV." He pointed at a particular scrawl. "That's my name. From the last time I prayed here. Not to be healed, of course. My grandfather can heal anything," he explained with pride. "But she can grant wishes, when she wants to."

"Huh," I grunted noncommittally.

He narrowed his eyes suspiciously at me. "Why're you looking for her, if you don't know who she is?"

"The old lady in the waiting room yesterday morning prayed to her when she saw the guns. I was just wondering," I said, and he made a face like he was disappointed in me. "She is beautiful, though," I added, because as artwork, she was.

He nodded in agreement, and I could tell I was slightly redeemed. "Well, now you know who she is. We should get back now. We're still at the edge of safe territory."

Olympio took us back down another street while I tried to think. I wondered what Reina de la Noche meant. I reached back in my mind for comparable Latin words. Reign, nocturnal—ruler of the night? An apt name for Santa Muerte, I guessed.

"How's your grandfather heal people?"

Olympio squinted at me. "Trade secrets."

"What—really?"

"Yeah. You don't have the *don*. You couldn't even do it if you tried."

"So why not explain it to me?"

He sighed exaggeratedly. "It would take up too much time."

"Can you do what he does—what he claims to do?" I corrected myself.

"Some of it." He picked up a rock in our path and chucked it across the street. "But I'll be the best in the world, eventually."

I looked around at our surroundings, all cement and hot sun. This was an unlikely place for anything to grow, much less a peerless folk healer. Olympio must have guessed what I was thinking. He puffed out his chest like a pigeon and glowered at me.

We were back at the clinic shortly. "So how far could we walk in this direction?" I asked, trying to rescue myself in his eyes.

He resumed his station outside the clinic door, like a dark cloud against its wall. It must be no fun working all day during the summer, all summer long.

"Only place you should be walking is back and forth from the train." He'd changed from a sensitive kid who liked attention to a proto-adult carrying world-weary exhaustion and heavy pride. I remembered being his age, sitting on the fence of puberty, not sure which way to jump, torn between desperately wanting people to like me and being angry all the time.

"Hey, don't shut me out like that," I complained.

"Why not? I hardly know you."

He had a point. I didn't know him either. But I knew his type. I shrugged one shoulder. "I just get the feeling, if we were someplace else we might be friends."

His eyes narrowed at me, the shy kid still coming through. "Yeah, well, I don't know how to get to that place from here."

Catrina leaned out of the clinic, interrupting us, and waved at him. "Olympio, I've got your grandfather's test strips."

Diabetic test strips. I recognized the box. Olympio snatched them from her hand and gave me a hot look before running off.

Guess for all of his powers, Olympio's grandfather hadn't mastered the art of healing diabetes yet.

# CHAPTER EIGHT

I stepped back into the clinic. There was a family in the waiting room now, a woman with three kids and a man with gang-looking tattoos.

I waved to the receptionist, who buzzed me into the back, and I reported to Catrina because she still seemed in charge of me. "What now?"

"Now you do some paperwork."

And that's almost all I did for the rest of the day, until Eduardo, one of the other medical assistants, introduced himself and rescued me from my desk.

"Come explain to my patient why he needs to take his blood pressure meds."

I looked at his numbers—150/105, oy!—and started talking as Eduardo translated me.

"No—of course they make your headache feel better. But you need to take them every day, not just when your head hurts. Has anyone in your family died of a heart attack? Or a stroke?" I leaned back against the counter behind me so I'd be eye level with the man. It was important he took his pills, or he'd leave his children fatherless.

From my new vantage point, I could see just inside his collar, to a tattoo on the left side of his neck. I tried not to stare at it while I gave him my blood pressure spiel. Two dark tattooed holes, with ink blood dripping down. They could have been tattoos of bullet wounds, but the fact that there were two of them, and on his neck, made me think that they were supposed to be from fangs.

I wanted to ask him about them, but I knew from working at County that it wouldn't be right.

Not for white kids, who mostly got anything on them that looked pretty on the wall. The hibiscus that reminded them of their trip to Hawaii, a bird because their spirits were free. But for people who had gang lifestyles, tattoos were a code, and you couldn't just ask them what things were. And you wouldn't get a straight answer if you did. I'd had to see three people with clown-type comedy–tragedy mask tattoos at my old job to realize that there was a local gang that used those masks to identify themselves. Before that I'd just thought it odd—and somewhat creepy—that middle-aged men were into clowns.

Vampires were a popular motif among a lot of people. Just because not many people knew that vampires were real didn't mean they weren't in the popular subconscious. It wouldn't have been the first time a gang thought that vampires were cool. I supposed they were, up until you actually met one.

I made sure he understood the reasons he needed to keep taking his medicine, as Eduardo translated his questions back to me, and then we let him leave the room.

"You could have told him all that, couldn't you?"

Eduardo gave me a sly grin. "It sounds more official coming from you. Some of them prefer to hear it from a *gringa*."

I snorted and pushed forward. "Hey—" There was a test tube of blood on the counter behind me. I pointed at it. "What's that for?" It wasn't labeled. He popped it into a plastic bag and opened the door.

"You'd have to ask Dr. Tovar." Eduardo shrugged, shuffling off into the back.

I waited for Dr. Tovar to come by, to ask him about the test tube, but when it hit five fifteen, my urge to go home—and maybe nervousness about the trip, after walking with Olympio—outweighed my curiosity for the day. The part of me that was trying to be rational thought I was overreacting, a little hyper-attuned to the type of thing that mattered in my now very-former life. As far as Santa Muerte went, that elderly woman hadn't come back. I could find a Three Crosses gang member and ask about their beliefs, but that sounded potentially injurious and I wasn't likely to get a better answer from them than I already had from Olympio. I'd have to wait and ask Dr. Tovar about the blood tomorrow.

I couldn't overlook the irony that I was grasping at anything to give me hope when my mother had already given up. Personally, I blamed her belief in a happy afterlife.

When I left the clinic, Olympio was gone. But I could hear the whispering sound I'd heard in the morning. I looked both ways before crossing the street and crouching to look into a storm drain.

"Drop something?" I startled. Dr. Tovar was locking the clinic door. "Or lose a gun? I'm sure there's half an armory down there, rusting away." He stood stiffly, his hands in his pockets, wearing his tweed coat on even this hot day.

"I thought I heard something."

His right eyebrow raised in a question. "I don't hear anything." He jerked his head toward the station. "Care to walk?"

While a doctor wasn't my preferred companion, walking with him wouldn't hurt. I made sure to stand far enough apart from him that it wouldn't look like we were together. Even so, ladies returning from the station made clucking sounds as we walked by. I wished there was a way to signal to them that no matter how handsome he was, I was not interested in him, nor would I ever be. At all.

"So how was your first day?" he asked.

"Interesting, except for the paperwork."

"I'm glad Frank's wound didn't make you run away."

"Am I going to get hazed every day I'm here? Or is that just your regular clientele?" I asked in a way that I made sure sounded like I was joking.

He outright laughed, maybe the first time I'd seen him pleased. I wondered what it would be like to be him, at the helm of a perpetually sinking ship, bailing water with all his might. We might have more in common than I'd thought.

"As regular as the rising sun. Why did you even apply for this job in the first place?" His eyes tried to read me as we walked, even before I could respond.

"If you'd told me this was going to be an interrogation, I'd have walked on my own," I said with an obviously fake grin. He snorted and I relaxed some. "Really, I just needed a change. I thought I wanted to take it easy, and the sleep clinic was great for that. But easy gets dull." No need to tell him about my mom's time bomb or any legends. "Why do you work down here?" I asked instead.

"If I don't, who will?" He shrugged, taking his coat pockets up and down with the gesture.

"Did you grow up here?"

"Nearby."

"Where do you live?"

His lips quirked up into a soft smile. "Nearby."

"How many stations away?" I asked quickly, before he could evade me.

"Past the station. I don't take the train."

"Oh." I kept on course, hoping I was on to something. "Do you live alone?"

He drew up short and looked at me. "Why?"

"Because people are looking." I indicated behind myself with a head gesture. "Either you're very single and they're making assumptions, or you're very married and they're imagining the worst."

He almost rolled his eyes. "I live alone. You?" he asked in a tone that made it sound like he was only asking to be polite. But in my experience men didn't ask questions like that if they didn't want to hear the answers.

"I have a needy Siamese," I told him. I tried to sound a little cute. Not that I was interested, but I could be flirtatious when the opportunity presented itself. "Did you report that guy from yesterday?"

He snorted, the beginning of a laugh. "I see how you are—try to get me to lower my guard with personal questions, and then in for the attack."

I shrugged and gave him half a grin. "There's only one of me. It's transparent when I'm the good cop and the bad cop."

He eyed me and turned serious, shaking his head softly as if to say there were a lot of things I didn't understand. "You'd probably find a lot of bullets inside that storm drain too," he finally said, which still wasn't a direct answer.

"Why?"

"Because reporting things to the police won't change anything. Not down here. You haven't seen one yet. Nor will you. We're off their maps, unless there's been too many bodies to ignore. But," he said, leaning his head forward, looking directly at me, "you seem willing to be very lax with rules."

"Heh." I hadn't exactly been reaching for the phone

yesterday. I felt a little sheepish—he had a point. "The place where I used to work, it didn't always pay to ask questions."

"And yet here you are, interrogating me," he said. He gestured me forward, and we began walking again.

"You haven't even gotten me started yet, really." We had just half a block left. Now was my chance for the most important question—we were too close to the train station for him to abandon me. "Eduardo drew some blood on my last patient, but you didn't order lab work. Did he make a mistake? Do I need to talk to him about that tomorrow?" I asked as casually as I could, trying to make myself sound managerial.

He shrugged and shook his head, too fast. "Don't. I'll say something to him."

"He did tell me to ask you, when I asked him about it," I pressed.

"We see a lot of patients each day. Mistakes happen. We should be lucky if they're all so benign."

I regretted his choice of words. It was too easy to slide in my mind from things that were benign to things that weren't, currently growing inside my mom.

"I will talk to him," Dr. Tovar assured me after seeing the look on my face.

"It's not that—" I began to explain, but saw my train coming down the line. I knew I hadn't seen a refrigerator full of blood-draw mistakes—but I wasn't sure they were worth throwing down with my day-old boss over just yet. For his part, he looked like he wanted to ask me what was wrong, but I could see him restraining himself. Maybe I wasn't the only one worried about crossing lines. Behind me, I heard the air brakes start. "Sounds like I should go—" I waved and started trotting backward.

My leaving decided him. He went back to being a doctor again, surely as closing a door. He stood a little straighter and nodded at me. "Have a safe trip home, Nurse Spence."

# CHAPTER NINE

I took the train all the way to my parents' house. Not the same train—they lived in the nicer part of town, off a different line—but it only took about thirty minutes. I got off at their stop, and it would still be a walk to their place, then—

I looked down. I was wearing the same outfit I'd worn at the clinic. When I'd been seeing patients. Frank, in particular. I may be immune to everything this side of TB, but my immunocompromised mother was not. There were germs all over my clothes. Shit.

I stood at the station—probably the safest in the city, as my folks lived in a gentrified zone—and called her.

"Edie—are you coming by?"

"Tomorrow." I told her who I'd seen today, and where I was. She was disappointed, but also amused.

"Weren't you just working at the sleep place?"

"It got boring."

She laughed. God, I loved to hear her laugh. "Well, I'm sure you're doing the Lord's work, wherever you are."

Yeah, about that. *Actually, Mom, I'm there because I'm trying to find a sympathetic supernatural creature to save your ass.* Too late to argue now. Plus, I loved her. "Can we do dinner again tomorrow? Don't cook. I'll bring food in."

"That sounds lovely. We'll expect you tomorrow night."

"Give me till seven thirty so I can go home and take a shower first."

She said, "See you then, dear," and hung up.

Still feeling foolish, I swiped my card to get back up to the train.

By the time I stopped off for takeout and took the train back, it was almost eight o'clock. I set the food down as soon as I got home and shooed Minnie off when she got too close. I didn't think I needed to take a shower before dinner—I was starving, my PB&J had been a while ago— but a change of clothes and washing any exposed skin would be nice.

I was running a washcloth over my arms and feeling silly for not just showering already when the doorbell rang.

It was eight o'clock at night. And to say I didn't typically have visitors would be an understatement. No one knew where I lived now, except for my family. Goddammit, if it was Jake . . . well. Maybe it would be good for us to talk about Mom.

I set the washcloth down and came out to look through the peephole.

"Hey, Edie," said a familiar voice as I looked through. He must have heard me lean against the door.

Ti. My zombie boyfriend from last fall.

All the stomach acid that had drenched my stomach at the thought of my brother visiting shifted slightly, continuing to rise. I could ignore him, like he'd ignored me for going on seven months now. Being forgotten had hurt.

"Edie," he said from behind the door, his voice dropping.

"Can't help but think of the last time we met like this,"

I said quietly, from my side of the door. We'd been going to a trial then, and he'd been wearing half of someone else—a part of their face, and their arm.

"I'm all me this time, though."

I opened the door up just a crack and whispered, "Where have you been?" I kept my face hidden by the door.

"Around. You were kind of hard to find, once you moved."

"And no one told you I was being shunned?"

"Do you think I care what any vampire says?"

This apartment unit, unlike my last one, was on the second floor. My porch light made him cast a shadow on the wall beside my door. His skin wasn't much lighter than his shadow, a dark even black, though his eyes were the color of amber hidden from the sun. The last time I'd seen him, he'd been recovering from injuries received as a fireman inside a burning house, and his skin hadn't healed back all the way. Now he was whole, the rippling scars were gone, and his hair had grown back, tightly clipped against his scalp.

He put his hand on the partially open door. "Can we talk?"

I looked up at him, at the face I'd kissed once, even when it hadn't been all his. He'd risked his life for me. He was still that same man. I nodded.

"Indoors?" he asked gently, not teasing in the least.

I took a step backward and let him in.

He took a look at the silver cross hanging on my wall. "I'd ask if you were religious now, but I think I know the answer to that."

"You never know who's going to visit," I said, well aware that neither crosses nor silver worked on zombies.

There was an awkward silence. I waited for him to fill it. I figured he was here for a reason, and I didn't want to give him any outs.

He walked into my living room and looked around. "I can't tell. Is this a step up or down?"

"It's a lateral move." What does one normally do when one sees exes whom one perhaps wants to stay on congenial terms with, but only for five minutes or so? I walked over to my kitchen. "Tea? Coffee?"

He smiled softly. "I'm fine."

Of course he was. Zombies didn't need to eat or drink, except for show, and to regrow—and besides, he'd gotten to do the leaving, not the being left behind. Of course he was fine.

"Edie, I didn't mean to—"

"Yeah. No one ever means to." I walked past him and sat down on the far end of my couch. He sat opposite me.

"This is a nicer couch than your last one."

"It is. So why're you here?" I was actually more interested in where he'd gone, and why he'd left, but the answers to those questions were more likely to piss me off.

"I wanted to check in on you. The last time I saw you, you were in pretty dire straits."

"You mean when you left me."

"At a hospital. Your hospital."

I crossed my arms again, this time over my stomach. The last time Ti'd seen me, I'd been stabbed by vampires and was bleeding at a prodigious rate.

"I was wounded too, Edie. I had to go . . . and heal." We both knew what that meant for him. Killing people. Eating them. Not nice people, but still. "I didn't leave town, though, until I knew you were going to be okay. I asked around."

"You could have asked me."

He rubbed his knees with his dark hands. "I should have. But—you know what I am, Edie. What I do. I should have never been with you."

"Didn't I get a vote in that?" I asked, my voice small.

He slowly shook his head. "No."

"Ti—"

"I tried to tell you. I don't know why I thought it could be different with you."

"Maybe it could have been, if you'd just given things a chance." I didn't want to hope that things could change now, did I? I was still mad at him for leaving me, right?

"When we were in the back of that limo together, when you were bleeding out, and I was falling apart—you smelled like death." He paused, and I could tell whatever he was going to say next would pain him. "And it smelled good."

I started shaking my head. "You never would have, Ti, never ever—"

He cut me off without meeting my eyes. "No. And yet, I can't deny what I am. What I'll always be."

"I don't judge you, Ti—"

"You did once. And you should." He shrugged softly. "It's the right of the living to judge the dead."

I bit my lips to keep quiet. Anything I said now would be the wrong thing. And yet— "Why're you here now, Ti?" If he was back for me, I wanted to hear it. I didn't know what I'd say at that point, but I wanted to hear him say the words. And if he wasn't back for me, well, I wanted to know that too.

"I was out of town for a while. And when I came back, I wanted to check on you."

"I'm not the reason you came back, though, am I." It wasn't even a question. If he'd wanted to come back for me, he would have done it already.

"No. There's a magician here who says he can give me back the rest of my soul."

It wasn't me. It was never me. Ti'd been looking for the rest of his soul ever since he'd been freed as a zombie. He had half of it—enough to keep him him—but whoever had changed him had the other half, and had used it to control him. Getting or growing a whole soul was the only way he could really die. Not just be-dismembered-die, but really die and go to heaven, where he thought he would see all his old friends. His dead wife.

I crossed my arms again.

"I don't know if he really can, but he's working on it. He has power like I've never seen—no, I don't see it, I feel it. He can do magic, Edie. Like my old master. The real thing."

"What're you trading him?"

Ti's lips split into a rueful grin. "Money. Lots of it. But I don't need it, like I am. And if it doesn't work, I can always get more."

I guessed employability wasn't a big concern when you were immortal and didn't always need to eat. I shook my head. "Why are you *here* here, Ti? Not in the metaphysical sense—why are you in my living room?"

He wouldn't meet my gaze. "I wanted to make sure you were all right."

"You didn't need to talk to me to find that out."

"Heh." He ran a hand through his short hair. "I guess I thought I owed you answers."

"You could say that. Seven months ago—you totally could have said that."

"I feel really bad for the way things happened, Edie." He shook his head. "I'm sorry. I mean it. Not that I can pretend to know if that even helps."

It was the only apology I would get from him. Take it

or leave it. I stared at my far wall, where a spider emerged from the corner, ran up, and, as if blinded by the lamplight, dove back into a crevice in the hardwood floor again. "I guess I should say that I'm glad for you."

"It's what I want. What I've always wanted. I just didn't mean to hurt you along the way. I feel really bad about that."

"You feel really bad about it?" I asked, my voice rising. "Yeah. I'm sure you do."

Ti tilted his head. He was still handsome, no denying. Strong, responsible. I'd felt safe when I was with him. There'd been a crazy moment in time when I thought that maybe I'd loved him. I'd spent the past seven months shoving that part of me down.

"I'm glad you're okay," I said. "I'm pissed that you didn't let me know sooner. And I'm sad that I was stupid, back then."

He looked wounded, but he recovered too quickly for me to know precisely which part of my statement had hurt him. "What's this about you being shunned?"

I leaned back. "I got into some trouble after you left. There was a werewolf problem, and a vampire problem—I wound up destroying all the extra vampire and werewolf blood at County Hospital."

Ti's eyebrows crept up his forehead. "When you get into trouble, you don't do it halfway."

I snorted. "Seems so."

"Is that creepy little girl vampire still around?"

"Anna? Yeah. I haven't talked to her since New Year's Eve, though." No matter how much I might like to, to somehow make her help my mom. "She's the one who made everyone shun me to keep me out of trouble. No one's allowed to talk to me now, on threat of death, I think. She set me free, by making me leave."

He snorted. "I've never known anyone to get away from them before."

I shrugged. "Seems I have. Nothing supernatural's come knocking at my door since I moved. Until you. Although I admit, I don't go out at night as often as I used to."

"That's probably for the best." Another awkward silence passed between us until he spoke. "It's almost dark. I should go."

I didn't have a way to convince him otherwise. I felt helpless again, like I had the last time he'd left me behind.

I cannot express strongly enough how much I abhor being left behind.

He rocked to standing, and this time I didn't fight him. "I'm sorry I can't give you what you need, Edie. Humans and zombies just aren't—"

I cut him off. I didn't want to hear it. "The time for that would have been a while ago, anyhow." I walked around him and opened my apartment door.

He swallowed—the vestiges of another human habit— and nodded. "I think the shun is a good idea, Edie. I want you to be well. But I don't want to see you around." He reached out and put his hand against my cheek. "I mean that in the best possible way."

I wanted to turn my head into his hand like a cat and lean into his strength, but I forced myself to stay still. "Thanks, I think," I said as drily as I could.

"Good-bye, Edie." He took a step back, and I closed the door after him.

Seven months is long enough to get over someone you loved who saved your life, right?

# CHAPTER TEN

I didn't sleep very well that night. I tossed and turned and Minnie got tired of putting up with me—when I woke up she was sleeping inside my closet, on the floor.

By the third time I'd snoozed my alarm, I was doubting the wisdom of signing up for a daytime job. It wasn't too late to call up the sleep clinic and say I'd been pulling some sort of dickish prank, quitting without notice. "They'd love that, of course," I mumbled to myself in the shower. But I got out the door on time to make the train, and I found myself rolling downtown, yawning through the first five stops.

"Ah, *enfermera*." Dr. Tovar was standing at the bottom of the station stairs. "Decided to be on time today?"

I wasn't sure where he got off acting so much older than me when he wasn't. "You haven't scared me off yet," I said, trying to sound brash.

He tilted his head, as though acknowledging that fact, while still making allowances for it to happen sometime soon. As I caught up to him, he started walking, and I walked beside him.

"So what is this place? A traveling market?"

"People need to buy food on the way to work in the morning. And those who come in each day whose jobs require the train are better able to pay for food than others." We ducked through the crowd. I tried to stay close enough to listen to what he was saying without being *close*-close. "Your old work shirt might have been torn, so you need another. Or you might have been paid well for the day, so you can buy new shoes for your child. It ebbs and flows with people's paychecks, firsts and fifteenths."

The sales spaces were marked by strings tied from structure to structure, some with clothing hanging down. One of them had a pile of individually wrapped toilet paper rolls, stacked up like a pyramid. I was pretty sure I hadn't seen that one yesterday, and I might not see it tomorrow. "I buy dinner here sometimes, on my way home," Dr. Tovar said. "And breakfast too. If you'll wait a moment—"

"Sure." The grilled stuff did smell pretty good. Better than my PB&Js, for sure. There was a stall here I hadn't seen previously, with T-shirts silkscreened with messages in bright colors. Feeling emboldened by Dr. Tovar's presence, I walked over to look at them. More images of Santa Muerte, with the words REINA DE LA NOCHE in elaborate script above her like the mural had featured. The woman running the show was at the back, rehanging shirts so that the artwork was facing out, no matter the direction of the wind. When she turned around, the shirt she wore had what looked like a vampire bite on the collar, in red ink, bleeding out.

No way. "Miss—" I opened my bag, hoping that pulling out cash would attract her attention. She was walking to me with a smile when something over my shoulders made her eyes go wide.

I turned back just as Dr. Tovar reached my side again and began pulling me away.

Three men were pushing through the marketplace,

with crosses tattooed on both sides of their necks, from windpipes to collarbones. They confronted the shirt-selling woman, saying something I couldn't understand. I could read their body language, though—they were looming. It wasn't good.

"This doesn't concern us." Dr. Tovar kept pulling at my arm. The rest of the market had gone quiet, focusing on the work of paying studious attention elsewhere. One of the men yanked down her shirts, sending them to the ground. The woman was complaining loudly. Another man grabbed for her, and in doing so pulled down the collar of her shirt.

Either she had two moles on her neck where fang marks would be, or they were scars, or strange tattoos—just like the man with high blood pressure yesterday. "Come on." Tovar pulled me more firmly, and wouldn't let go. "You go messing in other people's business here, and it won't go well for you."

"We have to help—" I fought with him.

"No, we don't. It isn't our job," he said angrily, yanking me along. Halfway down the street to the clinic, getting dragged like I was an errant child, I stopped and pulled my arm back.

"If it's not our job, whose is it?" I practically yelled at him.

He was quiet for a moment, fuming at me. "They'll get what's coming to them. Trust me."

Says the man whom I already know is lying to me about test tubes full of blood. "How can you be so sure?"

He stood there in front of me, pissed off. I could see him mentally forming the words he wanted to say—so close to telling me the truth—and then restraining himself again.

"Goddammit," I protested. "You know something you're not telling me." The blood, Santa Muerte, the rulers of the night—it was all adding up to vampires down here. Somewhere.

His eyes met mine, steely and dark. "I know that it's a good thing I waited there this morning for you. Otherwise—"

"Otherwise what?" I interrupted him.

"I'd probably be seeing you in the clinic, with a broken nose."

I frowned, waiting for him to back down, or explain. My arm throbbed. I looked down, and there was a red handprint around my wrist where he'd pulled at me. He'd been really scared for me. His eyes followed mine, and widened. "I'm sorry. That was irresponsible."

"What it was, was assault." I wrung my arm in the opposite direction, to get feeling back in my hand.

He took a step forward, still angry. "I just didn't want you to get hurt."

"What about her?" I pointed up the street with my good arm.

"I don't care about her!" he yelled at me. There was an awkward lurch where he gathered himself once and for all, regaining his temper, becoming the doctor that everyone here knew and loved. He continued on more sanely. "She's not my employee."

I ground my teeth together while I tried to figure out what to say next. I was angry at him, my arm hurt from being yanked on, and him holding out information was infuriating me. "What's going to happen to her?"

He inhaled and exhaled before answering me calmly. "They'll probably destroy her goods. They were there to make a scene. They wouldn't have to rough her up much for it to work. She was probably behind on her taxes."

"Oh, so they were from the IRS?" I said, my voice heavy with sarcasm.

"There's a lot of gangs in the area. That's a profitable open space. You can't just set up shop there without bribes."

"We still should have called nine-one-one."

He was his controlled self now, practical through and through. "Do you really think they would have come down here in time?" he asked snidely.

I didn't like what the answer to that might honestly be. "They're supposed to."

"You're too used to where you live." He jerked his chin back the way my train had come. "The world doesn't work that way here."

"I get that." I didn't understand it fully, but things down here operated by a different set of instructions, ones that hadn't been issued to me. I'd felt like this before, though—back on Y4. "Why'd she have a bite tattoo?" It was too telling for her to have one, and those shirts, and my patient from yesterday too. Plus, the Three Crosses had permanent *crosses* for protection tattooed on their *necks*.

Dr. Tovar looked at me like I was making things up. "You mean bullet hole marks. Bullet holes. How many times they've been shot."

I looked back behind us at the market that was becoming smaller with each step we walked, and then I looked at him, and he wouldn't look back at me. I didn't believe him farther than I could throw him. Everything pointed to vampires being here somewhere; the only question was how much did Dr. Tovar know—and could I get him to tell me in time to heal my mom.

# CHAPTER ELEVEN

I was a little cowed at work that day. Between witnessing violence and being dragged away from it, and the feeling that I had more questions than answers, especially about Dr. Tovar—I tried to keep busy. Knowing myself, it was the only thing I could do.

If Dr. Tovar was a daytimer, then the blood was going to someone. Who? Who was the Ruler of the Night that the Three Crosses were tattooed in fear of? I watched Catrina dive in and out of patients' rooms before and after me. I never saw her with test tubes full of blood in her hands, but her scrubs had pockets, didn't they?

*Keep your head down, Edie,* I told myself. I didn't have the protection of my former job or my former friends anymore. And I was supposed to be shunned—there was a chance I would blow my cover here and get ushered out the door. Then where would I be?

There had to be a way to get Tovar to confess, though. Something simple. Like holy water, or crosses. Only I didn't have either of those on me. I snorted, alone in a room while I was waiting for a patient.

Eduardo saw two people in, two women who bore a familiar resemblance to each other. The younger was my age, and she helped her mother up onto the table.

"I don't need your help, the *curandero* cured me," the older woman informed me as soon as she was settled.

Her daughter was filled with rage. "Oh, yeah? Then why was your last blood sugar four hundred and three?"

"The *curandero*?" I asked. The older woman emphatically nodded, and then started speaking in Spanish to her daughter. It was clear they were retreading an argument they'd already had many times before.

I didn't want to rat the *curandero* out as needing blood sugar test strips for himself, but if he was telling people with uncontrolled diabetes they were healed, he was doing more harm than good. No matter how nice his grandson was.

The daughter waited for their argument to subside, and then summed things up for me. "She thinks that he's cured her. He's prayed over her twice, and now she's cured."

*"¡No, si me visita dos veces más, me va a curar!"*

"You can go every day, Mom, for all I care—just keep taking your shots!"

Together they were a mirror image of my mother and me. And as with my own mother currently, I felt at a loss. I was sure the older woman had heard all the reasons why she should keep taking her medicine, and the daughter was tired of making her try.

I went for extreme science. "There's no miracle cure for diabetes. Just rigorous control. Without that, the sugar crystals in your blood will rip up your kidneys and the blood vessels in your hands and feet. You'll lose your nerves; you won't know what's hot or cold. And if you get an infection, because of all the sugar in your blood for the germs to feed on, you might die."

Although I felt like the mother already understood me, her daughter translated, adding her own inflection, especially on the you-might-die part. Her mother stayed proud and obstinate, and addressed me in English. "I believe I will be better. And so it will happen for me."

"That's not how it works," the daughter said.

The mother jerked her chin up. "That's how it will work for me."

I jumped in before things got any worse. "I know it's hard to accept that there's nothing that will fix the situation." I realized as I said it that I could be talking to myself. I could ignore everything strange I'd seen here and just try to be normal for once, to have a normal life, doing normal things, helping normal people. And my mom would die, like people with stage four breast cancer mostly, normally, do.

"You were saying?" the daughter prompted me.

I turned to face the mother and focused my attention on her. "You have to take the medicine. Your daughter loves you; she doesn't want to be without you. You can't blame her for wanting you to live, can you?"

The older woman's face crumpled a bit at this, but then she recovered and gave a dramatic sigh. "For your sake, I suppose I can pretend that the shots work."

"Good." The daughter shook her head and rushed her mother off the table, happy to take any victory she could. She ushered her mother out of the room, then leaned back to roll her eyes in commiseration with me. *Aren't stubborn old people crazy?* her look said. I nodded, yes, yes, they were.

I went outside for lunch and found Olympio there. I pulled out the extra sandwich I'd made him, and today he sniffed at it.

"No thanks, I already ate."

"Fair enough." I opened up mine and wolfed it down. "Your grandfather cure anyone lately? Practioner-to-practioner?"

Olympio grunted. "Of course. He cures everyone he touches."

"An older lady? Diabetes? Recently, from the sounds of it?"

His eyes narrowed. "Why?"

"You have to tell him not to say things like that, Olympio. What if that lady had gone home, not taken her medicine, and died?"

Olympio turned and began walking away from me. "Who's to say he didn't heal her? She's not dead if she came down here, right?"

"That's hardly an excuse, Olympio. And even if your grandfather doesn't know that, you do." I caught up to him, waiting for him to look back. No matter what bizarre claims Olympio made, he had to know his grandfather was telling lies.

Olympio inhaled like he was going to explain things to me, then turned and punched the wall behind him lightly. "Just leave me alone, okay?"

"Okay." I stood there as he faced away from me. I wished I hadn't pissed him off. I didn't want his grandfather hurting anyone, but there'd probably been a more sensitive way to convey it, one I hadn't explored in my flustered-from-this-morning mind. I sat down on the ground and sighed. He didn't walk farther away.

I waited what might be an acceptable period of time—and then longer than that, just to be sure—before asking him, "Do you know anything about Reina de la Noche?"

He was still facing away from me. "Why?"

"I saw a woman selling their shirts get hassled this morning, by the Three Crosses crew."

Olympio snorted, inhaling deeply, to spit out a wad of phlegm. "That's just like them. Scared."

"Which ones?"

"The Three Crosses. Beating up ladies. It's like them."

He was finally warming up to me—or the topic—again. "What are the Rulers like?"

"Rulers?"

"You know. The Reinas."

Olympio rolled his eyes. "Reina de la Noche—it means 'Queens of the Night.'"

"Oh." Well, that put a lot of things in perspective. Including vampire bite T-shirts and tattoos. I wondered who the Queen was. The only person I currently knew who could lay claim to that title happened to actually be a vampire. Anna, the vampire who'd gotten me shunned. "Olympio, can you do me a favor?"

"What?"

I fished two twenty-dollar bills out of my purse and held the money out. "Can you go buy me a small silver cross?"

"Why? You don't seem religious."

"I could be."

"But you're not."

I couldn't lie. "No, I'm not. It's for a friend. Look, you can keep the change, can you get me one, or not?"

Olympio eyed me for any signs of trickery. Finding none, he went back to his version of a businessman, suave and smug. "No guarantees that there'll be anyone with those down there today. I keep a twenty just for seeing, okay? Because I could be missing people to send my grandfather's way here."

"Okay. That's fair."

He prepared to set off, then turned back. "You have to do me a favor in return, though."

I blinked. This was new. "Sure, what?"

He gave me a wry look. "Stop pretending that you know Spanish. It's embarrassing."

# CHAPTER TWELVE

I saw myself out the door at five on the dot. While waiting for Tovar, I found Olympio. The storm drain moaned quietly behind him.

"Did you get it?" I asked him. He handed it out on his palm, a small silver cross, no bigger than my thumbnail.

"Had to look for it. So you don't get any change."

"That's okay." It didn't have a chain attached, and I didn't even know if it was actually silver, though it was shiny.

Olympio tsked at me. "Your *susto* is getting even worse," he informed me. "If you don't get a *limpieza* soon—"

"I still have that extra sandwich," I cut him off.

"Whatever." He crossed his arms high on his chest and looked away from me.

Stubborn, and mad at me. I had to respect him. I looked down at the sandwich. It wasn't attractive anymore. I hadn't been paying attention to my lunch bag on the train and it'd been squashed thin. I didn't want to take it home, and I wouldn't bring it back to eat it tomorrow.

I stood up, crossed the street, and chucked it into the storm drain. Maybe I'd plugged the hole, because the distant howling stopped.

The rest of the staff left—Catrina glaring at me—and

then, last, Dr. Tovar came out. "How nice of you to wait for me."

"Well, you know." I shrugged. "I wouldn't want to accidentally get involved in local politics while I was unsupervised."

Olympio, who was ignoring us both, chose then to look over his shoulder and roll his eyes at me.

I had the silver cross in my palm. I doubted Dr. Tovar was a daytimer—a daytimer would never do anything as selfless as work at a downtrodden public health clinic—but there was the blood, and the tattoos, and too much else unexplained. I'd been thinking about it all afternoon, and this was the least-worst idea I'd had so far. I just wished I had had a chain to put the cross on; that'd make hiding what I was about to do easier.

"Dr. Tovar—" I began, as a warning, and then reached out to grab his nearest hand in both of mine, pressing the cross flush against his warm brown skin.

He looked down at our touching hands and his eyebrows rose in bemusement. "Are you trying to have your way with me?"

I studied him for any reaction, any hint of a sign—and got none. I sighed, and let go carelessly, and the silver cross dropped to the ground. He knelt and picked it up for inspection with a frown. "Really. This? Again?"

"How do you know?" I asked him.

He held up the cross and twirled it between thumb and forefinger like it was a freshly plucked daisy. "Crosses and silver, everyone knows. I do watch TV." He shook his head while watching me closely. "You really thought I was a vampire?"

"No. You're standing in daylight. I thought you might be working for one."

Olympio fully turned back at this, eyes wide, and began watching our conversation, head swiveling like he was following a tennis match.

"Because of some blood?" Tovar's expression grew darker, and his voice rose. "You jumped straight to vampires? You're a nurse, you're supposed to be scientific, aren't you? If I'd wanted someone who believed in things like that, I'd just hire Olympio."

"Hey!" Olympio protested.

"You can't deny that it's weird," I went on, taking a step closer. "There's so many coincidences. The bite tattoos, the cross tattoos, the blood—"

His hand caught mine, and I stopped talking. "And you can't deny that you're obsessed with it," he said.

"Maybe," I admitted, and I didn't yank my hand away. He pulled my hand up and slapped the cross back into my open palm.

"I don't know what you believe, Edie, but we're not trapped in *The X-Files* here." He looked from the cross to me and back again. His eyes softened with pity for me. "Whatever you think you're seeing, whatever ghosts you're chasing from your past, you need to forget about them. You need to move on."

*It's not as simple as that. If I move on, my mom will die* was what I wanted to scream at him with all the breath in my chest. But what came out was a spiteful, "Okay. Fine."

He let go of my hand and took a step back, still watching me. "I need to go now. I have some personal business to attend to this evening. But I'm sure Olympio here can take you to the station and see you off safely."

My hand was wrapped so tight around the cross in my palm it was poking me. I shoved it in my pocket and took a huge breath of air, like I was surfacing from a deep pond. "Sure. I'm fine." *I don't need you, or your pity, anyway.*

"Okay then." He nodded, like we'd decided something together, and turned to go.

Olympio waited until Dr. Tovar had outpaced us for half a block before running ahead of me and turning back. "You really believe in vampires?"

I sighed and ignored him. Of course it would lead to this. The cross was in my pocket now. If only all of me could fit so neatly into another place, hidden from here.

"Is the Donkey Lady real?" he asked as a follow-up.

"Who's that?"

"She's a lady with a donkey head—if you're under the train station bridge at night, she'll come out and get you."

I concentrated on this instead of my current set of problems. "Why's she got a donkey head? And where does she find hay to eat?"

"She doesn't eat *hay*—she eats little kids who believe in her. Which is why I don't. I mean, I didn't, but—" Realization dawned on him like the sun over a smooth ocean, full and bright. "Should I be? Is she real? Oh, if she's real—"

I held my hand up, and Olympio went silent. "Vampires are real. The Donkey Lady is likely not."

"Whoa." He squinted at me. "How do you know?"

We were almost to the station now, and crowds of people were getting off trains, walking home. The woman's stall that I'd seen disrupted this morning was replaced by another stall, as if it'd never been there at all. And the pyramid of single rolls of toilet paper was almost gone. "I'm in a rush right now—lunch tomorrow? I'll explain, okay?"

He danced back and forth with frustration, but finally

nodded. "Okay. Tomorrow. You promised. Don't forget."

"I won't," I said, and dove into the exodus of people coming down the stairs so I could get up to catch the next train.

# CHAPTER THIRTEEN

After a shower and a drive, I was hauling a car full of groceries out at my mom's. I'd brought her favorite kind of frozen pizza because I wasn't a good cook.

I rang on the doorbell and then tried the door and found it unlocked.

"Honey, I'm home!" I called out as I wedged myself and my groceries inside. I had to go through the living room to get to the kitchen—I began waddling along, after kicking off my shoes, only to stop at the living room. "Oh. It's you."

My brother sat on the couch, beside my mom. He gave a short wave. "Hey, sissy."

"Hey," I said, flat. I'd been so worried about giving my mom MRSA that I'd gone home and showered first. And here was my homeless brother, with whatever germs he'd picked up on the streets, breathing her air with abandon.

"I should have called to tell you Jake was here," my mom said. "The meds make me forgetful."

She hadn't called because she'd known that it would be like this between us, although I'd be disappointed if she thought that knowing he was here would make me leave. A dark part of me thought there'd be plenty of time to give him a piece of my mind after my mother died.

I wanted to take that part of my mind out, stomp it to death, and then throw it through a high window.

"Well, I brought Hawaiian pizza over. If I'd known he was here, I'd have brought some pepperoni along."

"Pineapple, ugh," my brother said.

At least I had that to hold over him.

Hating pineapple didn't stop my brother from pulling it off the pizza and eating most of the slices. There wasn't much to talk about at the table. No need to ask Jake how he was doing—the answer? Bad—or what was going on with me—same as the last time I'd seen her, when I'd first found things out. No need to tell my mom that I was hot on the vampire trail on her behalf, if me pressing things didn't get me fired first.

"So what's up with your boyfriend, Edie?" Jake asked casually.

I blinked. "Um—"

"The guy from Christmas? Kevin?" he helpfully provided.

"Nothing. We broke up." "Kevin" had been my shapeshifter friend Asher, pretending to be my date so he could be nosy. He'd been a little more than a friend, if I were honest about things—but after the shun went into place, I'd had to leave him behind too.

My mom reached out to pat my hand, bringing me back to the present. "That's okay, honey. You'll find someone who appreciates you someday."

I patted her hand back. "Thanks."

She gave me a wry smile. "You know I'd make an extra effort to live if I had grandkids on the way."

"Mom!" I protested.

"What?"

"You can't say things like that. It's not fair."

"Sorry, sorry, you're right. I just always assumed I'd live that long. Now—" She didn't finish her sentence, and she let the thoughts drift.

I glared across the table at Jake. "I'm not the only one with reproductive organs here."

"Hey, remember that time you walked in on me and Debbie and yelled?" Jake said. I groaned, knowing where he was going with this. "I'm just saying, if you hadn't interrupted us, Mom might have had her chance."

"Oh, God, don't remind me." I put my hand to my forehead as my mother laughed. Debbie had been my best friend in high school, until I'd found out she had the hots for my brother. "I'm permanently scarred by that, you know." I turned toward my mother, who was still chuckling. "I thought you wanted us to be all celibate and stuff? You're supposed to have my back on this."

Her expression melted from amused to sick, and her pallor changed from pale pink to yellow. She put a hand to her mouth, and rushed for the downstairs bathroom door.

"What—look what you did, Edie." Jake instantly blamed me. Old habits die hard.

"I didn't *do* anything." I slowly stood. The sounds of my mother hurling in the other room began.

Jake glanced back toward the bathroom, fearfully. He lived a rough life now, but I'm not sure if anything could prepare him for this. "If you didn't stress her out so much, she'd have been fine," he lashed out.

"Me? Stress her out? The daughter with a real career? Who do you think she stays up at night crying over? Me, or you?" I stood up, ready to take it up with him once and for all. But he looked as scared as I knew I felt about Mom. The anger washed out of me. I was a nurse; when people were throwing up, I knew what to do. I turned and went into the bathroom with my mother and closed the door.

Here I was again, being the good kid, in a bathroom too small for two people at once. I couldn't even kneel beside her, so I just sat on the patch of countertop by the sink and reached down to stroke the back of her head.

Being the good kid never brings any rewards. A good life is its own reward, people tell you, and you in turn try to tell yourself that, but when you're the good kid and someone else is the black sheep, and they get all the extra attention and energy—it's hard not to be jealous of them.

I waited until she was done, and we were both quiet. I took a washcloth from the cabinet over the toilet, got it wet with the faucet wedged beside my ass, and wrung it out to hand down to her.

She took it and ran it across her face. "I hate being like this."

"I hate it too. The cancer," I clarified, after a second's extra thought. "I could stay in here with you puking all night. Not that I'd look forward to it, or anything."

She laughed and coughed, and handed the washcloth back up to me.

"Isn't there anything they can do?" My voice was smaller out loud than I thought it'd be, in my mind. Now that we were alone in here, no Peter, no Jake, I wanted my mommy to tell me everything was going to be all right. Even if it wasn't.

"I'm sorry to do this to you, Edie." She gave me a bittersweet smile.

"It's not your fault or anything. I just want to be sure—"

"I'm sure." She looked around at our bathroom's close walls. "I'm tired of being like this."

"The whole thing is so unfair." She was supposed to be

the one protecting a sick me. This role reversal felt wrong. "In my head, it only happens to grandparents. Not parents, you know?" She gave me a pointed look. "I'm not going to have a kid just because you have cancer, Mom. Sheesh. You'll get one someday. You just have to survive this is all."

She gave me a weak smile. "I'll try," she said. For the first time, I realized *I* was being unfair. Telling people to survive terminal illnesses was kind of a dick move. Like telling addicts to just quit their habits already.

"You just . . . do what you have to do," I said, leaving things open-ended. She would do what she had to do, and I'd keep searching for something that could heal her. Really heal her, all the way.

She sat on the bathroom floor now, her back against the wall, and reached up to put her hand on my knee. "You don't even have to have a kid, Edie. Just promise me that you'll be happy," she said, and I nodded. I could do that. "And that you'll try to look out for Jake."

That was easier said than done. I didn't want to make promises I had no interest in keeping. Looking into her face, though, what else could I say? "I'll try." The same promise she'd made me. It was the only thing I could say that wouldn't stick in my throat.

"Thanks, honey," my mom said. She opened the door and pulled herself upright by its handle. Leaning back in, she kissed my cheek with her sour stomach-acid breath and then walked out, leaving me alone.

After I'd said good night, I got into my car. First thing, I checked through my purse—which I'd unwisely left in the hallway alone while I'd been taking care of my mother—to make sure all my cash and ID were still there. They were. Maybe even the great and selfish Jake had been humbled into pure living by Mom's cancer. Or, more likely, he'd already shaken down my mom for money before I'd gotten there, and she'd leniently given in.

I drove home and got ready for bed. Today had been too long. I'd showered earlier, so all I had to do was brush my teeth and crawl under my sheets.

I still took an Ambien. My body wasn't used to switching to days yet, and if you could harness the power of sleep into a convenient pill form, you'd take it too, wouldn't you? Especially if you didn't want to lie there and think. None of the things I had to think about were good.

I was woken by a thump outside my door. A glance out the window proved it was still night—the middle of the night even. Full streetlight, no haziness of dawn. I closed my eyes. It was nothing, or a neighbor. Sleep had released me momentarily, but if I waited here quietly, it would retake hold.

Another thump. And then a third. They weren't knocks—definitely thumps. I reached for my phone. It was three A.M.

I still felt bleary from the Ambien. People saw things on Ambien, and drove cars up telephone poles. Was this Ambien, or was it real?

Another thump. I looked down, and Minnie was at the foot of my bed, standing up, looking into the hallway with concern. The sound was real. She leapt off the bed and dove underneath. That sealed it.

I got up and went as quietly as I could to the door, which actually wasn't very quiet as I stumbled along in my hall. Walking on Ambien was like walking on a boat. I didn't have any windows out to the second-floor landing, just the peephole. I pressed my hands to the door and leaned forward.

My outside light was on, casting something gray in shadow. The peephole's refraction made it hard to see what was really there; it kept focusing in on individual parts instead of the whole. Or maybe that was just me, woken against my will, the Ambien refracting my vision. I concentrated, hard.

Another thump, and I jumped back. Dammit. I still couldn't see. And I didn't dare open my door.

There was a whuffling sound of disgust, a massive indignant snort, the sort of thing you'd think a *T. rex* would do. And then one final angry thump, and the sound of something padding down the stairs.

I assumed it was the last thump. It'd had that sort of pissed-off quality. But really, there was no way of knowing. I waited for a time, and neither the sound nor the creature came back.

I made a short list of things that would be able to find me, cross-matched with things that looked like what I'd partly seen outside my door, and came up with an answer I didn't like very much.

Jorgen.

Fuck me.

On my way back to bed, I pulled my decorative silver cross off my wall.

# CHAPTER FOURTEEN

It would have been easy for Jorgen to find me, no matter where I moved. He knew what I smelled like. He was a vampire's Hound now—it was his job.

He hadn't started off as a Hound, though—he'd been a minor werewolf, a human bitten on a full moon night. This past winter he'd been involved in the same confrontation over vampire blood that'd gotten me shunned, and this was his punishment. He wasn't a free wolf anymore. He couldn't even go back to being human. Trapped as a Hound, he was enslaved to a particularly frightening vampire named Dren.

And it was my fault he was a Hound now, if you went back far enough. I'd been the one who'd stopped his pack's plan and destroyed all the extra supernatural blood. I had no idea what he wanted to see me for, but I couldn't imagine any reason that was good.

He was a piece of my old life, the one I was so foolishly, desperately trying to get back to. I pressed the cross to my chest and it chilled me through the fabric of my nightshirt.

"Goddammit." The reason I'd moved was so things like this wouldn't happen to me. At least at this new place, I'd never given any vampires permission to come aboard.

It was a good thing, though, right? If Jorgen wasn't

shunning me . . . what did that mean for me? Did it mean I was allowed to talk to vampires and other supernatural creatures now, and they to me? Or was I in trouble for refusing to accept my shunning? Was his visit a punishment, or a warning? If Jorgen was here—could Dren be far behind?

I tossed and turned until dawn.

My alarm went off at six thirty and I woke up and showered without much enthusiasm. At least today was Friday. It was easy to forget about Jorgen in the daylight—if I hadn't woken up with the cross beside me and Minnie still under the bed, I might have brushed the whole thing off as a bad dream.

I rode the train in and walked down the stairs, half expecting Dr. Tovar, my recalcitrant chaperone, to be waiting for me at the bottom. He wasn't there, though. I waited a minute, and then prepared to make the walk in myself.

Yesterday's shirt stall was still gone, but another clothing store had taken its place. Pink scrubs with a purple trim hung flat, straight as day, without any wind. They looked familiar . . .

I started walking quickly to the clinic.

The front of the building was covered in graffiti, looping swirls of complex writing that I couldn't decipher. The front door was open. I went inside and found it empty.

"Hello?" I looked around and realized all the chairs in the waiting room were gone, and the walls were painted with huge multicolored crosses. The room reeked of fresh paint. "Is everyone okay?"

Hell, was anyone but me even inside? The door to the back had been busted through. "We're not seeing patients today!" came a yell from beyond. Dr. Tovar followed it, his coat finally off. He was wearing a white T-shirt with his normal dark slacks. When he came out his hands were tight in rage, which made the muscles of his arms stand out. When he saw me he relaxed a little. Without his coat he looked surprisingly human, and more frail.

"What happened here?"

"We were looted last night. We're lucky they didn't burn the place."

Suddenly my urge to help that woman yesterday—this attack put it into focus. My mouth went dry. "Did I—"

"No. This is about them, and me."

"The Three Crosses?" I guessed.

"It's not like they tried to hide it," he said, pointing to the walls. "They took all the chairs, and anything left out in the break room. They broke into all the lockers. And they cut up an exam room table, autopsy-style."

"Should I call the police?"

"Already called. I have to report this, for insurance's sake."

I pointed back outside. "I saw Catrina's scrubs at the station. Should I go get them, and report who the seller is?" Maybe there were other chairs there for sale.

"No. I doubt Catrina would want them back. They took things to trash them. That person probably just picked them up out of the trash. That's where the receptionists and MAs are, looking for the waiting room chairs."

"Ugh." I would sit down, only there was no place to sit. I spun, looking from wall to wall—and the front wall, the one visible from reception, had looping numbers written on top of the crosses. It took a moment for my mind to resolve them into a date. Seven-seventeen. Like I'd seen on the mural on my computer map, that first day on the phone. "Why the date?"

He flushed darker. "No reason."

I pressed my lips together. I didn't want to refute him, but they hadn't written a huge date on the wall for their own health. Today was Friday, the eleventh of July. The seventeenth was next Thursday. What would happen then?

He started stalking back and forth, and finally answered my silent question. "They want me to make a tithe. To openly join their cause—to take their side."

"What side is that?" I couldn't see Dr. Tovar under some gang leader's thumb. "They don't want you to help anyone but their people? Or work for free?"

"It's more complicated than that." He stopped and got a pensive look. "They didn't go in back this time. Or burn us down. This was just a warning."

"And the seventeenth?" I tried again.

"It's meant for me." He walked over to the wall painted with the numbers and planted his hand against them. He rubbed against it and the top layer of wet paint smeared. He sighed and rubbed his hand against his pants.

"But why you?" I had my suspicions. Perhaps they wanted him to stop giving blood to vampires. "The crosses, and the blood," I slowly began. I'd seen Jorgen last night—I knew there were vampires around. I was sure of it.

He cut me off with a shuddering sigh. "Stop it."

He looked so exhausted and angry—exhausted by being angry—that I had to. It was my turn to take pity on him. I walked around the room. The two flanking crosses were ornate multicolored affairs, part Celtic, part Greek Orthodox, elaborately colored and twisting. The center cross was stick-straight and stark gray. I wondered if they hadn't gotten a chance to finish it, but its lines were crisp and the edges were shaded. Maybe its simpleness offsetting the others was the point?

I opened my mouth and inhaled to ask him a question,

but he cut me off with a gesture. "Please. Go." He waved me out of the waiting room, and went in back.

I sat down on the front stairs, not sure where else to go. If I went out very far I'd only get lost, and I didn't have any paint to begin covering the crosses up.

I felt bad for him, even if he was a doctor. This clinic was his baby, and Three Crosses had gone and ruined it—not just for him, but for everyone. That's why they'd hurt him here and not at his home, wherever it may be. Violence done to him personally, he'd just shrug off or take silently—he was that kind of man.

But violence done here, to his place and his people? It was the lowest kind of blow.

I'd never once seen him do the wrong thing, not where his people or patients were concerned. And it dawned on me that I was among their number, another wayward chick tucked under his wing. He'd hired me to protect me. And he'd been walking back and forth to the station with me. Normally that sort of thing would chafe, but I was having a hard time minding. It was nice to feel like someone else gave a damn. It made me feel safe.

What if this was the page of the Choose Your Own Adventure novelization of my life where I just picked to forget everything that came before and take everything at face value, as it was told to me? And not pry and just let sleeping dogs lie and not feel bad for realizing my boss sort of seemed interested in me, and also was hot? Apart from the part where my mom died, it sounded nice.

Eduardo returned holding a waiting room chair. "Chair delivery," he announced, and I scooted over to let him in, saving me from any more strange thoughts.

* * *

One by one, chairs filtered in throughout the rest of the morning. They'd been left in odd spots: on roofs of buildings, in deserted lots. My co-workers had put the word out, asking anyone who found a chair to bring it in.

The insurance adjustor came surprisingly quickly to take pictures of the place. After that, I spent the rest of the day laying drop cloths on the floor—reams of the paper we used to keep exam room tables clean—and putting coat after coat of white paint on the walls.

We were deep into the afternoon when a man appeared in our door. While he didn't have tattoos on his neck, the men who came in to flank him did.

He had close-cropped black hair, and held himself like he was used to being listened to. He had on a black button-down shirt, black jeans, and black cowboy boots. A gold chain hung outside his shirt, with a large pendant whose shape I couldn't make out. Catrina ran back to get Dr. Tovar as soon as she saw him, and afterward she stayed in the back. The others stayed but stilled. People put their paintbrushes down.

"I came as soon as I heard there'd been damage here," he said, once the doctor entered the room.

"I appreciate your concern, Father Maldonado," Dr. Tovar said flatly.

"Pastor Maldonado," the man corrected, looking around the room. "Clearly the crosses are meant to implicate us, when we were not responsible." He held his hand to his chest, as if gravely injured by the vandal's artistic implications. Once there, his hand stroked the pendant as if it gave him permission or powers. If I squinted and used my imagination, I could see the figurine holding a scythe.

"Clearly," Dr. Tovar repeated, with sarcasm.

The man looked around at the destruction of the room, his eyes lingering on the sad wall half covered in white.

"I could offer to have my men paint a mural here, you know. Testifying to Santa Muerte's greatness." He lifted up his pendant to kiss it before carefully setting it back down.

Dr. Tovar grunted. "If she's so great, why didn't she stop them from doing this last night?"

"Perhaps she was not aware she had your patronage," the man said in a conciliatory tone. But that was the only thing regretful about him. His eyes looked around the room, as proud as if the art here were created by his own child. "You have yet to tithe to us. The seventeenth approaches. We can't finish our new church without the support of every member of the community. How will she know we love her, if our new church isn't grand?"

"You and I both know this has nothing to do with that."

At that moment, Eduardo returned with another liberated chair. The pendant-wearing man, whom I guessed was the leader of the Three Crosses, but also some sort of Santa Muerte priest, smiled at seeing him awkwardly lugging it in.

"In the words of Jesus himself—if you're not with us, you're against us." He smiled, revealing teeth as gold as the necklace he wore.

I sighed aloud, and started vigorously painting. I wanted to flick white paint all over his black clothes, but if this is how they retaliated—well, my walk back and forth to the station was a long one. But I'd fought with vampires before and won. I had the scars to prove it. Evil wins when good steps down—and I was tired of stepping down.

I dropped my paintbrush, loudly. "Are you proud of yourself? What you did here?"

"Me?" he said, turning to look as if seeing me for the first time. "I did nothing."

"How many people who need medical attention won't

get it today, because of you? Kids who need vaccines, and their moms who took time off work to bring them in—are you going to pay them those days back?" I inhaled and exhaled deeply, seething with anger. "People here have it hard enough without incidents like this."

The man smirked, focusing his attention over my shoulder at Dr. Tovar. "And yet, they could have it harder."

At some unseen signal, the men behind him retreated, and he followed them out.

From behind me, Dr. Tovar said, "That was stupid of you."

I was still breathing heavy. "I know." I turned around to face him. "Sometimes I can't help myself."

He looked bemused. "I think you need someone with you at all times, to stop you." He exhaled and shook his head, but he was actually smiling now, warm and true. That and the T-shirt and the paint splatters on his slacks made him finally look his age. Too young to face a lifetime of this.

"I don't know why you put up with that. I mean, I know why—but it sucks." His amusement faded into a sad half smile, and I thought maybe I'd hurt him. If I had, it made me feel bad. This wasn't his fault. I inhaled and tried to extricate myself. "I'm sorry, Dr. Tovar. I'll just be over here, finishing my wall."

He shook his head at me. "You can call me Hector. When we're not in front of patients, that is."

I picked my paintbrush up from where it'd landed on the floor, and kept my smile to myself. "Thanks."

We both worked as the other medical assistants brought back chairs—people from the community brought them in too, once they'd heard what'd happened. By the end of the day, we were only down five.

We were both covered in splatters of paint. My scrubs were ruined. Luckily, scrubs were pretty cheap. I looked down at them—they were some of the green kind I'd snuck home in from Y4. It felt like a very long time ago.

Hector made us all leave when it turned five. "Anyone who wants to come back tomorrow can."

A few people nodded, then he looked at me.

I wanted to sleep in some first, on my first day-shift weekend. "Nine?"

Hector smiled at me. "I'll meet you at the station."

# CHAPTER FIFTEEN

I hadn't learned anything new today—not where vampires were concerned. Maybe Maldonado was a daytimer? He had the self-possession of one. It would explain why he didn't have the tattoos his followers did. Plus, he was an asshole, which fit the mold. Hmmmm.

I got off at my station, walked to my car, and drove to a hardware supply place, where I picked up a cordless drill and some extra chain locks.

I didn't go to sleep that night. No Ambien for me. Instead I lay in bed and waited. If Jorgen had found me once, he'd find me again, and I bet Dren would be with him this time. If I had to pick the person from my past most likely to break the shun and return to make trouble for me, Dren would win. He was a Husker, a type of vampire that specialized in finding people and, if paid to do so or sheerly for the pleasure of it, husking out their souls. I didn't understand what he did with them afterward; it was some sort of vampire numbers game.

Minnie hopped up on the bed, and I stroked her soft belly. Dren had tried to husk my soul out once, and it'd cost him one of his hands. I'd like to think that if we went back in time, knowing the consequences of his actions would have stopped him, but I doubted it—Dren wasn't the kind of vampire who learned. He'd just have tried crueler, harder.

One evening cup of coffee easily kept me awake until three. My body was thrilled to be staying up past ten o'clock, and my night-shift nature came rushing back. But by four, I was crashing again, and by four thirty I was doubting my will to live, wondering why the hell I'd said I'd go back to the clinic tomorrow. Oh, I know—Hector had asked me. I pulled the covers up over my head to hide from myself.

And then I heard it. A solid thump.

I sat up, and all foolishness left me as Minnie skittered off the bed. I picked up the cross I'd set beside myself at sundown and rushed to my front door.

"Who's there?"

No answer from the other side of the door. I looked through the peephole. My outside light was on, triggered by motion, and Jorgen's head, malformed by his transformation into a Hound, angled outside, looking back at me with first one black eye and then the other. His head was huge, like a horse's in size, only it looked like a wolf's.

"I'm going to open my door," I announced. "You know you can't hurt me, right? I'm being shunned," I added, just in case.

I'd installed five extra chain locks that evening, for all the good it would do now. I unlocked the main bolt and pulled the door open the width of the chains. I knew as a vampire Dren couldn't come inside, but I wasn't sure if the rules that applied to vampires also worked for their familiars, or whatever it was that Jorgen technically was now, as Dren's Hound.

"What do you want? Who's there?" I could only see Jorgen in four-inch-wide pieces as he moved outside. His fur was gray and scabrous—he walked on all fours, and his skin hung down around him so loosely it looked like he could turn around inside it. He was like a half-leper, half-wolf Shar-Pei.

More pacing. No response.

"Jorgen?"

The beast outside came closer and sat down. In the blink of an eye, it shoved a paw inside the gap of the door.

"Gah!"

I made to slam the door on his fingers, and barely stopped myself in time. They weren't fingers, and weren't paws either—it was like he was trapped between the two polar opposites of his transformation, between wolf and man, with all the disgusting qualities of both.

He dug at the door frame, taking away splinters, like a big bad dog.

"Go away!" I wasn't getting any answers from him. It was possible he'd tracked me down just because he could, to torment me. No matter that it was his fault he'd been trying to steal supernatural blood this past winter—the fight that'd gotten me shunned, and him punished and bound—I knew he'd feel I'd done this to him. I wondered which was worse, knowing he could never again be fully wolf or human, or knowing he was stuck permanently subservient to Dren.

I didn't want to hurt him, but I didn't want this—I only wanted to save my mom. I had a wild thought. "Jorgen—where's Dren?"

The scrabbling stopped, and the paw pulled back. Now it was a nose, dog-wet but pink like a human's, that shoved at my door. He took two long sniffs of the air inside my room, smelling my things, smelling me, and then retreated to look over his own shoulder. He looked again at me, his eyes human, and then exaggeratedly behind himself.

"Is Dren trapped in a well?" I asked, then shook my head. I didn't want to know why Jorgen was here—there was no possible reason that was good.

But Dren was a vampire. And my mom still needed blood to heal.

"Is Dren out there?"

Jorgen growled in frustration at me, a frightening low noise.

I highly doubted Jorgen was here with people who could drive. Surely they'd have sent a person who had hands to come and knock on my door; besides, there was no way he could fit himself into a car.

"Make him come up here to talk to me. I'm not going down there." I wasn't sure how protective my shun actually was. If there was a vampire in the parking lot, I'd rather meet him from inside the safety of my house, where no-entry rules applied.

Jorgen's paws reappeared, pushing against my door. He rattled it inside the frame, and the chain locks groaned under the strain. He reared back then slammed forward again, and one of the freshly installed locks popped.

"Jorgen!" I reprimanded him, for all the good it would do. I swooped up the cross and swiped it across his claw-tips. He howled and jumped away from the door.

"What's going on?" My neighbor opened up his door. He was a family man, with two kids and a wife, living tightly packed inside a one-bedroom like mine. At this, Jorgen ran away, snaking down the stairs and running off into the night. My neighbor looked at me through my jungle of lock chains. "Are you okay?"

"Yeah." I nodded to prove it.

"What was that about?"

"A bad ex-boyfriend," I lied.

He grunted, crossing his arms over his gut. "We don't

want any trouble here. If he comes back, you'd best involve the cops."

"I will."

He squinted at me, then nodded and retreated into his house. His manly work here was done.

And mine was just beginning.

# CHAPTER SIXTEEN

I tried to go back to sleep after Jorgen's intrusion, but it was hard. I'd never seen a Hound without the owner close behind, and it wasn't like Dren to taunt in absentia. I knew from our shared past that he was more the hands-on-personal-touch type. Or hand, singular, since I'd accidentally taken one of his. It was unfair that I'd become the enemy for life of a creature that never had to die.

I strongly doubted that Anna, the vampire who'd instituted the shun to protect me, would change her mind without warning me first, which made me wonder if she was okay. Was that maybe why Ti had broached the subject the other night? I should have asked more questions when I'd had the chance.

I didn't sleep again that night. I watched the clock tick by until the sun rose, and then I got up. Maybe I could be a day person after all—if I pretended the day was another night.

By the time I brushed my teeth it was seven thirty. I could go out and get breakfast. The best diner in Port Cavell was two stops up the train line. Close enough that I could go there and drink a lot of coffee, and come back to the clinic station by nine for my escort with Hector. I singsonged his name a little bit in my mind, and I snorted

at myself. I needed to get over my schoolgirl self. I'd
managed to stuff down my libido for the past seven
months. I could go a few more. Nothing had changed.
Nothing. I put on clothes I wouldn't mind getting indelible
paint on, and walked out to the train.

On the weekend, it was almost nice this early. The train
was nearly empty—there wasn't anyplace exciting to go
in the next two stops north, not on a hot weekend in July.
Most people were staying home, sealed tight in air-
conditioned bubbles, or standing in front of open fridges. I
hopped off at the right stop, walked three blocks over, and
went into the diner. I spotted someone wearing hospital
green in a booth, facing away from me.

I did what I always did when I saw someone in scrubs—I
hurried up a bit, in case I knew them. I walked past their
table and glanced back casually—this time, I did. It was
Gina, leaning over to put her wallet inside her purse.

"What're you doing up this early?" I teased. I hadn't
seen Gina in seven months. My face lit up without thinking about it. She didn't seem to hear me, so I tapped her
table and waved. "Hey! What're you doing here?"

She jerked her head up, looking night-shift tired, and
she reached out to protect the tip she'd left her waitress
like I might steal it. "Getting breakfast."

"Gina—"

"Hey." Her hand found the Y4 badge on her chest, and
she shoved it into her scrub's breast pocket.

"How're you doing?" I pressed on.

"What's it to you?" Her bangs swung forward as she
jerked her head in a slightly threatening way.

"Gina—"

"Just because you can read a badge doesn't mean we're
friends."

"You don't remember me?"

She frowned deeply. "No. Should I?"

I blinked. Oh, no. I'd told the Shadows I didn't want them to change my memories—maybe instead they'd changed everyone else's?

"I'm sorry—I must have had you confused with someone else," I said. It wasn't worth Gina wondering who the Shadows had stolen away from her for the rest of her day. I'd been the one to choose remembering. I didn't think she would have chosen to forget.

Gina deflated. "Whatever." I backed off, and she scooted out of her booth and walked toward the door.

I stood there watching her, all my memories struggling to get free. We'd been friends, good friends. I'd helped her out a lot—we'd trusted each other. And now . . . she didn't remember me. At all.

I wished I'd thought to check if there was a ring on her ring finger now, if her were-bear boyfriend had finally proposed. I hoped she was happy, without me.

"Miss—would you like a table? The next one down's already been cleaned." A waiter stopped in front of me and gestured to the next booth over.

"Sure." I stood by the booth meant for me. If I sat there alone after seeing Gina, that'd be no good for me. I reached out to tap the waiter's shoulder as he walked away. "Actually—I'll just get some coffee to go."

I made it to the Divisadero station early. The fact that it was a weekend hadn't stopped the marketplace at all; in fact, there were more people here, buying and selling goods.

Waiting seemed dumb, and two blocks wasn't that far. I angled around people, feeling much more at home among them in normal clothing instead of scrubs, and heard a familiar voice at the end of the aisle.

"Who among you has not felt the evil eye? How long can you take the risk that someone has cast bad luck upon you?"

I walked over to Olympio, and he waved low with his hand in acknowledgment that he saw me. So this was what he did to drum up business on weekends when the clinic was closed. He pointed at me. "You, woman—you look like you've seen a ghost!"

Because I had? The ghost of my former life. I made a face at him. "I couldn't sleep last night."

"The *curandero* can give you a candle to burn to make you sleep like a contented child. He can chase the ghosts away from you."

"Can he prescribe me Ambien?" I asked.

Olympio groaned and walked away. Something smelled like garlic over here—there was a grill running. I inhaled deeply and looked around. The rest of the people were ignoring Olympio. Either none of them needed ghost relief, or all of them had heard Olympio go on like this before. He sighed and dropped his act and came over to talk to me. "Man, I hope all these people meet the Donkey Lady. I wouldn't feel bad if she ate all these *disbelievers*," he said, louder at the end. The other people still ignored him. He rolled his eyes at them.

I was close enough to him to smell garlic. "Olympio— what did you eat for breakfast?"

"Nothing. I just slept with a head of garlic last night. And ate five raw pieces this morning."

It was his breath. Definitely his breath. I leaned away from him. "Did it occur to you that that's why people are ignoring you?"

He frowned. "You're the one who told me there were vampires down here."

I held up my forefinger. "I never said anything about down here. I just meant in town."

"Same difference."

I hated that phrase—and I hated the fact that Olympio remembered our conversation about vampires. I'd been hoping that the Shadows would erase his memory of our conversation, but apparently they were too busy wiping minds of people whom I wanted to remember me. "And anyway, garlic doesn't work on vampires."

"But silver and crosses do?" He raised his eyebrows, ready to throw anything he could back at me.

"I've created a monster," I said flatly.

"You said you'd tell me more today."

"Here?" I looked around at the people surrounding us.

He followed my gaze and grunted. "Later. But today, okay?"

"Okay," I agreed.

Olympio jerked his chin up. "Hey—don't you want to ask if I know anything about your clinic? Your doctor was here earlier, asking."

"He's not my doctor," I shushed him, feeling my cheeks turning red.

"When will you all be done? By Monday?" Olympio obliviously went on, luckily for me.

"I don't know. Maybe?"

"I like it better when all the sick people come to the same place. It sucks bad enough on weekends here—I don't want to have to do the market on weekdays too. The owner of the pharmacy won't let me stand in front of it. Says 'no solicitors,'" Olympio said, obviously making fun of the other man's Indian accent.

"Yeah, well. We're repainting today. If Dr. Tovar hasn't done it all by the time I get there." I could see him doing just that—coming in at five A.M. and doing everything before any volunteers arrived.

Olympio nodded. "Let me know if you need an extra hand. *Para el pago,* of course." I stared at him blankly. "For pay," he said, for my sake.

"Hell, I don't think I'm getting paid for this. I must have been high on paint fumes when I agreed to come in extra."

Olympio laughed and pointed. I turned around, and Hector was walking up from behind me. "Ahhh, there you are, Nurse Spence. Eager to start off the day?"

"Something like that," I said, and walked in with him.

He was wearing a dark green button-down workshirt and jeans. It felt strange to be walking beside him without his tweed coat on. A few other people at the market offered him condolences about the clinic; others shot dark looks at me. I found myself looking for excuses to talk to him, ones that weren't related to vampires.

"So what was that tithe thing yesterday about?"

Hector sighed. "You don't give up, do you?"

"I've been told it's part of my charm."

"By who?" he asked, with a rueful smile.

"People," I deflected. "Possibly crazy people. But— about the tithe—"

"Okay, okay." He waved his hands to stop me. "You've worn me down. The Three Crosses are building a new church in a warehouse two miles down."

"I take it Maldonado isn't a Catholic?"

Hector shook his head. "No. He believes in Santa Muerte. Which I normally find hard to condemn—if people find comfort in her, I won't take that away from them. Lord knows we get little enough comfort down here. If faith helps, and they feel the real church isn't helping, I don't care where they find it from. It's better than drugs or booze. But I do mind the extortion."

"What, it's not really a tithe?" I said, feigning disbelief.

Hector snorted. "When your priest is also a gang leader, it's usually a bad sign. Maldonado is not what he seems." Hector slowed and I slowed with him.

"How well do you know him?" I asked.

"What makes you think I know him?" Hector stopped entirely and looked at me.

"The love notes on the clinic walls. Unless he does that to everybody . . ." I let my implications fade. There was the deal with the cross tattoos and the vampire tattoos, of course, but it went beyond that. That, plus Hector's face right now—it all came into focus for me. "He seems like the kind of person who does what he wants, takes what he wants. If he wanted you dead, you'd be dead already." I paused to think. "So instead he must want something from you. Which implies that you have a relationship."

The look on Hector's face said I'd hit a raw nerve. I decided to go for broke, minus vampires. "Hector, what happens on the seventeenth?"

His expression, already clouded, became more so, and he hung his head. "I'm sorry, Edie. I don't want to talk about it." He started walking again, and was quiet on our way in.

At least for once he didn't try to tell me I was crazy. And I noticed he didn't deny a thing.

# CHAPTER SEVENTEEN

The volunteers who'd arrived before me had already gotten started on the next wall. It was taking several coats of paint to cover up the vibrant artwork, and while I knew we needed to cover them up on principle alone, not to mention for gang-affiliation reasons, it did seem a shame to ruin them all.

Then I remembered the sliced-up table in the first patient receiving room, which sobered me. It was a clear warning that anyone who worked here, or wanted to come here as a patient, could be sliced up like that too.

Hector had brought us face masks to wear, and a fan, which we'd set up in the corner for all the good it'd do. We left the front door open, and as we worked, applying coat after coat, other people trickled in to help.

Even with the work to do, I was getting sleepy. I hoped Jorgen visiting wouldn't become a nightly affair. It was weird on a lot of levels. Where was Dren? I held the brush the wrong way, pressed too hard against the wall, and it slipped out of my hand. Like a fool, I tried to catch it as it fell, and wound up making a bigger mess.

Catrina danced away from the paint spatter and tsked at me. "I don't know why he stands up for you. You're a drain on all our time."

I had had to ask one of the medical assistants—usually Eduardo, because he was nicer to me—to come in and translate a lot for me this past week. I retrieved my brush and turned toward her to apologize, but she went on.

"You couldn't even stay in last night and rest up for this—even though you slept in two hours longer than anyone else. No, you had to go out and party, and now you're useless here. Can't even put paint on a wall."

She turned back to her spot before I could contradict her. Her hand flowed up the wall expertly, and I could see the strange tattoo on the ring-finger knuckle of her right hand as she brought the brush back down.

"He . . . stands up for me?" I said aloud, more to myself than her.

"Rationalizes you, more like." She whirled on me, her voice low. Her short dark hair held a snowfall of white paint. "Don't you be getting any ideas—" she warned, punctuating herself with the brush.

I exhaled loudly. "I'm trying hard to fit in. Honest."

She puckered her face in disappointment. "Try harder," she said, then turned back toward her piece of wall.

At noon, I was going over the last cross for the first time when Hector came in with food and beer. People congregated in groups, like they knew one another, because they all did. Feeling awkward, I took my burrito and slunk outside.

Olympio sat on the steps, eating chips and holding a to-go cup from the place that we'd gotten lunch. "Hector hook you up?" I asked him.

"Yeah. You all done?" he asked, looking back.

"Almost." I sat down beside him. "You could have come inside to help too, you know."

"I can't go inside. It'd diminish my *don*."

"What is that, even?"

"It's my gift, as a *curandero*." He gestured grandly out at the street in front of us.

"Well, then, of course." I looked back at the wall outside. The paint didn't cover as well out here as it had inside. It'd need another two coats for sure. "We'll probably be back to normal on Monday. Whatever normal is."

Olympio cocked his head at me. "I wasn't kidding about the ghost. You sound down, *mija*."

"What's it to you, *mijo*?" I asked back.

His eyebrows rose.

"That's right. I know three words of Spanish. The other two are curse words, though."

Olympio grinned, showing me a mouth full of chips. "I could teach you more."

"Curse words?" I laughed out loud, and he did too. It felt good.

"More Spanish. Not curse words," he amended.

"Sure," I said and nodded. "It'd be useful."

"There'd be a small fee, of course."

"Of course." I took a big bite of my burrito and chewed it.

"Can you tell me about the vampires now?"

I sighed with regret. I should have watched myself better. "They're sort of like the ones you see on TV. Or read about in books. You'll probably never meet one. The end."

Olympio screwed up his face. "You have to tell me more than that. How many are there? Where did you meet them? Did they bite you?"

I twisted my lips sideways. "There's a bunch of them. More than you'd care to think about. I met them where I used to work, at my old hospital."

"They were there for the blood?" Olympio guessed.

"Something like that." I folded the wrapper back over the end of my burrito, my appetite gone. "I got fired, and now I don't know where they are anymore."

"But you're looking for them now. Why?"

"I didn't promise to tell you that," I said, setting the burrito down. I wished I'd brought out my Coke. "Your turn. Are the Reina de la Noche really run by a queen?"

His eyes widened, and he got a silly grin. "Oh, yeah. But here's the thing—no one's ever seen her."

"Really?"

"Seen her and lived. Even her own people don't know what she looks like. She's like a ghost." He squinted at me. "Or a vampire? The teeth and the blood of the Reinas—is that what you think?"

I shrugged mysteriously, trying to act like I knew more than I did, while still desperate to hear him go on. "You tell me."

"Whoa. Whoa." He set his cup down. "Then all the stories would be real. They say she killed all of the Port Boyz gang in one night—that's how the Reinas got their territory."

That did sound like a vampire, if, and only if, it were real. I could see the stories he'd heard through his mind.

"They said she ripped their heads off. I didn't believe it—how could a girl rip off anyone's head? But—"

I waved my hands for him to slow down. "People make up stuff all the time. And it's always been cool to have other people scared of you. Right?"

He closed his mouth, trapping all his previously outlandish stories inside, and nodded. "Yeah. Right."

We were quiet then, eating. The sun was beating down, and everything was still. People were walking in and out of a small store a few corners down, and behind us was a low hum of conversations I couldn't understand, but right now it seemed like it was just the two of us sitting outside, Olympio, me, and a few brave ants.

And whatever was moaning across the street from us in the storm drain.

"You cannot tell me that you don't hear that," I told Olympio.

"What?"

The day was completely still. The only other sounds were from people inside the clinic.

"That," I said, pointing to where it sounded like it came from, the drain. "Maybe it's my ghost. Or the Queen." I gave him a look.

Olympio seemed like he was trying to listen. He leaned forward, tilting his head. "Nothing." I heard the moan again.

"Oh, come on. What good are your *curandero* powers if you can't hear that?" I said, but the moaning had stopped, and Olympio shook his head.

I stood and walked out to look back to where the train was. Could the train be moving air? Or was the sound of it running on its tracks echoing back off a certain spot? The sound began again. I silently pointed at the drain, and Olympio made a face but slowly began nodding.

"Okay, that is creepy." He shoved the rest of his chips into his mouth and set his soda down.

I walked closer and squatted down beside the drain's mouth. "Is someone down there?"

"*¿Aquí abajo?*" echoed back to me.

"It's creepy, but it's not—" Olympio began, coming near.

"*Pero no es—*" echoed back to him, from a different voice. And then what sounded like a sob. We both jumped back and heard sounds of actual crying—someone choking back tears.

"We have to go down there," I said.

Olympio shook his head violently back and forth. "Call nine-one-one."

I knelt closer. "Can you hear me?" The crying continued. Louder. "Olympio—how do we get down there?"

He reached for my mouth with his hand. "Don't tell her my name!"

"Sorry, sorry." I stood and dusted off my knees. There had to be some way to get down in there. "Show me where. Please."

"We can tell the others," he said, pointing back to the people in the clinic.

"I could barely get you to believe me," I said. "And how often does nine-one-one get people to come down here?"

He closed his mouth and looked back and forth from me to the storm drain, where the crying kept on. "Fine. I'll show you, for ten dollars."

# CHAPTER EIGHTEEN

We walked down the street together, a little back toward the station, then to the left before Olympio stopped in front of the pharmacy. "We need five dollars."

Not in a position to deny him favors, I handed the money I hadn't used on breakfast this morning over to him.

"Good. Wait here," he said, and went into the store without me. I waited, the sun beating down. Just as I started to suspect that he'd ditched me and run out through the back, Olympio returned. "Here."

He showed me a small flashlight, free of packaging, with batteries already in it, and handed me a fistful of change. I shoved the change back in my pocket as he led on.

We went down a few alleys, and then between buildings and behind another alley, before storm drains opened up into one final wide cement ditch in the ground, like a footpath for giants. There were makeshift tarp tents along either side of the open ditch. We wove through these quickly as people slumbered inside. "This is *Tecato* Town," Olympio announced. "*Tecatos* are—"

"I know what *tecatos* are." We started walking down the steep graffiti-covered hill, leaning back as we did so, and I was glad I'd worn tennis shoes today. There were shards of broken glass everywhere—I wished I had my gloves. "Can your grandfather cure them?"

Olympio grunted in thought. "No. I don't think so. To be healed, you have to want to be healed. I've never met a *tecato* who wanted to be healed all the way. They're all a little in love with the drug. Why do you ask?"

I glanced up at the tents that were disappearing above the cement horizon. "My brother. He could be sleeping up there." He probably wasn't—he was probably at a homeless shelter—but I hadn't asked him where he was staying the last time I saw him. On purpose. My foot skidded, and I almost had to put a hand down. "Gah!"

"That's your ghost, then. He's haunting you." Olympio reached the bottom, taking a few running steps to land on mud-stained cement. I followed him, much less gracefully. "Maybe you should see my grandfather. Even if he can't help your brother, he could help you."

"Why do I need help?"

"He's haunting you—your worry. He's causing your *susto,* stealing your spirit."

I snorted. "He's been *susto*-ing me for years, then." I almost told him about my mom, then caught myself. He was just a kid; he didn't need my problems.

"Why don't they sleep down here?" I asked as we reached the ditch's flat bottom.

"Flash floods. Wash everything away. Us too, if it rains."

Huh. It was humid today, as always, but the sun was still out. At the bottom, we started heading toward the three circular metal tunnels that led beneath the street and then down. They looked like the beginning of some joke, where the devil asked you to pick a door. "How come you know so much?"

"Everyone plays here as kids. When you're little, you tell each other stories about La Llorona, the stories that your mom told you, to scare you away from here. When you're older, you take other kids here to beat them up." We took a few steps into the tunnel. "It dumps out on the far side of downtown. I know where it comes out, but I've never gone all the way through." The entrances to the tunnels were colored with graffiti, the floors strewn with rocks and glass. I saw the orange cap from an insulin syringe.

Olympio went on. "There's a lot of echoes in here. It's haunted, for sure. I did wonder, though, if all those times I thought you heard someone, it was just some other kid getting his ass beaten at the end of the line." He turned on his light. "Now we just walk back the way we came. Only underground. Watch out for needles."

We walked slowly, crouching, shining the flashlight before each and every step. The smell here was metallic, almost like the taste of fresh blood, the tang of wet rust. There were small tree branches—I wondered how far away those had been swept in from; where the hell was the nearest park?—condoms, bent spoons, and the occasional bullet case. Graffiti warned us that this place belonged to the Three Crosses, then the Reinas, then other names I couldn't read with faded colors—enough different scripts that it was clear no one really ruled here.

"Why does she cry? In your stories?" I whispered to Olympio, and heard it sussurate around me, like listening to a breathing lung.

"Someone killed her kids."

"The Donkey Lady?"

"No. The Donkey Lady—she's under the train station at night. She's different. Someone shot her donkey, and then she became one—don't ask me." He turned to look back, shining the flashlight up at his face, casting it in frightening shadows as he started talking again slowly, like it was an effort to explain things to someone as unimaginative as me. "La Llorona fell in love with someone who didn't love her back. She killed her children to follow him, but he still didn't love her. So she killed herself, and now she haunts rivers and snatches children away. And this place can be like a river, sometimes."

He swung the flashlight down to the ground and began walking.

"Isn't that an old story? Like it happened far away from here?"

"So?"

"So—I'm just saying, chances are she's not haunting a storm drain someplace where it snows in the winter."

Olympio glared over his shoulder at me. "I'm not hearing anything anymore—let's go back," he said, and then the wailing overtook us, echoing in the small tunnel. I yelped, Olympio jumped, and the flashlight fell to the ground, clanging on the tunnel's metal floor.

"Shhh!" I grabbed up the flashlight.

"Let's go, let's go, let's go—" Olympio started pulling at me, his hands scrabbling over mine for control of the flashlight.

"Hang on, okay? Who's there?"

*"Una abuela,"* came the sound back. *"¡Una abuela necesitada!"*

I looked to Olympio to translate for me. "She says she's a grandmother who needs help."

"Well then." That didn't make it any less creepy, but I'd take talking ghosts over disembodied crying any day. I took a few steps farther up the tunnel, and Olympio followed me. When I slowed down, he bumped into my back. We reached a fork in the tunnel, where it branched in two.

*"¿Vas a venir?"* said the voice.

"She wants to know if we're still coming," Olympio said. It seemed like her voice was coming from the darker path, of course. Olympio stopped me. He picked up a branch and set it down pointing in the direction that we'd come from.

"So we'll know which way to pick when we come back."

And then we went into the black.

The woman just kept asking if we were coming, over and over again. It got so I bet I would know those words too, in addition to *sangre* and *mija*. I might hear them in my sleep. They might be the last things I ever heard, if Olympio's imagination was accurate.

I tried not to let on that I was scared, but my imagination was just as good as Olympio's; worse, I'd already seen awful things before. Swirling Shadows that tried to suck you down, the teeth of an angry werewolf, vampire fangs, cancer. All sorts of different things that wanted to gnaw on you.

It got hotter, smelled worse, and suddenly there was light.

*"¿Vas a venir?"*

Sunlight poured in from a grateless storm drain above, but it illuminated only a square on the opposite wall. Hector was wrong about there being guns down here, but there was trash; everything from the street had been swept in. It stank. No clouds in the sky, but somehow water lingered here, in disgusting pools hidden by—or made of—trash. I stepped into the strange room, hunched over so the moldy ceiling wouldn't touch my head.

*"Usted está aquí."* The woman who'd called to us was in the far corner. The sunlight robbed me of any night vision, making it hard to see her in the shadows. I could only distinguish the crumpled shape of her form.

Olympio spoke to her first. *"¿Abuela por qué estás aquí?"*

*"Me perdí y me lastimé,"* she answered him.

Olympio looked to me. "She's probably from Tecato Town. She got lost and hurt."

I motioned with the flashlight for her to come nearer. She threw up her hand against it and withdrew. "Sorry, Grandmother," Olympio said.

She was huddled up, wrapped in a black blanket. Her eyes were hollow, and she had sparse white hair in greasy ringlets around her face. "Can she come out to me?" I asked Olympio while keeping my eyes on her. While I doubted I was going to become part of a horror movie right now, I'd seen enough of them to know better than to look away.

She said something, and Olympio translated. "She says her ankle hurts."

"Can she show me her ankle?"

Olympio asked her, and she did so, putting it out and pulling up the blanket to expose it while making little cat-like hisses and cries.

It was swollen and red. Cellulitic for sure. "Shit."

She spoke some more. "She says she can't walk."

I swallowed. It stank in here, and we'd walked so far, and there was no way this little woman was going to be able to walk back out.

"Oh, no. You aren't even thinking that, are you?" Olympio asked me.

"I am." Suddenly, despite the heat, I wished I was wearing long sleeves and jeans. Isolation gear. Maybe a full biohazard suit. I handed the flashlight over to Olympio. "It's going to be a long walk back."

"You're telling me."

I came nearer to her, where she sat in the one spot of shade. I gestured for her to stand as best she could. And then, despite the stink and my rising horror, I reached out for her.

Her blanket, where she'd been sitting on it, was damp. I didn't know if it was water, or urine, or worse. "Oh, God,"

I said, for strength, and then closed my mouth to keep out the smell. She scrabbled at my neck with her bony arms, fingernails clawing me. I took a shuffling step, and—by pulling down on me, my back already screaming from crouching in the tunnels all the way down here—so did she. She yanked my neck, and pulled herself forward, and exhaled what I knew was a curse word.

While the tunnel had seemed long enough going into it . . . walking back out, helping to hold up someone who stank and was damp and was climbing all over me . . . the only thing that stopped me from gagging was the horror that in doing so, she might get something into my mouth, a corner of her blanket, a piece of stringy hair. So I suffered in silence as Olympio led us back out, step after laborious step, as the dirt ground into me and the woman's dampness soaked through my clothes.

The last turn, and we were facing the tunnel's exit. The circle of sun looked so sweet, and with the fresh air rushing in, I didn't care if it was piping-oven hot. Freedom was so, so near.

*"No quiero ir por ahí."*

"She says she doesn't want to go out there," Olympio told me, forcing me to finally speak.

"Tell her she'll die in there," I muttered out of the safe side of my mouth, hauling her forward one more step.

*"Odio el mundo, me dará la bienvenida a la muerte."*

"She says she's okay with that. That she doesn't like the world."

I couldn't agree with her more right now, but letting her die in a storm drain was not an option.

"Tell her I'm horrible and mean, and I'm going to carry her leper ass out anyway. Only make it sound nicer when you say it."

Olympio snorted, and presumably did as he was told. She didn't stop fighting, and I pulled her, still struggling, out into the sunlight.

Thank God—we were free. I stood there for a bit, breathing the fresh air as carefully as I could. I didn't drop her, not because I was afraid she'd crawl back into her storm drain cave, but because I knew if I did I would never manage to talk myself into picking her back up again.

"What now?" Olympio asked.

What now indeed. The walls of the storm drain were steep. I was tough, but I wasn't strong. "Got any bright ideas?"

"Wait here." Olympio pocketed the flashlight and scurried up the wall.

She was talking—nattering even, I'd say—to herself. I wondered how old she was. Old people could get dehydrated easily, and then they'd become demented from sheer dehydration. Or urinary tract infections—those could take an old person from normal to demented in no time. There was nothing to do for that but get in an IV line and give fluid—but not so much that her questionable lungs or kidneys got flooded. Treating old people was hard, and there was nothing I could really do for her down here.

Olympio returned, rolling a shopping cart down from over the horizon. It careened down, with the rubber on his shoes barely braking it from slamming into the cement floor. Then he rolled it, with one wonky wheel, over to us.

"Put her in here, and then we can take her up."

She fought me—she fought us, since Olympio started to help. We got her in, and then it took me pushing and him pulling and us going up the hill at an angle to finally reach the flat top. We rolled the woman toward the clinic, where I prayed to God that Dr. Tovar had not gone home for the day.

# CHAPTER NINETEEN

Luckily for me, he hadn't.

Olympio told him the story after I'd set the woman inside and run in back. I didn't have an extra shirt to change into, but I washed myself up as best I could in the clinic's small bathroom. I soaped myself up to my armpits, and washed my face, and splashed my neck. She had clawed me, dammit, when she'd slipped on the tunnel's curved bottom, oh, every other step. I couldn't tell what was friction burns on my neck and shoulders, and what was claw marks. The whole area was bright red. I washed with soap and water, and soaped and rinsed again. I didn't want to put my old shirt on—I wanted to burn it.

There was a knock outside the bathroom door. "You want an extra shirt?" Hector asked from outside.

I opened the door up fractionally and stuck my arm out. "Yes, please." He handed it over, and I pulled it on. It smelled lightly of men's deodorant, like it'd been worn before, or had been packed near something that had. It wasn't a bad smell.

I came out, feeling slightly cleaner, and found him waiting in the hall. "Thanks."

He nodded, as if he loaned shirts to employees all the time. "We're waiting for an ambulance. She's significantly dehydrated, and she needs antibiotics now. And I'm not taking her in in my car."

"I don't blame you." I put my fingers to my neck where she'd clawed me, and felt the raised edges of the wounds, like speed bumps on my neck.

"Let me look at that—you cleaned it, right?"

I didn't answer him, I just gave him a look.

"Sorry. Had to ask."

"Hmmph." I did feel better showing it to him, though. This way, if I died of something tragic and curable, like cat scratch fever, someone would know how and why.

"What on earth made you go down there?" he said, stroking his fingers along the edge of the wound on my neck. I shivered, surprised by his touch, and then crossed my arms, trying to pretend that I'd somehow taken a sudden chill in July. "It was foolish of you."

I looked at him. His warm brown eyes were familiar—I recognized the same compassion in them for me that I'd seen him have for his patients.

What could I tell him? That I needed to save someone, because it was looking like I couldn't save my mom?

I looked away, conscious of how near he was. "I thought I heard someone."

"In the storm drain? But of course." His voice was light and teasing.

"It just sounded like someone was down there. And then Olympio heard it too."

Hector shook his head in dismissal. "I already talked to him. Told him he should have more sense next time. That's a dangerous part of town. You both could have been killed."

I rolled my eyes. "Thanks, Mom."

"Your life may not mean much to you, but Olympio's whole family relies on him." I didn't have anything to say to that. My cheeks flushed in shame. He finally stepped away. "Anyhow. The ambulance is on its way."

I followed him back into the waiting room, where the old woman sat. She clutched her black blanket around her, despite the heat, and I could only imagine how badly the seat she was on would need to be disinfected on Monday.

"Are we done here?" Olympio said, looking back and forth from Hector to me.

"Yes. Thank you." Hector pulled out his wallet and handed Olympio a ten-dollar bill. Then Olympio came over and looked at me. I found a ten and gave it to him. He looked me up and down, and hmmphed. I fished in my pocket and gave him the rest of my flashlight change.

"You want to know how I knew we wouldn't die?" he asked me as he pocketed my money.

"How?"

"La Llorona couldn't be a grandmother since she killed all her kids."

"Ha." I grinned at him. And then our shared moment was broken by the sound of water dripping—from the woman's chair onto the floor. She was peeing herself.

Olympio blanched. "You don't pay me enough for that, though." He sprinted for the door.

The paramedics lifted her onto the gurney. She fought, clawing at them like a wildcat. Without the black blanket, she was naked—they covered her up with a sheet from their ambulance. I knew they were driving her over to County, the only facility that would take someone like her. Even now that health insurance was becoming more common, hospitals weren't exactly going out of their way to open up their doors. And old habits died hard. Ambulance drivers who'd driven the sickest or meanest people to County for half their careers weren't going to change overnight.

Once she was gone, Hector threw her blanket away. I felt bad watching him trash what was probably her only possession in the whole wide world, but there was no way we could keep the thing; it was a petri dish. I promised myself I'd buy her another one, if I ever saw her again—but I bet she was going to stay a few weeks someplace with IV antibiotics, sedatives, and possibly restraints.

Then we closed the place, and Hector locked the doors behind him.

He walked me back to the station. "You should put some Neosporin on that. And change the bandage frequently."

"I am a nurse, remember?" I said. He gave me a look that made it clear that this afternoon, I'd crossed the line. "Okay, okay, I will. And I'll wash your shirt, and bring it back to you."

"Don't worry about it. Just get better. You should call me if anything changes." He patted himself down and found a business card inside one pocket. He handed it to me.

I'd gotten phone numbers in less romantic ways, barely. I grimaced and took it from him.

It was only five by the time I got home, but I was exhausted. Between two days of painting, and then my hunchbacked trip through the storm drains, I had more problems than just my neck.

I took a long shower, and every drop of water that hit or trailed down my neck wound stung. I fought to stand there, scrubbing away the rest of the grime, going through what felt like half a bar of soap.

After that I slathered Neosporin on my neck, gauzed it

up with supplies swiped from my last job, and crawled back into bed to take a short nap. I set my alarm clock and everything.

When I woke up Minnie was purring by my side. I petted her while I woke up, like always—and realized it was dark. I could have kicked myself. All that effort to get on a day schedule, and here I would be up all night.

Worse yet—I'd missed dinner with Mom. Shit. Shit shit shit.

I looked at my phone. It was ten o'clock. Too late to call. Of course, she'd called me, and sent a worried text message. I checked the volume on my phone. It was up. I'd slept right through her calls too. Should I text? Text Peter? Or what? Shit!

I sent an email, hoping one of them would check it in the morning. They'd be up for church; maybe they'd check their emails before that, or after? I could call at nine. I didn't think my mom was in any shape to leave the house, but I knew if she couldn't leave she'd watch one of those sermons on TV.

I had limited mother–daughter time left in my life, unless I managed to shake down a vampire—one that didn't want to kill me, which meant Dren was out. *Fuck.*

And my neck still hurt. Goddammit. I got up and stumbled over to the bathroom. I tripped and stubbed my toes.

Fucking fuck fuck!

Maybe if I stopped cursing at God, he'd treat me better. Then again, a fair God wouldn't be offing my mother with breast cancer, now would he?

I sighed and sank down onto the floor of my bathroom rather than face myself in the mirror again. My neck burned—and so did my pride. What was I doing? I was chasing the hope of healing my mother like it was some kind of frantic butterfly. Anytime I thought I got close enough to try to catch an answer, my hands wound up empty again—or worse yet, my dreams were smashed inside.

Maybe I should just quit the job at the clinic and spend what little time was left with her. No one could blame me if I did. I could move back in for a little bit. She and Peter had turned my old room into a guest bedroom. I knew they still had my old bed.

I hauled myself up by the edge of my sink.

I leaned on my sink and tugged the tape off my neck dressing with my free hand. The gauze slid away, colored with the yellow of purulent drainage, and the claw marks were red and oozing. "Ugh." And now that I was standing—I did not feel well. Or look well, by the dim bathroom light. I was still sore from earlier today, I'd slept wrong, and now I was fighting off this infection too.

I had faith in my nurse's immune system—I couldn't count how many times I'd picked up something at the hospital and felt sick going home, only to wake up the next morning well. Plus, the only emergency room I could think to go to in the middle of the night would be County, and damned if I'd end up there. I tied up my hair, hissing as raising my arms above my head made my neck hurt, and got back into the shower.

I couldn't rinse my neck off directly—it hurt too badly for that—but I held my head so that it'd catch all the water running down, and tried to dab at myself with a soapy washcloth. I dried myself off, regauzed my wound, and stumbled back to bed, where I dry-swallowed an Ambien. My last memory was of it being bitter on my tongue as it made its way down.

# CHAPTER TWENTY

Thump thump thump.

What what what?

I blinked in bed. If Jorgen was back here to eat Minnie, I was going to punch him.

All my covers were tossed off the bed. I sat up as the thumping continued. Who did that? Why? Who unmade my bed? Jerks.

Thump.

"Go away!"

Thump-more-thump.

Shit.

"I have neighbors, you know. I'll call the police."

I scrabbled for my phone, watched the numbers on the screen flicker and dance. Stupid numbers. Always betraying me.

The thumping kept going on. Was it coming from inside me? I looked down at myself, and oh-my-God my neck burned. Maybe it was my neck knocking. Telling me something. I sat on the edge of my bed.

"What? Go!"

I heard talking, outside, as though someone was answering me.

Not Jorgen then. Unless he'd learned how to talk. Had

he learned how to talk? I tried to imagine him talking, and saw a comical dog in my mind, one with a tweed coat and a smoking pipe. I snickered at this, and the thumping began again.

"Whatever!" I stood up, naked, and picked up my robe off the floor. I walked down the hall to my front door and swung it open.

Hector was standing outside.

"Why're you here?" I asked him.

"The more I thought about it, the more I was worried about you. No telling what diseases that old woman had."

I squinted at him, choosing the version of him I thought was really him, and not the shadows the porch light made him shoot off to either side. It was hard; there were a lot of him to choose from. "How do you know where I live?"

"You did fill out some forms when I hired you. Can I come inside?"

Nervous laughter spilled out of my mouth like a river. "No. I mean yes. Wait. No."

Who was this person talking? Not me. I pressed my hand against my hallway wall. The cross there, it was cold, it felt so good. I took it off the wall and held it against my chest.

"Are you okay, Edie?"

"I'm fine. I've always been fine, and I'm going to always keep being fine."

He looked doubtful. "You don't look so fine. Can I come in?"

I leaned forward and put a finger on his chest. "Are you a vampire?" I had seen him in the daylight, but who knew?

"No. I wish you'd get over your vampire delusions."

"You would be deluded too if you were me!" My voice rose, and I realized I was shouting. Neighbors, *dammit,* neighbors! I lowered my voice to hiss, "You'd be looking for a lot of excuses to delude yourself, if you were me."

He took my hand, and pushed me gently back. More like he was holding me upright. "I thought you said you were fine?"

"Dammit." I took a step back, and the hallway tilted, sending me spilling to the side. I hit the wall with my shoulder. It reverberated up to my neck, and I hurt so bad I wanted to cry. "Here, hold this." I handed the cross to him, this one made of real silver. If he touched it, I'd be safe.

He took it, and took a step inside. "Edie—you look really bad." He reached his hand out and touched my forehead. His hand was nice and cool. Maybe it'd taken all the chill from the cross and channeled it into me. I reached up and pressed his hand tighter against my forehead.

"You're hot. You should sit down." Fully inside my house now, he took my shoulders and directed me toward my couch.

"I'm totally, utterly okay," I said, letting him push me down. "Can I have your hand again?" Looking at me strangely, he offered it over, and I pressed it to my face again. "This is a good hand. I like this hand."

"Okay. Edie. You need to calm down. Wait here, okay?" He freed himself, closed my door, and went down my hall. I was there for an hour or twelve, but then he came back and handed me a wet washcloth.

"What were you doing with my cat?"

"Edie. You're sick."

"No I'm not." I would totally shake my head to tell him no, only my neck hurt so so bad.

"Yeah, you are." He reached into his phone for a pocket. Or the other way around. "We need to get you some help."

"Fine." I was tired. Now that I was sitting down again, the sleepiness was taking me.

He smiled at me, a warm light in his eyes. "See? You're still fine."

"I'm not sick." I looked up, petulant as any child fighting sleep. "I hate you."

"You are sick. I know you don't hate me." He held his pocket to his ear.

I remember saying, "Don't tell Olympio anything," and then I thought I was going to pass out.

I'm pretty sure I did.

# CHAPTER TWENTY-ONE

Wherever I was when I woke up, it smelled like smoke—not like cigarette smoke, but like hippie smoke, herbal stuff, and pipe tobacco. A dim lightbulb hung overhead. The ceiling was dingy, stained yellow with smoke and neglect, the walls mostly hidden by colorful banners with phrases in Spanish. I recognized the names of a few saints, and there were posters for soccer tournaments from 1973. There were statues on a cheap table at the back of the room, skeletons wrapped in robes and holding scales and scythes, like the background of a pretentious metal album. Something crinkled beneath me as I moved my head—and sitting up, I realized I'd been lying on tinfoil.

"What the—where—" I patted at my pockets, looking for my phone. My mom. I had to call my mom—but the last things I remembered didn't involve putting on pants.

*"El durmiente despierta,"* said a voice in Spanish. A man I didn't recognize was watching me. He was smoking a pipe, sitting among the statues, and the light in here was so dim I'd thought he was one. He had one whole leg and one that jutted out and ended, amputated at the knee; a crutch leaned on either side of his chair.

"Where am I?" I skittered backward from him, wrinkling the foil.

"Edie—" A familiar voice from behind me. I turned around and saw Hector at the door.

"What is this?"

"You were sick. So I brought you here."

Olympio peeked in behind him. Suddenly I knew where I was at. "Oh, God. Take me to a real hospital."

"You don't need a real hospital now! My grandfather cured you!" Olympio pointed at the strange man behind me. I looked back, and he tapped out his pipe into a wastebasket by his good knee.

There were no windows in this room. "What time is it? Tell me."

Hector found his phone inside his coat pocket. "Three A.M."

I'd taken an Ambien at ten P.M. No way I was awake now. Oh, shit. "How long was I out for?" I stood, unsteady, my feet slipping against the tinfoil I'd been lying on. Now that I was standing, I could see it was in the shape of a cross.

"A whole day. You were very sick."

My mother had probably been freaking out for almost two days. She already had one derelict child—she didn't need two. "I need to get home. Right now."

"It's only been a day. I'm sure your cat's fine. And I'm your boss, it's not like I'm going to fire you. You were really ill."

There was a wetness on my neck. I reached up and found a poultice there. I pulled it off, and it crumbled in my hand. It smelled like tobacco. "Jesus Christ!" I flung the remnants of it down. "If I was *really ill,* why the hell did you bring me here?"

Hector's face darkened, but it was Olympio who spoke first. "Hey! I told my grandfather that you were cool! Worth saving!"

There were still pieces of what looked like wet spinach stuck to my hand. I looked back at Olympio's grandfather, who was stoically contemplating what an asshole I was. I took in a few huge gulps of air to calm down. "It isn't— I'm sorry." I made sure to look at his grandfather. "I'm really sorry. Thanks for healing me. I think. But I've got some other things I need to be doing with my time."

He leaned forward and held out an egg to me.

"Don't touch it," Olympio said. "He's just showing it to you."

I thought it was stone, black marble in the shape of an egg, until Olympio went on. "The egg holds what my grandfather took from you. The badness, *muy malo,* very bad. He put it into the egg to protect you. And when you leave, he'll take care of it, so it'll never attack you again."

Olympio's grandfather spoke, and Olympio translated. "But he won't be able to stop you from putting new bad stuff back inside yourself."

"Thank you," I said, as sincerely as I could, then turned to push my way through the door.

Hector followed me down the hallway and stairs as I raced my way out. I didn't know where I was going, I just needed to get home.

Halfway down the hall I realized that those had been statues of Santa Muerte in his room. I should have asked him about her. Of course. If anyone had a direct line to obscure supernatural entities, it was a man who took bad-ness out of people and put it into gothic Easter eggs.

I made it out of the building, hitting the street almost at a run. "Hey—slow down!" Hector called after me. I darted through a group of people standing, and they laughed, either at some joke or to see a lost white girl on the lam. Hector caught up to me.

"Where are we? I need to go. I have to get home." He reached out to feel my forehead, and I ducked away. "I'm fine. I just have to go."

"What is wrong with you?"

"Me? Why did you take me to him? What was that about?"

We were underneath a sputtering streetlight, and Hector's face was full of concern. "He was the best doctor for the kind of illness you had."

"Does he cure cancer?"

"No." He pulled back as if I'd hit him. "Do you have cancer?"

"No. My mom does. I was supposed to go see her the other night." I went through my pockets, looking for my phone or anything at all, but then realized that when Hector had gotten me out of my house, he probably hadn't thought to bring my purse along. "I'm sure she's worried sick. Sicker. You know?" I laughed at my own poor joke.

"Edie—I didn't know. I'm so sorry."

"It's why I started working at your place. I couldn't bear to be at the sleep clinic one more night, once I knew. I couldn't just sit there, not doing anything. It'd drive me insane." I looked around, trying to figure out where I was, where the nearest train station would be, only I didn't have any money on me. I whirled on him. "I need to go home now. I have to call her tonight, even if it wakes her up."

"Or you could just ask me for my phone?" He held it out to me.

He was right. I'd had my mother's phone number memorized since we'd moved in second grade. I stuck out my hand without saying anything. Hector dropped his phone into it, and I dialed.

"Mom? Peter—Peter, yeah, I'm fine. I'm sorry. I was

really sick. No, I'm better now, thanks. Really sick. This is actually a doctor friend of mine's phone." I glared at Hector. In case my parents called back to check on me, he'd better cover for me. "Yeah. Tell her I love her, and not to worry, okay? Okay. Thanks."

I hung up, a small portion of my guilt lifted, and gave Hector back his phone.

"If I'd known, Edie—" he said, his voice heavy with apology. "What about just taking it easy for a week? Letting the news settle in?"

"Because. I suck at being alone with myself. And I'm the most alone person I know."

He looked down at me. "I find that hard to believe." His arms were open, palms facing up. I could step into them, just for human contact, for human warmth.

I took a step back so I wouldn't do anything foolish. "Believe what you want. It's true." I couldn't let him hug me, so I hugged myself. Now that we were outside, it was cooler, and the shirt Hector had picked out for me was thin. Oh, God, he'd put my bra on me. Yes, he was a doctor and all—I knew that for me penises were a dime a dozen, I'd seen so many at work—but he was still my boss. Ugh. "What happened to me?" I touched my neck, where the claw marks had been. They were still there now, but fainter, and they didn't hurt to touch.

Hector's arms dropped; our moment was gone. "*Susto.* In layman's terms, some of your spirit leaked out. The *curandero* caught it, and put it back in."

I snorted. "Is there a cork on me somewhere I should know about?"

"No. But you need to go easier on yourself." He stepped nearer and stood quietly, as if by being calm he could force me to be still. He didn't have his coat on, and from this near I could smell him. Deodorant, and the sweat it fought. He smelled like a man. The night was cool and I would bet his hands were warm.

"How'd you know to check on me the other night?" I looked up at him, without stepping away.

His eyes searched mine, and I didn't know what question he was trying to answer there. "I just had a feeling."

"At eleven o'clock at night?"

"I'm like Olympio. I see things." He shook his head and looked away from me. "Sometimes when an addict comes in, I can see their addiction, like a black snake tied around their chest. Not every addict—and it's not always a snake. Sometimes I see other diseases. When I see those people, I do what I can, and then I tell them to go see the *curandero.* Their problems are not entirely of this world—and they'll need more than medicine to solve them."

I looked down at myself. "So all those times he told me I needed healing, you saw it too?"

"To a lesser degree. I suspect he's got stronger sight than I do. And better training. I'm sorry—I didn't know it would get so bad so fast with you."

"Heh. Don't feel too bad, you've still got all of Western medicine on your side. And penicillin. Which is what I was pretty sure I needed. Or Cipro. Bactrim. The big guns." I looked back up at him, and he was still too near to me. He was close because he wanted to be. "What do you see when you look at me now?"

He was still for a moment, and then tapped my breast-bone. "There was a black flower here. Unfurling, like an anemone." He waved his fingers in the air. "Sucking your life away. You were already barely hanging on—you didn't have any strength left to fight it."

"Is it still there?" I asked, my voice small.

Hector nodded, and held up his fingers, an inch apart.

"He shrank it, but it's not gone. It'll just grow until you solve whatever causes it."

*My life?* I wondered, and then laughed aloud. He opened his mouth, like he was on the verge of making a confession, and then he looked hurt.

"You don't believe me?"

"No—I'm not making fun of you. I already know there are strange things in this world."

"Like vampires?"

I nodded.

"Why do you want to meet a vampire?" he went on.

"To help my mom. Their blood can heal almost anything."

A gamut of emotions ran over Hector's face, from wisdom to disgust. I wasn't sure how he'd wind up feeling—if despite his seeing things he'd think that I was insane or if he knew better and would finally break and tell me.

"You give that extra blood to someone, right?" I pressed, hoping I could help him decide.

He nodded, slowly. "Yes. I do."

"*¡Médico!* Doctor! You forgot your coat!" Olympio came running out of the building behind us, yelling for us to stop, like we'd been going somewhere. We turned to watch him, and he drew up short, wide-eyed, pointing behind us. "Donkey Lady!"

He dropped Hector's coat and ran back inside.

I looked over my shoulder and there was Jorgen, reared up on two legs.

# CHAPTER TWENTY-TWO

I didn't think he looked like a Donkey or a Lady at all—but I knew what he'd once been.

Standing made him at least seven feet tall, with an angular wolf-like head, looming over me. I should have known he'd find me again. That's what a Hound was for. He jumped after Olympio, and I threw myself into his path.

"Jorgen!"

The Hound drew up short. "Are you here for the kid? Or for me?"

Jorgen tilted his head down, and oh, how I wished for a doorway between us. He took a step forward, shoveling his nose at me, as if to push me back. I held my ground.

Hector whispered. "What . . . is that?"

"You can see it?" I wasn't sure if Jorgen's powers to hide depended on his proximity to Dren, or if he was generally hidden. Jorgen looked over to Hector, and then back to me.

I could see him running after kids to scare them since they could see him, like a bored junkyard dog. "You don't eat them, do you?"

He looked at me through one of his too-human eyes. He didn't blink.

"I don't want to know. Why are you here?" I asked

Jorgen. He came very near, slowly, and it was hard to
steel myself not to back away. He was even more grotesque up close, and since my shun hadn't protected me
from him so far, I wasn't sure what he was capable of. I
stood very, very still as lips, slightly more human than
Hound, grabbed my wrist and tried to pull me down the
street.

"Hey!" Hector said in warning. I gently pulled my
wrist away from Jorgen's mouth and wiped it on my
shorts.

"Jorgen, I have no idea what you want—or how I could
even help you."

Jorgen growled, a human-sounding expression of frustration. He reached for my wrist again, and Hector
stepped up. Jorgen eyed him with pure hatred, and his
lips curled into a snarl.

"What is that?" Hector asked, trying to stand in front
of me to protect me.

"It's a Hound. I didn't always work at your clinic—or
the sleep clinic before." Now was the time to lay all my
cards on the table, if I was going to get the truth. "I used
to work on a floor for supernatural creatures that needed
help. The Hound belongs to one of them." Not the entire
truth, but enough. "He belongs to a vampire. Which I
wish I could find right now."

At this, Jorgen stopped growling.

"That's what you want from me, isn't it?" I asked Jorgen. "To follow you."

Jorgen's oversized wolf head bobbed, the patches
where he was missing fur gleaming in the streetlight.

"Where?" Hector asked.

"I don't know. To Dren, I assume." Jorgen bowed down
at this, and his teeth slunk toward my wrist again. I pulled
it away.

Dren was a vampire; finding him would solve my problem, right? Maybe. "I'd rather find a vampire that doesn't hate me, though." I couldn't really imagine my mother spending her life indebted to Dren now, could I? God.

"How did he find you?" Hector jerked his chin at the nightmare by our side.

"It's what he's cursed to do." I used a knuckle to push my cheek in to chew on. Could I get Dren to help me? Somehow? Was it worth the risk? Of course it was. It was my mom.

Just as I was talking myself into following Jorgen, even if I already knew I wouldn't like where he would lead, Hector nodded. Subtly at first, but then grander, as if convincing himself of something. "All right. I'll take you to her. I'll show you."

"To who?"

Hector raised his hands to the sky. "To who else? The Queen of the Night."

This was a much better option, inasmuch as any option was better than dealing with Dren, a vampire whom I already knew had a grudge against me. Now a willing guide, Hector took us deeper into the city, with Jorgen following along like the Hound of the Baskervilles come to life. Jorgen whined periodically—it was clear we were not going the way he preferred, from the noises he made, and the way he wove at every corner—but he didn't put his lips on me again, thank God.

We reached a place where there were women standing on the corners of the streets. Not dressed like hookers, or fiending for dope—normal women, in groups of two or three, talking, standing in place. Watching. When the first group saw us, they smiled at Hector. And one of them whistled out a call that I heard repeated far away. The graffiti on the walls changed—Reina colors for sure. "Are we in their territory now?"

Hector nodded.

"So I was right, there was a connection between the people with the bite mark shirts and the tattoos all along?"

"Presumably. I've never seen her myself. I've only heard about her."

"Why did you go in with her lot, then? The blood is for her, isn't it?"

He nodded again. "Catrina explained it to me."

"And you believed her? Wait—she knows?"

"She does. Our visit will probably wake her up."

"She told you she was getting blood for a vampire, and you believed her. Wow." I at least had Jorgen to prove that I was for real. What had Catrina had?

"Hey, I see things too," he said.

"But—you've never *met* her," I tried again.

"No. I don't have to. I can walk through here and see the changes she's made. Look around. There's no trash on these streets. All the businesses here close at the end of the day, and no one ever breaks into them. The kids who live inside her lines get fed. I have no idea how she's doing it, or what laws she's breaking, but this is what I want for our entire community." He looked around the empty street we were walking down, all of the people living in it happily at home, watching TVs that we could hear through open windows. Vampires weren't typically helpful like that. All the vampires I'd ever met had three plans. What they wanted, what they wanted, and how you could help them get what they wanted.

"Plus," he went on, "something goes bad—she's strong enough to fight."

"Fight who?" I asked, but I realized I already knew. "Maldonado."

"And his men, if it comes to that. She's stronger than I am. She'll live longer, for sure."

That sounded ominous. "Hector—" I still had to figure out how to save my mom. But we were less than a week away from the seventeenth and whatever badness it meant for Hector and his home. I thought my mom had longer than that. We turned a corner and he drew up short.

"We're here."

The street we turned onto had been truncated halfway down, turning the road into a courtyard. There was a barricade across the entire block, the road cut in half by cars stacked on top of one another, junkyard-style, like Legos made of steel. No mere human had done that.

"Whoa."

"Almost there," Hector said. "They're unlikely to let me inside, but they might let you in if I vouch for you."

I nodded. "Please, try." Whoever was inside was legitimate. No plain human could move cars like that without a backhoe. Following Jorgen, presumably to Dren, was my worst-case scenario. If there was any way I could get a seemingly decent vampire to help my mom, one that wasn't self-centered and insane, I would do it.

We reached the front of the structure, which wasn't as solid as it had seemed from the shadows at the end of the block. It was a double-walled fortress, and there were tunnels inside where I could see women walking—patrolling—back and forth, between the rows of cars.

Hector and I waited until two women emerged.

"It's a bit late for *la entrega de sangre, el médico*."

"No blood tonight. I've brought a friend who needs to

see the Queen." He gently pushed me forward. From my new vantage point, I could see that both of the women were casually wearing submachine guns.

"We don't allow visitors." Neither of the women apparently saw Jorgen, standing beside me.

"Please, bring someone with the *don* out. She's special, and she needs to see her."

They talked among themselves, passing the message up the line. I used that time to wonder what exactly the submachine guns were for. Someone inside yelled out, "Hey, *médico*!" then companionably came around the corner and saw me.

"Oh, not you—" Catrina, from the clinic. Then her eyes found Jorgen and her jaw dropped.

"What the—" She crossed herself.

"Hey, Catrina." I gave her a low wave.

"Explain that." She pointed at Jorgen.

"He's like a pet. To one of *them*," I said with particular emphasis, hoping she'd know what kind of creature I meant. "He doesn't belong to me. I'm trying to return him." Whatever I needed to say to get inside the door and meet this Queen.

She squinted at me. "You have the *don*, too?"

"No. I knew his owner in a former life." I didn't want to say the word *vampire* here—despite the blood thing, I didn't know how much people out here would actually know. If they were daytimers, they would have been able to see Jorgen. Hell, if they were daytimers they probably wouldn't need submachine guns.

"Perhaps the Queen can rid her of him. *Él encuentra las cosas.* Maybe the Queen could use him herself?" Hector asked.

Catrina grunted. "He's not coming in here."

To be honest, I didn't want to take Jorgen in with me

either, but I didn't want to find out what he'd do if I didn't eventually go along with his mysterious plan. I gestured at the wall of cars and made an excuse I hoped he'd understand. "I don't think he could safely fit."

"All right then. We'll take her in. You two wait here." She pointed at Hector and Jorgen.

I looked back at Hector, apologetically.

"Don't worry." He looked over his shoulder at Jorgen, who was on all fours now, too long to be normal, drapes of skin and fur hanging down. "I'm sure we'll both enjoy it."

Catrina let me in. The other two let her, and acted like she wasn't crazy—even though they couldn't see Jorgen, they accepted that there were strange forces at work in the world, and were prepared to try to handle them with gunfire. I wondered if Catrina had always been able to see the soul-sucking flower in me.

She patted me down more thoroughly than the TSA, and when she was done, she gave me a grudging nod of respect. "I guess you know more than you let on. Welcome to *casa de la noche.*"

Word traveled ahead of us. First we moved through the precariously balanced maze of junkers. I looked overhead and realized we were walking under deadfalls, created by non-engineers. I took a few deep breaths, tried to chase away my claustrophobia, and kept my eyes on Catrina's back.

It got darker as we went in—and then we reached simple Christmas lights, sparkling like stars, netted overhead. It gave the tunnel we were traveling through a dream-like quality, and took away the edge of a thousand pounds of rusting junk.

Then we reached the building everything was attached to. I felt better once I was under solid brick. The main doors were guarded, and Catrina had to do a call and response in Spanish before she was let back in. Inside was quiet, as befit a place without drugs or hooliganism to keep it awake. A few people getting up for early jobs—they were wearing uniforms, and I could smell the coffee on their breath as they walked the way we'd come down the hall. They looked at me but didn't ask any questions.

We passed one person as she was closing her door. I could see into her rooms—they looked normal, tight but tidy—with the exception of a bricked-up window on the far wall.

"Bricks?" I asked Catrina.

"No open windows on the bottom two levels. It's not safe."

If you were allergic to light. Or maybe were expecting smoke grenades from rival gangs. I kept my mouth shut as I followed her farther in.

We reached the end of the hallway, and there were stairs going down. To the basement. There was a gate across the hallway, bolted into the cement. A series of locks of all different types ran down it, circled with padlocked chains through the bottom rungs.

"We'll have to wait here. I don't have the key." She sat down on the stairs.

"Is she normally out late?"

"Until almost dawn. You have an hour."

"You could—" I gestured back up the stairs. No need for both of us to kill time here.

Her eyes narrowed. "Are you trying to ditch me?"

I shook my head. "No—not at all. It's just that it's late. Not everyone's as used to staying up at night as I am."

She reached behind her neck and unclasped a necklace I hadn't noticed there. A small cross swung out of her shirt, and she patted me with it.

"Wouldn't it have been smarter to do that up above?" I asked when she was done. She reclasped her necklace, satisfied.

"You're right—I should always check." She looked away, lips tight, like she'd missed something she ought not to have in recent past. "Even Reina doesn't mind me checking."

So. The plot thickened. If I'd known I might meet a real vampire, I'd have brought something useful. Like a syringe, or an IV start kit. I snorted at myself and rubbed sweaty hands against my jeans.

Catrina was quiet. Any questions I wanted to ask would give away information on my part. I didn't want to tell her anything else about myself or my situation until I found out who I'd be dealing with tonight.

Waiting here I could feel the moments ticking away. I hoped that Jorgen hadn't eaten Hector, that Olympio wasn't cowering under his bed worrying about the Donkey Lady, that I hadn't left Olympio's grandfather with the impression that I was a bitch, and last but not least, that Peter had woken up my mother just enough to explain to her that I was all right. Let's add the hope that my mother might not die at the end of all this to my laundry list too. That maybe I could get some fucking answers here from a fucking real vampire, one that just happened to be nice enough to hand over a small amount of blood.

There were footsteps on the stair above us. "Catrina, who is there?" a voice called down.

Of course the vampire could smell me. She could probably hear me breathing.

"She's a nurse, she works at the clinic with me. Hector

brought her. She says she needs to see you, to help her get rid of the thing outside. Hector says it may help you in your search."

Had he? Hmmmm. If this vampire was searching for something, maybe we could work out a trade. "My name's Edie," I helpfully provided, my name echoing up the stairs.

There was a sigh from up above. "I was hoping it wouldn't be you."

Black boots appeared on the stairs, then tight jeans, black shirt, and then a face that I knew. She was a real vampire. I'd been there when she'd been marked to be turned. "Luz."

*"Enfermera,"* she said, closing her eyes and shaking her head.

I'd been her nurse—no, her boyfriend's nurse—for a stretch when I'd been working on Y4. He'd been gravely injured by a gunshot wound, and she'd been adoring him to the end. Anna, the vampire I was a friend of, had changed him into a daytimer, and Luz into a full vamp, to save both of their lives. Mostly. Seeing as I'd found her as the ruler of a gang, hidden in the basement of an apartment-bunker, I wasn't sure this was what Anna'd had in mind.

"Catrina, you can go," Luz said.

"But—" she began, reluctant to be dismissed. She looked to me, then back to Luz, and asked, "Any news?"

"Not tonight. I'll look again tomorrow."

It was clear Catrina didn't want to leave. Luz reached out and grabbed her shoulder. "I'll find her. I won't rest until I do. Don't lose hope."

Catrina nodded softly, and then ran back up the stairs. Luz watched her go with pity, and then looked to me. "I suppose that we can talk. Perhaps I owe you that. Or perhaps you owe me?" Her eyebrows rose, and the gaze that had been so wide and soft with Catrina narrowed to predatory.

"I didn't mean for this to happen." She'd begged Anna for her boyfriend's life, and this was the payment Anna had required. Changing her into this, here. "I had no idea."

"What's done is done," Luz said, her lips snaking up into an ironic smile, showing fangs, as she reached into her pocket for a ring of keys.

# CHAPTER TWENTY-THREE

After enough locks to successfully win a car on *The Price Is Right* were opened, Luz pushed open a very squeaky gate. "Rust, my last defense," she said, closing the gate behind us—and, to my dismay, redoing all the locks. Once finished, she repocketed the keys.

She flipped on a light and gestured me farther in.

The basement was small and open, with cement floors and walls. A couch, a coffee table, an unmade bed. A single lamp hung over the bed, a tissue paper heart stapled to its shade, casting a pink shadow down. With the exception of her excellent collection of capless test tubes scattered on the floor, Luz had fewer belongings than me.

"Luz, this is a pit."

"Call me Reina. Everyone else does," she said as she kicked test tubes aside. Thank God the things were made of plastic, not glass, or this'd be like some sort of torture-porn horror film.

"Okay, Reina, what—" I watched her sink onto the cement floor, and went to kneel beside her. Her eyes were flat and cold, like a shark about to bite. I scooted back a bit, and she nodded. "What the hell happened to you?"

Focusing on me, she pushed herself up on one elbow. She stirred the test tubes nearest her until she found one with its contents still intact. "Since this is all your fault, I'll tell you the truth."

I cleared a spot from test tubes on the floor, thanked God that Hector had dressed me in jeans not shorts two nights ago, and carefully sat down.

"After I was bitten I slept for three nights. When I woke, I was unguarded and hungry. So I went out." She cracked the cap off the test tube and daubed the contents out with a dainty fingertip. "My first thought was to use all my power to tear apart the gang that'd crippled Javier. I went to see him immediately after I was reborn.

"He didn't understand what had happened. No one had explained things to him. He just knew he was well now and that I'd been gone, that was all. No one told me that I was asleep. Dying. Then becoming alive again." She tilted her head and finished off the blood in the tube like it was the last gulp of beer from a bottle, then she tossed the empty tube away. "I found him at a party."

I imagined her, starving, entering a room of humans, the sound of their blood singing in her ears.

"He said I'd been cheating on him, and went to hit me. I stopped him. For good."

I wondered if Javier had realized the mistake he'd made—right before Luz had broken his head off. "The party ended after that. I ate him. It was awful, in retrospect. At the time?" She picked up another test tube and looked at it as though it paled in comparison, then threw it aside. "At the time I was hungry. And then she arrived to claim me. Your friend."

I wasn't sure *friend* was the best term to describe the bond between Anna and me. I'd saved her life once, and that was a very big deal, but *friend* was pushing it.

"I think she wanted me to do what I did. I think she knew I would do it, and she wanted me to, to show me what I was capable of. So that I would believe her. I would know what I'd become, and feel her power over me. But even after that I still fought her." She looked directly at me. "I don't like being told what to do. By anyone."

I snorted. "I remember that about you."

"We made a deal. As long as I don't out vampires, or create followers—if I don't bite anyone human or share any of my blood with them—she will leave me be. So far I have been true to my word."

I wondered if Anna had given Luz her freedom as a test. And if so, had she ever imagined that Luz would manage to hold out this long? Luz was strong-willed indeed. I looked around at the test tube pit we were in. "How long'd it take you to come up with this workaround?"

"Longer than I would have liked. There were not many dogs out to feed on in winter." I imagined Luz, half mad with hunger, wandering the streets at night. Her eyes were distant, probably remembering the same. "The only thing keeping me alive—and not under her sway—was my pride. Pride is not a very filling dish."

She began to sink back against the cement floor, her black hair spilling out like the roads on a map. "And then Adriana found me. She was the most beautiful thing I'd ever seen. She knew Catrina, and Catrina . . . helped."

If this was helping. The jury was still out on that one.

"I have been true to my word. And I may kill people, as long as I don't bleed them. When I realized that—" A sly smiled crossed her face. "I took charge. I punished the gang that had hurt Javier in the first place. Then I started to take their place. Only in different ways. Hopefully better." Luz finished lowering herself to the floor. "Morning is near. *Enfermera,* why are you here?" She was fading before my eyes, with the arrival of the sun.

"I need to talk to Anna."

"If she wanted to talk to you, she'd find you. Next." Her eyes were halfway closed, like a resting cat.

"My mother has cancer. I want some of your blood."

She paused, and then laughed and laughed and laughed. "Please say you're kidding me. No. You're too earnest to kid. I remember that about you." She rolled to her side and closed her eyes, nuzzling into the chill cement floor. "Do you really think that's wise?"

"I don't know what else to do."

"I couldn't help you, even if I wanted to. If I did that, I would break my word. If I give you my blood, I would break my promise to Anna, and that would be the end of my freedom. I have no doubt that she would come herself to take me back."

"There has to be something I can trade you. Or something that you want."

She snorted. "You? No. There is nothing more for us to discuss." The sensation of her presence in the room kept fading.

"Goddammit! Luz!" I crawled over to her on the cement floor, empty test tubes rolling out of my path. I grabbed her shoulders and shook her. It was unwise, but I had finally found a vampire that wasn't going to kill me and she was turning out to be fucking useless. She didn't move. I twisted around, looking around her room for anything to grab hold of, leverage to get her to help me. Her unused bed, bathed in heart-shaped pink, mocked me. I frowned and looked down at her now peaceful face. I shook her again. "Luz! Who else lives down here with you?"

One eye opened and fixed on me. "Who told you?"

"No one. Pink hearts aren't exactly a vampire decorating theme." I'd gotten a reaction, so I decided to press my luck. "Where is he? Who is it that you're looking for?"

She groaned, shaking herself, trying to fight the sun. She pushed herself up on her elbows, and I quickly scooted back. "She," Luz corrected me. "Where is *she*. She isn't here." She breathed like a dying person, raspy and with long pauses, except in her case she was fighting to stay awake. Luz fixed her eyes on me and panted. "There is no way you can find her if I cannot."

"If it's a deal—if it's for your blood—I can. Try me."

Luz squinted at me, her head beginning to sink down. "Ask Catrina. She can tell you what you need to know."

I nodded at her relaxing form. "Okay." I stood, dusting off my knees, as Luz faded. Lightning-fast, one of her arms snaked out and her hand caught my ankle, fingers tight. It would be nothing for her, even half asleep, to crush my ankle and rip off my foot.

"Don't come back unless you've found her," Luz warned.

"Okay," I said, my voice pitched higher. She finally went to sleep, and her hand released me.

# CHAPTER TWENTY-FOUR

I stared at Luz's prone form. Could I condemn my mother . . . to this? I didn't want her to be a vampire, just a daytimer; I wanted her to get just enough blood to be healed and stay that way. But there were no promises after that, no way I could predict how things would go with 100 percent certainty.

Catrina was waiting outside on the stairs, on the other side of the locked gate. She called out to me. "Get the keys."

I looked down at Luz again, trying to imagine my mother sleeping there instead of her. "Really?"

"Really." Catrina crossed her arms.

I slunk back over to Luz and tapped her. She was well and truly gone now—I didn't know if she was mostly dead, or dead-dead, or what. It was creepy. I reached into her pockets and yanked out the keys too quickly, shaking her. I jumped back, just in case, and then ran back to the doorway.

Catrina snapped her fingers on the other side. "Give them here."

I imagined her taking them once I did, leaving me locked in here with Luz—there were so many locks, it'd take me hours to free myself on my own. She snapped her fingers again, and I tossed the keys through. From here, I had a good view of the tattoo on her right-hand ring finger's first knuckle. It looked like a stylized bone.

She began opening the door. I talked while she worked. "Reina said you would help me. She's looking for someone—"

"I know." Catrina knelt to get at the last locks on the gate.

"I need something that smells like her, to give to the Hound." She frowned again at hearing this as I stepped out. I wondered if I would ever see her smile. She closed the door and started relocking the gate.

It wasn't too late. I could stop Catrina and run back in there and somehow bleed Luz while she slept. But pledging my mother to a vampire that hated her wouldn't do any good—it was likely to get her killed.

"Come on," Catrina said as she finished locking the door. She threw the keys back inside, where they clattered on the cement floor and landed by Luz's thigh. "I'll take you to her room. We'll find something for your devil there."

I took one last look at Luz's sleeping form. I tried to imagine being in love with a vampire, and drew a blank. Anna and I had done right by each other—but *love* was not the word. Whatever human had cut out that paper heart for Luz was crazy. And brave. "What was her name, anyhow?"

"Adriana." Catrina glowered at me. "And she's my sister," she said, before going up the stairs.

Because of Luz, I knew it was already past dawn. I couldn't see outside, but there were people moving around, the sound of showers being turned on through thin walls, opening and closing bedroom doors. Catrina led me upstairs, and then down a hall.

"When she wasn't down there, she was up here." She opened up a door and we stepped inside. Natural light from a window across from us flooded the room. The walls were cream; one had a red couch, the other a small black TV. A black bookcase didn't have books on its shelves—it had tiny figurines in bright colors, and gold medallions artfully arranged. A streamer of tissue paper with elaborate designs cut into it swung from shelf to shelf.

Catrina pushed past me to go into the next room. I didn't follow. There was no need for me to be too nosy. She came back with a dark blue sweater. "Will that thing be able to find her—even if she's—" She didn't want to say the worst out loud.

"I don't know. But tonight I'll ask it if it can." Her eyebrows rose at my response. "It used to be human. It understands," I said, and she shook her head.

"Just when I thought I'd seen everything there was to see." She looked from the sweater she held to me, and pulled it back. "I'm going with you."

"What? No way."

Catrina started nodding and wouldn't stop. "She's my sister—I have to go. I want to be there when you find her. You don't know what she looks like—and that thing might eat her—and—"

"Okay!" I held up both my hands to stop her. "I want to go on record as saying I think it's a bad idea, but okay." I didn't think it mattered how I found Adriana—and besides, Catrina had the *don,* whatever the hell that was. It might be nice to have someone on my side who could see things I couldn't, and who could talk.

"Tonight?" she asked, holding the sweater to her chest.

"Yeah. Meet me at my place at sundown."

"All right."

I gave her my address, and she led me out.

# CHAPTER TWENTY-FIVE

I trotted down the stairs and out into the car-filtered daylight. Following people who already knew their way through the maze led me out to where Hector was sitting, waiting for me.

He stood up when he saw me. "How'd it go?"

"Oddly." I looked around to make sure no one was listening as we began to walk away. "She *is* a vampire." I figured I could tell him that much. "Her floor is littered with a thousand or so test tubes from Divisadero, which I think you knew." I made a face at him.

"I'd rather pay her kind of tithes, seeing as she's doing useful things here. Not making everyone pray to a bony statue and extorting bribes."

I looked around. "When'd Jorgen leave?"

"He disappeared before sunrise. He wasn't pleasant to look at, and so I didn't for a while. When I turned back next, near dawn, he was gone."

I wondered where he roosted during the day—if he ran back to Dren's side, literally disappeared, or hid out . . . underneath the leaves of trees. Like a butterfly in the rain. Not. I snorted at the thought.

"So will she help you?" he asked. I nodded. "What's her

price?" I gave him a look, and he shrugged. "Nothing is ever for free."

Which begged the question why Hector was helping me. Had been helping me, ever since the day he'd seen the black flower on my chest and hired me to keep an eye on it. I really should have asked Catrina about that, dammit. I guess I'd get a chance to, tonight.

"She said if I can find her friend, she'll trade me the blood for my mother."

Hector made a groaning sound and shook his head.

"What?"

"Edie, that's impossible. Adriana's been missing for more than a month. Sometimes—rarely—kidnappings work out, but after a month? No way."

"Oh, man." I groaned. Hector had no reason to lie to me that I knew of, and besides, I'd watched enough true crime shows on TV to know he was right. A month was a really long time. Throw one more slim chance of saving my mom onto the pile. "Was it Maldonado?"

"Who else could it be?" Hector's lips drew into a grim line. "But he must know what Luz is. That's why he only comes out during the day and hunkers down at night."

I couldn't imagine Luz not shredding anything that moved to get to Adriana—no. Maybe once she'd been kidnapped, the threat of violence against Adriana had held her hand. She must really not know where Adriana was . . . and cruelest of all, she still lived in hope.

"How long does he think that'll work?"

"Long enough."

"Through the seventeenth?" I pressed. We were nearing a train station.

Hector drew his hand up himself like he was catching bad thoughts and throwing them away.

"I don't understand why you won't tell me what's happening on that date. Do you have a cage match scheduled with him then, or what?"

"My fight with him wasn't supposed to involve anyone else." He sighed deeply, started patting his pockets, and retrieved a fistful of change. "Take it. Go home."

I didn't know if he meant home, like to my apartment home, or fired-go-home-forever, home. "What's that?"

"Train fare."

"You can't fire me—" I protested.

"I'm not. The clinic needs you. You're a good nurse. Just go home."

I eyed his palm suspiciously. "Will you tell me everything later?"

"If I can. Give me one more night." His eyes searched mine, and I hoped he would find what he was looking for there. "I have to get to work now, Edie. Make my life easier for once, and do what you're told."

I frowned but held out my hand, so he could pour the change in. As I relented, he relaxed, and I realized he must be exhausted. "You have to be as tired as I am—you should take today off." I bit my tongue before I asked him to come home with me. Not to take advantage of him, but just to take care of him for a bit. Like he'd spent the past two days taking care of me.

His bearing softened. "I wish I could, but I can't." And then he stood straighter, picking up all the burdens he'd momentarily left behind. "Go home and get better. Doctor's orders. Especially since I don't think I can talk Olympio's grandfather into taking you back."

I was tired. I needed a shower. I still smelled like smoke and I was pretty sure my shirt had a stain from that disgusting poultice. "But what're you going to do? You have to be as tired as I am."

He smiled softly at me. "I am. But I've got to go to work."

I took the next train. I got off at my stop and went home. My front door was closed, but Hector had left it unlocked.

Minnie was exorbitantly glad to see me and meowed aloud as she followed me around my house. "I know, I know." I knuckled her head, and then stripped for my shower.

When that was through, I plugged in my phone. Three worried calls from my mother, and a private one from Peter to tell me I was being awful. I'd caught as much in his tone last night, and deleted it without listening all the way through. I called her back, tried to sound the right combination of sick and safe on the phone, and rescheduled an early dinner with her tonight.

Five hours of sleep and twelve snoozes later, I got up again. It was only three. I tied my hair up, bent at odd angles since I'd slept on it wet, and headed for the train. I got off at the stop before my mother's to get her a small bouquet of flowers from an upscale liquor store. Then I hopped back on and off and walked up to her door.

Three knocks, and I waited. Nothing. I was reaching up to knock again when the door opened. Peter.

"Hey—"

"Your mother's sleeping." He stepped outside and closed the door behind him.

"I can wait—"

"She was up all night, worried sick about you. I'm not waking her up, after the stunt you pulled."

"I'm sorry," I said, trying to reach for the door handle. He didn't slap my hand away, but I could see him thinking it. "I really was sick!"

He looked me up and down. I looked tired, maybe, but not ill. He knew what ill looked like. Ill was sleeping inside, right now.

"I'm not lying!" I protested.

"Keep your voice down," he snapped at me.

"Peter—she's my own mother. You can't stop me from seeing her," I said in clipped tones.

"She needs her rest right now. More than she needs to see you." He inhaled and exhaled deeply. "Look, Edie, you and I have always gotten along. So you get another chance. But not today, not right now. I'll tell her you came by."

I could not believe I was being stopped. I wanted to yell at him, but what would that do? Wake my mother, so she'd stumble to the door and see us fighting? That wouldn't do. "Here." I shoved the bouquet forward. "They're for her."

He looked down at the flowers, but didn't take them. "She's neutropenic. You should know better." And with that, he went back inside and closed the door.

# CHAPTER TWENTY-SIX

Neutropenic people couldn't get flowers or fresh fruit, or anything else that might have germs on it. I knew that—flowers weren't allowed on ICU floors. And of course my mom was neutropenic, after all her rounds of chemo. She'd be lucky to have four intact white blood cells left to rub together, like the last few floating Cheerios in a cereal bowl.

I couldn't believe it had happened, all the way home. That I'd forgotten, and that Peter'd rebuffed me. I went back to my apartment on the train, stunned and angry, and barely remembered to get off at my stop. It was drizzling as I walked in. I was halfway up the stairs to my apartment when I realized I'd left the flowers behind on my seat.

I forced myself to eat a dinner of whatever was left in my fridge. Just before nightfall, I heard a knock. Catrina was standing outside my front door. I held it open for her. "Welcome to casa de la crazy."

Snorting, she walked in to sit down on my couch. "What now?"

"We're on Jorgen's time line. I'm sure he'll show up." He still wanted me to go with him—and now I needed something in return. I sat down on the opposite end of my couch. I'd already gotten ready. I was wearing mostly black. I'd taken the cross I'd had Olympio buy and strung it on a long string hung around my neck; my old badge from work was in my back pocket. I was super prepared to make bad decisions.

Catrina had Adriana's sweater out, across her lap. She'd worn sensible boots, and I thought I could see the outline of a knife hilt at their top. Of course.

"How'd your sister meet Luz anyway?"

"You even know her real name."

"Yeah. We go back awhile."

Catrina's eyes narrowed in thought as she looked at me. "I underestimated you."

"I'm . . . sorry?" I guessed. I didn't know what to say.

She hugged the sweater to herself and leaned back into the couch. "My sister used to have some problems. She hung out with the wrong crowd. One night, things weren't going well for her. Luz rescued her from a bad situation. And Luz wasn't doing so well herself, on her own. They . . . started hanging out. Together." I tried to fill in the gaps in Catrina's story with my imagination. Leaping from saving someone's life to being on a pink-heart basis. Catrina watched me closely out of the corner of her eye. "They are in love."

I already knew as much. It wasn't the pink heart that gave it away, but the look on Luz's face when she spoke of Adriana, and the warning bruise she'd left on my ankle. "When'd you know she was a vampire?"

"When she tried to kill my cat." Catrina snorted. "I didn't want to believe, but the stories Adriana told me, and how she'd saved her—I have the *don*—I didn't want to believe, but I could see. After that, it was easy for me to help them by supplying Luz with blood. And after that, things started getting better for our block."

Well, I'd had no idea Luz would become the world's first socially conscious vampire when I'd met her. I wondered if Anna had had a hand in that. "What'll happen if your sister doesn't . . . come back?"

"I honestly don't know." Catrina was interrupted by a thump. She jumped, and Minnie bolted from the kitchen to the bedroom.

"Sorry. That's our ride."

We went to the door and Jorgen was there. "Hey. You're here because you need me to help Dren, right?" I didn't want to think of what was wrong with Dren that he couldn't help himself, or that Jorgen couldn't waltz in and fix. Jorgen nodded, his black eyes fixed on me.

"Okay—well, we need to make a deal." I really hoped that my neighbors weren't looking out right now, seeing me talk to empty space. "I need you to find someone else for me first. Then—and only then—can we go help Dren."

Jorgen went back to all fours and leaned forward, his face very near to mine. His breath stank, and he tilted so that I could see into his nearest black eye. In that one eye was all the hatred Jorgen felt for me, for the situation he was in—where I had put him. He'd kill me if he could—but he needed me right now. We'd get along until then, was what that eye told me, but afterward? Who knew.

I looked back into my apartment and waved to Catrina. "Okay. Let's go."

She let Jorgen smell her precious sweater. I'd never seen a Hound do what one does before. He was still for a moment, waiting. And then I'd have sworn he seemed pleased. He bounded to the bottom of the stairs, rippling like a weasel or ferret or some other creature with an extra half a spine, then looked back, waiting for us.

I figured we were walking toward the station halfway there. Catrina was quiet, just watching Jorgen pace along. The Hound could be faster than we were, but there was no point in jogging after him when we didn't know how far we'd have to go.

"How long have you known him?" Catrina asked me.

"I first met him in December." I didn't want to go into the details of my past with Jorgen. "How long have you known Hector?" I deflected instead.

"Since December."

I was a little stunned. "Really? He seems so entrenched here."

"Oh, he is. He's done a world of good. He was a friend of the original doctor, who was getting quite old."

"Hmm." That didn't fit the picture of Hector's life that I'd created in my head.

When we reached the station, I wondered how Jorgen would get through. I fed in my card for myself and Catrina, and the turnstile clicked as we passed through. I looked back at Jorgen, trapped on the other side. Leaning back, I passed my card through again, and he reared back onto two legs, waddling through the turnstile in a creepy half-human fashion, jerking spastically forward like a monster chasing me in a bad dream. When he was through he fell to all fours again, his ill-furred loose skin swinging down after him.

There was no way not to see him in the station's brighter light. His human skin was pale and blue-veined where it was visible in patches through his fur. He looked so wrong it made it hard to talk to him. "Where to now?" I asked aloud.

He got his bearings, and we waited quietly for the southbound train.

Why wasn't I surprised when we got off at the clinic's stop? The homeless people were sleeping in their make-shift shelter. I hoped that neither of them had the *don* like Catrina—I didn't want to have to explain Jorgen to any-one. At the same time, I felt safer traveling at night with a nightmarish creature beside me. I hoped that just because normal people couldn't see him didn't mean he couldn't affect them. I'd hate to get into trouble and not be able to count on my horrific imaginary friend.

"Here?" Catrina asked, plainly disappointed when we reached the bottom step.

"You wanted somewhere more exotic?"

"I just figured she wouldn't be so close."

Because close . . . was probably bad. The best answer for why Luz hadn't been able to find Adriana was that she was dead after all. I could see Catrina steeling herself to find out the truth, any truth, just to finally know. I didn't respond.

We walked in a direction I hadn't gone yet on my short tours with Olympio and last night with Hector. At night, this side of town seemed much grimmer. The colors were washed out, and all that showed up was dirt and darkness. A few dogs ran up to us as we passed an alley—half feral and growling. Jorgen leered at them, and the shy ones ran away. The braver ones trailed us with a litany of barks, until yells of frustration from the closed windows we passed shook them off.

"Can he tell us what we're in for?" Catrina asked.

"I don't think so." At County Hospital, for patients who couldn't talk or write, we had boards with likely com-plaints. They could point to a picture of a toilet, and we'd know to bring a bedpan. What kind of board of horrors would Jorgen need to tell me what we were going into? A knife, in the alley, with Colonel Mustard. Heh.

There were some people sleeping in the street—on a hot night, you didn't need a shelter. And if you were too drunk or crazy to get into one, odds were that no one would mess with you.

Other people were lurking in corners. I could feel them watching us. I didn't know if it was Jorgen's presence that kept them at bay, or if we possessed some frightening luck.

We turned onto a new block, and there was a bright light at the end of it. My first thought was of a train. I couldn't help but stare.

"Here?" Catrina whispered in disgust. "All this time—here?"

An effigy of Santa Muerte was standing in the window, draped in a purple robe, trimmed in gold, with embroidered gold-thread stars. The street was strewn with flowers and petals. I had a suspicion where we were.

"Maldonado's current church?" I guessed. She nodded. The altar's light illuminated the grimace on her face. We walked toward the church, Jorgen bold, us more slowly behind.

A person raced out in front of us, crossing the street, and started sweeping up the flowers with both arms.

"Oy!" A man I hadn't noticed stepped out from beside the altar, hidden by the shadows of the building behind. "Stop that!" He shoved the other person down, and pulled back his leg like he was going to kick whoever he'd shoved. I saw a bony arm rise up in supplication.

"Hey!" I said, without thinking about it first. Catrina yanked me back. The man stopped, mid-kick, distracted by me, and the person I'd saved scrambled over. In the altar's light, the bony flower thief had stringy hair and was wearing two hospital gowns, one in each direction, only three buttons snapped between them. "Oh, God. Not you." It was the woman I'd saved, who'd infected me.

"*¿Quién eres?*" the man said, coming over.

"You're kicking someone's grandmother!" I said, emboldened by Jorgen's presence beside me.

"She's stealing flowers to resell. It's against the law. Those flowers are Santa Muerte's." I could see the three cross tattoos on either side of his neck.

"The flowers are in the street. Technically they're trash," Catrina said, stepping forward, into the altar's light.

"*Cállate, no sabes lo que estás hablando,*" he said, and stepped forward. I really hoped Jorgen was looming somewhere behind. "Wait—I know you—" He looked Catrina up and down, then put a hand to something at his waist.

Jorgen bowled him down. The man fell with a grunt, and Jorgen's mouth stretched comically wide. His jaw unhinged, like a python's, and he barely had the man's head in his mouth before the man began to scream. Three bizarre gulping bites and the man was gone; only Jorgen remained.

What had that man been reaching for? A gun? A knife? A phone? Too late now, we'd never know.

"Where did he go?" Catrina whispered, horrified.

"Do you really care?" I said, my voice rising higher. Jorgen's formerly slack-skinned stomach was stretched taut like a drum. I thought I could see a foot pressing out from the inside, like a perverted kicking baby.

The elderly woman started babbling between us, holding her hands up in a placating fashion. I gladly concentrated on her instead.

"Grandmother—*Abuela*—" I said, trying to calm her down. She must have made it to County; I recognized the pattern of her hospital gowns. I reached out and touched her forehead, and she didn't jerk away. She didn't have a fever, that was good—hopefully she wasn't contagious anymore. "What happened to you?"

She began speaking in fast Spanish that I couldn't understand. Catrina translated quickly. "She doesn't like it here, everyone is mean to her, there is no respect left in this world. And she's scared of that dog."

Well. She had every right to be. She bent over and started scrabbling on the ground, rooting through the discarded flowers like she'd lost a contact lens. I didn't want to leave her behind here for the next Three Crosses guard to kick. "Catrina—is there somewhere you can take her?"

"Why?"

"We can't just leave her here is why."

"Doesn't she have a home?"

"Look, Jorgen will only listen to me. And we're near where your sister is. Maybe you can just trust me to find things out." I didn't want to state the obvious: that we both knew what the answer would be—that Jorgen would most likely lead me up the street so he could dig away at a shallow trash pit in a narrow backyard. I gestured to the elderly woman. "She needs your help. Can you take her back to the Reina's? Get her some food?"

Catrina looked from the old woman to me, and then past us to Jorgen, whom we'd both just seen swallow a man alive. Even though she had the *don,* the weirdness tonight was mounting in a way I could tell made Catrina uncomfortable. Maybe that, and being too close to the final truth. She frowned but agreed. "Okay. But you better come to work tomorrow and you tell me what you find out."

"I will. I swear it."

Catrina reached out and gently herded the old woman away.

# CHAPTER TWENTY-SEVEN

"This whole night is hard to swallow. But you know all about that, huh?" I asked Jorgen in an attempt to be light-hearted. He had just eaten a person. It was weird. Should I offer him some Tums, or should I go off and violently puke out my disgust in a corner? I didn't know, so I decided to press on. "Where to?"

Jorgen took off toward the far end of the street, and I followed him. We reached an alley, and Jorgen dove in. I chased after him. "Hey! No eating people!" I whispered as loudly as I dared.

We snaked to the back of the building we'd just been in front of. There were dogs in cages out back. They started whining as soon as they felt, or maybe saw, Jorgen. Trapped in cages, all of them were cowed.

A man came out of the back of the Three Crosses building and kicked the nearest cage. "Stop it! ¡Cállate!"

I waited against the wall, hidden by an overflowing Dumpster, and Jorgen stood in the middle of the alley, huge and invisible.

Jorgen looked to me, then looked to the man and leapt forward, catching him in the back. I knew the landing knocked all the air out of the man—I heard it leave him in a rush once Jorgen pinned him. I raced up as the dogs whined even louder, clawing at the backs of their cages.

"Don't kill him!" I hissed. "Just keep him from follow-ing me."

Jorgen reached out with a massive back leg and stepped on the Three Crosses man's leg, breaking it with a crunch-ing sound.

"Jesus!" I yelped. The gangster's eyes widened, and now, able to breathe he inhaled deeply to howl in pain. "No no no." I lunged down and planted my hand over his mouth. "Can you understand me?"

His eyes were wide. He could see only me in the alley; he had no idea how I'd managed to knock him down and break his leg.

"Don't yell." His eyes were watering with pain. "If you yell—I'll have my ghost here kill you." Jorgen crouched in and exhaled on the man, breath rancid as rotten death.

He nodded, and I released his mouth.

"If you move even one inch, my ghost will eat you."

"Like upstairs," he whispered.

He knew other hungry ghosts? Great. Leaving Jorgen to guard him, I turned toward the door.

The man had left the door open when he'd come outside. I hoped Jorgen wouldn't eat him while I wasn't looking—I wasn't sure I could handle that on my conscience. I swung the door open and looked inside before entering. It was dark. Disconcertingly so.

This was for my mom. I'd find out what had happened to Adriana, and then Luz would owe me, no matter what. The small voice that kept telling me what a bad idea this was in the back of my head—I told that voice to shut the hell up.

I reached in and fished past the doorjamb for the light switch. As my hand passed into the darkness, I felt an odd static in the air. About as far as I could reach my hand into the room, I felt the chipped plastic switch against the wall and flipped it. It wasn't wired to the light overhead, but to a light at the top of the stairs that rose from this bottom entryway. I stepped fully in, and felt enveloped by the charge—as if it were crawling up and down my skin, inside my clothing, like electric pins and needles.

It smelled in here too. Worse than Jorgen's breath. Like rotting meat. Not good. I was prepared to find one dead body, but the smell promised more.

Jorgen had followed me from the alley to look inside. He leaned forward through the door, but it seemed to be blocked to him. Maybe by whatever I was feeling right now.

"Can you come in?" Screw the man in the alley. I'd feel better with Jorgen at my back.

The Hound shook his head. Whatever felt weird about the air in here was actually barring him. "Shit."

The room I was in was just a communal room, a landing for the rooms that branched off it. Two doors to either side, and then the stairs leading up. I didn't know where to go next; I was going to just try the door on my right when I heard a groan.

Up the stairs. Of course.

I'd left the door open behind me, in the hope that Jorgen would follow me or stay in my line of sight. I took the first stair, listened to it creak, and then took the next three stairs more slowly before looking back at Jorgen's disappearing form.

Whatever I'd thought I'd be doing tonight, I didn't think I'd actually be doing it alone.

# CHAPTER TWENTY-EIGHT

I reached the top of the stairs as quietly as I could. As I walked up, I could see there was another landing, and again, more doors.

Another groan. Louder. Longer. But I couldn't locate it—there was a door in front of me, and a door to my left. I opened the one in front of me first.

This place reeked. As a nurse, I'd smelled ten different kinds of death before, seen maggots feasting on someone's gangrenous leg, and this smelled worse. It was dark inside too, of course. It felt humid, probably from the rain, but my skin imagined it as the dampness of spoiled things. With extreme reluctance I fumbled inside for a light switch. My hand found something smooth and round instead. I patted up and down, more strange things, and started panicking. I inhaled, exhaled, imagined where the hell the light switch would be if this fucking place were built to code, and went in for it, finding the tiny plastic nub of a switch between two smoother surroundings.

This time, the light illuminated the whole room. Which let me see that the things I'd been touching on the wall . . . were bones.

"Oh, God." The entire wall I was walking out of was faced in bones. Long femurs and short tarsals, and bro-

ken-up pieces of skull wedged between. The entire wall—
and half the ceiling. And part of the floor.

I took a few steps in, careful not to touch anything else.
Not all of the bones had been bleached, which was the
reason for the smell. Nuggets of flesh, strings of tendon,
all remained attached.

"*¿Hola?*" said a very weak voice, hoarse.

I couldn't figure out where it was coming from at first.
The jagged outlines of the bones on the walls prevented
me from seeing what was there, like an optical illusion—
a cage made of bones, set on the room's far side.

"*¿Que está ahí?*"

Whoever was talking sounded frail. I walked nearer,
reminding myself that cages were a two-way street. They
could be cruelly used on good dogs—or used on bad dogs,
to keep good dogs safe.

The bones were wired up with curling rebar, ornate,
disgustingly beautiful, Giger-esque. I stopped a body
length away from the cage to peer inside.

"*Por favor, ayúdame.*" It was a woman, dressed in a thin
nightgown. I thought she was a child at first, but then I realized she'd been starved. Her hair was in front of her face,
her arms were stick-thin, and—"*Por favor, por favor.*"

"Please?" I knew *por favor*. She started speaking, more
quickly, and I held up my hands. "I don't know what else
you're saying. Are you okay? *Se habla ingles? Dolor?*"

"*Mucho dolor.*" Much pain, she agreed. She reached
for the bars of her cage, and I knew what I thought I saw
was true. The outlines of the bones under her skin had
been tattooed on her arms. There was a tattoo on the back
of her ring finger on her right hand, one that I knew I'd
seen before, but her hands were so thin, so thin.

"How can I help you out of here?" I had never wished
so hard to know another language in my life.

She turned toward me, and the hair slid away from her face. The outline of her skull had been tattooed on her, the outlines of teeth pulled up on either side of her mouth, forcing her face into a cruel smile, just like Santa Muerte in the altar outside.

"We have to get you out," I said more loudly. I didn't know how, but—I touched the cage carefully. The bones weren't solid, but the rebar beneath them was. I searched for any cracks.

"Come on—" I found a loose bone, and pulled, and it came off with a crack, but the rebar below didn't budge. The bars were welded too close together for me to manage to pull her through. I groped over bones not long removed from their owners, searching for a door—Maldonado had gotten her in there somehow, and that's how I'd get her out again—then I found it. A knot of rebar, double-wrapped, in between pierced vertebrae.

It wasn't a lock, and there wasn't a key. Whoever had twisted this cage shut on Adriana never meant to open it again.

I put my hands on either side of the knot's tail and prayed that I somehow could Hulk out and get Adriana free. "Come on, come on—"

"Edith?" came a weak voice from outside the room. Almost no one called me Edith anymore. I stood up straighter and looked around. The woman in the cage, nearly skin and bones, pulled herself halfway up.

"I'm so sorry—hang on—I'll be right back." I started backing out of the room. The woman in the cage reached a bony arm through its bars out at me.

She didn't cry. She might have been too dehydrated to cry.

\* \* \*

I made it back to the landing without fishing around inside bones to find the light switch again. I went to the second door and opened it up.

"Edith—I smell you."

"Dren?" Jorgen's owner, my erstwhile Husker, the vampire who'd tormented me, whom I'd cost a hand. "Dren?" I asked again, my voice rising.

"Don't turn on the light. Just come here."

I stood in the doorway. "Dren, what's going on? Why are you here?"

"It took Jorgen long enough to find you. Come here."

Was this where Jorgen had wanted me to come all along? Nice. And ironic. No wonder he'd been so pleased.

"Come here," Dren demanded again.

"No." He sounded weak, but that didn't mean that it was safe to wander in blindly and say hi. "How about you come here? I need your help to free this girl."

"I'm not in a position to free anyone right now. Get in here." There was a long pause, and then a word I never thought I'd hear. "Please."

That was weird—and frightening. "Dren, tell me what's happening. Now."

"Edie—I'm weak. They've . . ." His voice sunk low. "If you turn on the light, we might be seen. We don't have much time before he comes back. Hurry."

"Hurry and do what?"

"Help me, goddammit! Please!"

A piece of vampire lore returned to me. Honor and whatnot, when sworn. "Swear not to hurt me."

There was a dry laugh. "I swear it. I couldn't hurt a fly. Come closer, Edie. I'll need to lean on you."

There was movement at the back of the room, him, fabric, the bang of something metal. I took a step inside, and another, waiting for my eyes to adjust to the darkness ahead of me. He was laying on a metal table, draped in a sheet not unlike a gown, one hand folded in across his lap, the other hand missing.

"Come on already." I waved him to come forward. The charge around me, what I'd felt when I first came into this cursed place, was increasing now. The pins and needles were beginning to feel more like teeth.

"I can't. I need your help." He reached out to me, with his arm that ended in a stump.

"And swear to help my mom," I added.

"I swear, but only if you hurry the fuck up," he hissed.

I'd wanted to save my mom, right? And I'd found Adriana. Only I couldn't get her out. I was torn between the two rooms, like a kid frozen between horrors at a haunted house. Neither of the rooms was a good option, and everything felt like it was getting worse, fast—it was *act, or run, and don't stop running, don't think of looking back.*

I ran toward him instead, and drew myself up short at his bedside. He was lashed down, restrained across his chest, abdomen, thighs, and feet. I ratcheted the ties off him, unlacing their ends, freeing him. He gasped as the last one came loose, and pushed himself up.

He lurched up, swung his arm around my neck, and shoved himself off the table. He hobbled, as if one of his legs didn't work. Because it didn't. I looked down at his other flaccid arm.

"The bones. They take them out each night. Alternating. And then I heal, and then they take them out again." His voice was dancing on the edge of mania.

I grit my teeth to not puke, and took a step forward. Stumbling, he came with me. *Okay, okay, okay. Do this. Don't run.*

"Jorgen's outside."

"Good. Let's go." Dren said, his face tucked in against my neck.

I would have rather saved the old grandmother again than Dren. This place was so much worse than the storm drain where I'd found her. It'd only been trash there, things forgotten. This place was full of bad intent. Someone had done this to Dren—was doing that to Adriana.

"Is there any way—" I started to ask, even though I had no idea how I'd manage to carry them both out. And Dren couldn't even use both his arms.

"No. She's as good as dead. Just hurry—go—" he pleaded.

I was saving the vampire instead of the girl. I heard her whimpering as we crossed the upper landing. She must know we were leaving her behind. She deserved saving more than Dren, but he was the only one I could get out. It felt so wrong, but I couldn't think of how I could undo her cage's knot.

How much more moral ambiguity could I take? I'd work on sorting it out tomorrow.

"I'll come back," I whispered to the girl, praying that she could hear me, that she'd understand—that no one had ever lied and told her that before.

I just needed to get Dren over to Jorgen. Who knew where the hell they would go together, but after that, he would owe me. This had to be worth some blood.

And then maybe I could come back for her. I didn't know what I could do against welded rebar and magic, but there had to be something, something, something—we reached the top of the stairs, and the door opened below.

Fuck.

Dren started panting into my neck. "Don't let him hurt me, Edie. Don't let him hurt me again—" His voice was rising like a boy's.

"Shhhhh." There was nowhere for us to hide, only one way out. I thought about throwing Dren down the stairs—it wasn't like he could die, right?—and somehow tumbling after him, getting the door open again, somehow hauling Jorgen inside to help us.

That was a lot of somehows.

The bottom floor's new occupant arrived at the bottom of the stairs, putting his foot on the first creaky step. He stepped into the half-light the downstairs switch provided. And I knew him.

"Ti?" My zombie ex-boyfriend. I almost dropped Dren in surprise.

"Ti—this is awesome timing—can you help?" I shouldered Dren up higher as he hung limp against me, like a rag doll. "Dren's been hurt, and there's this girl upstairs—" I began, and I realized my great luck. "You're strong enough to open her cage, awesome!"

"Edie," Dren warned, with true fear in his voice.

Ti was silent as he came up the second and third stairs.

"Ti?" He had to have seen me. Right? "Come on. Hurry up and help."

Dren started quivering, trying to control his disobedient limbs and lurch away. "See if you can get us past him—hurry!"

"What—" I looked down at Dren, who was trying to let go of me and brace himself against the wall, and then back to the still-ascending Ti.

Who was holding a long butcher knife.

"No. No no no. This is not happening," I bartered aloud. I backed us up an awkward step as Ti rose. "Ti—you can't do this. This isn't you."

The Ti I knew put honor above almost everything else in life. Wanted to help people, not hurt them, not unless they deserved it. Wanted to get to go to heaven when he died, once he'd earned back the lost half of his soul. "Ti, please—"

I could see his expressionless face. There was nothing of the man I'd once loved there, nothing of anyone, nothing at all.

"Ti—stop," I ordered, hoping it would trigger something in him. "Stop this right now. I'm Edie. You remember me. I know you do."

The electric currents of this place were roiling now; it felt like my hair was on end. I pushed Dren sideways, into the wall, and blocked him from Ti with my body. I was going to be killed by my zombie ex-boyfriend, and my bones put into the room with that poor woman. Silver didn't work on zombies. I pulled out my badge and prayed to someone, anyone, that it might still protect me the way it used to when I was on Y4.

It struck up like a lit match, and Ti paused one stair down from us.

"Dren—go. Somehow. Just go."

Dren fought against my back, and I moved forward. He fell down a few steps, tumbling past Ti, and then started crawling forward, dragging himself down the stairs with his one good arm.

Ti made to follow him. I raced down the stairs until I was below him, badge still out. The electric jolts were sharper, running up and down my body in sharp snaps, like the charges from a violet wand. My badge sputtered like a dying sparkler, and Ti took a step down, implacable, following Dren. I put myself in his way.

"Ti, say something," I pleaded, but he wouldn't. Or couldn't. I was close enough now to see that his eyes were glazed. He was not himself here. He took another step forward, and I took another step back.

"Please, Ti. No." The butcher knife was still at his side. I was in striking range now. I had to believe that Ti wouldn't kill me—I put my dying badge against Ti's chest, breathing heavy, the electricity in the room buzzing in my ears. We danced together down another stair.

"Ti—I know you remember me." His eyes tracked me. Was that good, or bad? I hoped that whatever in him was human was listening. "You broke up with me once. You do not get to kill me again." He stopped advancing. The knife was still low. I could hear Dren behind me, pulling himself against the linoleum floor.

"I'm out!" Dren called from below, just as the light from my badge disappeared.

I took three steps back. Ti didn't follow me. His body might belong to someone else now, but his eyes were still his, watching me. I didn't want to leave him here. "Ti—"

"Edie—hurry!" Dren called from the alley.

I dropped my badge, turned my back, and ran for the door.

# CHAPTER TWENTY-NINE

Outside, Dren was scrabbling along on the wet ground, and Jorgen was standing guard over him. What had happened to Ti?

"Okay, okay—" If I stopped telling myself what to do I would panic. I reached down and pulled Dren up. He hissed at me, fangs out. "Don't you dare—"

"Just get me out of here."

The man who was still lying back there with his broken leg started trying to crawl backward at the sight of Dren.

Dren's shirt slipped through my fingers as I tried to haul him up. I'd only imagined springing him—it hadn't occurred to me that after that, we'd somehow have to run and that he wouldn't be able to walk. I hadn't thought about bringing a wheelchair along.

Jorgen knelt awkwardly, and I tried to hoist Dren up onto his back, but Dren kept sliding off. There was surprised shouting from down the alley. Perhaps the disappearance of Jorgen's first victim had been discovered. I couldn't understand their words, but I could hear their angry tone.

"Dren, we're going to have company soon. Can you send them away?" We were still trying to scrape our way down the alley, the three of us, unsuccessfully. But I'd been with Dren before when he'd made everyone ignore him, entire train cars full of normal people.

"Can't. Too weak. Too close to the *bruja*'s power." He hauled himself up Jorgen's side desperately and planted his fangs into the Hound's neck. Jorgen snarled and twisted, dislodging him.

"Horrible beast!" Dren yelled, back on the ground.

"This is not the time to be feeding, Dren—"

"I need blood!" Dren yelled.

The man we'd threatened earlier had crawled backward to hide behind the dog cages, and then he started yelling for help.

"Shit!" I hissed. "Come on." Jorgen looked behind us and took a flying leap back toward the dog cages. "No!" I shouted at him. The dogs squealed. Jorgen stopped, but he was standing over the man who'd given us away. The man started praying at the top of his lungs. Santa Muerte this, Santa Muerte that.

"You'd be better off praying to me!" I hauled Dren away, dragging him down the alleyway like a dead body. Three Crosses men raced out of the building like angry ants, weapons drawn. At a command from someone among their ranks, they held fire and moved aside. I'd never seen so many guns before. My stomach turned to ice.

"What's happening here?" I recognized his voice. From the clinic—Maldonado. Somehow he was even more frightening than the weaponry.

"I'm rescuing my friend." There wasn't any point in lying.

Maldonado smiled. "He was always free to leave. All he had to manage to do was walk out." Some of his cohorts laughed as Maldonado continued. "He's the kind of beast we protect ourselves from. Him and la Reina. He deserves what he got."

Under other circumstances, before this, I would totally agree. But after what I'd seen tonight? No. The bone room had gone above and beyond.

"And what about her?" I pointed back up to where the bone room had been. Dren kept crawling away behind me. I could hear his good arm splash into puddles and the rest of him slide.

"She was with la Reina. As, clearly, are you. Which makes many things of yours forfeit." Maldonado closed the distance between us. "First your bones, then your life." He raised his hand, and many of his men put guns away to pull out knives. Somehow the knives seemed worse. I took a step back.

I was cast in sudden shadow by headlights behind me, and I heard the squealing of tires. Some of the Three Crosses men raised their hands to protect their eyes, and I heard "Get in!" from behind me. I whirled and saw Hector, frantically waving at me from inside his car.

"Jorgen! Now!" I yelled at the Hound. He ran back through their numbers, clawing and biting, shoving them aside.

I ran until I caught up with Dren, and hauled him toward the waiting car's backseat. Shots rang out; I prayed to God that they hadn't made contact. I hopped in beside Dren, almost on top of him, and slammed the door.

"Go go go!" I looked behind us, at Jorgen, running away.

Hector raced backward down the alley, then went flying down the street.

"How did you know?" I asked his reflection in the rearview mirror.

"As soon as Catrina got home she called me and told me where you'd been." Hector looked into the backseat at Dren. "Where are we taking him?"

Dren seized his chance. He lunged forward and wrapped his good arm around Hector's neck, the headrest in between them.

"Dren, no!" I yanked at the vampire. His arm nearest me was too flaccid to get traction on, and his good arm was too strong. I reached out and grabbed hold of his head, hauling it backward by his ears and hair.

"I need blood to heal—" Dren said, and it was clear that he didn't care where it came from.

"He has to drive! Let him go!" Hector wove from side to side in the empty street, reaching for the glove compartment with the hand that wasn't on the wheel. He teased the latch with his fingers and it slid open. He grabbed whatever was inside, and then bashed Dren in the head with it. The vampire hissed like a rattlesnake and recoiled, sinking down behind the driver's seat.

Hector held up what he'd hit Dren with so that it was visible in the rearview mirror. The good old King James. "I was raised Catholic, motherfucker. Stay in the backseat."

The rest of our ride passed in silence. I'd done it. I had some help—but we were gonna be okay. No one had gotten hurt. My mom was going to be just fine. To borrow a phrase from Hector, I had saved the motherfucking day. As the streets got nicer and it was clear we were out of Three Crosses' realm, I began to beam.

"Why are you so pleased?" Dren asked from beside me.

"Because." I inhaled and exhaled deeply. "Just because."

# CHAPTER THIRTY

Hector pulled the car into a well-lit place—the parking lot of a Catholic church. As soon as we parked, he got out and slammed his door.

I hopped out after him, leaving my door open.

"We're going to kill that thing." He popped the trunk of his car, bringing out duct tape and a tire iron.

I took a step back. "We're not going to kill him, and I'm not going to ask you why you're driving a kidnap-mobile."

"He tried to kill me," Hector said, shaking the tire iron for emphasis.

"I need him! To save my mom! Remember?"

"Technically, I only wanted some of your blood," Dren said from his slumped position inside the car, eyes glittering in the night. "I didn't need all of it."

I pointed at him. "Do me a favor, and don't try to help." Then I moved to stand between Hector and Dren. Normally, a vampire would have no problem fighting back, but since Dren was missing half of his long bones and starved for blood and Hector was pissed, I gave humanity an even chance. "Let me explain. Some. As much as I can. Hector—that place up there—it was awful. They were torturing him. Taking out his bones and using them to decorate—" My voice failed me at the memory.

"Adriana's up there, Hector. She's trapped in a cage of bones and rebar. It is literally insane."

Then I looked to Dren. "And you swore to help my mother. I need some of your blood. She's got cancer. I want to heal her."

Dren's eyebrows rose up on his forehead. A smile pulled up the edges of his lips, and then he gave a barking laugh. He laughed again, and again, sounding like an overexcited dog, until he started coughing, and the coughing won out.

"What's so funny?" I stood outside the car with my hands on my hips. "You promised—you swore!"

Dren recovered himself from the coughing. "You need to make your oaths more precise. Trust me, you do not want your own sweet mother to be bound to my blood."

"Fuck you, Dren." I took a step nearer to the car, strength building in me. "You're doing this."

He slunk forward in the car, crawling out of it with his one good leg and arm, and both Hector and I scooted back. "If she were bound to me, I would make you regret giving her my blood until the day you died. She would come to hate you as the person who enslaved her to me." He paused to arrange himself on the pavement once he was on the ground, straightening out his messed-up leg. Then he appeared to think, and smiled, full of fangs. "Just think of all the things I could order her to do. Oh, my."

My fists curled in impotent rage. "But I saved your life!"

"And I thank you for that. But I also swore an oath not to hurt her, whoever she may be. Trust me that my blood would only do that. I would see to it, in fact."

I leaned forward and screamed at him, "I did not come all the way down here just to save you! If I had known, I would have tried harder to save the girl instead!" I whirled on Hector. "Give me the tire iron."

He took a step back. "I thought we weren't supposed to kill him?"

"That was before," I said, my hand still out.

"Edie—he has a point."

"Fuck both of you, then." I walked in a small circle. I ran my hands up through my hair. "We have to go back for her."

"Not tonight. We're not going anywhere tonight." Hector brought the tire iron down with finality.

"We may not be—but Luz, I mean Reina, is going to be all over Maldonado when she hears about this. Do you have her phone number? Does she have a phone?"

"And what do you think she will do to your precious zombie when she finds him there, girl?" Dren said from his position on the ground.

"You shut up."

"Go on. Tell him about the zombie," Dren crooned. "I'd love to hear you explain him away."

I knelt down to be on a level with him. "How is it you were stupid enough to get caught?"

"What's it matter to you?" he challenged me.

"More mouth from you, and we're going to wait out here for the sun," Hector threatened, waving the tire iron. I blinked, startled that he knew how to kill a vampire. Then again, it was on every other TV show right now. At least Hector was still on my side, even though he had to know I was holding out information on him.

Dren sighed in exaggerated exhaustion. "I came looking for Santa Muerte. The Shadows sent me in. She's got a high bounty."

"Did you find her?"

"No. Those fools are trying to summon her. The girl in the cage is meant to be some sort of sacrifice." He shrugged his weak shoulder, which yanked his limp arm up in a grotesque fashion. "Santa Muerte herself is still loose—and they've almost got enough magic to draw her there. I'll give them that. I sorely underestimated the magician inside."

"That's because he's a *bruja*," Hector said. I didn't know what that meant yet, but somebody was going to be explaining it to me soon.

"Someone is helping them," Dren went on. "You don't get knowledge like they've gained through experimenting on your own. You try magic that strong without practice and you'd blow yourself up." His eyes narrowed. "I suspect House Grey is funding them, or helping them outright. I didn't meet any of them personally, but my torture did have the feel of poetic justice to it."

The last time I'd seen any vampires from House Grey, Dren had been lopping their arms off at Anna's command. His torture had a grim symmetry to it. Vampires didn't forgive, and they sure as hell never forgot.

"What would they want with Santa Muerte?" I asked aloud.

"She's hugely powerful. Who wouldn't want death on their side?"

"Why didn't the Shadows send anyone in after you?"

"And admit defeat? Or that they'd sent me to begin with?" He snorted, pushing himself up against the car's open door with his good arm. "I sent my Hound out for help—and the stubborn thing spent a month trying to run away before admitting defeat and realizing it couldn't. I think it was hoping I would die. Little does it know, that wouldn't free it. Our fates are linked."

"Why did it find me?"

Dren rolled his eyes. "It wasn't like the weres would help me now, was it? And I'd kept him away from other vampire kind. In the circles of the people he could find, and the people who were likely to be stupid enough to help me, the only overlap was you."

"You always know how to make a girl feel special, Dren." I rocked back up. My calves ached from all the crouching and pulling I'd done tonight. "Look, where can we take you? You need to go somewhere."

"I need blood is what I need." His eyes shone in the car-door shadow, backlit like a cat's.

"Neither of us is going to give you any." I did feel bad for him. He was a shade of his former self here. Still frightening, but also sad.

Throughout all this, Hector was surprisingly nonplussed. He still held the tire iron at the ready, but he didn't seem as ready to use it as when he'd first gotten out of his car.

"Once, I made it halfway down the stairs," Dren went on. "The sun began to come up. I had to crawl myself back up again before I passed out in the light. And your boyfriend—he's a piece of work."

"He's not my boyfriend, Dren." Whatever we saw on the stairs tonight . . . it was not Ti.

"You should have seen him, rooting around inside my thigh every other night. Like he was gutting a chicken." Dren played with his damaged leg, rolling it back and forth on the ground. It flopped from side to side like a twisted toy. "What did I ever do to him, other than threaten to kill you?"

Hector turned to me. "Where are we taking him? We need to take him somewhere, before I beat his head in."

"Okay." I fanned out my hands. As much as I didn't want to take him back to my place, I inhaled to offer it up. Then Jorgen appeared, racing back down the street, a nightmare in full flight. "Oh, thank God."

Hector groaned. "Goddammit, not that thing again."

We moved out of Jorgen's way as he came to kneel down, offering his neck to Dren.

"You'd better behave this time, or I'll skin you, I swear I will," the vampire warned.

Jorgen closed his eyes, and Dren bit in. Hector made a repulsed face, and there was no way not to hear the slurping noises while Dren sucked at Jorgen's neck. Just when I thought the noises alone would make me wretch, Dren pulled back and tottered up to standing. Hector and I jumped even farther back. "How can you—"

"I'm a vampire. I heal quickly, when fed. Even on blood as disgusting as a Hound's." He was still emaciated, but at least his bones were whole. A trail of Jorgen's blood stained his chin. "That's why they used the zombie. I couldn't feed on him." Jorgen lurched up, and Dren leaned against his side.

"Where are you going, Dren?"

"Away. To shun you," he said, and laughed. "To heal. And sleep. And leave this place for good."

"Whatever magic those people are using—it's powerful, Dren. You know it yourself." I took a step nearer to him, hands out, pleading.

"Please don't try to appeal to the altruist in me. There is none." Dren started walking away, one arm slung around Jorgen's neck.

"Don't kill anyone tonight, Dren," I called after him.

He turned back to smile wickedly. "You're not the boss of me." And then waved weakly with his healing arm.

Dammit. I still wanted him to help me. If only I'd made him promise more precisely—and if only he weren't a jerk. I didn't want to admit that maybe he was right, maybe by denying me he was actually helping my mother. And yet I didn't want all this to be for nothing. I'd almost gotten killed, I'd left an innocent person behind, and I still hadn't saved my mom. I wanted to run after him, yelling at him until he changed his mind. But I couldn't. He was running now. Not to avoid me, but because he—a vampire, fearless and occasionally psychotic—was afraid.

I watched him rush down the street until he was hidden in shadow.

# CHAPTER THIRTY-ONE

"Good riddance." Hector rounded his car, tossed the tire iron back into his trunk, and slammed it shut.

"What time is it? We've got to go tell Luz." I started pacing. I didn't want to get back into the car. It felt like maybe three or four. Plenty of time for Luz to go in and rescue Adriana.

"You can't tell her, Edie—you'll start a war."

I stopped and stared at him. "Luz wouldn't be starting anything—she'd be finishing it. You did not see what I saw."

"Innocent people would die, Edie—"

I pointed back the way we'd come. "There's an innocent person up there being starved to death and tattooed with bones. I don't really care if some other people die, as long as she gets free."

"No," Hector said, decisively.

"Why are you protecting them? I thought you hated Maldonado?"

"You don't understand—"

"Because you haven't told me!" I yelled. After tonight, I had no patience for games.

"Edie!" He took hold of my shoulders and shook me.

And then his face changed. His tan skin lightened, and his dark eyes went blue.

It took me a moment longer than it should have to place what was happening, it had been so long. Hector wasn't Hector anymore. His face was changing, into the face of someone else I knew. "Asher? Oh, my God." I put my hand to my mouth to muffle a scream. "Why—why didn't you tell me he was you?"

He let go of me and stepped back. "I was trying to hide." His face changed, more slowly, toward the Asher I used to know.

"No. Don't. Just stay Hector, okay?" I didn't need any more blasts from my past tonight.

"Okay," he said, his voice low.

I couldn't believe that Hector had been Asher this entire time. That he'd known me, from before. We'd been friends, and more than friends, and he'd hidden himself from me—why?

"Have you been him . . . all along?" I asked. He nodded slowly. "Why didn't you tell me?"

"It wasn't supposed to be like this, Edie."

"Oh. Tell me. How was it supposed to be? I would have wanted to know!" I wanted to lean in and hit him. I couldn't believe he'd lied to me. "All this time I've been trying to do things and get help, and you knew who I was, and you knew what I'd seen—you could have fucking helped me."

"No. I couldn't have." He stepped back closer to the streetlight and arched his back, running his hands through his dark hair, changing fully back to Hector. "You don't know what I've been through—"

"Because I didn't know!" I accused him.

He turned and I saw him fight to keep his emotions in

check, stopping himself from yelling back at me. "You're not the only one who has problems, Edie."

That shut me up. I was still pissed off, but leery. "What's wrong?"

His eyes scanned the ground, as if he were looking for where to begin. "Do you remember when that shapeshifter punched you on Y4?"

"Yeah." Gina and I had been taking care of him, and he'd gone wild, trying to escape. He'd lost control of his ability to shapeshift, and had wound up going through everyone he'd ever met before. "He was insane."

"Funny you should put it like that." Asher inhaled and exhaled deeply. "What was happening to him happens to all shapeshifters, eventually. If they don't take steps."

I frowned, and thought back to the event. "But you said he'd been tortured by vampires, I remember—"

"I lied." Asher cut me off. "That was only half the truth. I didn't want to explain at the time." His frown deepened as he stared at the ground. "No one likes to talk about how they're going to die."

I waited for him to go on.

"You can't be a shapeshifter forever, Edie. You either touch too many people, or you get too old, and something starts to break inside." He touched his chest. "You can't hold yourself together like you used to. The person you know you are fades, and if you're not careful, you get replaced by all the people you've touched—by everyone else you have inside. There's only two ways out: Either you go crazy, or you pick someone else inside to be." Asher stretched his hand out and looked at it as if the fingers there were unfamiliar to him. "It happens to all of us eventually."

"I don't understand." Asher was supposed to be gone, just like everything else from before the shun. And now he was here—and I was going to lose him again, already? "So you picked being Hector? Over . . . going crazy?"

Asher nodded.

"Is Hector real?"

"He's a clinic doctor in Miami. I touched him years ago, and started being him in Port Cavell after New Year's. We were the same age, and he has no family. The real Hector doesn't know he has a doppelgänger here, and he never will."

"And so . . . who are you then, now?" I asked, squinting at him.

"Asher all the way. Still. But I've been trying to be Hector. To let him win." His eyes finally found mine again. "I need to let myself go. But seeing you every day has been making it hard."

I bit my lip for a moment before asking him my next question. I wasn't sure I wanted to know. "How long do you have?"

He looked away from me. "Not long now. Every day I wake up, and everything's cloudy. It's hard to sort out what's me and what's him. And I shouldn't even try, because if I don't forget, if I don't give myself over to really being Hector, I'll—" His voice drifted off.

"Go insane," I finished for him, remembering the tortured patient we'd had to tranquilize back on Y4. I hadn't realized that being a shapeshifter was like having the supernatural version of Huntington's. "Is there any way to stop it?"

"No one in the entire history of shapeshifters has ever managed to escape before." Asher sighed. "Except for maybe one."

I pounced on the idea. "Who? Can we find them? Talk to them? Get them to tell you how?" I couldn't stomach the thought of losing Asher again so soon.

"He's already been trying to contact me. He found me a few months ago." Asher stared stonily at the ground. "Sometimes he sends thugs over to paint my birthday on the clinic walls."

"No way—Maldonado's a shapeshifter?"

"Yeah. Who also happens to be my dad."

My jaw dropped. Maldonado being a shapeshifter made sense; it explained how Adriana had been duped. But him being Asher's father— "How can that be?"

"I don't know. It shouldn't be possible." Asher tensed as he faced his past. "He left when I was a kid, abandoned me and my mom. She said he knew his time was coming, and he was going to try to find a way to survive. What my mother didn't tell me was that it happened all the time— and that everyone who went out like that almost surely went insane. I spent my whole childhood waiting for him to come back." He snorted softly. "Talk about a waste of time."

I sat on the hood of his car, giving him room to pace. "How do you know it's him now, though? Do they look alike, or what?"

"No. It's his interest in me. Things he says, the way he acts. And the fact that everything is going to happen on my birthday, on the seventeenth? It's his way of letting me know he's still in there, even if he's not completely in charge. I always wondered what happened to him . . ." Asher frowned and shook his head. "He must have gone out and looked for the most powerful person he could find, to touch them so that he could mimic them before he went insane."

"And now he's pretending to be him—like you're pretending to be Hector?"

"Like I'm becoming Hector." Asher made another face. "Although for all I know, he killed the original Maldonado and took his place."

I blinked. "That's a thing? That you all do?"

He shrugged one shoulder. "I'm not proud of my people all of the time, Edie."

"Remind me to never hang out with you in a dark alley."

Asher gave me a look. "Why would I want to be a nurse when I could be a doctor?"

I narrowed my eyes at him. "You're gonna need to be someone else entirely when I'm through with you."

"I kid." He snorted softly. "I've been trying to figure out how he did it, ever since I realized he'd managed to. It's not like we can have a tea party where he tells me all his tricks. I don't think he's able to come out all the way yet, not without breaking his mind, so his interest manifests repeatedly in shitty ways. Graffiti, personal threats, the birthday timing."

"Nothing personal, but your dad is kind of a jerk."

"Agreed."

A silence passed between us, in which I couldn't believe I was hanging out with Asher again. I wish it'd been under different, better circumstances. But despite the cloud hanging over us both, it was nice to be on the same team again. "Do you know what his plan is? And why now, anyhow?"

"Because he thinks he can control Santa Muerte. And because if he can, he wants to save me. I think. As much as I can guess at anything. I know he thinks Santa Muerte's the answer. And after the way you described seeing Adriana—she must be the key."

I swallowed at this. I couldn't forget Adriana's suffering, but I didn't want to condemn Asher. He held his hand out to me, and it was changing, rippling, strange. I willed it to be a trick of the lamplight, and not him losing his form. "I don't want to know what's inside my heart on this, Edie. I don't want to live over the bones of some girl's corpse, but I don't know how much longer I can manage to be both Hector and me." He clenched his hand into a fist, and brought it back to his side. "I don't want to condemn Adriana to die. But if there's some way Maldonado can save me—it's not the kind of choice anyone should ever have to make." He hung his head. "I honestly thought she was dead, Edie. I had no idea."

I nodded, even though he couldn't see me.

"I don't want to lose myself. That'll be like dying. And I don't want to go insane, either. I can feel the voices getting louder, inside my head. They're all so . . . angry. It hurts me."

I didn't know if he meant emotionally or physically. I didn't think I wanted to know.

"I spent my whole life doing what shapeshifters were supposed to do. I saved money up, I contributed to the safe houses—the sanatoriums—we send our kind to when they lose their minds. I thought I was ready to go, at peace with my fate. And then Maldonado appeared, telling me to do things like my dad used to do—and then I saw you and—I don't know what happened to me." He took a deep inhale. "It's not too late for me to just give in to Hector. I could just sink into him, and let him win."

"And that Hector won't remember me, will he," I said. It wasn't a question.

"He wouldn't know anything about my past. Just his. He might remember this conversation—but he'd write it off like a bad dream. I've seen it happen before." He snorted and looked up at me, the emotion on his face raw. "My own mother doesn't even remember me. She thinks she's a housewife upstate."

I swallowed against the rising knot in my throat. What was happening to Asher was awful. But was it more aw-ful than what was happening to a kidnapped, starved, and tattooed girl? I couldn't swallow that down—and from the look on his face, neither could he.

I didn't know what to say, so I opened my arms to him. Asher came over to me and stepped in. I wrapped my arms around his waist, and pressed my head against his chest, as his arms looped over me. I could feel my hair catching on the stubble on his chin. "I don't want you to go away again."

He didn't say anything, just held me close.

If it'd been up to me we would have stayed there forever. I didn't want to let go. But sooner than I would have liked, he squeezed me one last time and began pulling away from me. I sighed and leaned back.

"I swore to Catrina that I would let her know today, Asher. I'm not going back on that. She deserves to know."

He nodded above me. His face was Hector's face. "Today is technically after dawn, and Luz will be asleep. Just give me until tonight. We can regroup and go in with Luz instead of her racing off half-cocked, not knowing what she's up against, right before sunrise. I don't think he'll kill Adriana if he needs her for his ceremony."

*Don't think* didn't equal *know*. I bit the inside of my cheek. We were betting somebody's life either way. Why shouldn't I bet on Asher's?

Who the hell was I to make that choice?

I evaded my shadowed conscience by talking. "Why didn't you tell me earlier that it was you?"

He snorted. "You were being shunned."

I waved my hand to draw a circle around us. "You're not doing a very good job of it."

"Don't forget you were the one who came to be interviewed," he said. He was close enough that it would have been so easy for me to touch his face. "When I saw your name on that résumé I didn't know what to think. And then when you walked in—I tried to not hire you."

"So me getting the job was some pretense? To keep me in your memories?"

"I don't know what I was thinking. Maybe I didn't want to let go." He gave me a smile full of regret. "If those gang-bangers hadn't come in, you would have been out the door. But when they did, I thought maybe it was a sign. You're good in dangerous situations. You're foolish sometimes, but you don't back down from a fight. And if something happened to me, you'd actually keep working at the clinic. I know you're the type that'll go down with the ship."

I kicked my heels against the side of his car. "Gee, I don't know if I can take much more flattery."

"I'm sorry, Edie. I wanted to say something to you so badly. Every single day. Seeing you struggle to find answers hurt me more than you could know." He looked solemn and sad and worn out. Despite all the lies before, I knew he was now too tired to tell me anything but the truth. "I just didn't want to drag you down with me. I wouldn't wish this on anyone."

If I was going to split moral infinitives tonight, I needed some guarantees. "From here on out, I want to go with you. I don't want you doing anything without me."

At this, his face lightened a degree. "Good. I want you there." He inhaled and exhaled deeply, all the while staring at me like he might not see me again. I couldn't imagine being forgotten—or being forced to forget everyone I ever knew. "Living like this," he said slowly, "knowing what's coming for me—it's been so lonely."

I nodded to agree. Being shunned was bad, but his fate was so much worse. "Can you give me a ride home?"

He shook himself, as if coming back to the present, and backed up to give me room to hop off his car. "Of course."

# CHAPTER THIRTY-TWO

I was quiet in his car while he drove us. The car, which I hadn't noticed much of before, was a Datsun from last century. I watched his face in the rearview and his hands, one on the wheel, one on the stick shift beside me. I reached out and laced my fingers through his for old times' sake. Who knew if we would ever get to make new memories? He nodded, though he didn't turn his head.

"So why Hector?" I asked him, when the silence had gone on too long.

"I've spent most of my life being either a dick or a rogue. I figured it was time to give something back. I saved up a lot of money—my bank account can coast."

I watched Port Cavell pass by outside in the night. "How old will you be on the seventeenth?"

"Thirty-three. Assuming I can remember that." We made a left-hand turn onto the highway. "What Dren said back there—was it really Ti?"

"Yeah. And speaking of forgetting—" I blew air through half-parted lips. "I don't know what he was. He didn't know me, and he wasn't acting like him."

"How long has he been like that?"

"I don't know. He came over to see me the other night, and he was normal then." His grip tensed slightly—if I hadn't been holding his hand I might not have felt it. Or maybe I was reading too much into things; maybe it was just another gear change.

"What happened to him?"

"He said he was in town because someone here could cure him and give him back the other half of his soul so he could finally die. A great magician," I said more slowly, adding two and two. "Shit."

"Yeah." Asher merged into the fast lane of the highway, and then we didn't have anything to say at all.

He pulled into the parking lot of my new place, and I tried to pull my hand back casually. He caught it. "Wait."

"Okay." I turned to face him. My brain was still having a hard time merging Asher's personality with Hector's body. Was this the first time this had happened, us in a car together, or the fortieth? He swallowed before speaking to me.

"It's just really good to see you again is all, Edie. I've been wanting to tell you that for a while."

"It's good to see you too, Asher," I said, because it was. "No matter who you look like." I leaned back against the closed car door. "I'm going to call the clinic and leave Catrina a message to call me—and when she does, I'll tell her everything."

"That's fair. Don't tell her about me, though—or this. And call me Hector. It's easier on me."

"When I talk to Catrina this morning—doesn't Luz deserve to know what she's up against?"

"Luz already knows Maldonado's a shapeshifter. It's how they captured Adriana in the first place, I think. He went as someone she knew—Catrina, Luz, or me. Who knows. And the Three Crosses wouldn't be freaked out by him showing off his powers. They already know he's magical."

"Don't you think she would have searched his current home first?"

"You saw how weak Maldonado made Dren . . . maybe she couldn't get close enough to see?"

Which brought up a good point. "If Maldonado is so strong he scares vampires, and he's trying to control the saint of death, how can we succeed?"

Asher shrugged. "You're not asking me anything I haven't already asked myself. There's a chance I could get in with him, but there's no guarantees."

I tried to think out different scenarios, pushing players around on a chessboard inside my mind. "Luz might get killed if she goes in alone. Us going with her isn't much better, but there's a chance."

"I could get us in the door, get his guard down— maybe," Asher offered.

I nodded. It wasn't much of a plan, but it was better than Luz running in to replace Dren on Maldonado's cutting board.

"Just get her to wait for the rest of us, once she finds out. Tell Catrina it's vital to keep Luz at the Reina's fortress after sundown tonight until we get there. Tell her you're bringing Jorgen if you have to. I'll act surprised when she tells me at work, and then agree to go along with it, and that way we can both encourage Luz to accept our help."

Encouraging and convincing vampires. Wow. I didn't know if either of those things was possible. "I feel so much better now that there's only a fifty–fifty chance she'll go off and get killed during a rampage."

Asher snorted. "Me too." He glanced over my shoulder at the apartments behind me. "I still have to get to work. See you at sundown?"

I smiled softly at him. "I wouldn't dream of being anywhere else."

# CHAPTER THIRTY-THREE

I called the clinic and left a message for Catrina—I hoped by the time she called back I'd still have some tact. It'd been a long night and I was going down.

I got a call shortly after eight A.M. "Well? What?"

I'd been dozing on my couch. It took me a second to remember who it was on the other end of the line.

"Was she there? What did you find?" Catrina's voice rose, taking my silence for bad news.

"She's there. She's alive."

Catrina whooped on the far end of the line. "Where is she? Is she okay? Did you get her out?"

"Go into a closet, will you?" I told her, and I heard doors open and slam in her path. "Okay. You need to promise me something before I say anything else."

"Anything. What?"

"I couldn't get her out, Catrina. She was caged. But she's alive—she saw me. I told her I'd be coming back."

"You? Pffft. Reina will have her back tonight!"

"No no no. That's what you have to promise me. Maldonado's a *bruja*—he's more powerful than you think he is. I only made it out alive because I had Jorgen with me. If you send Reina in there alone, there's a chance she'll die, and then where would we be?"

"But we're going in—we're getting her."

"We are. I just want you to tell her to wait for us. So she's not alone." I could feel her weighing my advice against her urge for expediency. At least she couldn't tell Luz anything until it was dark. "Please, Catrina. I don't want to see Luz get hurt."

"All right. I'll tell her that. I can't make promises, though."

"Not many people can, where vampires are concerned." I inhaled and exhaled. All my chores for the night were finally through. "I'll meet you at Reina's at sundown, okay? And then we can set off together. I'll bring the Hound." It was a white lie, but maybe another reason to get Catrina to make Luz wait—she'd already seen it gobble one man alive.

"Okay," Catrina said, and hung up on me.

After the night and morning I'd had, I thought I'd be too wired to sleep, but no—the second I was out of my shower, I fell into my bed. I set my alarm for three, and I woke up in almost the same position I'd landed in. I'd slept like the dead.

I got up and walked to the train station. The humidity was worse, and there were thunderclouds overhead. It was fitting it would rain.

I arrived at my mom's house before the first fat drops. I crouched under the overhang above my parents' front door, and I almost fell in when Peter opened it.

"You look a sight," he said.

"Is she up?"

He nodded and let me in.

I walked into what had once been my home. Pictures—some of me—hung on the walls. My mom had framed a drawing I'd made of a fall leaf in the fifth grade. There was a picture of all of us, me, Mom, Jake, minus Peter, plus bio-dad, at the Grand Canyon, when I was like four.

I didn't remember that trip anymore—if I ever had, four's pretty young—but I remembered the picture of it. The picture was the real memory. Where would it go if it wasn't here—at my mom's? Put into a box? Only exist in my head?

This world was so far removed from where I'd been earlier today. Nothing here was cement. Nothing here had ever been covered in bones or blood.

I felt the friction that I'd had frequently when I was beginning as a nurse, trying to hold two worlds inside my head. The world that I'd known my entire life—the one with nice couches you could sit in, watching the daily news as it happened to *other* people, distant on TV—and the world where drunk people tried to hit you, where people turned orange once their livers blew out and then shit themselves until they died.

It was a little like being a prisoner. Once you'd seen the inside, the outside was never really the same again.

"Edie!" My mom spotted me as I walked into the living room.

"Hey, Mom." I smiled at her, bending down for a hug, stepping through the tunnel from my current life, violent and strange, into this, the recollection of my past. Two-dimensional pictures. Painted leaves. Carefully labeled jars of vacation sand.

My mother smiled at me. "How was your day?" she said, and she patted the couch beside her.

"Good," I lied, and sat down.

I spent the afternoon chatting with my mom. She seemed smaller now, even smaller than at our dinner earlier this week. I remembered that Greek myth about Tithonus, who lived forever but was always aging, who eventually shrunk down to the size of a cricket. My mother wasn't there yet, but she would be, if the cancer didn't get her first.

"You know, Edie, I've been thinking about your childhood. I'm sorry it was hard on you . . ." She kept talking, but my mind went blank. Oh, God. *This* conversation? I'd heard people have it at work. I'd lurked in rooms while it was happening, or had been sitting right outside their doors, but I'd never had it myself. Half confession, half absolution. The ordering of affairs.

"I don't really want to rehash the past," I blurted out, louder than I meant to. She blinked. "You've been a great mom. I'm a pretty awesome kid."

"But—"

I shook my head. "Shut up."

It wasn't that she couldn't die if we didn't have that talk . . . but having it was one more step on the path of inevitability. Accepting what was happening. No turning back. I didn't care what growths were raging in her right now, I still hadn't given up.

Even if she had.

She shook her head, gave me a smile, and patted my hand with hers, all bone-thin and skin translucent-white. "Tell me about your new job. Is the doctor there handsome?"

My mom had asked me that at every job I'd ever had as a nurse, ever. "Gah." I rolled my eyes for comic effect, and grinned at her. "Okay. Yeah. He is."

My mother chuckled in triumph. "Tell me about him."

"Okay."

We hung out until she faded, talking about small things under Peter's watchful eye. When she wanted to take a nap again, I left. Peter even gave me a hug. I tried to be genuine when I gave him one back.

By the end of my return trip home it was raining in earnest. I ran from the station to my door, and once I got inside I started to gear up. I put on my belt with a silver buckle, and a silver cuff that Asher'd given me for Christmas what felt like a lifetime ago. I took the silver cross down off my wall again and plunked it in my bag. I wasn't sure how to get to the Reina's. I pulled out my phone and prepared to text Asher.

There was a knock at my door. Maybe he'd saved me the hassle of a text, heh. I walked up to my front door and looked through the peephole outside.

As soon as I saw who was there, I began latching all the lock chains I'd installed.

"Edie!" Ti protested, from the far side, hearing me work. The Ti of last night hadn't been able to speak to me, right?

"Ti—where were you last night?" I asked through the closed door. Though the better question to ask might have been who he'd been.

"Edie, come on. Let me in." He hit the door, and it made me jump.

"Why're you here?" I yelled through the door.

"I found your badge. In my pocket." There was a long pause. "Why was it there?"

"Just stay on that side of the doorway, okay?"

Silver wasn't any good against zombies. Nothing was, except for guns and knives, and I couldn't imagine hacking Ti up. Plus the most dangerous thing I had in my house was a steak knife.

I opened the door slowly and peered through the chains. He loomed on the other side.

"Do me a favor and try to look harmless, could you?" I asked him. He deflated, taking a step back. "Thanks."

"Edie, what's going on here?" Honest confusion played on his face.

I stepped forward and peered out and up at him. "You really don't know?"

"No. And I don't like feeling like that."

"You're not going to like what I have to tell you then." I looked to the side, where my neighbor's front door was closed. "Last night, I saw you with a butcher knife. You'd been cutting bones out of Dren. For a while now, it seems. A month or so."

Ti blinked. I waited for him to tell me I was lying. If he did, then I'd slam the door in his face. My hands tensed, waiting.

"Go on."

"I was rescuing him. From where he was trapped. Being tortured. By you, as it turns out. And then you were going to come after us, and somehow you changed your mind. I think you remembered me. You could have hurt me but you didn't—so maybe you knew who I was. Even if you can't remember it happening now."

Ti ran his fingers through his short hair. "Why would I hurt you? And why would I torture Dren?"

"You really don't remember anything?"

He shook his head slowly.

"What's the last thing you do remember?"

"Yesterday. I did some construction work for the guy I'm working for now. It's what I do in the day, while he works on getting me back my soul." He stared down at his hands. "I remember from sunup to sundown, but not after that."

"Do you sleep at night?" We'd never done any sleeping when we slept together, when he was with me.

"No. I don't need to." I watched him think about the gaps in time. "I don't remember what I've done any night . . . for a while now."

"Is the magician you're with named Maldonado?"

Ti's brow furrowed deeper. "How did you know?"

I sighed. "Hang on." I closed the door and undid all the locks. "You're sure it happens around sundown?"

"Yes. Whatever *it* is."

I let him into my apartment and closed the door before I went on. "I saw you with a butcher knife. You'd been filleting Dren." I sat down on my couch.

He stood there for a moment, processing. "You're sure?"

I nodded quickly. "There was a chance that you were going to debone me. That's why I had my badge out. I hoped it still had some magic left in it. And I think you remembered me—you didn't raise the knife."

It was clear from the look on his face that he couldn't believe it. "I would never hurt you, Edie."

*Well, that's debatable.* I kept my witticisms to myself.

Ti looked at his hands like they had blood on them. "How could I have been so blind?"

"Do you remember anything about a girl there?"

"Oh, God, no—what else have I done?"

"She was trapped in a cage. The room she was in was plastered with bones. I couldn't get her free."

"Why—why any of that? And why me?"

"I'm not sure, to be honest. You helped him torture Dren—and Dren couldn't feed off you. Maybe that's why."

Disbelief still roiled on Ti's face. "You rescued him? Why?"

"Because I couldn't figure out how to rescue her. And

even though Dren's awful, Ti, no one deserves what happened to him."

Ti flexed his strong hands. "I know where he is. I'll kill him."

"If he's been controlling you, Ti, you can't go back to him. Who knows what'll happen to you tonight." I looked at my phone. It was six o'clock now—not that far away from sundown. "We have to figure out how to fix you, how to get you cured."

"How?"

How indeed? I made a face. I only knew one person who could cure the incurable.

# CHAPTER THIRTY-FOUR

Ti came willingly with me to the train station. It was so hard not to remember the last time we'd done this, when we'd been on the way to my trial, where the fate I shared with Anna had been sealed. I stood near him, but not too near him—I wanted to protect everyone else on the train if he did go away, but I didn't want him to get the wrong idea about him and me.

For his part, he seemed lost in thought. I bet he was poring over each and every day he remembered, searching for lost memories.

I stepped away and texted Asher. "Hey. I need more time. Ti's here—he's safe right now. I'm taking him to the *curandero*." Asher didn't respond to me.

When we got off at the clinic's stop, the marketplace was winding down; everyone had taken their wares home as it wasn't safe to sell at night. We walked down to the clinic itself, where a bright blue Three Crosses flyer had been nail-gunned to the door, promising the opening of a grand new church for Santa Muerte's mass on Friday night. The eighteenth—the day after whatever Maldonado was starving Adriana to do. The street was littered with them—I wondered if there'd been a fight.

"Where to?" Ti asked, looking around.

"I was hoping we'd see Olympio." I felt safe traveling with Ti. We walked down the street. I tried to remember the way I'd come that night, but it'd been dark, and we'd gone to the Reina's hideout besides. I recognized one side street and took it, taking us to the mural of Santa Muerte. The sun was beginning to set, giving her an eerie glow. How long did I have? What a wonderful plan this was. I stood in front of her picture. "Hey, you—I'm doing a lot of work here. You want to help me?"

Ti looked from the mural to me. "Edie?"

"Edie!" I turned toward the new person shouting my name and saw Olympio, riding along on a bike too small for him, waving at me. "Hey—Edie!"

"Olympio!" He parked the bike and got off. I hugged him, and he hugged back for a second before he realized it was uncool and pulled away. "Olympio—I need a really big favor."

Olympio looked over my shoulder at a brooding Ti. "Who's he?"

"He's being possessed by Maldonado every night. Can your grandfather cure that?"

He looked Ti up and down, and I wondered what he was seeing with his *don*. "Of course he can," Olympio said, but his face was unsure.

"How do we get there from here?"

"I'll take you the short way. Follow me." He hopped back on his bike and led the way.

Ti and I walked quickly after him. "This was your plan?" Ti murmured.

"Pretty much." I crossed my fingers that it was a good one.

# CHAPTER THIRTY-FIVE

We reached Olympio's grandfather's building not long before nightfall. Olympio ditched his bike and raced ahead to announce us.

"How is he going to heal me?" Ti asked.

"I'm not sure. But he fixed me up when I was in dire straits. I wouldn't bring you here if I didn't think he could help." I took his hand in mine as we walked in the door.

Olympio came back down to find us as we were taking the first set of stairs. There was a child crying behind one of the thin walls. I tried not to think about what would happen if I was wrong; if Maldonado's power over Ti couldn't be broken, just where would I be setting him loose? It was hard not to yank him down the hall.

Olympio opened his grandfather's door and waved us in. "He said yes. Come on."

Ti ducked under streamers hung from the ceiling near the door. "Edie," he chastised, seeing all the candles and statuary lying about.

"He's magic. In a good way. I promise."

Olympio's grandfather was tearing off strips of tinfoil to lay on the floor while muttering what I assumed were prayers to himself. When he saw Ti he made an exclamation.

"What?" I asked Olympio. Olympio turned, eyes widening.

"I saw, but I didn't see—" He was gawking at Ti. "You didn't tell me he was really dead!"

"You didn't ask. I thought you could see—"

"I thought it was a dead man's curse. Not that he was actually dead."

"He's a zombie. Does that change things?"

Olympio's normally confident expression crumpled. "My grandfather says we're charging you triple."

Ti snorted softly.

The *curandero* said something aloud, and Olympio translated. "Bring him over here. There's not much time."

Ti stood where they showed him to stand, facing us near the door, although he was giving me exasperated looks. The *curandero* went around the room on his crutches, lighting candle after candle. It was getting later; I could feel it, even if I couldn't see the sun going down. The *curandero* started chanting while he moved, crutch-hopping from place to place, gathering herbs strung up from his ceiling to dry.

Any moment now Luz would be waking up. I hoped she listened to Asher and Catrina. And any second now Ti could be going away for the night.

"First the Donkey Lady, and now this—" Olympio tsked. His grandfather glared at him and started praying loudly.

As the sun disappeared outside, Ti became still. His countenance changed from a grimace as he tolerated my elaborate prank upon him to slack, unemotional smoothness.

"He's gone," Olympio whispered to me.

"And Maldonado?" I whispered back.

Olympio shook his head quickly. "Don't say his name while you're in here."

The *curandero* swung over to Ti, beating him with a bunch of herbs tied together, whisking first at his exposed skin, then starting from the top of him, slowly beating lower, increasingly awkwardly, dangling from one crutch. When he reached Ti's feet, he stood straight to start over again. I had no idea what he was saying, but he was loud.

"It's going to be difficult," Olympio narrated to me. "He's made of magic—it'll be hard to pull the *malo* magic out of him while leaving him whole. How do you know him?"

"He's an old friend."

"You and your friends," Olympio said.

At least Ti was still for the procedure. He hadn't moved an inch since the *curandero* had begun. I was getting tired of standing and went to lean back against the wall. Ti's amber eyes tracked me. Angry, accusing, scared? They were impossible to read, and then they closed, as slack as the rest of him. I hoped Asher was okay.

When the *curandero* had finished hitting him with herbs, he lit them on fire and set them in a metal pan. *When's the last time the fire marshal visited?* I wondered darkly. Then the *curandero* pulled out a white egg.

I was surprised to see it wasn't already black. I assumed that part of the procedure was sleight of hand— still might be, I realized. I kept an eye on the egg while the *curandero* waved it over Ti's body, praying even more loudly, as if he could shout Maldonado's influence away.

I nudged Olympio. "What's the point of this?"

"Same as when he did it to you. My grandfather's pulling the bad energy out of him and putting it into the egg."

"Poor egg," I said.

"Better it than us. The energy has to go somewhere."

Between the candle smoke in the room and the endless chanting, I started feeling claustrophobic. But I didn't want to disrupt the ceremony. Gah, did I really believe in magic now? Was I one of those people? I always wanted to punch those people at the hospital, when they'd brought their crystals into their sick friends' rooms and hung Tibetan prayer banners from the walls.

It wasn't even the paraphernalia so much as the type of people who enthusiastically believed in it, and tried to convert you to their tantric chanting ways. When you're performing actual science, those people get irritating fast. And I didn't want to get started on the patients who believed crazy things, like water was poisonous, and mosquitoes were recording their conversations. Some people's brains were porous due to stupidity, damage, or drugs, and once bad ideas got in there, they were impossible to shake out again.

But there *was* magic in the world. The vampires and were-things and shapeshifters, I could blow off as alternative life-forms. But whatever held Ti together was truly magic—hell, he'd been alive since the Civil War.

Magic, and a strange hope he could be happy someday, even if he had to wait until he got to heaven. Ti was strangely like my mom. I snorted and smiled at him, and his eyes opened.

The *curandero* splashed what must have been pure alcohol on the herbs in the pie tin at Ti's feet, and lit it into flame with a cheap plastic lighter. It would figure that there was no smoke alarm in this room, and that Ti used to be a firefighter.

"You okay?" I whispered to him, hoping he could read my lips. He didn't respond. The *curandero*'s prayers went quiet and intense, then loud again, repetitively, as if his words were ocean surf. He lunged in and pressed the egg against Ti's forehead.

At first I thought it was smoke from the fire he'd already illegally lit—the blackness swirling around the white eggshell. Then the egg changed color like it was being dipped in weak dye, turning a gray so faint I could hardly see it, then progressively becoming darker, until the shell was night black.

Olympio raced around me into the back room, then returned with another egg. He ran up to exchange this one with his grandfather while carefully setting the black one into the charred pie pan. I could swear it started rocking from side to side.

It was really black. I sat on my haunches against the wall, trying to figure out how the *curandero* had done that.

The second egg changed colors now. Olympio produced a third fresh egg and set down the second, which began to spin. The *curandero*'s hand with the new egg in it began to shake.

Ti leaned forward, pressing the *curandero* back.

"No. Ti—" I ran forward, so if Ti raised his hands I could put myself in harm's way. Olympio's grandfather hadn't asked for this.

The black eggs in the pie tin cracked and things slithered out of them, pouring over the edges of the shallow metal pan. Like snakes made of smoke, endless numbers of them writhed out of the broken shells, trying to crawl toward Ti's legs. I tried to kick them out of the way. It burned where they touched me, and they bit me like tiny vipers, striking again and again with small black fangs. The *curandero* stayed still, the final egg trapped between Ti's forehead and his palm. Ti blinked, coming to eerie life.

"Ti," I whispered.

My legs were on fire—I could feel their bites through my shoes down to my foot bones. I didn't know if the snakes were poisonous. I knew this couldn't be good for me, but I couldn't leave Ti.

He leaned forward and lifted up one leg like he was going to walk off the foil cross.

"Ti, don't."

I got as close to him as I could. His lifted foot dropped, touching down on the carpeting outside the cross.

"Ti—you remember me. I know you do. It's why you didn't hurt me the other night." I reached out for him, and electricity snapped between us like winter static. I grabbed his wrist and it thrummed, quivering like one of those carnival games where they say they'll test your love power.

And that's sort of what this was, wasn't it? Even if we were through. There had been something there between us, once upon a time. It was gone now, but not erased. I'd never let go.

"I know you remember me."

His other arm swung wide, sweeping the *curandero* to the ground, crutches and all. Olympio's grandfather kept praying, even as he landed on the floor, the blackening egg he held smashed. I took his place, centering myself in front of Ti. I couldn't give up on him, not when him being here was my fault.

"I know you can hear me, Ti. You're in there some-where." His amber eyes were staring down at me. I reached up to touch his chin with my free hand, like the last time he'd touched me. There was electricity there too, as if where we touched we completed a circuit. "Come back to me."

The door to the room opened up, and Luz flew in from the hallway outside. Her teeth were out, and she raced in the way full vampires can: from *not there* to *in your face* in half a second.

"You liar!" she shouted at the top of her lungs as she lunged for me.

Ti ripped his arm free from my grasp and punched her. She flew across the room and landed against the wall.

She stared down at her concave chest, where Ti's violence and her prior speed had caved it in. Snap by sickening snap, she reknitted before our eyes.

"Don't ever hurt Edie," Ti said, and then sagged forward. I caught him.

# CHAPTER THIRTY-SIX

Luz stood as soon as she could and jerked her chin at Ti. "What is that thing?"

"*He* is a zombie." I helped set him to standing again. I stood on the side of him opposite from Luz. Even though she was injured, she was still pissed and fast. "What happened tonight? Why are you here?"

"I went there and found nothing!"

"You didn't wait for Hector or me?"

"Catrina told me—and I have waited long enough!" She pounded her fist into the wall behind her. It shook.

I didn't want to ask if Adriana was dead. If she was, it was something that'd be written on my conscience until the day I died. "What did you find there?"

"The whole place was emptied out. I could smell the blood—I could smell that she'd been there. But she and everyone else, and everything, were gone." Luz sounded mystified with herself. "I don't know how they were keeping me from seeing it before . . . when she disappeared, that was the first place I checked. I know I checked it. Repeatedly. I know I did." She sounded more like she was trying to convince herself than us.

People remembering actions they'd never done had a feel of familiarity. Either the Shadows were here, mucking things up—unlikely, seeing as it was in their best interests that I somehow complete my quest—or it was House Grey, as Dren had suspected, loaning or teaching Maldonado their powers. They wanted Santa Muerte for themselves, even though they wouldn't get their own hands dirty to do it—just help out Three Crosses and Maldonado.

Ti was still leaning on me when Hector arrived with Catrina. Olympio helped his grandfather to stand. Ti turned toward the old man. "Is it broken? Am I fixed?"

The *curandero* spoke, and Olympio translated. "Fixed for now. No guarantees, though. Once you've been touched by a *bruja*, he can always find a door." He looked at me and said something else, but Olympio didn't translate it. The *curandero* laughed aloud, triumphant, holding the smashed remains of the last black egg. The snakes—or whatever it was that they'd been—were gone. I looked at my ankles and they were covered in red welts, oozing serous fluids. I'd worry about that later.

"Luz—are you okay?" Luz was touching herself like she couldn't believe what had just happened. Either Luz'd never seen herself heal as a vampire before, or she was used to beating on people a lot more fragile than a zombie.

Catrina and Hector arrived. "What happened?" Catrina asked.

"I went there, and she was gone." Luz glared at me. "If you'd come to me sooner, last night—"

"Then you'd have been killed. He's more powerful than you think," Hector said, surveying the room. His gaze landed on me, still holding Ti, and looked displeased. "We came as soon as we could."

"Thanks." I turned toward Ti. "Are you better?"

"I'm not homicidal anymore. Better might take a

while." He pushed himself up. "What's the vampire's deal?"

"Ti—now that you're fixed, what do you remember?"

"How does this help?" Luz demanded.

I ignored her. "Ti—there was a girl incarcerated with you. The one I told you about. Do you remember any more now than you did earlier today?" *Incarcerated* sounded better than *jailed*. They'd both been prisoners, in a sense. Unwilling.

Ti's brow furrowed as he tried to retrieve information that House Grey magic had shoved aside. "Just the bones. So many bones." He looked down at his hands as if they still might be covered in gore. "Rooms that there was no daylight in, and bones. That's all I see when I think of her."

"I went to that room. She was gone," Luz said.

"Ti—rooms?" I gently prodded.

He nodded. "There was . . . more than one. Only one girl, though." His eyes fixed on mine. "What kind of monster was I that I helped keep her there?"

What kind of guard would be more fearsome and invulnerable than a leashed zombie? I took his hands in mine. "It wasn't you, Ti. You weren't yourself."

"I swore no one would ever control me again, once my old master died—that I'd never be how I used to be. Used. Again." He slowly shook his head. "I can't believe it happened to me. That I came here to offer myself over to him—"

"Only because you wanted to be healed. How were you to know?" It was hard to see him in so much pain. He wouldn't be the first person to fixate on a goal so much that he lied to himself about its outcome. If anyone about knew that, it was me.

"If there was more than one room, where's the second

one?" Hector asked. I looked back at him—at Asher—and he wouldn't meet my eyes.

"Their new church. The one I was doing construction on during the day. It's behind the main altar there."

"That's where they've taken her?" Luz stood, pushing Catrina aside, but Hector blocked the door.

"We go together, Reina. You cannot do this alone," Hector said as she prepared to shove past him. There was irony in the situation. If only Luz had bitten Adriana, Luz would know exactly where she was now—vampires could find anyone they'd ever bitten before. But because she'd followed Anna's instructions to the letter, she was blind. And healing my mother was that much farther away from me, still.

Luz deflated. "I've searched there too, and missed her before."

Olympio's grandfather said something, and Olympio translated him. "Because they would not let you see. But someone who has had the bridle taken off their mind will not so willingly put it on again."

"She has a bridle, but I have a door?" Ti asked ruefully.

Olympio held up his hands and shrugged. "It's magic. Do you expect it to make sense?"

Ti looked around the room. "I'm going with you all. I know the layout of his new church. And I want revenge."

Luz's lips lifted in a feral grin. "Then you're on our side."

# CHAPTER THIRTY-SEVEN

Hector drove us. It seemed for the best. He knew where we were going, and that way I could sit in middle of the backseat in case I needed to stop Ti from going crazy again, in theory. Hector was silent, and I wondered if he had anything in his glove box that'd stop a zombie. Luz sat in the front seat, and Catrina sat beside me. Outside, it started to rain, hard, and I wondered if Maldonado was somehow behind the storm.

"How was she? Last night, when you saw her?" Catrina asked me.

I didn't want to lie, but I was afraid Luz would throw herself out of the car and race ahead without us if I told the truth. I wondered if Hector had had the sense to child-lock his car. "She was starved, but still alive. And covered with tattoos of bones."

Catrina pulled her head back at this. "Why?"

"She couldn't say. I don't speak Spanish."

Catrina's hands found each other in her lap, and she touched the tattoo on her right ring finger. "I wonder if—"

"Don't," Luz advised from the front of the car.

"What?" I asked.

Catrina finally held her hand up for me to see. The tattoo there was hard to make out with only streetlamps outside the car for light. "When we were eighteen—we went out and got them done. So we'd be sisters forever. To the bone." It was a stylized drawing of a finger bone, tattooed on her first knuckle, like the funny bone from an Operation game, only fatter. "Maybe that was why," Catrina went on.

"No," Hector said, looking back at us in the rearview mirror. "Who better to serve the house of Santa Muerte than a dead man? And who better to steal away than the love of a dead girl?"

"I'm not dead," Luz protested.

"You are. You just don't get it yet," Hector said. "Look—whoever they are, they stole Adriana out from underneath you. Edie tells me that probably means Maldonado's a shapeshifter," he added, leaving himself out of it.

"That explains a lot," Ti said, making a fist and cracking the knuckles of his right hand.

"What it means for us, though, is that we shouldn't touch him. We should try to corner him and disarm him, but not touch him skin-to-skin. And we should stay line-of-sight to one another, so that no one gets lost or left behind."

Luz groaned. She could be much faster than any of us. It would pain her to be so close, and be slow. I wondered if she'd still give me blood at the end of this; if my participation on this trip was enough to count. She turned back, as if she felt me thinking about her. "I know why she shunned you now."

I nodded in the dark. People who were islands couldn't get hurt.

"How do you know where it is?" Ti asked Hector.

"They nailed a flyer to the clinic door this morning with the address. Made it hard to miss." Hector turned off the headlights and coasted to a stop. "It's at the end of the block. If I get any closer, they'll know we're here."

"They're going to know we're here soon, anyhow." Luz sat straighter in her seat. "I'll see you all on the inside," she said, and she leapt out of the car.

"Reina!" Catrina called after her. I leaned over Ti to look out, but I couldn't see her; she'd already run away.

"Think we can count on her to take out snipers?" Ti asked aloud.

"They don't snipe down here. They spray," Hector yelled, just barely louder than the rain coming down on the car roof. A lightning bolt illuminated him gesturing his hand back and forth, like a running machine gun.

"You two should stay here then," Ti said, looking at Catrina and me. I wanted to go in with them, but I wasn't supernatural, or bulletproof. And if I went, there'd be no way to convince Catrina to stay behind.

"Okay." I looked back and forth between the two of them. It might be the last time I'd see one or both of them alive. "Protect each other, okay?"

Hector nodded and Ti grunted—and as one they went into the rain. There was a distant shout—louder than the rain—and shots were fired.

"Come on." Catrina huddled behind the driver's seat, where Dren had been last night, and pulled me down to do the same. "This isn't the first gunfight I've been in," she explained.

It killed me to wait there, to hear sounds of violence, guns, and not know what was going on. When I peeked up like I shouldn't, and a lightning bolt shot down, all I could see was a warehouse down the block and gates that were wide.

"Stay down!" Catrina hissed.

"How can you be so calm?"

There were more shots. I tried to convince myself that

it was thunder, but I hadn't seen any lightning bolts to cause it.

I wanted my friends to be all right. I wanted my mother to be all right. I just wanted everything to be right in the world for once, for one soul-shattering moment of calmness when I wouldn't have to worry about anyone else, or even myself.

Another gunshot, a scattered grouping. I pressed my forehead to the window like I shouldn't, trying to see anything through the rain.

A bloody hand slapped against the top of the glass. I screamed and jumped back.

The hand slid down, horror-movie style, like a drowning man's last wave good-bye. The unrelenting rain made the bloody droplets race down.

Ti wasn't going to bleed, and Luz bleeding was unlikely. "Hector?" I said, my voice cracking in fear.

"Don't do it!" Catrina warned me.

I ignored her and opened up the car door, glad to find it was someone I didn't know. With the help of the overhead car light, I could see a young Latino man with three cross tattoos on the visible side of his neck. He was prone on the sidewalk, and the rain was washing his blood away.

"Oh, God." I reached for my phone. I didn't know where we were, but Catrina did. I handed my phone to her. "Call nine-one-one. Tell them someone's been shot."

Maybe I should have pre-reported our arrival here, seeing as gunfire was almost a given. This kid was technically a bad guy—but we were the ones who'd come in asking for trouble. I couldn't just watch him die.

Hector was a doctor—he had to have a first-aid kit in his car somewhere. All self-respecting doctors did. I reached and felt under the chairs, found nothing, then hopped into the driver's seat to pull the lever for the trunk. A spare tire, the tire iron and duct tape from last night, and lastly a paper bag full of medical supplies. I looked inside it as the rain pelted the bag and started soaking the equipment inside.

What good was gauze going to do right now? Not very damn much, in this fucking rain. I took it back to the prone man.

"Where did you get hit?" I asked. He didn't answer. He was far away from the compound—I assumed he'd run this whole way. Or maybe crawled. I pushed him so he was on his back, and tried to look him over. There was a welt on his arm. I unspooled a roll of gauze, lassoed it around his armpit, and tied it tight. Until I could figure out where he was bleeding, I was going to cut off blood flow to all his extremities on principle.

His shirt was full of holes. The crosses hadn't protected him from anyone but Luz—and even that was iffy. I started when I thought I'd found a gun—but it was just the outline of a gun, tattooed on his stomach, roughly done. This kid wasn't much older than Olympio was. Jesus.

"Hey!" I shouted at him, shaking him. He groaned. I could feel a pulse at his neck. "Help is coming, okay? Just hang on."

I went through his limbs more systematically now, looking for holes in the fabric in addition to blood, and undid one arm and a leg. Then I planted the rest of the gummed-up gauze over a wound on his thigh. I hoped it wasn't his femoral—I didn't think I was strong enough to haul him into Hector's car.

There was another burst of gunfire. "Edie!" Catrina shouted at me.

"Hang on. I'm almost done, okay?" I wasn't sure whom I was addressing, him or her.

"Edie—Edie?" Catrina made a question of my name, and I turned around. "I think I got shot."

She was still crouched behind the seats, but she was holding her side. "Oh, God—can you lie down on the backseat? Lie down right now." I tied down the dressing on the gangbanger's leg, and took my soggy bag of gauze back into the car. "Shit shit shit—where?"

"Here." It was the side of her stomach—could be a flesh wound, could be halfway to peritonitis.

"Okay. I want you to lie still." I opened up as much gauze as I could. "Is there an exit wound?" I slid my hand under her back to feel for any other, potentially worse, openings. Finding none, I shoved all the gauze into the bleeding spot on her stomach. "Shit. Catrina—hold this here, okay?" I fished my phone out of my pocket with bloody hands. Not that now was a great time to text Asher, but he had the fucking car keys and I didn't know what else to do. Emergency vehicles should already be on their way. *Should.*

"How did it happen? I was being careful." She was gritting her teeth from the pain. I wondered where the bullet had wound up inside her. God-fucking-dammit. If anyone should have gotten hit, it was me, gallivanting around outside.

"What have you done?" Luz was outside, standing in the rain, looking at the bleeding man. Her eyes went wide when she saw Catrina.

"Did you find her?" Catrina reached a red hand out.

"No. She wasn't there—" Luz looked between the gangbanger and Catrina and made an assumption. She put her foot on his tattooed neck.

"No! He didn't shoot her!" I yelled into the rain.

"So?" Luz yelled back. "He's one of them!"

"Tell her he didn't hurt you, Catrina!" I sank down to her level inside the car. "Tell her!"

Catrina's eyes narrowed. It was clear she didn't want to care.

"Catrina—" I begged.

"Reina—don't," Catina whispered.

"Bah!" Luz kicked the man and knelt down, holding his eyelids up with her thumbs and looking into his eyes. He woke up then, when he hadn't before. Seeing her looming over him, he started to talk—I assumed she was using her glamour on him. She reached for the bandage I'd placed on his leg and pulled it aside. "He doesn't know where she is. He says he's never seen her. Let him bleed to death like he deserves to." I reached out and fought her for control of his leg. "Whose side are you on?" she yelled at me, fangs out.

"The side where no one dies!"

Luz rocked back on her heels and laughed at me. "It is too late for that."

Acid flushed through my stomach. "Where's Hector and Ti?"

She smiled, showing fang. "Your zombie friend makes a very effective human shield. They're slower than me, but I think they're fine."

"And she wasn't there?" I asked again.

"No. All this, for nothing. And Catrina shot." Luz looked into the car where Catrina was. I couldn't read what was written in her eyes. "I wanted to save one person. That's it. Just one. The rest of the world can go fuck itself, if I can save this one. And they still keep her from me. There was a pile of bones there—but no girl."

"I'm sorry, Luz." I didn't know what else to say.

Catrina screamed from inside the car. I didn't know if it was anguish or pain.

"We've got to—" I said, looking at Catrina. If I had to

pick between her and the man outside, I'd choose her. "Do you have keys?"

"No. The doctor does." She squinted into the distance. "He's on the way."

Hector and Ti arrived just as sirens started down the street, ambulances and police cars fighting through the rain.

"Who is that?" Ti asked.

"Oh, no—Edie—" Hector said, looking at the man and then at Catrina. He leaned into the car and quickly assessed her.

"She needs help—but he might die. He's going into shock."

Of course he was; he'd been bleeding out in the cold rain. Hector pulled his keys out and threw them at me. "I'm a local doctor. I can say I heard shots and came out to help." He shook his hand, and I handed him his emergency bag.

"In the rain?"

"I know the police. They'll believe me. Take my car— get Catrina to County. You know where to go."

I didn't want to leave him behind with this mess. There was no guarantee more Three Crosses members wouldn't come out. I almost said his real name, and just barely caught myself in time. "As—Hector—be careful, okay?"

Asher nodded, and Ti put his hand out. I handed him the keys. I knew he'd been to County before.

# CHAPTER THIRTY-EIGHT

Luz rode in the front seat while I cradled Catrina's head on my lap and applied pressure to her side in the back. Was it a good thing there was no exit wound? I didn't know enough trauma medicine to know. I petted Catrina's hair with my free hand while she moaned.

"Can't you just—" I asked Luz. She pulled her head back, as if I'd suggested something offensive to her. "Goddammit, Luz, it's only a little blood."

"If I give blood to her, I'll wake up Anna—and if Anna takes me back, who will rescue Adriana then?"

"How do you think Adriana will feel if you kill her sister?"

"Don't," Catrina whispered.

"You stay out of it," I told her. Her blood was seeping up, gluing her shirt to my thigh. "Ti—what happened in there?"

"Nothing good. Maldonado wasn't there. And the girl we were looking for wasn't either. They seemed surprised, so it wasn't a trap, but nothing was gained."

It was still pouring outside. Inside, the car smelled like humidity and rain, and blood—and rot.

"Did you get hurt?" I asked Ti.

"A few shots. Nothing I can't heal." He pulled us onto the highway, and the rain didn't stop.

* * *

We were silent on our way to County. I wondered what
was happening with Asher, if they would keep him for
questioning, if they'd find other members of Three Crosses,
and what they would say. Catrina had been quiet—her
eyes were open, but I could tell she was thinking, watching lampposts go by, upside down, outside the window in
the night. I watched her breathing, and my free hand held
her wrist to feel the strength and speed of her pulse.

We pulled into the emergency roundabout, and Luz
got out of the car. "I'll go in with her. You two go on."

I looked to Ti. He shrugged, and then I looked back to
her. "Are you sure?"

"There's still half the night to go. I can take her in and
answer any questions—or stop them from asking them."
Luz tilted her head to indicate what, as a vampire, she
could do with her mind.

"Is that okay with you, Catrina?"

She nodded and I relinquished her to Luz, who picked
her up easily, although she gasped and groaned. Once she
was in Luz's arms, she looked up at the other woman.
"You'll search again tomorrow night?"

Luz smiled down sadly at her. "Of course."

Ti drove me home. I didn't know what to say, straight up
until he put the car into park. I turned toward him. "Do
you want to stay here? I've got a couch."

"Sure." He opened up his door and got out. I trotted up
to my apartment and opened the door. Once he was in, I
latched all the chain locks again. Ti looked bemused.

"Am I supposed to be keeping an eye on you, or are
you supposed to be keeping an eye on me?"

"To be honest, I'm not sure. Both, maybe? I need a
shower, and I need to sleep. How about you?"

"Just the one. I don't think I ever want to sleep again." He waved the thought away. "No offense to people who need to."

"All right then. Dibs on the shower, because it's mine." And because after a wounded zombie showers, there might be . . . clots. I got a towel out of my linen closet and threw it down on the couch for him. "Wait here."

I couldn't help but think about how in other circumstances, if our lives had been different, the chance to take a shower with Ti might have been sexy. Now—no. That door had closed. I wasn't sure when it had happened, or how, but when I searched my heart, I knew it was true. Maybe because someone else was there instead. My heart always liked to bet on the darker, more damaged horse. I sighed and looked down—my ankles still had red marks on them that were tender to touch after the snakes. At least Asher wasn't full of snakes—just other people. I got out of the shower, dried my hair, and threw on clothes. Ti stood up when I entered the room.

"Your turn."

"Are you sure?"

"Yeah. You can't stay out here like you are now." I pressed a smile on, as if the events of tonight had never happened. As if I hadn't had my hands covered in other people's blood.

"Okay." He nodded and stepped around me. A few seconds later I heard the water running. I went into the kitchen and made myself coffee. There was a knock at my door.

"You have got to be kidding me." I set my coffee down and walked over to the peephole, barefoot. Asher stood outside, looking bedraggled. I started unlatching the locks.

"Hec-tor." I stuttered while saying the right name. "Are you okay?"

"Yeah. Are you?" His eyes were scanning me, as if to make sure I was still whole. Knowing who he was inside, and who he might be after the seventeenth—I wanted to say more, but the seventeenth was only two days away. Technically, it started at midnight tomorrow night. I shouldn't want to fall on my sword again, like I had with Ti. "Are you sure you're okay?" he went on, worried by my silence. "I couldn't ask you back there, but if anything happened to you—"

"I'm fine. Honest." I nodded quickly to make him believe.

There'd been familiarity between us before, a willingness to touch each other without fear. I wanted that back, no matter who he looked like now. Screw being afraid of getting hurt.

He stepped in, and I didn't move—I wanted him to step into me.

"Edie?" Ti asked from the hallway, emerging with a towel wrapped around his waist—and several flesh wounds visible on his chest.

"Ti—" I looked back at him and gestured toward Asher, who was perilously close. "This—Asher's here—" I explained lamely, then swallowed. Ti didn't know Hector was Asher yet.

"It's okay." Asher looked from Ti to me, and stepped back outside again. "I was just coming for my keys."

I shook my head. I didn't want to shout out that it wasn't like that, but I could see his assumptions on his face. "Asher—"

"Asher?" Ti began. I could see the beginning of a change on Asher's face, as if his other form was being summoned by his name.

"You'll keep her safe, won't you?" Asher asked of Ti, taking a step farther back on my stoop, into shadows.

"Asher, don't go."

"Don't apologize, Edie. In a few days—" He held his hand out, not for me to see anything, but because I would know what he meant. On the seventeenth his hands would be fully Hector's . . . or no one's at all. "Keep the car. I'll take the train." He turned and went down my stairs.

Maybe I should have run after him. Or maybe he was right. I was exhausted by too much too fast tonight.

"That was Asher?" Ti asked me. "How long has he been pretending to be the doc?"

"Seven months or so." I stood in my doorway, looking out, willing Asher to return.

"I didn't mean to startle him, Edie."

"No, it's okay. You were just trying to keep an eye on me is all. And I'm still keeping an eye on you." I tried to sound as light as I had earlier and failed. There wasn't enough coffee in the world to help me fake it.

"It's been a long night. You should get to bed."

"Yeah. I should."

"I've wrung out my clothes. I'll leave them in your shower to air-dry overnight."

"I'll get you sheets for the couch." I came back with them. He was still wearing just a towel.

"Edie—I'm sorry." He jerked his chin at the doorway where Asher had been.

I held up my hand and passed the sheets over. "I don't think I can take any more apologies tonight."

# CHAPTER THIRTY-NINE

It was noon when I woke up. The rain had stopped, but it was still gray out, thick clouds with the promise of more to come. I stumbled into my living room, where Ti was lying on my couch. He nodded when I came in.

"Did you have a good night?" I asked him.

"I remember all of it. It's a start." He was on top of the sheets and had his clothes on, though they looked worse for the wear. He still had the faint smell of rot. "I need to go now. I thought you should know. I wanted to stay to tell you." He swung his feet down so he was sitting. "I think we're going to be fighting again tonight, and I don't want to be at half speed."

I read between the lines. He was telling me he was going to go out to feed. If he and I had stayed together, how many times over would we have had that conversation in code? Would I be okay with it? Was I okay with it now? "Thanks for letting me know."

He stood and started walking toward me for the door at my back. "I didn't want to just leave this time, you know?"

I nodded and hugged myself with my arms. Better late than never. "Thanks, Ti. I appreciate that."

"Edie—" he began, drawing up his face to one side like he was going to say something else.

I leaned back and quickly opened up the door. "You should really be going. I have to visit my mom soon. I'll see you tonight." I didn't want to let him in, not even a little bit.

He sighed.

"Okay." He nodded at me and walked out. I watched him go until the rain began again and hid him from me.

Once Ti was gone I folded into my couch. Was Asher at work today or not? I sent him a text message, one I probably should have sent last night. "That wasn't what it seemed," and "Again, tonight? Reina's?"

Tonight was likely the last night we could save Adriana. It was officially the seventeenth at midnight tonight. And if we didn't find Adriana, then I wouldn't have any leverage over Luz, and Santa Muerte would belong to Maldonado, costing me the only thing I could trade to the Shadows for my mom. Tonight was the night. Wherever we went tonight, whatever we did—I wasn't going to stay behind again.

I got up, went into the bathroom, brushed out my hair, and put on clothes. And then I made the hardest phone call of my life.

She picked up on the third ring. "Hey, Mom."

"Hi, honey!" She sounded happy to hear from me. "What's up?"

"Nothing much. I just wanted to tell you that I love you."

"Awwww, that's sweet of you. I love you too, dear. Are you coming by tonight?"

"No. We've got a meeting scheduled after work." If I went by now, and I was scared, she'd root me out. Mothers had a kind of magic too. "But I'll come by tomorrow afternoon, if that's okay."

"Sure. I've got a doctor's appointment at three—come over before then, or after six?"

"Can do."

"I always love hearing from you."

"Thanks, Mom. I love you."

"I love you too," she said again, and I hung up. If she knew what I was doing for her, if she understood everything that was involved, she'd tell me to stop it, that she wasn't worth it.

She'd be wrong.

My next phone call was going to be to County—I still had their main information line in my phone. But I didn't know Catrina's last name, and she might not be able to speak right now besides. I put on all my silver again, grabbed my purse, and ran out to my car in the rain.

The information desk wasn't much help when I got there, without a last name. But County was a big facility—even though I hit one dead end, it wasn't hard to leave and loop back in through another unguarded door. I had a suspicion where she'd be at, and it was late enough that some of my old co-workers might remember me as an occasional float nurse there. Through a combination of persistence and luck, I found her in medical ICU. I waved, and she waved back, and it was good enough for her nurse to let me in.

"What's happening tonight?" she asked slowly as soon as I was close enough to hear her.

"Nothing you're going to be a part of. How do you feel?" I read the numbers on her monitor. Everything looked fine.

"They found the bullet. It took them a while." She was pressed flat against the bed like someone who was on the good drugs. I knew if I started fondling IV bags I'd draw her nurse's ire—but her pupils were wide and her movements slow. Even if she wasn't on a narcotic drip, she'd been getting them frequently—and understandably, if they'd been fishing inside her guts for a ricocheted round. "What's going on?"

"You didn't miss anything else last night. I just wanted to check on you was all. Do you need me to tell your family that you're here?"

Her dilated eyes slowly fixed on me. "Family? What family? Adriana's all I have."

"I'm sorry." I glanced up at the clock. I probably had an hour, provided I wouldn't get in the way here. I pulled up a chair. "I can't believe you got shot."

Her lips pulled into a low grin. "Me either. Should have been you." I'd found the small hole in Hector's door on my way out to my own car. The bullet had gone through the door, through the passenger-side chair, and straight into Catrina.

"Yeah, I know." I looked around the room—it'd been a while since I'd floated to medical ICU, and a while since I was last here, period. "They treating you right?"

"I don't hurt much, as long as I don't move." She stared off into space. I wondered how long I should stay, if she was tired. Her eyes closed, and I made to stand. The sound of the chair scraping back startled her awake again. "I keep fading off. Sorry."

"It's okay. I'll go now. I'll come back tomorrow and let you know."

She didn't respond, but her eyes closed again. Chances were she wouldn't even remember my being here. I turned around and took a step toward the door.

"Edie?"

I turned around knowing she might not say another word. People on good drugs were sometimes like that. "Yeah?"

She fought to open her eyes again. "She left me there last night, Edie. She didn't stay."

"What?" I turned around and crossed the room to stand at her bedside. She was too wasted to lie.

"Reina set me on a chair in the waiting room, bleeding. She left the second after you did."

"Are you sure?" Bleeding could cause unconsciousness. And unconsciousness felt a lot like time travel when it was happening. "She had to leave before the dawn."

"No. I could see the windows—it was dark outside. She just left me behind."

"That's not like her."

"I know." Catrina's dark gaze wandered around the room, until it finally landed on me. "I just needed to tell someone. It wasn't . . . kind of her."

I took Catrina's hand into both my own. "You're right."

Information shared, she relaxed again, and soon she began to snore. I stopped by the nurses' station on the way out and gave them my phone number just in case, and told them I was a family friend. And in the elevator on my way out, despite the fact there were other passengers in it, I knocked on the wall with one hand.

"Hey—Shadows. You've got to protect her. Make sure she's okay."

They didn't respond, and as we reached the first floor, all the other passengers avoided looking at me.

# CHAPTER FORTY

In my car again, with hours left to kill before sundown, I wasn't sure what to do or where to go. It wasn't too late for me to drop in on my mother, but . . . no. If I went there, she might sense something was wrong and start to worry. Surely the story of last night and tonight was written on my face. Without thinking, I followed the train on street roads, heading farther downtown.

While it wasn't raining now, last night and this morning had filled in the potholes with water, making their depth hard to judge. My little Chevy swayed from side to side as cement rubble caught alternating tires. The market was closed, due to the weather, I assumed, and I drove down to the Divisadero clinic proper.

Maldonado's blue sign had been ripped off the door, and a new one put in its place: CLOSED.

Of course the clinic was closed. With Hector barely himself, and Catrina gone, there'd be no one left to run the ship. The real question was, would it open again? I drove on.

The distances were shorter, now that I wasn't on foot, and landmarks were easier to find during the day. The rain seemed to have washed everyone away with it—that, or the gunfight last night, made everyone else but me wise enough not to go out.

I canvassed streets until I found the one we'd been on the night before. I recognized the fence Hector had parked his car next to. The rain had washed away all of that boy's blood. I should have looked at County for him too.

I slowly cruised up the street to where the new Three Crosses church had been. In the day, without the rain, it was much less menacing than the lightning-freeze-frame picture I'd had of it last night. The gates were torn off their hinges—that was all Luz there—and had been re-constructed using woven locked chains. Police tape fluttered, torn down from the places it had been tied, and a lone janitor was shoving water around with a street broom inside.

I stopped the car. The janitor looked up at me nervously; then, seeing only a girl inside the car, shook his head and got back to shoving water around. I eased off the brake and stepped on the gas—and there was a thump from the front of my car. I hit the brakes again and leapt out to see what I'd hit.

The elderly woman I'd saved from the storm drain was huddled in front of my car. "What the—I cannot believe you!"

"*¡No te creo!*"

"Did I hit you? Are you okay?" She was still wearing County Hospital gowns, soaked to the bone.

"*¿Estás tan ciego qué no puedes ver?*" she complained.

"Lady, I still can't understand you. What the hell are you doing out here?"

The woman put her hands on her hips, and I took her meaning.

"Okay. Maybe if I can't understand you, I shouldn't keep asking you questions. But sheesh." I looked around. "Where did you come from? I'd swear to God you weren't here just a second ago."

She squatted back down and played her hands in the water streaming down the gutter from higher ground.

"No no no, you can't do that. You'll catch a cold."

She angrily hit the water, and splashed it at me.

"Hey! Come on—that's not right."

She shoved her hands back into the water—there was another storm drain down the street. Some of the water the janitor was brooming out of the Three Crosses compound had made it up to here, a waterfall over the sidewalk's edge. Looking like some sort of creepy elderly otter, she fished out a handful of rubble and showed it to me.

"Look—" I began. She shook her hand again, spattering me with cold drops. "That's disgusting! Stop it!" I walked away from her and opened up the driver-side door of my car. I was done with trying to save her by force. Either she'd get in willingly, or I'd just drive away. I didn't have to save everyone right now—in fact, my saving-people dance card was fucking full. I pointed from her to my car with an intention that could be understood across tongues. "Get in."

She shook her hand again, playing her opposite forefinger against the stones in her palm, as if she were panning for gold.

"Get in," I repeated. Surely she knew how door handles worked. I got in my car, and she hit my car hood with one hand.

"Are you coming?" I asked her. She tottered back and opened up the door. When she sat down she threw the wet stones she held across my dashboard. Trails of thin mud poured down from them. "Hey!"

She dusted her hands off on her wet gowns, and crossed her arms. "Gah." Clearly, the Reinas hadn't been able to keep her safe somewhere—and before that, neither had County. That left just one place we could go.

I went back toward the clinic, slowly, the only car on the road, searching for the path Olympio had taken Ti and me on yesterday. I made a few wrong turns but eventually wound up in front of Olympio's tenement and parked my car.

"Look," I tried to explain to the old woman. "You just need to be safe for a night. No one should be on the streets tonight. Bad things are going down." The only thing I saw on her face was frustration, likely with me. "I'm sorry. I wish I could explain." I ran through what little Spanish I did know and went for broke. "*Noche muy malo, mucho dolor.* Stay indoors!"

She lunged forward, grabbed up one of the rocks that hadn't rattled off my dash, and shoved it at me.

I took it. At least it was dry now. And it didn't look much like a stone to me.

"That's not a stone. Is it?" I held it up to the fading light outside. "It's a finger bone."

Not a lot like the tattoo Catrina and Adriana shared—it was long and slender, gracefully curved. It'd been stained gray by mud, but there was no denying what it was.

I picked up another stone from where it'd fallen on my floor. It was just a rock. All the rest of them were. But not this one.

"Okay—we're going up to the boy's house. And then you can talk, all right?"

Wherever she'd gotten the bone from, I'd get Olympio to make her tell me.

* * *

It took time and effort to herd her up the stairs toward the *curandero*'s door. I knocked three times, and Olympio peeked out. "I knew I saw you outside!" he exclaimed. "You never told me you had a car!"

"You never asked," I said, and stepped back so he could see the woman I'd brought with me.

"Ugh, her again?"

"Yeah. Sorry. Can she stay here?"

Olympio released a huffing sigh of protest. "I'll just add it to everything else you owe my grandfather. Don't forget, you owe him for last night."

"I'll write him a check. Honest. Just this one more thing."

"Fine." Olympio pulled back and opened the door all the way, so that we could step in.

He went off to get the old woman a towel, and we stood in the same room I'd been in yesterday, only there was no tinfoil cross, and no snakes. The *curandero* sat on his chair in the corner, surrounded by candles and statuary. When Olympio returned, he looked me over. "Are you okay?"

"Yeah. I just need you to translate for me. And then to keep her safe overnight."

"Big. Check," Olympio warned.

"I totally understand." I looked to the old woman, and pulled the finger bone out of my pocket. "Where did you get this, Grandmother?" I looked to Olympio. "It's very important. Make her tell me."

Olympio translated my question, although I got the impression that the woman understood me on her own.

"Mictlan."

Olympio waited for her to go on. When she didn't, he asked the question again.

"Mictlan," she answered again, with a strong nod.

Olympio shrugged. "It's not a word. I don't know what it means." Then the *curandero* spoke and Olympio began to frown. "My grandfather says . . . it's like a word for hell."

I looked from Olympio to the *curandero* and back again. "I would guess that whoever's finger that came from agrees with you." I went over and put my back against the wall, much as I had the prior night while watching the *curandero* heal Ti. There was some thread of commonality here; all I had to do was see it. I squeezed the bone in a fist while I tried to think.

The place where I'd seen Adriana trapped had been full of bones—and by the next night, when Luz had gotten there, completely emptied. And the new Three Crosses church, where we'd made our abortive attack, had been empty too.

Adriana and all those bones were somewhere. I'd bet they were still all in the same room.

Ti had said he'd been working at night someplace dark. With no lights. Maybe there was a third location? But if so, where?

The old woman was standing in front of me, her eyes burning, trying to make me understand something that I couldn't see. I shook my head like the janitor had shaken his head at me earlier, to see her playing in the gutters, while he shoved around all that water that wouldn't drain away.

Because the gutters were blocked. The same gutters I'd found Grandmother playing in, where she in turn had found bones—and not unlike the ditch where I'd found her in the first place, hidden underground. In a dark place, not unlike hell.

"Olympio." My eyes took a second to focus on the boy again. "I need you to explain to me how to get to that ditch by Tecato Town."

"Oh, no—" Olympio began shaking his head violently.

"I need to get over there."

The old woman started clapping her hands in glee, like a psychotic cymbal monkey.

"If you're going there, then I want to go with you," Olympio said.

"No way."

"You don't know where you're going. It could flood—"

"All the more reason that you can't come."

"No—I have to!"

I looked to his grandfather and pleaded with my expression for the man to talk some sense into his grandson.

*"El siente la llamada, debe contestar,"* the *curandero* intoned.

"See? My grandfather agrees. He says it's my calling to go with you," Olympio interrupted as his grandfather went on, and Olympio made a face. "Ugh. Really?"

The *curandero* nodded, and Olympio looked up at me. "He says you have to take us both."

I blinked. How were we going to get someone with crutches down the steep cement side of the ditch to the bottom? Much less inside the tunnels afterward?

Olympio read my mind. "Not him. Her." He made a face at Grandmother.

That was almost worse. "To a flash-flood zone, underground, while it's raining out?" I looked from one to the other of them and waited for someone else here to be sensible, because it wasn't going to be me.

"It's the only way. I was meant to go. So was she," Olympio said.

"You're sure about this?" I asked Olympio's grandfather, and he nodded. I let out a sigh. "I guess you can't fight prophecy."

# CHAPTER FORTY-ONE

To my dismay, no one had stolen my car while I'd been at the *curandero*'s. Then I'd at least have been able to leave the hospital-gown-wearing grandmother behind. Olympio, though—the thought of predestined adventure had him clinging to me like a barnacle. Before we left he'd gotten two flashlights from his neighbor for our trip. Now he sat in the passenger seat and played with my radio in between giving me directions. When he realized I didn't have any Spanish presets, he started slowly twisting the dial. I didn't enjoy listening to him hop from station to station like he was cracking a safe, but it was a good way for him to kill time. Listening to him made me not stop and think how insane this was. Taking them with me, destiny or not, was like going to war in a clown car.

"I can't believe you didn't tell me you had a car," Olympio said.

"I wasn't keeping it from you. It just never came up. Why? Where did you want to go?"

"I couldn't go anywhere, until I was called." Olympio found a station he liked and finally sat back. "I've been waiting for my whole life to find my calling. Now, though . . . who knows? I have to see where the calling takes me."

"I thought you'd been seeing things your whole life?"

"Yeah. So? So's Catrina. You never know if you'll really be called." He nodded along with the song.

"And you can't tell it yourself?" I asked, wondering for a dark moment if Olympio's grandfather had taken out a large life insurance policy on him.

"No. It comes to you in dreams. Or another *curandero* can see it. Like I see things on other people." He pointed for me to go right.

"Speaking of, how's my gaping chest wound?"

"Your black flower?" he asked, and then squinted at me. "It's smaller. Almost gone."

I made a thoughtful sound. "You're just being nice to me in case we die, aren't you?"

He grinned. "I'm not going to die."

I stopped at a dented stop sign. "God. If I'm going to die, don't tell me." I looked back in the rearview mirror as I made another right-hand turn. "What about her?"

"She's just a cloud. Can't make a thing out about her. I've seen people like her before, though. It just means she's undecided."

"About what?" I couldn't imagine the old woman having big decisions to make. It was clear she didn't have a house, a lover, or a 401(k).

"No clue. And I don't think she'd tell me if I asked her. Park here."

"Great. Just great." I pulled alongside the entrance to an alley. "Is this the kind of place where I might as well leave them my keys?"

Olympio looked around my car in dismay. "It's not like you have anything in here worth stealing."

"True. All right. All aboard that's going aboard."

"What's that mean?" Olympio asked.

I jerked my thumb out the window. "Time to get off the train."

* * *

It was almost sundown. I made them wait while I texted Asher quickly. I should have texted him earlier, but I think I knew he would try to leave me behind again—along with the Three Musketeers that I'd become.

*At the edge of Tecato Town. Think Maldonado's bone room is underneath. Have guide.* Better to tell him that than get into specifics. I eyed Olympio again. "You're sure about this?" The old lady could suit herself, but Olympio . . . I wished I could make him stay behind somehow. I hadn't gotten a choice about a lot of things as a kid—but nobody had told me I was destined for greatness either. Olympio worked harder and deserved a fairer life.

He nodded brusquely. "I'm sure."

"Okay then. Where to?"

"Through here," Olympio said, and led the way.

We threaded through the tarps the *tecatos* had strung up to keep out the rain. The air here was thick with the smoke of wet fires. Skinny men huddled around them, blowing on them to keep them lit, with socks strung overhead. The old woman kept up surprisingly well.

We reached the edge of the wide cement ditch, half a football field across, filled with a muddy stream. We were closer to the metal mouths this time than we'd been before. I could see them down there, and hear water pouring through them and on into the dark.

"You ready?" Olympio asked me.

"I was born ready," I said, teasing, trying to sound like an action hero. Olympio snorted, and then we started down the steep cement bank.

I didn't have time to watch the old woman; I was too busy concentrating on my own feet. The sides were slicker now after last night's rainfall, making the entire thing feel like we really were going into a mouth.

I reached the bottom with a splash at the same time Olympio did. I wished I'd known when I'd left my house this afternoon to wear rain boots, though the water felt good on my smoke-snake sores. God only knew what I was going to contract tonight. I heard a splash behind me, and the old woman was standing there. I was glad she hadn't tumbled down.

"Which one?" I yelled. The sound of the water running over the corrugated metal was loud.

"I don't know! What does your intuition tell you?" Olympio shouted back.

My intuition said it wished that it was dry. I stared, looking from one tunnel entrance to the next, wondering if Olympio was right, if I'd be able to feel the right one.

I was just like those people at the hospital with their stupid crystals.

"I have no idea!" I shouted back to him.

The old woman shoved by both of us. "¡Éste, éste!" and went into the nearest mouth.

Olympio shrugged. "She says this one!"

"Fine." She was probably at least as magical as I was, or anyone else could be. Our chances were one out of three.

We hobbled behind the woman in the dark. Olympio pulled out one flashlight for himself and handed the other one to me.

The old woman was part mole. She didn't wait for our light, she just dove through the tunnel, her hunchback perfectly suited for our journey. Olympio and I had to cling to the walls to stay upright while the ankle-high water tried to trip us. I got in front of Olympio and started using my bigger size to block him from falls while he tried to shine the flashlight far enough ahead to keep the woman in their spotlight. She took a right-hand turn and disappeared.

"Fuck," I whispered when she went out of sight.

"Come on, keep up," Olympio urged me on.

Together we waddled to where she'd taken the turn. Olympio shone his light in the tunnel she'd taken. "Where did she go?" I asked.

"*¿Abuela?*" Olympio called.

"Wait for us, lady!" I shouted after him.

We took the turn, but she didn't wait. We reached a T in the tunnels and shone our lights each way. "Where now?" he asked.

"I don't know." One of the tunnels looked higher than the other. I couldn't imagine Maldonado pulling off a ceremony while fighting getting swept away down here. "That way." I pointed my flashlight toward the slightly drier tunnel.

"Okay."

We shimmied along it, one step after another, until it took another turn. This new tunnel was longer than the flashlight beam. Could she have really gotten that far in front of us?

"Keep going." Olympio nudged from behind me.

"Fine."

The tunnel floor rose, and we had to crouch farther down. The only benefit was that the water we walked through was shallower. Each shuffling step sloshed less and kicked more. There were hard sharp things below us that we were walking on; they ground against one another, making our footing harder to find. I toed up one of whatever it was, my foot numb with prolonged exposure to the runoff.

It was rounded and flat, and curved just like a rib.

"*Huesos*," Olympio whispered behind me. "Bones."

I nodded and put my finger to my lips. I turned his flashlight off and kept the other one, keeping its beam low as we went in.

# CHAPTER FORTY-TWO

There was a bend in the tunnel, and the walls turned from metal to stone . . . to bone. We'd found it. The last bone room. Olympio gasped.

"Shhhh," I cautioned. I raised the flashlight slowly, scanning around the ground. Scattered bones covered the floor and were affixed to the walls. The same cage I'd seen before, or its sister, sat against one wall, its occupant hard to spot inside. From somewhere in the room came a sound of running water, a faint hissing like a faucet left on.

I didn't see anyone where the flashlight could reach. I took a few more steps in, and Olympio stayed glued behind me. Together we crept up to the cage. "Adriana?" Olympio guessed.

"*Dejala ir,*" the girl in the cage whispered back.

I ignored him. "We have to get her out of here—"

"No. She's saying 'free her,' not 'free me,'" Olympio interrupted. He took the flashlight away from me and shone it down to where Adriana lay collapsed inside the bone cage. Her whole body was wedged against the side, and her arm was reaching out. He shone the flashlight where she was reaching to—and Luz was there, chained to the ground.

"Luz!" I ran over to her at the same time as Olympio did. "Luz—wake up—" She was sprawled across the floor, chained at both wrists, and I realized with sickness that the hissing sound I'd heard was her—the cuffs were silver and sawing through her arms as fast as she could heal. I dragged her back and pulled the silver cuffs out of the divots they'd worked into her wrists.

"Luz, when did this happen to you?" Without Catrina around to guard Luz, had someone attacked the Reinas during the day? Who better to know their schedule than the Three Crosses? I'd hoped the guards I'd seen with submachine guns had been able to defend the people inside the Reina compound.

But it was still daylight outside. Despite the fact that it was pitch-dark in here without our flashlight to see, the daylight above still held sway.

"Why won't she wake up?" Olympio asked me.

"She's Reina—and it's still light out overhead." I snapped my fingers and pointed to the nearest pieces of bone. "Grab me those, will you?" Olympio did as he was told, and I shimmed them between her skin and the silver cuffs.

There was the sound of boot heels on cement, footsteps louder than the water outside. And another Luz appeared, from a crevice of shadow in the far wall.

"How?" Olympio whispered.

How indeed! My mind panicked, and then I realized I knew. Last night, when Luz had run in first to look for Adriana, or maybe even before then, during a prior fight—she'd touched Maldonado. And he was still a shapeshifter. He'd been able to capture her and take her form.

It was probably how he'd captured Adriana in the first place.

We'd taken Maldonado himself home last night. No

wonder he'd left Catrina behind. And because he wasn't really a vampire, he wasn't constrained by the sun.

The shapeshifter's eyes saw us, and he put a hand that wasn't his on his hip. "So now you see." The upright Luz looked to her twin on the ground, and then at me. "I knew if my son loved you, you were smart," said the shapeshifter with Luz's face. And then he transformed into Maldonado.

Luz's clothes were tight on him, until they disappeared, changing with him into Maldonado's black robes, pendant and all. I didn't know if his transformation was shapeshifting or magic or what.

"So you're . . . Asher's father?" I asked, looking for some way I could appeal to him.

"Only part of me. It's very complicated in here." He tapped his forehead with a gloved finger and watched me with glittering eyes. "We only use the shapeshifter when we need him. We do as I say, the rest of the time."

"Can you," I began slowly, not sure who I was addressing or how to address him, "let her go?"

He grinned and laughed. "We have a plan, and she's a part of it. It's too late to go back now."

"But she's just a girl—" I pleaded. "You have to let her go."

He knelt down a distance away, so we were on the same level. "Why would I do that?" He swept his arm back to indicate the room we were in with the girl in the cage and the bones on the walls. "I have a glorious plan, and you expect me to ruin it over your conscience? Because you think you have a tenuous connection with someone from my past?"

Maldonado was waiting for an answer. The longer I played stupid, and the longer we talked, the greater the chances Luz would wake up, or Asher would come down here and save us. Maybe.

"Do you know how many pasts I have inside me right now?" he asked.

All I could do was shake my head.

Maldonado leaned forward. "I'll tell you. Thousands. And they're all so mad. And the shapeshifter, your friend's father, is the worst of them all." He grabbed a loose bone off the ground, and scraped its sharp edge across his forehead. "He screams and screams until I want to cut him out of me from the inside. When all this was his idea. His idea!" He jabbed the bone at his forehead with force, and when he moved his hand, a bruise and drops of blood were left behind.

Maldonado regained control of himself, casting the bone aside. "When he's the one that found me to implement it."

"Why? What possible reason could you have for all this?" I looked desperately around the room, with the deaths of so many written on its walls.

"This location lends itself to magic. This place is as old and angry as the land your Shadows call home, and is more watered with fresh blood. It was nothing to buy the warehouse above and block off this storm drain, and easy to use the pathetic *tecatos* outside. Your zombie friend went among them at night, while they were high, like a junkie reaper." He paused to consider this, and then continued. "And then this room—even in his sleep, look at the artistry. He's good with bones."

I needed more time. Luz needed more time. "But why all the bones? Why here? Why the girl?"

"So we could call Santa Muerte to us and control her." Maldonado rose again to standing. "It's a brilliant plan."

"You can't own Santa Muerte!" Olympio shouted from behind me. *"¡Eres un mentiroso, hijo de la chingada!"*

"Shut it!" I ordered Olympio. He didn't know what I

did about Maldonado. The flashlight he held, our only light, shook in his hands.

"We'll kill you!" Olympio went on.

Maldonado smiled. "There you are wrong. I can see into the future sometimes. And I see myself becoming very powerful shortly."

Luz stirred beside me. I didn't see it, but I could feel it, like a presence returning to fill the space, the reverse of dying. I'd never seen a vampire wake up before. I knew she was going to be pissed—and still chained, unable to help us just as she hadn't been able to help herself before.

The only thing I could think of to do to save us was what she'd been forbidden to do. I carefully spotted Luz's lips in the near dark. I'd once sworn I'd never let anyone else bite me—I'd already been bitten by Anna once, and feeling vampire fangs slide into your flesh once is enough. But if I didn't get Luz to wake up soon and even the odds, Olympio and I weren't going to make it out of here.

"Olympio—run!" I shouted at him, and reached for her mouth. I yanked her lower jaw down, smashed my wrist between her fangs, and slammed her jaw back shut. Olympio took off, his light shining with him toward the tunnel.

Maldonado spotted me half a second too late, as the light disappeared. He laughed. "*Dama*—there's no key for those cuffs." There was a snapping sound, and then bright flames appeared, without anything to burn, in the high corners of the room, illuminating all the bones. There was a pattern on the walls: They swirled from large to small, all sweeping in toward the cage. Maldonado walked over and yanked me back, making Luz's teeth lacerate my wrist.

He grinned down at me, his face a rictus. Both hands on my shoulders, he shoved me back with more motion than force. It was his magic that followed through, sending me skidding like a strong wind into the wall, extra bones on the floor clattering away from me. I was pinned to the wall, a great weight pressing against my chest. "Stay here," he commanded. "Someone should get to see."

And then he returned his attention to the woman in the cage. *"Adriana, mi niña esqueleto, mi mujer delgeda, la más pálida y rubia."* He stroked his hands up and down the bars of the cage, bone and metal both. Bones on the wall behind me were jabbing into my back, but his power held me still. Maldonado leaned back and started waving his arms in the air in front of the cage in a pattern, like he was conducting a symphony. His voice rang out, as the *curandero*'s had on the previous night. I couldn't get free.

A dirty face appeared in the tunnel entrance. Maldonado seemed not to notice. It was the old woman returning. *Go away!* I tried to shout at her, but the *bruja* had stolen my voice.

Grandmother walked in like a charmed snake, weaving back and forth. Maldonado's hands included her in his gestures, and he crooned to her, encouraging her, pleading, begging, telling her where to go. And she listened. She came nearer—not to him, but to the cage.

Inside it, Adriana had risen up. She was impossibly thin, cachectic, and the sleeveless white dress she wore hung off her. The outlines of her bones were clear to see, running just beneath their matching tattoos, and her face was tattooed into a grinning skull mask.

Like a bird dancing for itself in front of a mirror, Grandmother and Adriana mimicked each other. Grandmother came closer to the bars of her cage, and Adriana followed, holding up her weakened body by leaning against the bars. Maldonado's voice rose in a song-like prayer, and Grandmother stood up straight and leaned in. Adriana met her there, and their lips touched.

Old and broken, and young and broken, different but paired, two halves of the same whole. I realized what I was seeing just as a strange light enveloped the place where they touched—if I squinted it looked like they were merging. Maldonado's magic was uniting Santa Muerte: the old lost woman, the goddess held prisoner by the Shadows for so long that she was a hollow version of her own self, and putting her into Adriana's starved, trapped form. Adriana's hand went up, and Santa Muerte's matched it, two hands pressing into each other until magic combined matter and only one hand remained.

Maldonado's voice went from whispers to shouting, and behind him Luz sat up. Night had finally arrived. She licked her lips, tasting my blood, and she looked at me with angry eyes. I'd betrayed her to her maker—but Anna was the only person who could save us all now. Then she saw Adriana and Grandmother, and the strange thing they were becoming, conjoined.

"No!" She lunged at the end of the chains—I heard the bones I'd slid into her cuffs shatter.

If Luz had just woken up—so had Anna. Would she get here in time? Where was she? Was she even still in town? I didn't know. I started beating against the magic that held me, and it kept slamming me back into the bone wall, tighter each time.

Another voice joined Maldonado's. A flashlight beam illuminated the tunnel's entrance, and then Olympio was there.

*No! Run!* I tried to shout at him, but my voice was still gone.

He came into the room like the boy I'd first seen outside the clinic, confident, and his prayers met Maldonado's with a cocky tone. He didn't wave his hands, just set his flashlight in his armpit, lining it up so it'd beam into Maldonado's face, and kept repeating himself.

Maldonado rebounded—I expected him to attack Olympio physically, but he redoubled his efforts toward controlling the women he held in thrall. The light where Grandmother and Adriana met got brighter—no matter what Olympio tried, Maldonado was too strong. Olympio realized it just as I did, while Luz was screaming obscenities in two languages, lunging like a rabid dog at the end of her chains.

Olympio grabbed the flashlight from under his armpit and threw it at the cage.

It flew end-over-end and only hit the corner of the cage. But it hit the bone there solidly, and knocked off one tiny flake.

Maldonado began waving his hands madly, as if he was sending his orchestra toward destruction. He flung his hand out toward Olympio. His magic slammed into the boy, sending him reeling back into the wall beside me.

I watched the tiny piece of bone drop as I heard Olympio grunt, wind knocked out of him by the force of his landing. The light holding the matched women together began to flicker and shake.

"Edie—" Olympio whispered, gasping for air. There was a spear of tibia shooting out through his right shoulder—a bone from the wall behind us had pierced him through, back-to-front.

*Oh God*, I yelled, still without a voice.

Luz shouted a triumphant battle cry from behind the cage. She held up mangled hands—she'd broken the bones of her hands to free them from the silver cuffs. She ran for Grandmother and began to pry her back from Adriana with her arms. Maldonado stopped praying now, and started shouting. I dropped the few inches between me and the ground, yelped, and found I could talk.

"Olympio—" I scurried over to where he was pinned. We were the two least magical things in the room—we needed to get the hell out. I reached behind him, where the wall was slick with his blood, and tried to pull the bone free from the wall. It was attached—embedded into cement. I couldn't break it without hurting Olympio. With piercing wounds you were supposed to try to leave the object in—it might be applying pressure on arteries on the inside, stopping the person from bleeding out. But the shouting and fighting behind us wouldn't last forever, and in Luz's damaged state I couldn't guarantee who would win.

"This is going to suck," I told Olympio.

He gritted his teeth and nodded. "Do it."

I took him by his shoulders and yanked him off the wall. The bone slid into his wound again and out the other side. He collapsed into me. I balled his hand into a fist and put it up against his chest, and I pressed the back of him into me, picking him up.

"Come on," I told us both. "Come on." I started drag-carrying him to the tunnel's maw. Behind us, the shouting and sounds of fighting didn't stop.

# CHAPTER FORTY-THREE

I wasn't sure where we were going. The water fought against us, trying to steal Olympio away from me. We were lower here, so the water was deeper—I didn't know if that meant I was going the wrong direction, or if it'd begun to rain outside. He whimpered every time I yanked him, and my chest was warm with his hot blood.

"You can't die," I explained to both of us. "You can't." I felt along the tunnel's side with my shoulder, hitting it with the top of my head, the sound of the water susurrating around us, making me dizzy. What if I got turned around? What if Maldonado's magic twisted the tunnel somehow? What if there was no safe place?

"Come on." I pulled us both along. The air got fresher, and I had to fight the water more. I was soaked up to my thighs; I couldn't feel from my feet to my knees. The only thing that kept me going was that I was carrying Olympio.

The water rose and I stumbled, wrenching on Olympio's arm. He cried out then; I heard it echo. I pulled him up again and turned to start sidestepping against the rising water-wall, trying to give it less of me to push against.

"Edie? Olympio!" Our names, shouted from a distance.

"*¡Estoy aquí!* Here!" Olympio shouted weakly from my arms.

I couldn't spare a breath to yell. If I lost my footing now, there'd be no regaining it; we'd both be washed away, battered against the tunnel walls.

"Edie! Olympio!" The voice was more panicked. Closer.

I saw light just as hands snatched in. I fought them instinctively. Olympio yelped as he was pulled from my arms.

"We've got you—Edie—" Ti was there, pulling me forward against the tide, and Asher was at his side holding Olympio.

"She's down there—so's he," I whispered as soon as I felt safe. They hauled us against the current, out of the tunnel, back to the ditch's open space. Wider here, the water was shallower but not much slower. "He's insane." I reached for Asher. "Whatever he tells you—he is insane."

Asher held up a hand covered with Olympio's blood. "I know."

There was a crash of thunder and a lightning bolt nearby. In that frozen second of light, I could see that the man who held Olympio wasn't fully Asher anymore . . . or Hector either. His face was pulled between forms, asymmetrical, pieced together with parts from a hundred different beings.

"No—" I fought against Ti to stand on my own.

"Shhh," Asher whispered to Olympio, hidden again in the dark. Regardless of his form, he applied pressure to the wound like a doctor would. "Shhhhhhh."

The sound of water grew—rain from a hundred city blocks was slowly channeling down. We turned to walk up the ditch as one.

"Asher!" A man's voice yelled behind us. Maldonado emerged from the middle tunnel, apparently no worse for the wear. Adriana, Luz, Grandmother? Had magic or water taken all three?

Maldonado reached out his hand. "I knew you were out here. It's not too late for you!"

Asher stopped, Olympio still cradled in his arms. He turned toward Maldonado, his father, and I couldn't see his face.

"Asher—come to me," Maldonado demanded, and I remembered how inside the bone chamber he'd kept me trapped. "The ceremony can go on. They're all trapped in there. I can save you. Come with me, and see."

Asher started setting Olympio down. Was he choosing to do that? Of his own volition? Or was he under Maldonado's control, as I had been?

"No!" I struggled against Ti to find footing with my numb feet. He pulled me close for one moment, helping me stand straight, and his lips brushed my forehead.

"Be careful, Edie," he whispered. He made sure I had my footing, let go of me, and then ran in.

Ti reached Maldonado before Asher, and hit him like a truck. The *bruja* was flung back into the cement wall and collapsed into the water at Ti's feet. I wanted to cheer, but I had to get over to Olympio—maybe this would all be over soon and somehow we'd all survive. I tried not the calculate the odds as I reached Olympio's side.

Maldonado had recovered—I hadn't seen it happen, but he was locked with Ti now, arm-to-arm, chest-to-chest. As a zombie, Ti was the only thing a shapeshifter like Maldonado couldn't become. Asher was still walking toward his father, slowly. I hoped it was reluctance holding him back, but I honestly didn't know.

I scooped Olympio up out of the water. He was cold and pale. "Hey, hey." I shook him awake. "You'd better still be with me."

His eyelids fluttered open. "You haven't killed me yet."

"Where'd you want to go, Olympio?" I knelt down in the

water to keep him out of it, raising his chest up across mine. I hugged him in an attempt to provide pressure. "In the car, when we get out of here. Where do you want to go?"

He smiled at me. "Disneyland."

I snorted. "That's pretty far away from here."

"Yeah. I know." I squeezed him tighter.

Out of the farthest tunnel, Grandmother arrived. She was like some mystic cockroach that nothing could kill. As I had that thought, she turned and pierced me with her eyes.

Maldonado shoved Ti back, and Ti stumbled to one knee. Grandmother moved around their battle and walked toward me. As she did so, I noticed something strange about the fight. Asher was at its periphery, moving back and forth in one spot like a paused character in an old video game. Was he fighting his father, or had his father put him there, trapped, while he was wrestling with Ti? I crushed Olympio to my chest with worry.

As Grandmother neared she seemed taller, as if her spine had unwound, and I realized she was producing light, the bright orange-yellow of light pollution tinged with smog.

*"Elegir,"* she said when she stood nearby. *"¡Elige!"*

"What the hell are you saying?" I asked aloud.

*"¡Elige! ¡Elige uno!"*

"She says for you to choose. She says you get to pick one," Olympio translated for me. I could see the meat of his wound, where I'd mashed him to myself, turning white with no-blood. It wasn't just the rain that made him cold—he was slipping away from me.

"Ask her what she means!" I almost shook him in my frustration.

*"¡Elige!"* she yelled again, spitting the word at me. *"¡Elige!"* she commanded, and I knew.

If whatever Maldonado had been trying to do in the bone room had worked, with all the magic that'd been swirling around below—then she was *the* Santa Muerte. The Saint of Death.

I'd been praying to God for my mom to live for a week and a half now. Why not just ask the deity of the damned, the one that was actually here?

*"¡Elige!"* she yelled, and thunder cracked in time with her voice.

*Choose.* My mom. Or—Olympio.

God help me.

# CHAPTER FORTY-FOUR

What kind of horrible choice was that? What kind of uncompassionate fucking awful deity asked for you to choose between your friend and your own mom?

"I hate you!" I shouted out into the storm.

"¡Elige!" she shouted back.

My mom already believed in a good afterlife. I couldn't send Olympio, a punk-ass kid I'd dragged into this mess, to his, here.

God. Help. Me.

"Him! Save him! If you can!" I shook him in fear. "Do it if you can—do it now!"

Grandmother squinted at me, then made a thoughtful face and looked down at the boy in my arms. Then she stepped away, taking her phosphoric aura with her.

"Olympio?" I looked down at his face, wet with rain and my tears. "Come on. You have to get better."

"Déjame en paz, estoy bien."

"I can't understand Spanish, remember?" I shook him again. "Olympio?"

"Stop that. I'm fine." He blew air through half-parted lips and struggled to sit up. I released the wound on his chest—and his skin under my palm was whole.

A wave of water came our way. Maldonado had

toppled Ti. The electric feeling I'd had in the altar house returned—Maldonado's power regrouping around him. Asher stumbled when the wave hit him, falling to his knees.

"Asher—hurry! Come help me! It doesn't have to be like this. I can set you free!"

Asher put his hands to his head and bent down, as if in prayer. I could hear his anguished voice yell, "No!"

Ti recovered and yelled a mighty cry. He ran toward Maldonado again, only to be pushed back like I had been in the bone room. I could see him fighting against the magical force, leaning in as if he were wrestling a hurricane. Grandmother walked over to him.

Luz crawled out of the nearest tunnel, silver-ruined hands holding Adriana to her chest. She pushed to standing, cradling the other woman, and walked toward us with laborious steps.

"Is she okay?" Olympio asked.

I shook my head. "I don't know."

Grandmother reached out toward Adriana and Luz just as Luz tripped. Adriana clung to her, and Luz fought not to get washed back.

Maldonado shook his hand at Asher. Asher refused him, shaking his head, slowly. So painfully slow.

Lightning flashed nearby, and thunder clapped. A *tecato*'s tarp washed by. I snagged it, for all the good it would do, and gave it to Olympio. I set him down in the torrent, and he held his own. Then I moved with the current toward the tunnels, the water speeding my feet.

A rush of anger at being used fueled Ti now—he kept pressing forward against Maldonado's magic front, making incremental gains. I passed Grandmother helping Luz back up. I wasn't sure what I could do against Maldonado, but someone had to help Asher. He couldn't go insane alone. I couldn't just leave him there. As I walked toward him, he stood up and started moving away from me. Slow step after slow step, ever closer to his father's outstretched hand.

I took dangerous steps and let the current carry me, splashing down to my knees twice. "Asher, no!" I fought back up, coughing out foul mouthfuls of runoff.

Asher turned, and a lightning bolt showed me his face. There was little of the man I knew left behind—he was like a golem, made of clay. "Wait for me!" I yelled. "Remember! You said you wouldn't go without me!"

"Shut up, woman, before he is lost to us both," Maldonado commanded. I tried to yell back at him but he stole my voice.

I rushed through the water before his magic could shove me away like Ti. I reached Asher and blocked him with my body.

"Don't go." I could only mouth the words, but I took him in my arms and held him. "Just don't go."

He struggled with me, and I wasn't sure if I was making the right decision or not—he would go insane here, and lose all memory of me, but I couldn't let Maldonado win. The Asher I knew would not have wanted that.

His form rippled beneath me, changing through all the people he could be. I felt my hands down his arms to find his hands, pressed against the ditch's cement floor, and wove my frozen fingers through his. My chin was barely above water, and I pressed my cold cheek to his back. I called his name in a voiceless whisper, like I was summoning the dead.

The electric feeling in the air faded, and Ti ran for Maldonado. The *bruja* brought his hands up as Ti aimed one fist at Maldonado's chest.

"*¡Basta ya!*" Grandmother yelled. Lightning strobed

down and ignored all the higher places it ought to hit, striking on Maldonado's chest just as Ti's fist landed. Ti was blown back as thunder shook the world to the bone.

The lightning didn't leave Maldonado. The connection it made with his chest pinned him back against the ditch's cement wall. It bore into him, lasting longer than a lightning bolt should. The first things to go were his clothes; they burned away as if maybe they'd never been there, been magic all the time anyhow. Then it burned through his skin—like some terrible acid, the lightning kept eating things away. Maldonado shed form after form, like a peeling snake, each one appearing for a second, and then being vaporized. I realized they were faces of everyone he'd ever been—the lightning was forcing him to ripple through them all, and all of them were screaming.

"Don't look!" I told Asher, though I didn't know who he was now anymore. No matter how you felt about your parents, no one should see that. Rising up to a whine, the screams finally stopped. Ti hadn't moved from where he'd landed, and Grandmother—now incontrovertibly Santa Muerte—was turning from orange to white.

Beneath the water, Asher's hands gripped mine back. He'd stopped twitching, going through his forms. I wasn't sure what that meant, but I took comfort in his fingers wound with mine. He rose up, pushing me back.

He didn't look like anyone I'd ever seen him be. But he was one person now—hopefully whole.

"Edie—" I heard my name, but Asher's lips didn't move. I turned as I realized it was coming from behind me, from Ti.

"Hang on, okay?" I told Asher as his hands rose to feel his unfamiliar face. He nodded silently.

I waded through the freezing water to Ti, who was holding himself up. Santa Muerte's light was barely enough to see by—and what I could see wasn't good. Ti had been hit by the same blast that'd tortured Maldonado.

"Let me see." I turned him toward the light and pulled his hand away from his side. A chunk had been torn out of him, which shouldn't matter, because Ti was a zombie. And yet—he held his hand up, mystified. He was dripping red. "Ti—"

The sternness that had always haunted his face disappeared. "Can it be?"

"Oh God—oh God—" There was visible bone, rib cage, I could see it, and more pink underneath. He didn't smell like he'd smelled all the other times he'd been shot. There was no stink of ancient death here, just the rain, running through his wound, washing his blood away. "Oh God."

Ti reached out and seized me. "This is not your fault, Edie."

"Oh, no, Ti—" I whispered in a squeak.

He held me tight, forced me to look at him. "This is what I've wanted for so long. I'm okay."

"Ti—" I was racked with guilt. I should have never shut him out. My whole body was numb from the freezing water—every part of it except for my heart, which was cracking in two.

"This was what I wanted. She did it. She just knew." His expression was beatific. Soft. "You remember. I explained this to you. I meant it."

"If you don't go to heaven now, I'm going to go up there myself and kick someone."

Ti laughed aloud, until it ended in a cough. I reached forward and held him, and he held me back until he couldn't anymore. When I let go of him, he would be gone. I would never get to see him again. It was one thing knowing he was just gone, away from me, and another to know this was final, that he was dead. We sank into the water together, and I let his greater weight pin me down until it covered me entirely, baptized by my sorrow, anchored by what I'd lost.

Hands reached down from above and pulled me up. "Let me go—" I fought them as I resurfaced. "I belong with him."

"No you don't." It was the man I'd never seen before again. I knew it was Asher, but I didn't know how many more changes I could take tonight.

"Are you . . . still you?" I asked him.

He nodded and pulled me to him. "And I need you to stay here with me."

# CHAPTER FORTY-FIVE

I wrapped my arms around Asher and sobbed as he held me close. I heard his voice rumble in his chest as he addressed Santa Muerte. "Explain yourself."

I pulled back, still crying, to see.

Grandmother pointed at Olympio and began speaking. He translated instantly.

"You shall be my voice, young one. And I owe no one explanations, nor apologies." Olympio translated her words, but there was no mistaking her tone. The hospital gowns were gone now, covered instead by a translucent flowing light, but her hands and skull were visible, all bones. "I was trapped by the creatures below the ground, and the *bruja* sought to conquer me."

There was nothing left of Maldonado but a charred mark against the cement. Everything that had been him had been burned away and floated off, into the drains. She continued, looking at each of us.

"I have answered the prayers of those who have called to me—one prayer for each of you. I have been kinder to you than you could ever hope for me to be."

I realized that's what had happened to us. Ti—he'd always wanted to be human again, to get the chance to really die. I'd chosen to save Olympio, and Asher had chosen to save himself. I looked back to Luz and Adriana—Adriana was standing on her own now, without any of the bone tattoos. And Luz didn't seem as frightening as she once had. I wondered what Olympio had wished for.

There was a commotion from above us, in Tecato Town. A squad of people jumped over the side to land in the ditch upriver from us. The way they leapt and landed—vampires, for sure.

A cloaked woman was at the head of their number, hood high. But I saw her white skin, and one blond curl pressed out. Anna had arrived.

"Why are you no longer mine?" She pointed at Luz.

Luz pushed Adriana behind her—if there were to be punishments, they would be hers. "I wished to make her whole. And she wished to make me human again."

Anna took in our ragtag group, looking like drowned rats except for Santa Muerte, and her face softened. "I understand." She pushed down her hood. "I came as soon as I could, when I knew you'd broken your promise and tasted blood. House Grey attacked us as soon as we left." She stared at Santa Muerte. "I can only presume they wanted to control you."

And suddenly the reasons why people wanted to control Santa Muerte became clear. If she could turn a vampire human again—and a zombie—she could bring the dead back to life, as befit her name.

"What will you do now?" Anna pressed.

Santa Muerte spoke. "I do not owe you answers either," Olympio said for her as soon as she was done.

"Your people need you here—" Anna said.

Santa Muerte turned toward her, and her skull-mouth opened up and laughed, jawbone flapping up and down. "Do not presume to know me, undead one. I could control you too. Those creatures of the dark held me for too long, centuries, sucking away my power."

"Who will protect the Reinas from the rest of the Three Crosses then?" I interrupted while I was still brave enough to ask. Whatever had just transpired here, it hadn't magically ruined everyone else's guns. People like Maldonado had plenty of followers eager to take their place. Without Luz to be the Reina and instill fear, her people wouldn't stand a chance. I looked over to Luz and I could see the same thoughts cross her face.

Anna looked at me as though she was just registering my presence. "I should have known it would be you—"

I wasn't about to get shunned off now. "You can't abandon all those people, Anna. You don't know what it's like down here."

Santa Muerte clapped her bony hands, and another lightning bolt struck nearby. "Don't tell me what it is like to be abandoned. And don't dare tell *me* what here is like." Again, Olympio translated. Santa Muerte pointed at Anna. "My people no longer need your kind."

Anna took two steps forward. "You owe us."

Only Anna would try to call in debts from a saint.

"I've already paid them," Santa Muerte said, indicating us. "What do you think I should pay you?"

"We were attacked on the way here. I lost three servants to House Grey tonight." Anna looked unsure. She never looked unsure. "If—if they are not in a better place—I demand their return."

"You admit vampires fear the afterlife?" Olympio translated, his tone as arch as hers.

Anna spread her hands to include the area that surrounded us. "I admit that here may already be hell."

Santa Muerte cackled at this. "Oh, I have seen hells,

*mi amor, mi querida.* I have seen hells." Then she cocked her head and focused eyes that were just empty sockets on Anna. *"Pero ha hecho lo mismo usted,"* Olympio said. "But so have you."

Anna had been tortured for a century not long before. Maybe not as long as Santa Muerte, but——the older spirit nodded, as if to herself, making her robes flow. "Perhaps we may come to an arrangement."

Anna nodded. "I would like that very much."

The two women moved aside. I had no doubt that the flock of vampires that had followed Anna here could hear them speak in whispers, but I was too tired to try. I sagged, and Asher gathered me up. If I didn't look at his face, then I knew that it was him—I felt it in the way his arms held me, strong and close.

"Are you okay?" he whispered in my ear. He sounded like Asher. Some.

"Yeah," I whispered back, a lie. I looked around for Ti's body and couldn't find it. He'd already been swallowed by the drain. "I want to get away from here."

I could feel him nod against me. "Me too. Soon."

Anna and Santa Muerte's conversation ended. Santa Muerte proffered her skeletal hand, and Anna sank to kneel and kiss it, her cloak flowing out around her in the waters. I wondered what agreement they had reached. Standing again, together, they rejoined our small group. At an unseen signal, Anna's people started flowing away.

"But what about Three Crosses?" I shouted out. I needed to hear that the clinic would be safe.

Santa Muerte turned and fixed her dead sockets on me. Olympio translated as her mandible moved. "Do not worry. I have some business yet to do with them."

And then she walked past us. *Walking* wasn't the right word—she moved through the runoff without actually moving, her robes concealing any motion of her body below. She rose up the wall of the ditch, taking her light with her, and disappeared.

Anna watched her go, then looked over to me. "Are you okay, Edie?"

"It's been a long night," I answered honestly.

She came over to me, shaking her head like a disappointed auntie. "This is not what I had in mind when I started your shun."

# CHAPTER FORTY-SIX

Luz really was whole. She let me hold her hand, which let me feel her wrist. Her bones had been reknit, and she had a pulse. Adriana wouldn't let go of her—we three were all crammed into the leather backseat of one of the black cars the vampires drove. Vampires always traveled in style. Olympio was in the front seat, playing with the radio dial. Asher had asked to take a separate car home. I wished I'd gone with him, but he'd seemed worried and weird, and I wanted to make sure Olympio got home in one piece—

Adriana said something in Spanish. I hadn't realized she was talking to me until Luz elbowed me. "You knew him from before?"

"Who?"

"Hector."

"Yeah. I knew both of them before, actually." My hair was drying out in the car's lovely heat.

Adriana went on, and Luz smiled before translating to me. "When you find someone you love, you should never give up hope."

I gave them a halfhearted smile, but mentally amended, *Unless your name is Edie.*

We went into Reina territory first, and our grim vampire driver parked right at the edge of the junkyard maze. The guards with submachine guns held them meaningfully, waiting for the first signs of aggression as Luz and Adriana stepped out. Then there were shouts of joy carried up the line—and people swarmed out of the Reina apartments to see them, to touch them with their own hands. Witnessing their joyful reunion with their friends made me want to cry. Olympio was plastered to the window, watching them until he couldn't as we drove away.

"She really was a vampire?" he asked me.

No point in lying; he'd already seen much worse. "Yeah."

"Wow. And the Donkey Lady?"

"I don't think he's coming back anytime soon." It would probably take wild-undead-horses to drag Dren back to town after what Maldonado had put him through.

"Good."

"So what'd you pray for?" I asked him.

"When?"

"You know. Earlier," I said. I assumed when she said we'd all gotten a prayer answered, she'd meant him too. Unless he was too busy being almost dead to hear her.

His face furrowed into a frown. "You mean when I wrote my name on her mural?"

"Sure," I agreed, because it was easier than explaining anything else to him.

"I asked to be the greatest *curandero* of all time."

I snorted. "How do you feel about that now?"

He pondered it for a moment, then held up his hand. He reached into the backseat and tapped me on my chest. "You tell me."

There was no ticker-tape parade awaiting Olympio's return when we parked outside his building. He hopped out of the car and held the door open. "You'd better come back and visit me."

"I will. I might bring my mom." Who knew what semi-magical Olympio could do versus unmagical irrational cancer, but I should take the chance.

He made a curious face, then nodded with a grin. "Okay!"

I shut the car door. Had I made the right choice? I could have healed her tonight, for real. But what other choice could there be? I waved at Olympio through the window, and he waved back at me. My vampire chauffeur hit the gas and turned the radio off.

I forgot that my car was down by Tecato Town, and remembered that fact as the driver dropped me off at my apartment. It was too late now—what was done was done. I'd go pick it up tomorrow. When I got inside my place Minnie was happy to see me. There weren't any disturbing texts or messages on my phone. I started a shower, because God knew what I'd been drenched in in the storm drain tonight—probably toxic waste. I snorted, got myself good and clean, then dried off. I didn't notice when I poured Minnie a double helping of food because I was thinking too hard.

What now? Was everything worth it? Ti was gone. My mother wasn't guaranteed saved. I'd gone from normal to strange again in less than two weeks. What had I done? What had I become?

I paced around my bedroom, putting on clothing, trying to figure things out. I realized I'd gotten dressed again instead of putting on clothes for bed.

Hopefully the only other person who could help me answer things would be awake too.

# CHAPTER FORTY-SEVEN

I walked out and took the earliest train uptown. I didn't remember directions precisely—I'd only been to Asher's house twice before, in the winter and in a car. But I got off at what I thought would be the nearest stop and walked in a direction that felt right to me. The morning was cool— last night's rain had washed away all the clouds in the sky, and as I walked I could see the beginnings of dawn.

It took me a while, several side streets and dead ends, second-guessing myself after I'd walked entire residential blocks. But eventually I found a house that I thought I recognized even without the snow. I went up to it and knocked on the front door.

After a long wait, a man I didn't know opened it, and I was scared I had the wrong address.

"Edie?" He pulled the door wider, and unfamiliar lips gave me a tentative grin. "Come in."

I smiled nervously and nodded, and then painted the air in front of his face. "I'm not used to—"

"Me either," he agreed.

"Is it . . . permanent?"

"I don't know. I just asked her to save me was all. I didn't get an instruction manual. It didn't feel right to press." He shrugged. "I'll try it . . . in a few days."

"That makes sense." No reason to risk dying again so soon. He closed the door behind me and gestured me farther in. The interior of his house remained the same as the last time I'd seen it. We were in his living room, which was mostly a library; there was a fireplace but currently no fire. I walked over to the mantel and stroked a finger down it. "You've got a lot of dusting to do."

Asher snorted. "When I left this place behind six months ago . . ."

"What'll happen to your new place?"

"I don't know."

"Is Hector . . . coming back?"

"I don't know." He circled his couch and sat down, facing me and the fireplace. "It's only been a few hours. I haven't figured much out yet." Asher touched his own chest and pointed at me. "The thing haunting you—it's gone. I've still got some powers. I can still see."

I looked down at my own chest. "I think I can thank Olympio for that."

"Is he okay?"

"Yeah. He didn't die. And he didn't know anyone that did. He thinks we won."

Asher's eyes narrowed, and his gaze focused on me. "Did we?"

"As much as we ever do," I said, and then I walked over to him. "I'm not used to your hair." I stepped up to him and reached out for his hair, pulling down shaggy brown-blond bangs. They almost reached his eyes—he could be an emo guitarist if he tried, or with a little gel clean up to be a youthful accountant. He had the kind of face that would look better with glasses. He was still taller than me, but not very much more so, not too much to be comfortable to reach up and hold.

"What were we doing out there?" I asked the man who didn't look anything like my friend.

"We were doing what was right. What we thought was right at the time."

"But Ti's dead—and I didn't save my mom. Unless it turns out that Olympio can magic away cancer." I rolled my eyes.

Asher ducked his head, and his hair slipped through my fingers. "I should have asked to save her. I know you chose Olympio."

Save her—instead of himself? "That's absurd, Asher—you're a man, not a saint."

His eyes wouldn't meet mine. I took a step closer, took his chin, and pulled it gently up. It was the first time I'd touched him since the events earlier this evening—and instead of the brown I was used to, his eyes were now blue. What must it feel like to always see the world through different eyes?

I stared at him wondering for so long, he gave me a questioning look. "I'm sorry, I'm just not used to this," I apologized.

"Neither am I." He pulled away from me, and stood and shrugged with one shoulder. "Did you walk? Do you want a ride home?" He started walking for his door, and I followed him out.

I waited outside while he opened his garage and backed out a silver truck. He rolled down his window. "Get in."

He left his window down as he drove, and I rolled mine down too. It was summer outside and dawn air was rushing in. He didn't merge with the highway but went a side route in the same direction as my place, and I didn't complain. Anything I said would be pushed away by the wind, anyhow. Pieces of half-dry hair whipped my face; I held them back with one hand. I propped my feet up on his dashboard, and he took an unexpected right-hand turn.

"Hey—" I protested.

"You'll see," I saw him mouth as he shifted gears.

It was strange to sit beside him in the car when I wasn't used to this version of him yet. I stared out the window and concentrated on the wind. We wove down roads I didn't know until we were in the middle of nowhere, a dirt track overgrown with trees. He pulled in and put the car in park.

"Out."

"Where are we?"

He took his keys from the ignition. "Out."

I hopped out of the truck and walked around to wait for him. "Is this where I find out that you're also a serial killer?"

He frowned at me. "Do you really think that?"

"No." I squirmed, feeling awkward. Nothing out here but trees and his stare. "I just have a smart-ass mouth. Why're we here?"

"Follow me." He walked past me and into the tree line. The trees thickened and then thinned out again, exposing a wide pasture with a small wooden building in the middle of it, not much bigger than a shack. "This is where I was born. Shapeshifters live far away from everyone else when they can. To protect them as long as possible from what they are."

"To stop them . . . from touching people?" I guessed.

"Precisely."

No one had lived in the building for a very long time. Ivy had grown up the walls, and the chimney'd started to break; there was a small pile of brick rubble beside it on the roof. Too many rough winters, and no one here to care.

"This place is special to me." He stared at the lone

shack, lost in his memories. "Last night, I thought I was never going to see it again."

I smiled at him. "I'm glad you were wrong."

"Do you know how long it's been since anyone's tried to protect me?" he asked. I shook my head. "When I met you in my office without your badge, I touched your skin. I could see through you then. Your entire life. Everything."

I suddenly felt very naked and alone. "So?"

"I saw someone who always thinks other people's lives are worth more than hers." He took a step toward me. "You're wrong."

I made a face and rolled my eyes.

"I'm not kidding, Edie. Your brother, your mom. You're so busy saving the world that you forget to ask who is saving you."

I inhaled to protest, but I wasn't sure how to fight back.

"And then you there, last night," he went on. "I knew what you were thinking, Edie. Every time you touched me. Every time I touched you. Last night—last night, I held on to you like a rope. Thinking about you, thinking like you, they were the only things that kept me from going insane. I was so close, I was on the edge—but I still knew you."

I held myself and crossed my arms. "It's not fair that you know everything about me when I don't know anything real about you."

"That's why I brought you here. This is real. I'm real. And you do know me." His eyes were intense, and he was breathing deeply. "No matter what I look like. You will always know me."

Emotions fought inside me. I was confused. I didn't know what I wanted, or what he wanted from me, but this was almost too much. "I think you should take me home."

He waited a long moment, then deflated and inhaled. "All right."

* * *

I followed him back through the trees to his truck. He opened up my door for me, and I slid in while he walked around to the driver side. The wind and light through the trees overhead gave everything below moving dark spots, roaming pieces of shadow. He opened up the driver door and sat down, reaching out with his keys. If we drove away now—all this would be lost, in our past. I realized I didn't want to lose anything else right now.

"Asher, stop."

Holding the keys still, he slowly turned to look at me, with hope in his eyes.

"Edie, let me in. I won't go," he told me.

I nodded, so slight that he might not even have seen it.

He slid the short distance of the seat over to me and kissed me, pressing me up against the half-raised window glass. I was surprised by his intensity—I didn't know his lips or his chin, or the feel of his stubble grazing me, but I knew him. I closed my eyes and let myself feel back.

Skin, warm and lean. I kissed him as hard as he kissed me, pushing my hands up underneath his shirt, touching him. He ran his hands over me like he'd never get enough of my skin. When he came up for air he grabbed me and pressed me to him bodily, my face into his neck. I could breathe in the smell of his hair, and he wasn't vetiver-scented anymore; just shampoo and sweat and skin.

It was hard to breathe smashed against him. "You know I'm not going anywhere, right?" I told his shoulder, and he pulled back, shaking his head, eyes worried.

"I can't read you anymore. Not since last night."

I didn't want to think about what that meant for him just yet, if he was a stunted shapeshifter or a full human— right now I was glad for a little privacy. I let my head fall back onto the seat behind me and smiled at him. "That would explain why your pants are still on."

He smiled down at me and touched his forehead to mine. "Not for long."

# CHAPTER FORTY-EIGHT

There wasn't much room on his truck's seat. He pulled me down to lay on the seat and we wrestled with jeans until we were out of them, him between my legs, my right knee wedged against his steering wheel. After six months of nothing but my fingers I was tight. He concentrated, pushing himself into me, and when my body relented, suddenly taking him in, we both gasped.

"Did I—"

"No. Don't stop." I moved beneath him. This was what it was like, to be with someone I'd been with before. It had been so long. He moved with me and we found a rhythm together. There was no way for him not to be on at least some of my hair, and the morning sun plus our friction was turning the truck into an oven, making him drip with sweat. But he was real, and this was real, for as long as he was in me. His face over me was earnest, watching me like I was the magical one, breathing in time with his thrusts. I reached up and my hand slid over his sweaty back, feeling the muscles of his shoulders working to hold him up. I ran the backs of my nails up his scalp, and held my hands there, framing his head, watching him back. I put one hand back to push against the door so I could press harder against him. Every time I arched he groaned, and the more I arched the harder he rubbed against all of me. I gasped again and he moved with more intent, and faster. I pulled his head down toward me so that our foreheads touched, and we were breathing the same air. It felt like we were one, me beginning where he ended, him beginning at the end of me. His whole body moved over mine, stomach-to-stomach, chest-to-chest, and when I began to cry aloud and let go he thrust harder until he came with me, finishing with a hoarse breath, calling my name.

He collapsed against me, and it was hard to breathe, but I didn't mind. Asher carefully pushed himself up, half on, half off me, and slid an arm through my hair to hold my head. I nestled against him, watching the dappled light play off his shoulder and chest.

"You want to tell me your real name now?" I asked him, pushing a damp lock of hair off his face. Even though we were through he was still watching me carefully, as if at any moment I might change my mind and leave. "I mean, what if I want to say it next time?" I reasoned aloud.

"I don't want to be that person anymore. I only want to be Asher with you." Something tentative sparked in his eyes. "Next time?"

And suddenly, despite the fact that I already was naked, I felt even more so now. And trapped. "I mean—"

"No. That's what I want too," he interrupted before I could take it back.

My first instinct was to ask, *Really?* but before I did I realized I wasn't that insecure. So instead I said, "Good." He beamed down at me.

The real world crept in slowly, like eventually it always does. Now that we weren't moving I wasn't very comfortable, and I didn't think his truck had a towel, but there was no way I was pulling away from him. Not this time.

"You do realize one of us has to move first," I said after a while, when I was pretty sure I couldn't feel my leg.

"Never." He pressed his face down against my shoulder and chest and I ignored everything else to wind my arms around him and hold him tight.

# CHAPTER FORTY-NINE

"I'm so glad you didn't come over last night, Edie—you would have been trapped by that storm." My mother stood in the doorway of her home, looking frail. "Summer storms are the worst."

"Yeah, they are," I agreed, and she smiled at me.

"Are you staying for dinner?"

"No. I just wanted to drop by and say hi." Asher was waiting in his truck around the corner for me—I'd asked him to detour on my way home, and he'd obliged. "I'm actually running errands, but we can reschedule for later on in the week, any night's fine."

"Tomorrow night okay? Unless you have a hot date, that is," she teased.

I made a face. For once I actually might, but I knew Asher would understand. Besides, my mom went to bed pretty early. "Tomorrow night's fine."

Her face wrinkled, and she squinted with a little worry. "Can I invite Jake?"

"Of course. You don't have to ask, Mom. I'll even bring something he likes to eat this time."

My brother's weight lifted, she smiled even more widely at me. "Thanks, Edie. I like it when we feel like a family."

"Me too." I leaned in and hugged her close. "Hey—hang on, Mom." I pulled back a little and leaned out the doorway to wave down the street to Asher, gesturing for him to get out of his car and come down the street, and I gave my mom a silly grin. "I have someone for you to meet."

I went back downtown with a bouquet of flowers to get my car the next day, surprised to find it intact. What, no one wanted to see what treasures were hiding in a Chevy? I opened the door, and heard someone shout my name.

"Edie!" It was Olympio, again on his bike. "I was waiting for you! I figured you'd come yesterday."

"Sorry. I was busy." I hadn't left Asher's bed for one blissful day. Even just sleeping beside him was nice. But today was back to being a grown-up, and dealing with things.

"Who're the flowers for?"

"For Ti. I don't think they're going to find a body." And if they did, they wouldn't know whose it was. I'd try to find out where his wife was buried and put them together if I could, but I didn't have enough to go on about his past. I'd borrowed Asher's laptop this morning to try, but no luck. Besides, as my mother was fond of telling me, bodies were just our mortal shells. If there was any fairness in the world, Ti was already with his wife wherever they'd wanted to be. Now that I was with Asher, I was more inclined to believe things could be fair. Maybe.

"You want me to go with you?" Olympio offered.

"You got a lock for that bike?"

Olympio tsked at me. "Nobody's going to steal it."

"Because you're the world's greatest *curandero* now?"

"Exactly." He leaned it against my car, and together we went back down to the ditch's side.

*  *  *

The weather had gotten better immediately after our battle, and all the drainage had done its job. Now there were only long shallow puddles and muddy debris to prove it'd ever rained. We reached the bottom and walked up to the three metal mouths. The sun was coming up behind them, so the retaining wall cast shadows, and the tunnels—I didn't think anyone could talk me into going into a tunnel ever again.

"Do you want to say anything?" Olympio asked when we'd reached the shadow's edge.

"Not really." I didn't want to pray, and I didn't know what to say. Ti'd been a good man for almost a century. It didn't matter that his heart wasn't beating for half of it. I walked forward, leaving Olympio behind. I reached the middle entrance and threw the flowers inside it. I heard them land with a splash, and knew they'd be there until the next rain. "I'll always think of you when I see storms," I said softly.

"How sweet," a voice in the tunnel echoed back.

I jumped, but Olympio must have taken my movement for grief; he didn't rush in. Which was good, because I didn't want him seeing what I knew I'd see next. He'd already seen enough strange.

"Ahhhh," the Shadows hissed in an imitation of sympathy. "We didn't mean to startle you."

"Why're you here?" I wanted to tell them to get out—they didn't deserve to be anywhere near Ti.

"Because. We entered into a pact. You did find Santa Muerte after all," their voices murmured, interspersed with dripping sounds. "She is not ours, but we are bound by technicalities. So we talk now, as we said we would."

"What do you want?" There was no way they'd be talking to me if they didn't want something from me. I knew how they played the game.

"There's been a little accident on Y4. We could use you

there again. In exchange for helping your mother, of course."

Forty-eight hours ago I would have jumped at that chance.

But the events of the past two weeks had changed me. I stared into the blackness of the tunnels where the Shadows lurked, only now willing to offer their aid. As much as I still wanted to save my mom the easy way—probably the only way, whispered the darkest part of my heart—my mother wouldn't want her life to come at the cost of mine.

Which is what it would be, if I went back to Y4 under the Shadows' yoke.

I'd come so close to death this time. Next time—would I make it? It all came pressing down on me. I'd had to weigh so many options and choose between lives since I'd arrived here. How much longer could I press my luck before it ran out?

I was close to a normal life here, with my job and Asher, and I knew it. As close as someone like me would ever come. And that was what my mother really wanted for me.

I chose me.

"We'll see," I told the darkness inside the tunnel mouth.

"We'll see?" they mimicked back. "We'll see?" Their multivoice raised harshly, and then ended in a laugh. "We'll see, indeed."

I stepped away from the tunnel entrance. With Ti's body gone, there was nothing for me down here now.

Olympio still waited politely, just out of the Shadows' reach. "Everything go okay?"

"Yeah."

"I'll say an *oración* for him later."

"Thanks. I'd appreciate that." I smiled down at him. "You're awesome, Olympio."

He patted himself like it was no big deal. "I know."

# CHAPTER FIFTY

And so now things are normal. Ish. As normal as I've ever had them before. Shadows don't talk to me, I haven't seen a vampire in three months, and Asher wants me to move in with him, which is good because I practically live over there anyhow and Minnie is royally pissed off at me. Asher can change safely into Hector—we haven't tried anyone past that—and he still works at the clinic and no one else knows. Catrina was discharged from County into Adriana's waiting arms.

My mom's condition stabilized. The tumors are still inoperable, but they're no longer growing. I don't know who I have to thank for that—God, Santa Muerte, science, or luck—but I'll take it. It's good.

I still miss it sometimes, though.

I like to think I'd go back someday because I want to. Not because anyone owes me, or I owe anyone else, especially not the Shadows. But, well.

You never know.

Don't miss the next book in the Edie Spence series by

# CASSIE ALEXANDER

# DEADSHIFTED

Coming soon from St. Martin's Paperbacks

And for more of the nightshift don't miss...

# NIGHTSHIFTED
## and
# MOONSHIFTED

... the first two Edie Spence novels.

Available now from St. Martin's Paperbacks!

## "Are you accep

"Can you assure me that we can keep this businesslike?" Luca said thoughtfully.

"Absolutely."

He considered that for several moments, and Olivia's pulse went into overdrive. So much hung in the balance for her. There was so much this marriage would achieve—not least providing for her mother, securing their family home and protecting Sienna.

"Fine." He nodded once. "Then we will marry."

A shiver ran down her spine, even when he was giving her everything she'd wanted. Even when his acceptance was the first step on her pathway toward liberation. She forced her mouth into a smile, made her eyes hold his even when sparks of electricity seemed to be flying from Luca toward her, superheating her veins.

"Excellent," she murmured, even when she had the strangest sense, for no reason she could grasp, that she was stepping right off the deep end with no idea how to swim.

# Clare Connelly

——

## VOWS ON THE VIRGIN'S TERMS

# HARLEQUIN®
# PRESENTS®

Recycling programs for this product may not exist in your area.

ISBN-13: 978-1-335-56831-1

Vows on the Virgin's Terms

Harlequin Enterprises ULC
22 Adelaide St. West, 40th Floor
Toronto, Ontario M5H 4E3, Canada
www.Harlequin.com

**Printed in U.S.A.**

**Clare Connelly** was raised in small-town Australia among a family of avid readers. She spent much of her childhood up a tree, Harlequin book in hand. Clare is married to her own real-life hero, and they live in a bungalow near the sea with their two children. She is frequently found staring into space—a surefire sign she is in the world of her characters. She has a penchant for French food and ice-cold champagne, and Harlequin novels continue to be her favorite-ever books. Writing for Harlequin Presents is a long-held dream. Clare can be contacted via clareconnelly.com or on her Facebook page.

### Books by Clare Connelly

#### Harlequin Presents

*The Secret Kept from the King*
*Hired by the Impossible Greek*
*Their Impossible Desert Match*
*My Forbidden Royal Fling*
*Crowned for His Desert Twins*

#### *A Billion-Dollar Singapore Christmas*

*An Heir Claimed by Christmas*
*No Strings Christmas*
(Available from Harlequin DARE)

#### *Signed, Sealed...Seduced*

*Cinderella's Night in Venice*

Visit the Author Profile page
at Harlequin.com for more titles.

This is a book for every girl who's ever been told she's "bossy" but really just knows what she wants in life and isn't afraid to reach out and grab it.

# CHAPTER ONE

IF OLIVIA COULD have closed her eyes and disappeared to *anywhere* else in the world, then she absolutely would have done so. But, having tricked Luca Giovanardi's assistant into revealing that he would be attending this all-star event, spent money she could ill afford on a budget airfare to Italy, and actually turned up at the party on the banks of the Tiber, she knew she'd crossed the point of no return.

There was nothing for it.

Her eyes scanned the crowds, feasting on the unfamiliar elegance and sophistication, a churning in her gut reminding her, every second, that she didn't belong here. It was so removed from her normal life, so different from what she was used to.

The party was in full swing, the restaurant courtyard packed with affluent guests, the fragrance in the air a heady mix of night-flowering jasmine and cloying floral perfume. As she studied the swarming crowd of glitterati, a woman bustled past, bumping Olivia, so she offered a tight smile of apology automatically, despite having done nothing worse than stand like a statue, frozen to the spot, too afraid to move deeper into the crowd, despite the fact she'd come here for exactly this purpose.

Naturally, he was in the centre.

Not just of the party, but of a group of people—men and women—his obvious charisma keeping each in his thrall, so that as he spoke their eyes were glued to his chiselled symmetrical face.

Why did he have to be so handsome? This wouldn't be so difficult if he were ordinary looking. Or even just an ordinary man. But everything about Luca Giovanardi was quite famously extraordinary, from his family's fall from grace to his spectacular resurrection to the top of the world's financial elite. As for his personal life, Olivia had gleaned only what was absolutely necessary from the Internet—but it had been enough to know that he was the polar opposite of her in every way. Where she was a twenty-four-year-old virgin who'd never even been so much as *kissed* by a man before, Luca was every inch the red-blooded male, a bachelor ever since his brief, long-ago marriage ended, a bachelor who made no attempt to conceal the speed with which he churned through glamorous, sexy women.

Was she really aiming to be one of them?

Olivia licked her lips, her throat suddenly parched, and, despite the fact she was alone, she shook her head, needing to physically push the idea from her mind. She wasn't aiming to become his mistress; what she needed was to become his wife.

A drum seemed to beat inside her body, gentle at first, the same drum beat she'd been hearing for years, since she'd first learned of her father's will and the implications contained therein for her, and her life. But now, as she stared at Luca, the drum was growing louder, more intense, filling her body with a tempo that was both unnerving and compelling.

There must have been two hundred people, at least, in the courtyard, and yet, at the very moment she moved a single foot, with the intention of cutting a path through the crowd and getting his attention, his eyes lifted and speared hers, the directness of his stare forcing her lips apart as a shot of breath fired from her body, the searing heat of his appraising glance the last thing she'd expected. So much for making her way to him! Her legs were filled with cement suddenly, completely immovable.

She'd seen photographs of him—there were no shortage of images online—but they hadn't prepared her for the real, three-dimensional image of Luca, and the way his nearness would affect her. His eyes were dark—like the bark of the old elm that grew at the rear of Hughenwood House. But not in summer, so much as winter, after a heavy rain, when it glistened and shimmered. A tremble ran the length of her spine. Olivia blinked away, needing relief. But even as her eyes landed on the moonlit river that snaked through this ancient city, she could feel his eyes on her, warming her flesh, tracing the lines of her face and body in a way she'd never known before.

Almost as if they had their own free will, her eyes dragged back towards him, skating over the other guests, hoping to find someone—something—that would serve as a life raft. But there was nothing that could compare to the magnetism of Luca Giovanardi—and Olivia was sunk.

When her eyes met his, he smirked, as if to say 'knew you couldn't resist me', and then he turned back to his companions, resuming whatever story had held them in his thrall all along.

Olivia's heart sank to her toes.

This wouldn't work if she found her husband attractive. She wanted a businesslike marriage, ordained purely to free up her inheritance. There was to be no personal connection between them, nothing that could make their marriage messier than it already was.

And yet, how could she *not* find him appealing? Despite evidence to the contrary—a spectacularly uninteresting love life—Olivia was still a woman, and she recognised a drop-dead gorgeous guy when he was paraded right beneath her nose. Who wouldn't recognise how damned hot Luca Giovanardi was? From his chiselled features, swarthy complexion, hair that was thick and dark and rough on top as though he made a habit of dragging his fingers through it, to a physique that was half wild animal and half man, all sinew and lean muscular strength, a figure that was barely contained by his obviously bespoke suit. It fitted him like a glove physically, but his spirit was too primal for such elegant tailoring. He should be naked. The thought had her sitting up straighter, mouth dry, and before she could help herself an image of him *sans* clothes exploded into her mind—the details undoubtedly inaccurate for lack of personal experience with anything approaching a naked man, but it was still enough to bring colour to her pale cheeks.

One thing was certain: Luca was not the kind of man one simply propositioned out of nowhere. Even with the leverage she felt she'd found it was almost impossible to believe it would be enough. She was perfectly *au fait* with *her* reasons for needing this marriage, but why in the world would a man like Luca, who had the world eating out of the palm of his hands, accept what she was intending to suggest?

She forced her legs to move once more, but, rather than taking her towards Luca, they fed her away from the party, skirting the edges of it, until she arrived in a quiet spot near a table of empty glasses, with one solitary waiter sitting on an upturned milk crate, smoking a cigarette. Olivia pretended not to notice him as she made her way to the railing, curling her hands over it and staring down at the river, her stomach in a thousand knots.

*Coward.*

Are you really going to leave without even asking him?

Did you ever think you'd go through with this?

It wasn't as though she'd told Sienna or their mother, Angelica, what she'd planned, so they wouldn't hold the failure against her. Yet despite that, how could Olivia ever face them, knowing she had the power to fix their futures, and had simply balked at the first hurdle?

For the briefest moment, the threat of tears stung Olivia's azure eyes, but it had been a long time since she'd cried, let alone run the risk of anyone *seeing* her cry, so she bit down on her lower lip until the urge passed, focusing on blotting her emotions completely, so that, a moment later, she was able to straighten her spine and turn around, ready to return to the party and once more weigh up her options—or torment herself with the path she knew she had to take, even when she was terrified to do so.

The waiter had disappeared, leaving the upended crate and a lingering odour of second-hand smoke that made Olivia's nose wrinkle as she passed. She turned her head to avoid the aroma, and as a result of not looking in the direction she was walking, stepped right into a rock-hard wall of a human's chest.

'Oh!' She tore her face back, apologising before she could make sense of what had happened, so even before she realised that the strong hands curling around her forearms to steady her belonged to Luca Giovanardi, she heard herself say, 'I'm so sorry, I didn't see you.'

'Now, we both know that is a lie,' he responded, his voice deep and gruff, and so much more sensual than she had ever known a voice could be. Her heart went into overdrive as she was confronted with, in many ways, her very worst nightmare.

Olivia sprang back from him, needing space urgently. She looked around, wishing now that the waiter were in evidence.

'Are you leaving?' Her question blurted out. His answering response, a slow-spreading grin, was like being bathed in warm caramel. Olivia tried not to feel the effects of it, but how could she resist? Nothing in her life had prepared her for this.

'No.'

'Oh.' Her relief was purely because that meant she hadn't lost her opportunity to do this. 'Good.'

When his eyes met hers, the speculation in them was unmistakable. Oh, God. This was going from bad to worse. It was bad enough that she had imagined him naked, but that he might feel a similar curiosity about her...

'I take it you are not leaving, either?'

'I—no. Why?'

'This is the exit.' He nodded towards the garden.

'Oh.' She furrowed her brow. 'I didn't—no. I just needed space.'

He lifted a brow. 'And now, *bella*? Have you had enough space?'

*Bella?* Beautiful? A shudder ran through her. She was *not* beautiful. At least, she desperately didn't want to be. Not in the way any man might notice and praise her for. She was not going to be like her mother— praised for her looks, adored for them, and then re-sented for them and the power they wielded. It was one of the reasons she'd refused to dress up tonight, choos-ing to wear a pair of simple black pants and a cream linen blouse—nothing that could draw attention to her figure, nothing that could draw attention to *her* at all.

'Olivia,' she supplied quickly, stopping herself from revealing her surname by clamping her lips together.

'Luca.' He held out a hand, as if to shake hers, but when Olivia placed hers in Luca's grip, he lifted it to his lips, placing a delicate kiss across her knuckles. Delicate it might have been, but the effect of her central nervous system was cataclysmic. She jerked her hand away, her blood pressure surely reaching dangerous levels now.

'I know.' Her own voice was croaky; she cleared it. Don't be such a coward! Get this over with. 'Actually...' She dug her fingernails into her palms. 'You're the reason I'm here tonight.'

His expression didn't change, yet she was aware of a tightening in his frame, a tension radiating from him now that hadn't been there a moment ago.

'Am I?' There was dark scepticism in his words, and she wondered at that. 'And why is that?'

'I came to speak to you.'

'I see.'

Was that disappointment in the depths of his eyes? She'd been wrong before. They were nothing like bark. Nothing so ordinary. These were eyes that were as dark as the sky, as determined as iron, as fascinating as every book ever written. She was losing herself in their intricacies, committing each spec to memory when she should have been focusing on what she needed to say!

'Well?' he drawled, and now his cynicism was unmistakable. 'What would you like to discuss?'

Her heart stammered. *Say it.* But how in the world could Olivia Thornton-Rose stand there and propose marriage to Luca Giovanardi? It was so ridiculous that, out of nowhere, she laughed, a tremulous, eerie sound, underscored by a lifting of her fingers to her forehead. She ran them across her brow, searching for words.

'There are two reasons women generally approach me,' he said quietly. 'Either with an investment "opportunity"...' he formed air quote marks around the word

'…or to suggest a more…personal arrangement. Why don't you say which it is you have come to discuss?'

She sucked in a jagged breath, his arrogance wholly unexpected. But somehow, it made things easier, because he reminded her, ever so slightly, of her father in that moment, and that in turn made her feel just a little bit of hate for him—a hate that helped her face the necessity of what she'd come to do.

'I suppose, if we have to place this conversation into one of those two categories, it would certainly be the former, and not the latter.'

His eyes probed hers for longer than was necessary, then swept down to her lips, blazing a line of fire and heat as he went. 'Shame,' he murmured. 'I am not interested in any further business opportunities at present. However, a personal connection would have been quite satisfying to explore.'

Her stomach rolled and tumbled and her breath seemed to burn inside her lungs, making breathing almost impossible. Stars danced behind her eyelids. 'Impossible,' she managed to squeak out, wishing for her trademark cool in that moment. 'I'm not interested in that, at all.'

His features showed that he knew that to be a lie. Was she so obvious? Of course she was. She had no experience. How could she conceal what she was feeling from someone like Luca? She was a lamb to slaughter.

'Then I cannot see what we have to discuss.'

*Do it. Get it over with. What's the worst that can happen? That he'll say no?*

'I know about the bank you're trying to buy.'

He straightened, regarding her with a new level of interest. She'd surprised him, the words the last thing he'd expected to hear from her.

'Everyone knows about the offer I have made,' he hedged with admirable restraint, as though it were no big deal.

'Yes.' She offered a small smile, trying to defuse the tension that was pulling between them, and failing miserably. 'Of course, it's not a secret.'

He didn't say anything in response, and his silence seemed to stretch between them.

'You want to buy a bank, one of the oldest in Europe, and the board won't sell because of your playboy reputation. They're conservative and you're…not.'

His features—briefly—glowered before he resumed an expression of non-concern. His control was impressive.

'In addition, your father—'

'My father is none of your business,' he bit out crisply, surprising her with his vehemence. So those wounds still smarted, then? Despite the passage of twelve years, it seemed Luca hadn't recovered from the scandal that befell his father—his whole family— and the part he'd played in it.

'Actually, that's not exactly true.'

Luca's eyes narrowed. 'Ah. I see. Is this another debt of his? Money owed from him to you?' He frowned. 'But you are too young, so perhaps it is a debt to someone else, someone you love?'

Olivia's heart thumped. Someone she loved? Was there any such person? Sienna, of course, she thought of her younger sister with an ache in the region of her heart. But beyond Sienna, Olivia was alone in the world. There was no one else she loved. Her mother, she pitied, and felt a great deal of duty to care for, but loved? It was far too complicated to be described in that way, and impossible to express in such simplistic terms.

'It's not like that.'

Luca's nostrils flared. 'Then why do you not get to the point and tell me what it *is*, rather than what it is not?'

'I'm trying,' she promised from between clenched lips. 'But you're kind of intimidating, you know?'

Her honesty had surprised him. He took a step backwards, tilted his face away, drew in a deep enough breath to make his chest shift visibly, then expelled it slowly, before turning back to face her.

'I cannot help being who I am.'

'I know. But, just—bear with me. This isn't easy.'

He crossed his arms over his chest—hardly painting a picture of calm acceptance. She bit down on her lower lip then stopped when his eyes dropped to the gesture.

'Perhaps we should start with my father, not yours. I imagine you've heard of him. Thomas Thornton-Rose?'

Luca's demeanour shifted, his features changing, as he disappeared back in time. 'He was a friend to my father. During the trial, he supported him. There were not many who did.'

'They were very close friends,' Olivia agreed with a murmur, wondering then if he knew about the will. There was no recognition in his features beyond that which was perfectly appropriate to an acquaintance of his father.

'He passed away shortly after my father went to prison. I remember reading a headline.'

'Yes.' Olivia blinked quickly, focusing on the Castel Sant'Angelo, a short distance away, glowing gold against the inky sky. 'It was very sudden.' Her brows knitted together. 'He hadn't been ill or anything. None of us expected—' She swallowed, ignoring the lump in her throat.

'I'm sorry.'

She brushed aside his condolences. 'That's not necessary.'

Her cool response had him arching a thick, dark brow. Olivia didn't notice.

'Shortly after he died, the terms of his will came to light. You would know that we're part of the British aristocracy, with much land and money held up in various investments?'

He lifted his shoulders in an indolent shrug. 'I do not know much more than we have already discussed. Should I?'

Another maniacal laugh erupted from her chest. He didn't know anything about this, and he didn't know anything about her? Panic was swallowing her whole. She'd counted on a degree of insight, but that had been foolish. After all, his father had been in prison a long time. She doubted they had regular tête-à-tête regarding their lives.

She would need to start from scratch. Careful to keep the anxiety from her voice, she began slowly. 'When my father died, it was discovered that his estate was carved up in a particularly unusual—' *cruel*, she mentally substituted '—way. My mother was to inherit nothing, and my sister and I would only inherit if we met very specific circumstances, by the time we turn twenty-five.'

His features gave nothing away. 'And what circumstances are these?'

*Do it. Stop freaking out. He'll say no, and you can go home again. And do what? Kick your mother out of the family home? Hand the keys over to horrid second cousin, Timothy?*

'Well, it's very clear. You see, my father was very...' she searched for a word that was more socially acceptable than 'misogynistic' '...old-fashioned.'

He dipped his head forward. 'And this is a problem?'

She ignored his interjection. He'd understand, soon enough.

'He never believed women to be capable of managing their own financial affairs.' She couldn't look at Luca as she spoke, and so didn't see the expression of disgust that briefly marred his handsome features. And with good reason—since rebuilding his family empire, Luca had prided himself on employing a diverse workforce. His executive team was made up of more women than men. It had never occurred to him to discriminate based on gender.

'When my parents married, my mother signed over her life savings to him—she'd been an actress, quite successful here in Italy, and had earned well. But she was very young—only just twenty, whereas he was nineteen years older. She loved him.' Olivia's voice curled with a hint of disdain at the very idea of love, and Luca, who was an expert in nuance, responded to the subtle inflection by leaning infinitesimally closer. 'She trusted him.' It was impossible to flatten the emotion from her tone, but she didn't convey the depths of her anger—how her father had abused that trust, because young Angelica had made one mistake, had a silly youthful indiscretion, and for that she'd been punished every day for the rest of her life, no matter how hard she tried to fix things, no matter how often she apologised. Olivia turned to face him, her clear, blue eyes spiking through his black. 'My father managed everything, so that when he died, she had no idea how their affairs were arranged. She couldn't have known that he'd manipulated the estate to curtail everything away from her.'

'What reason could your father have had for doing this?'

His incredulity touched something in the pit of her stomach.

'He was angry with her,' she mouthed, clearing her throat, the barbarism of her father's final act something that had stung her for years. Olivia waved a hand through the air. 'It was ancient history by the time he died, a silly mistake my mother made, many years earlier. Clearly nothing can justify his decision.'

Luca compressed his lips, and her eyes fell to them, so something white hot radiated from low down in her abdomen, spreading through her body with fierce urgency, stealing her breath and weakening her knees. She wrenched her gaze away, unable to make sense of the emotions that were rioting through her. The truth was, the unmistakable rush of desire she felt for him made her want to turn tail and run, to hide from the things she was experiencing. Olivia considered herself to be an expert at hiding her feelings, but she was also used to her feelings making much more sense.

'He was never going to leave any part of the family fortune to our mother, nor to me and Sienna.'

'Nothing about that makes sense. Does he have other children? From an earlier relationship?'

'No.' An anguished smile tormented her beautiful face. 'If only it were that simple. There's only us. And in order to know that the money would be in safe hands, he had his will drafted to specify that Sienna and I must marry, by our twenty-fifth birthdays. Only then will our portion of inheritance become legally ours. Only then could he trust "his money" would be in safe hands.'

'And your mother?'

'She was granted a very small stipend. But it's been lessening every year and stops completely when we turn twenty-five. My birthday is next month.'

She caught the coarse swear word he issued from between clenched teeth. 'With respect, your father sounds like a jackass.'

Her eyes flew wide, and amusement bubbled through her. Were the situation not so very dire, she might have given into it and laughed, or even leaned forward and pressed her hand to his chest, to share the moment of agreement, but worry still dragged at her every breath.

'He was…very set in his ways,' she said, puzzling at the deep sense of loyalty that still ran through her.

Even after all he'd done, after the nightmare he'd made all their lives, she felt driven to defend him.

Luca made a sound that suggested her description barely scratched the surface.

'I wouldn't be here if I weren't completely desperate.' Her voice snagged a little and she angled her face away, wondering why she was finding it so difficult to hold onto her usual reserve. 'When my father died, I was only twelve. I had no control of our finances, no insight into what my mother was spending. She continued to rack up enormous debts, maxing out all the credit cards she had, as well as a hefty line of credit set against the house. By the time I was old enough to see what was going on, things were dire. I have tried, Luca. I have tried to fix things, but there is never enough money to make even a dint in the debt. I have to work jobs close to home, and that limits my options, plus I'm not qualified for anything.' She shook her head, surprised at how much she was confessing to him. It was as though, having started, she couldn't put a lid on her feelings.

Drawing in a deep breath, Olivia tried again. 'We have lived on the breadline for years. I have scrimped and saved and done everything I can to get by, but it's no use. If it were just me, I would walk out of Hughenwood House and never look back. But I can't leave my mother saddled with hundreds of thousands of pounds in debt. I can't let my father do this to Mum and Sienna.' Not on top of everything else he'd already done. 'I won't let him do this to us.' The words were laced with a quiet, determined vehemence, but it was clear that they came from the very depths of her being.

'As I said, your father sounds like a jackass.' A hint of sympathy softened the words, surprising her and bringing an ache to her throat. 'But I cannot see why you have sought me out to tell me all this, unless you think my father has some control over the will?' He scanned her face, and she had the strangest sensation he was pulling her apart, piece by piece. 'If that is the case, I must disappoint you. I have no sway with my father. You would be better to approach him directly, believe me.'

'No, no, that's not it.' She fluttered a hand through the air then brought it to the bridge of her nose, pinching it between forefinger and thumb. 'If I don't get married soon, per the will, then the inheritance defaults to my second cousin. It's not just the money, but our *home*. Our family home.' To Olivia's chagrin, her voice cracked, and she tilted her chin defiantly, angered by the weak emotional display, and even more so by the fact the house still meant so much to her, despite the unhappiness they'd experienced within its walls. 'It's the only home my mother has, and it would kill her to have to leave.'

He crossed his arms over his chest. 'I'm not a matchmaker, *cara*. Besides, I find it hard to believe you would have any difficulty finding a man willing to play the part of your groom.'

As he offered the compliment, his eyes slid lower, to the outline of her breasts, barely revealed by the boxy linen shirt she wore. Despite that, heat simmered in her veins and, to her shame, her nipples puckered against the fabric of her bra, straining—but for what? Her eyes flew to his hands and she knew what she wanted, needed. For him to touch her. Intimately. All over.

She swallowed a groan and looked away, using every ounce of her determination to maintain a frigid expression.

'It cannot be *any* man.' Her voice took on a wooden quality. 'My father was explicit about that too.'

Silence hummed and crackled between them, anticipation stretching her nerves to breaking point. Did he know what was coming? She risked a glance at him but was none the wiser; she couldn't read what he was thinking.

'I have to marry *you*, Luca. No one else. You.'

# CHAPTER TWO

IT WAS OBVIOUS just by looking at Luca that he was a man
who prized his control and strength, but in that moment
Olivia could have blown him over with a feather. It was,
quite clearly, the last thing he'd expected her to say.

'You're saying—'

'That I need to marry you,' she confirmed, forcing
herself to meet his eyes even when something sparked
between them that set her blood racing at a million
miles an hour. 'And that marrying me could be very
good for you, too.'

'This makes no sense.'

'I know.' She bit down on her lip. 'I was really hoping you'd know about this whole thing.'

'My father and I are not exactly on speaking terms.'

She pulled a face, sympathy flooding her. But then,
she knew more than enough about difficult family relationships.

'But they made the agreement so long ago. I just presumed, over the years…'

'It was never discussed with me.'

'Me either,' she promised. 'The first I heard about

it was when the solicitors appeared at Hughenwood, grim-faced and stern.'

'How did you learn about the bank I am buying?'

'Trying to buy,' she corrected valiantly, because his desire to acquire the bank, and their determined rebuffing of his offers, was at the heart of her inducement. 'I read about it online. Why?'

'So you researched me, prior to coming here tonight?'

'Given that I came here intending to propose marriage to a man I'd never met, naturally I did some preparation.'

A curl of derision shifted the shape of his mouth. 'Then perhaps you also read that I have already been married once. It was, in every way, an unmitigated disaster. I have no intention of ever—' he leaned closer, so close that if she pushed up onto the tips of her toes, she could kiss him '—marrying again. *Capisce?*'

'This wouldn't be a normal marriage,' she said quietly, glad that years of living in the war zone that was her parents' relationship had left her with nerves of steel—or the appearance of them, at least. 'I don't want a husband any more than you want a wife.'

'I'm sorry, I thought you just asked me to marry you?'

'Yes,' she responded quickly. 'For the sake of satisfying a clause in my father's will. But our marriage would be a sham—nothing more than our names on a piece of paper.'

He stared down at her, his features inscrutable, so she had no idea what he was thinking. With a sense she was losing her argument, she clutched for the only straw she held in her possession. 'My family's name is well respected. Marriage to anyone would increase your chances with the bank's uber conservative board—but marriage to a Thornton-Rose, in particular, would improve your standing.' She had made her peace with this offer many weeks ago, but as she said it now, as she heard herself actually trading on her father's hated, hated surname, she wanted the world to open up and swallow her whole.

But freedom would be worth it. If she could just get him to agree, the money would be hers and she could finally fix everything her father broke—her mother would finally have some security and stability. And, most importantly, Olivia's beloved younger sister Sienna would be saved from having to make her own arcane match to inherit any part of the fortune—they simply wouldn't need the money.

'And you are suggesting I could use your ancient name to curry favour with a group of prejudiced snobs? That this is how I operate in business?' His sneer of derision warmed her to the centre of her being. She couldn't have said why, but his immediate rejection of that idea was a relief. 'I do not need your father's name to succeed, *bella*, just as I have never needed my own father's name.'

Admiration expanded inside her. He was right—everything he'd achieved had been off his own back. And yet, from what she'd read online, he wanted the bank more than anything else—and she was sure their marriage would help him achieve it. She narrowed her gaze, focusing on that salient detail. 'You want to buy the Azzuri Bank, and I believe our marriage would make that easier.'

'I don't do things the easy way.'

Her heart skipped a beat and she realised, all at once, that this wasn't going to be enough. She didn't hold enough of an incentive for Luca to agree to this. Why had she even allowed herself a glimmer of hope?

'Well, that's a lovely privilege to have.'

'Privilege,' he repeated with disbelief.

'Oh, yes, privilege.' She turned away from him, stalking back to the railing and staring out at the river. It had seen so much over the millennia, so many tragedies and heartbreaks, so much joy and delight. Her own emotions spilled towards it, adding to the multitude of experience. 'What must it be like to be able to turn down offers of help?'

'You said it yourself, you come from a very wealthy family. Do you really think you have any right to complain to me about privilege?'

'Wealthy, in theory, yes,' she responded, turning to look at him over her shoulder, only to realise he'd moved to stand right beside her and was staring at her in a way that made her feel as though she was completely naked—not in a physical sense, but right down to her soul. 'But not privileged. And not free. Do you have any idea—?' She bit back the words, shaking her head.

'Finish what you were going to say.'

'Why? There's no point, is there?' Her shimmering blue eyes caught his, scanning them, hunting them for answers. 'You've already made your decision.'

'My first decision, yes,' he agreed. 'I want no part of any marriage.' Was she imagining the slight hesitation to his voice? Yes. Of course she was. Men like Luca Giovanardi didn't hesitate about anything.

'Then I'll go,' she whispered, accepting her fate, numb to the future that lay before her.

'Not before you have explained some more,' he insisted, with a firmness to his tone that made it almost impossible to argue.

But Olivia was used to being dictated to, and had learned how to harden herself to another's commands. 'Is there any point if you've made up your mind?'

'We won't know unless you try.'

Hope beat wings inside her chest, but she refused to let it carry her away. He was offering her a chance, but it was very slim. She searched for words yet her brain refused to cooperate. She groaned, turning back to the river.

'Start with this,' he suggested, the gentleness of his voice making her stomach churn. She hadn't expected anything like that, from him. 'How exactly did you imagine this marriage would work?'

It was something—a way in. But was he simply trying to make her understand how stupid the whole idea had been? She sucked in a deep breath and forced her nerves to slow down.

'Well.' She spoke slowly. 'I thought a businesslike agreement would be best for the both of us.'

His brows shot up. 'A businesslike marriage? Isn't that a contradiction in terms?'

'Not for people like you and me?'

'And what exactly are we like, *bella*?'

'Please, don't call me that. My name is Olivia.'

He nodded, brushing aside her request.

'Both fundamentally opposed to marriage.' She returned to her original train of thought. 'You don't want a wife, and I don't want a husband. Therefore, we can dictate the terms of our marriage, making sure they suit us completely.'

'And what terms would you suggest?'

Something like danger prickled along her skin. Desires she had no business feeling, let alone voicing, spliced her in half. She did everything she could to ignore them. After all, desire was at the root of her mother's downfall. Love. Allowing herself to be swept up in a man's promises, a man's charisma, blinding her to reality, had led to Olivia's mother's life of misery— Olivia never intended to be so foolish.

'That's the beauty of what I'm offering,' she said quietly, trying to pick up the threads of the speech she'd prepared on the flight over. 'This would be a marriage in name only. I'd live in England, you'd live in Italy, and when a suitable amount of time had passed, we would quietly, simply file for divorce. After our wedding day, we'd never have to see one another again.'

He studied her in a way that sent little barbs running through her body. His eyes seemed to see everything, to perceive everything, so years of practice hiding her emotion no longer seemed to serve her. She struggled to maintain a mask of composure in the face of his obvious interest.

'I can see you've thought this through, but you've

miscalculated. The promise of your name is not enough
to induce me into marriage, with you, or anyone.'

She swept her eyes shut, failure inevitable now. 'I see.'

'You said that if you don't inherit, your portion of
the family fortune goes to a cousin. Do you know this
person?'

She shuddered involuntarily. 'Yes.'

'Is he the kind of person who would act in self-
interest, to secure this inheritance?'

She bit into her lower lip. 'He would only stand to
inherit *if* you and I don't get married.'

'Or...' he let the word hang between them '...if he
challenged the validity of our marriage.'

She blinked up at him. 'But—could he do that?'

'It is my experience that people are capable of all
sorts of things, when large sums of money are involved.'

She crossed her arms over her chest, then immediately wished she hadn't when his eyes lowered to the
swell of roundness there. Anticipation ran like little
waves across her skin. 'So what do you suggest?'

'I do not intend to make a suggestion, Olivia. Only to
point out that the neat and tidy marriage you've imagined would never have worked.'

Of course, he was right. She should have seen all the
angles. They were talking about a multimillion-pound
inheritance. If they were going to fake a marriage, it had
to be plausible. 'Then, what if we were to marry—' she
thought quickly '—and live together, here in Rome, but
only as housemates. Separate bedrooms, separate lives.'

His lips curled with a hint of derision. 'I cannot see
what is in that for me.'

'Azzuri Bank—'

'I will acquire the bank, Olivia, on my own terms. Of that, I have no doubt.'

A shiver ran the length of her spine. His determination was borderline ruthless—she didn't doubt he'd succeed, and now felt a degree of foolishness for ever thinking a man like Luca Giovanardi could be tempted by something as flimsy as having her as a wife.

'If you want to tempt me to agree to this, you must think of something to offer beyond the bank.' A test? He was staring at her as if weighting her reaction.

Her cheeks went from paper white to rosy pink within a second. 'Are you saying you would want our marriage to be—intimate? Because I have to tell you, I have no interest in becoming another notch on your very well-studded bedpost.'

A cynical smile changed his face completely. The smile whispered things into her soul. *Liar.* 'I'm not so desperate that I need to blackmail women into my bed.'

'No, of course not,' she dismissed quietly, wishing they were more like equals when it came to relationships. 'You probably have a line snaked around the block.'

His obsidian eyes narrowed. 'I was not referring to sex.'

'Then what did you mean?'

He scanned her face, and she wondered if he was going to dwell on the suggestion of a physical relationship. 'If we were to marry, there would be no advantage to either of us in maintaining separate lives, under the same roof. News of our marriage would inevitably break in the press, and then, public scrutiny would follow. A housekeeper could be bribed to provide details of our living arrangements. These things happen.'

'I hadn't thought of that,' she admitted.

'We would need to create the fiction of a passionate, whirlwind romance, for as long as it took to satisfy the terms of the will—I would imagine thirty days would be sufficient.' He lifted his shoulders in a charismatic, indolent shrug. 'To that end, we would need to share a bed.'

Her lips parted to form a perfect 'o'. How she wished she had more experience with men in that moment! 'Surely that's not necessary.'

'I have staff.'

'Couldn't they take a holiday for the duration of our marriage? A month isn't very long.' Except when you were sharing a bed with a man like this!

His lips twisted into a cynical smile. 'Don't worry, *cara*. I have no interest in sex becoming a part of our marriage. It would be purely for show.'

She stared at him, aghast. She wanted to demur, to fight him on this point, but something was shifting between them, and she no longer felt that failure was imminent. If anything, he was positioning himself to accept. She tilted her head, not quite a nod, but at least not a denial either.

'It is a big bed. You'll cope.'

She swallowed, her throat visibly knotting, then jerked her head once more, this time in agreement.

'Are you saying you'll agree to do this?'

He considered her for several long moments. Could

he hear the rushing of her heart over the sound of the nearby party? Surely. It beat hard and fast, a fast-paced drum, hard against her ribs. He turned away from her abruptly, staring out at the river, his face in profile like something crafted from stone. She stared at him against her will, unable to draw her eyes away. He was captivating and magnetic, completely overpowering. It was not hard to understand how he had made such a success of himself and his life.

'There is something personal about me you would not have discovered on the Internet.'

She frowned, wondering at his tone, the darkness to his voice.

'My *nonna* is ill.'

The words were spoken quietly and yet they fell between them like rock boulders.

Olivia leaned closer, as if that might help her understand better.

'Not ill.' He turned to face her, the strength in his gaze sending a pulse radiating through her. 'She is dying.'

'I'm sorry to hear that.' Olivia's voice was gentle, sincere. 'Are you close?'

A grimace tightened his lips. 'Yes.' He paused, seeming to weigh his words. 'She has been my biggest support. I owe her a lot.'

'I'm sure she supported you out of love. Seeing you make such a success of yourself is undoubtedly all she wants from you.'

His smile showed a hint of affection. 'She is still an Italian *nonna*, and cannot help meddling. She has ex-

pressed, on many occasions, a desire for me to marry.'
The words wrapped around Olivia, steadier than steel.
'She worries about me.'

'Worries about *you*?' Olivia couldn't help remarking,
the very idea of this man being the object of anyone's
concern almost laughable.

He didn't look at her, nor did he respond.

'If we were to create the impression of a passionate,
whirlwind love affair, it might go some of the way to
easing her concerns.'

Olivia's eyes flared wide. 'You want to lie to her?'

'We would be legally married,' he pointed out. 'That
is not a lie.'

'But a love affair,' she said with a soft shake of her
head. 'No one would believe it.'

His eyes narrowed as he stared at her. 'They must.
This marriage must convince your cousin, your father's
probate solicitors and my grandmother. It must convince the world.'

Something twisted inside her. Surprise. Hope. It
wasn't exactly an agreement, but, for a moment, he
sounded as though he was seriously contemplating this.
She might actually be getting somewhere—and that
knowledge both excited and terrified her.

'If your grandmother wants you to get married, why
haven't you done so before now?'

'Marriage is not a mistake I intend to make twice.
Even for her.'

'But we're discussing marriage now.'

'A very different kind of marriage,' he pointed out.

'One with clear-cut rules and boundaries. One that precludes, by design, any emotion whatsoever.'

'Are you saying you'll agree to this?'

He stared at her long and hard, so long, so hard, that any pretence she might have liked to maintain that she felt nothing for him flew out of her soul and swam away on the crest of the Tiber. It was all physical—surely she could control that?

'I would have conditions of my own.'

Her heart skipped a beat. 'I see. Such as?'

He turned to face her now, looking just as he had the first moment they'd met, but with a hint of grief still stirring in the depths of his eyes, so Olivia was forced to re-evaluate her appraisal of him as a cold, ruthless tycoon. He clearly had a heart, and a large part of it, she suspected, belonged to his *nonna*. 'My grandmother would need to believe this is real.' He pressed a thumb to his middle finger on the opposing hand, counting off a list. 'There would need to be discretion and respect. No affairs for either of us.'

'Easier for me than you, I suspect,' she said, before she could stop herself. After all, the man's prowess as a bachelor was a well-established fact.

He let the barb sail by.

'This would be a marriage of practicality,' he continued with firm indifference, tapping another finger, not taking his eyes off her face. 'You'd get what you want, and I'd get what I want.' For a moment, his gaze dropped to her lips. 'This would not be a genuine relationship. We would not become friends. We would not have sex.'

A shiver ran down her spine as images of that sprang

to mind before she could stop them, and, for the first time in her life, Olivia experienced a headlong rush of desire.

She kept her expression neutral with great effort. 'I'm not interested in your friendship. Or in having sex with you.'

He didn't smile. He didn't nod. He simply stared at her as though she were a mathematical equation he could understand, if only he looked long and hard enough.

'And what about love?'

It jolted her straight. She shook her head fiercely. 'No.'

His dark eyes narrowed speculatively.

'Absolutely not,' she rushed to reassure him, suppressing a shudder of sheer panic. It wasn't him, but the idea of submitting herself to any man, as her mother had her father, that sent arrows of terror down her spine. She wanted independence—true independence—and this she wouldn't find by falling in love.

'I'm not kidding. I will not run the risk of you fantasising about a relationship with me. It is something I never risk when I sleep with a woman.'

'But we won't be sleeping together.'

'No, we'll be married. That has the potential to be far more dangerous. You might start to think—'

'Believe me, I won't. If it weren't for this damned will, I'd never, ever say those vows. And the happiest day of my life will be when the ink dries on our divorce. Okay?'

'I'm curious,' he said slowly, so close the words

breathed across her temple and she caught a hint of his masculine cologne. Goosebumps lifted on her skin.

'You are a beautiful, young woman. What happened to make you so opposed to marriage?'

'You don't hold the monopoly on disastrous marriages.'

'You've been married before?'

'No—I—didn't mean mine. My parents—' She shook her head, cleared her thoughts, and focused a steady, steel-like gaze on him. 'I was born with a brain,' she said after a beat. 'I don't see any reason to tie myself to a man. At least, not for real.'

'And do you promise me you will not change your mind? At no point in our marriage will you want more than I am willing to offer today?'

She tilted her face to his. 'Are you accepting my proposal?'

'Can you assure me that we can keep this business-like?' he said thoughtfully.

'Absolutely.'

He considered that for several moments, and Olivia's pulse went into overdrive. So much hung in the balance for her. There was so much this marriage would achieve—not least, providing for her mother, securing their family home, and protecting Sienna. And yet it would come at a great personal cost for Olivia. To give into her father's misogynistic, sexist demands from beyond the grave rushed her skin like a rash, and anger speared her, despite the fact she'd made her peace with the necessity of this long ago.

'Fine.' He nodded once. 'Then we will marry.'

A shiver ran down her spine, even when he was giving her everything she'd wanted. Even when his acceptance was the first step on her pathway towards liberation. She forced her mouth into a smile, made her eyes hold his even when sparks of electricity seemed to be flying from Luca towards her, superheating her veins.

'Excellent,' she murmured, even when she had the strangest sense, for no reason she could grasp, that she was stepping right off the deep end with no idea how to swim.

After his divorce, Luca Giovanardi had destroyed almost every single piece of evidence that he had ever been married. There had been catharsis in that. He was only young—a boy, in many ways—and so the act of throwing his wedding back into the ruins of the Coliseum had felt immeasurably important, as though he were reclaiming a piece of himself. He had destroyed every photograph they'd had printed, and wiped almost all of them from his digital storage. He hadn't wanted to remember Jayne. He hadn't ever wanted to think of her again. Not of how much he'd loved her, nor how happy he'd thought they were. He didn't want to think about the way his world had come storming down around his ears and then she'd turned her back on him, leaving him for one of his most despised business rivals, a man who had swept in and triumphed as Luca's father's empire had come crumbling down around them.

Luca had learned two lessons that day—never to believe in the fantasy of love, and never to trust a woman.

So what the hell had he just agreed to?

He gripped his glass of whisky, eyes focused straight ahead, without seeing the view. Olivia Thornton-Rose filled his mind. *'I wouldn't be here if I weren't completely desperate.'*

Besides, there was no danger here. No risk. This was nothing like the emotional suicide he'd committed the day he'd agreed to share his life with Jayne. This was sensible. Safe. And short-term.

More importantly, it met both their needs. For months, he'd been wishing he could do something to calm his grandmother, to ease her as she approached the end of her life. Her repeated entreaties for him to find that 'one someone special', to 'give love another chance', were offered kindly from her vantage point of having had a long and very happy marriage, but marriage was not even remotely on Luca's to-do list.

Until now.

He reached for his phone and dialled his grandmother's number before he could change his mind. 'Nonna?' He took a drink of Macallan. 'There's something I want to tell you.'

# CHAPTER THREE

IT WAS LIKE being in a dream, a dream from which she couldn't wake. But wasn't it better than the nightmare that had been life before this? At least some relief was on the horizon.

It had, however, been a mistake not to see him again before the ceremony itself. A mistake not to inure herself a little to the sight of Luca Giovanardi, dressed to the nines, in a black tuxedo with a grey tie, shiny black shoes, and hair slicked back from his face. She stood beside him in the unbelievably extravagant dress she'd been talked into buying at Harrods, after Luca's assistant had called to explain that he'd organised an appointment with the bridal team there. She was aware of his every breath, the husky tone to his voice, the magnetism of the man, and felt as if she wanted to turn tail and bolt for the door.

A wedding 'in name only' had seemed like a simple idea at the time, but, now that they'd come to the actual commitment, the reality of what they were doing bore down on her like a ton of cement. She glanced across at Luca, his sombre profile making her breath snatch in her throat, so she looked away again, panic drumming through her. She wished, more than anything, for Sienna to be with her. It would have meant the world to be able to reach out and hold her sister's hand, to see her smiling, kind eyes and know that this wasn't sheer madness. Only Sienna would *never* have approved. She wouldn't have smiled from the sidelines as Olivia committed herself to this farce—she'd have fought tooth and nail to get her to stop. Even if that meant losing their house. Even if that meant letting their father punish their mother one last, cruel, lasting time.

The priest said something, and Luca turned to face Olivia, dragging her back to this moment, in which it was just the two of them, and the lie they were weaving. He spoke his vows first, in English in deference to her, before slipping an enormous diamond ring onto her finger. The simple contact sent a thousand little lightning bolts through her; standing was almost impossible.

When it was Olivia's turn to say the vows, the priest spoke slowly, his accent thick, and Olivia stumbled on a few words. Nerves were playing havoc with her focus. She offered the priest an apologetic glance, before retrieving a simple gold band and pressing it to Luca's finger. Just like before, when he'd placed her ring on her finger, Olivia felt as though a marching band had started to run rampant through her veins. She pulled her hand away quickly, as though she'd been electrocuted, her eyes sliding to Luca's *nonna* without her intent. The happiness there was blatantly obvious—she had obviously bought the lie, hook, line and sinker. Olivia looked away again immediately, right into Luca's enormous dark eyes, their watchful intensity making her heart thunder.

'And that is it,' the priest said with a clap that completely undid the sombre nature of the ceremony. 'You may now kiss your bride.' He gestured to Olivia, and Olivia's heart seemed to grind to a halt. Oh, crap. How had she forgotten about this part?

Was it too late to back out? She stared at the priest with a sinking feeling, aware of Luca's *nonna*'s watchful gaze, then looked back up at the man who was now her husband.

Oh, God, oh, God, oh, God.

*In name only.* Except for right now.

Luca moved closer, one hand coming to rest on her hip, the other capturing her cheek, holding her face steady. His thumb padded over the flesh just beside her lip, low on her cheek, and goosebumps spread over her arms.

She wanted to tell him she couldn't do this, that she'd never even been kissed before, that too many people were watching, that she had no idea what she was doing, but then he was dropping his head, his mouth seeking hers as though it were the most natural thing in the world, and all she could do was surrender to the necessity of this. And the wonder.

Luca swore internally. His body had ignited, a flame of passion bursting through him the second their lips met. What had started as a perfunctory ceremonial requirement had blown way out of his control the second her lips parted beneath his and she made that husky little moan, pushing the sound deep into his throat. Screw ceremony. The hand that was on her hip slid around to her back, drawing her body hard against his, angling her slightly for privacy from his grandmother—not that he was capable of that degree of rational thought. Instincts had taken over completely. His mouth moved, deepening the kiss, his tongue flicking hers, and with every soft little moan she made he felt his control snapping, so within seconds he was fantasising about stripping the damned dress away and making love to her—not slowly and languidly, either, but hard and fast, as this passion bursting between them demanded.

Hell. This was a nightmare.

They had a deal, and at no point was he supposed to be attracted to his wife, of all people. At no point were they supposed to want each other like this. He wouldn't let this happen. Any other woman, fine. But not with his bride.

He wrenched his mouth from hers, and Olivia had to bite down on her lower lip to stop from crying out at the sudden withdrawal. Her eyes were heavy, drugged by desire, so that it took several seconds before she remembered where they were, and who they were surrounded by.

Mortification doused her sensual need. It had only been a kiss—albeit a passionate one—but in Olivia's innocent mind, they'd just done the first act of a live porno for Luca's grandmother and priest.

He was watching her in that intense way of his, eyes hooded and unreadable, his own face notably *normal*, not flushed and passion-filled, as she was sure hers must be. Of *course* he looked like normal. This was Luca Giovanardi. The man literally went through women as most men did underwear. Or bottles of milk, at least.

She stifled a moan and blanked her face of emotions—but too late, she feared. He must have seen how affected she was by the kiss. He must know how completely he took her breath away. How *easily*.

She sucked in a deep breath, and another. *It's okay. It's over now. You never need to kiss him or touch him ever again.* The thought was supposed to be reassuring, but her heart did a strange, twisty reaction, painful and impossible to ignore.

The next moment, his hand reached down and linked with hers, fingers intertwined, so she jerked her gaze back to his face. He smiled at her, but the smile got nowhere near his eyes.

'Come and meet my grandmother. *Cara.*' He added the term of endearment as an afterthought. It brought a rush of warmth to her. She ignored it. This was all for show, for his grandmother's benefit. That was part of their deal, and, given what he was sacrificing for her, he deserved her to play along to the best of her ability.

'Yes, of course.' Her voice sounded, blessedly, normal.

Pietra Giovanardi was past her eightieth birthday but she stood straight and proud, silver hair pulled over one shoulder, slender body wrapped in couture and diamonds, yet somehow she managed to look approachable and down to earth. Her lips were quick to smile, her face well lined by time, by life, and her eyes sparkled as the couple approached. There was no hint of the terminal illness Luca had mentioned, beyond a body that was painfully slim.

'Ahh, Luca, Luca, Luca, this is the happiest day of

*my* life,' she exclaimed, lifting a shaking hand and patting her grandson's cheek affectionately, tears dampening her eyes as she turned to look at Olivia. She smiled brightly, emulating a happy bride. That was, after all, their deal.

'Signora Giovanardi,' Olivia murmured, but the older woman batted a hand through the air then drew Olivia into a warm hug, enveloping her in a softly floral fragrance at the same time she dislodged her hand from Luca's, leaving a cool feeling of absence that Olivia wished she hadn't noticed. The older woman was painfully thin, her bones barely covered by fine, papery skin. Sympathy spread like wildfire through Olivia at this obvious indication of her illness.

'You must call me Pietra,' she insisted. 'Or Nonna.'

'Pietra,' Olivia rushed, softening her haste with a softer smile. 'It's a pleasure to meet you.'

'Ah, no, the pleasure is mine. I thought this would never happen, after…' Pietra's voice briefly stalled but she covered quickly, moving on. She hadn't needed to finish anyway; Olivia knew what the older woman had been going to say. After his first marriage. For the first time since they'd agreed to this sham, she wondered about his past, his ex, and why the marriage had left him so badly scarred. But Nonna was moving on, steering the conversation forward. 'And here he's been keeping you a secret all this time.' Pietra made a tsking sound. 'But it is no business of mine. I won't ask the details. I'm just glad it has come to this. Now, shall we have some Prosecco?'

Olivia blinked up at Luca, expecting him to demur—

the sooner they concluded their 'wedding', the sooner they could be free of the need to act like a pair of besotted newly-weds, and the sooner their thirty days of captivity could start.

'*Sì*, I have arranged it.'

Olivia's eyes widened, but she couldn't argue with him, obviously.

'You would be welcome to stay at Villa Tramonto tonight, as well,' Pietra offered as they walked from the church.

'My grandmother's villa,' Luca explained to Olivia. 'Nestled above Positano. You would love it, *cara*.' He was so good at this! With effortless ease, he made it seem as though they shared a genuine connection. His voice was soft, romantic, so her skin pricked with goosebumps she was sure his dark eyes observed, before he turned to Pietra. 'Another time. It is our wedding night, after all.'

Heat bloomed inside Olivia at the implication of his words—at how they would be spending tonight if they were anything approaching a real couple. But they weren't, this was just make-believe. Soon they'd be alone again, and she'd be able to put some space between herself and this irresistibly charismatic man.

'Of course, of course. Will you return to Rome?'

'We will honeymoon in Venice for the weekend, actually.'

Olivia stopped walking, and for the briefest moment lost control of the vice-like grip she held on her cool exterior. Luca saw, and moved back to Olivia, putting an arm around her waist and drawing her close, so all she was conscious of was the hardness of his physique, the way her side melded to his perfectly.

'A weekend in Venice?' Pietra wrinkled her nose. 'In my day, honeymoons didn't count unless they lasted three months.'

'In your day, it took a month at least to get anywhere interesting.'

Pietra laughed affectionately. 'This is true.'

Olivia was struck by the natural banter between the two, and, despite the happiness of their mood, a chasm was forming in her chest, impossible to ignore. When she saw their easy affection, it was impossible not to dwell on how different her own upbringing had been, how tense and fraught with emotional complications. Only with Sienna could she be herself.

The afternoon light was blinding as they stepped out into the square, and a flock of pigeons flew past them, low to the ground, looking for treats left by the lunch-time crowd.

'Here?' Pietra gestured to a restaurant with tables and chairs lined up on the footpath, facing the square.

Luca turned to Olivia, surprising her with his consultation. 'Yes. I reserved a table. Are you happy to share a drink with Pietra before we leave, *mi amore*?'

My love. Her heart skittled. He was very, very good at this. What was he like in genuine relationships? she wondered as she nodded and they began to make their way to the venue. Undoubtedly, his affection shone as hot and bright as the sun, but, if the gossip blogs were to be believed, his attention wandered faster than you could say supernova.

Her gown was a sleek white silk, ruffled across one shoulder, and as she entered the restaurant the diners paused and then clapped, their excitement at seeing a couple on their wedding day, on the celebration of the great Italian tradition of love, something they couldn't contain. Luca lifted a hand in acknowledgement, and drew Olivia closer, pressing a kiss to the crown of her blonde hair. *It's all for show.*

But that didn't matter. Knowing it was fake didn't stop the very real chain reaction spreading through her—heat seemed to bloom from the middle of her soul, so she was warm and almost dizzy, and desire flickered through her, lazily at first, and then, as he pulled away, more urgently, so she wanted to lean close and kiss him properly, as they had in the church, but this time with no one watching.

He held out a chair for Pietra first, then another. *'Cara.'* He gestured towards it. She swallowed hard as she sat down, aware of his proximity, so sparks of lightning ignited when his hands brushed her bare shoulders. He took the seat opposite and their feet brushed beneath the table—an accident, surely.

Pietra was charming, intelligent, well read and politely inquisitive, asking just enough questions of Olivia without seeming as though she were prying, and the questions were all of a reasonably impersonal nature, so Olivia could answer without feeling that she had to speak to the nightmare that her home life had always been. Conversing with Pietra was a welcome distraction, allowing her to almost, but not quite, blot Luca from her mind. Except there was the subtle contact, beneath the table, his feet brushing hers whenever she moved, so wiping him from her consciousness completely was impossible. He sat back, watching the interplay, taking only two sips of his champagne and a forkful of cake, while Olivia enjoyed a full glass and then half of another, as well as her entire slice of cake. She smothered a hiccough as they stood, and Pietra embraced her again.

'You'll come to Tramonto soon? I would love to get to know you better.'

Guilt was now a full-blown stack of TNT in Olivia's belly, ignited and ready to explode in a confession. She clamped her lips together, trying to remember what was at stake, and that Luca's lie to his grandmother was none of her business. It was the only reason he'd agreed to this.

But misleading the beautiful, older woman felt like a noose around Olivia's neck suddenly. *She's dying.* Sadness dragged down Olivia's heart. There was so much vitality in the older woman, it was hard to believe she was so gravely ill.

'We'll come as soon as we are able,' Luca placated. 'Where is Mario?'

'Across the square.'

'We'll walk you to the car.'

'I can walk myself.' She batted the offer away with an affectionate shake of her head. 'I live alone and still he thinks I can't walk twenty paces without his help.'

'She has an army of servants, in fact,' Luca confided as they left the restaurant.

'I'd like to walk with you,' Olivia insisted gently, linking arms with Pietra.

Luca's eyes met hers and her stomach dropped to her feet. They were going to be alone together soon, husband and wife. She looked down at her wedding ring, diamonds sparkling back at her, and her pulse shifted, lifting, slowing, thready and strong at the same time.

Luca opened the rear door to a sleek black car and Pietra gave them both one last hug before slipping inside. An unknown man—the driver, Mario, Olivia presumed—started the engine and pulled into the light afternoon traffic.

Luca turned slowly to face Olivia and it was as though time were standing still. Her heart began to throb; nerves made her fingers tremble.

'Well, Signora Giovanardi,' he said. 'It's done.'

She grimaced. 'Yes.'

'You're not happy?'

'I'm—' She searched for the right words, words that wouldn't make him sound like a heartless bastard. 'Having met your grandmother, I feel pretty bad about lying to her.'

'Even when you saw how happy we made her?'

'But our divorce…'

'It is doubtful she will live to see it.'

Tears stung the backs of Olivia's eyelids, completely surprising her. She was a world-class expert at hiding her feelings. She looked away, shocked at the raw pain his words had evoked.

'And in the meantime, it's worth it to see the joy in her face.'

Olivia pushed aside her misgivings. 'She must have

been very worried about the state of your life for you to have gone to these lengths.'

'I only took advantage of an opportunity that was offered,' he reminded Olivia. 'I would never have married a woman simply to fool my grandmother. But when you arrived, offering yourself to me on a silver platter, how could I say no?'

'I wouldn't put it that way,' she responded tautly. But it was too late. The vivid imagery of her sprawled out on a platter just for Luca's enjoyment filled her mind's eye, and her cheeks flushed bright red.

Luca had no idea what had caused her to react so vividly to his words, but it was clear he'd offended her. Anger glowed in her cheeks, and she didn't meet his eyes. It shouldn't have bothered him but, all of a sudden, all Luca wanted was for Olivia to look at him. Not simply to look. To touch. To lift her hand to his chest, as she'd done during their service, to grab his shirt and pull him closer, to part her lips and moan softly into his mouth.

But wanting his wife wasn't part of this deal. It *couldn't* be.

'This way.' He spoke more gruffly than he'd intended, gesturing toward the doors of a building, pressing a button for the elevator then standing a safe distance from his wife. Maybe it was the dress? Unlike their first meeting, when her outfit had offered only vague hints as to her figure, now he could actually *see* her body, her tantalising curves, could see every delectable ounce courtesy of the clinging silk fabric, so that even before their incendiary kiss he'd felt a jolt of need surge through his body.

The elevator doors pinged open, and they stepped inside, without realising that the elevator was incredibly small. He hadn't noticed when he'd travelled down, but being caged in here with a woman he was doing his damnedest to ignore on a physical level, having her so close their bodies were brushing, was the last thing he wanted.

'I thought you said we were going to Venice,' she enquired, but huskily, softly, and when he looked at her face, her eyes were trained on his lips, as though she couldn't look away. Oh, hell.

'We are.' His own voice was gruff in reply, frustration at their situation emerging in the force of his words. They were trapped by the agreement they'd made. Neither of them wanted this to get complicated, but damn it all to hell if he wanted to push her back against the wall and make love to her here and now.

She blinked, but didn't look away. 'Isn't Venice at sea level?' She swallowed, her throat shifting, and his groin strained against his pants. Hell.

'Sinking below it by the minute,' he managed to quip, despite the charged atmosphere.

'Then we'd better hurry.'

'That's my intention.'

'You're being serious?'

'What about?'

'A honeymoon in Venice?' She formed air quotation marks around the word honeymoon.

'Is that a problem?'

'Well, I mean, isn't a honeymoon sort of redundant?' Heat fizzed between her ears.

'Not if we want to convince the world—and particularly your cousin—that our marriage is genuine. I don't think anyone would believe me to be the kind of man to marry and not take my bride away for a time. We will go, take photographs as evidence. It may matter a great deal, if there is a legal challenge to your inheritance.'

Her lips formed a small 'o', because he was right. It was a small, but likely important, detail, in terms of making their marriage look real.

*'Va bene?'*

Okay? She blinked up at him, wondering why she was fighting this, why she was dreading the idea of a honeymoon with this man in Venice, but unable to put her finger on it.

The doors pinged open but neither of them moved. It was as though their feet were bolted to the floor, as though there were something about the confines of the lift that required them to remain. Olivia felt as though she were about to move into a different realm, as though the moment she moved, everything would change and be different.

A steady, rhythmic whooshing sound broke through the spell, so they both turned in unison to regard the helicopter, with its rotor blades beginning to spin.

The luxury craft had a high enough body that there was no risk from the blades to either of them, no need to bend down as they approached. 'Are you ready?' he asked, not sure what the question referred to. The small frown on her lips showed she didn't either.

'I think so.'

And despite the fact they'd agreed to a hands-off

marriage, it felt like the most natural thing in the world to reach down and take her hand in his, to guide her to the helicopter. The most natural thing in the world to hold her hand as she stepped up, only releasing it when she was seated, and then his own hand seemed to tingle, as if the ghost of her touch remained. Luca had conquered a lot in his thirty-three years, and desiring his wife was just another thing he would need to manage. But the strength of his desire was unexpected. For the first time in his life, Luca felt as though possessing a woman, this woman, was essential to his being. It had never been like this before, even with Jayne, even though he'd loved her. Perhaps, he rationalised as the helicopter lifted up into the sky, it was simply the temptation of forbidden fruit.

Yes, that was all he was dealing with—a simple case of pleasure denied. For a long time Luca had got everything he'd ever wanted in life. Not by accident, but through sheer hard work and grit. Having lost everything once, he'd made sure that would never happen again. As for women, he only had to show a hint of interest before they tumbled into his bed. He had never felt a rush of desire and known he couldn't act on it. Until now.

Understanding himself better, Luca was sure he could ignore the rampant throb of need twisting inside him. He was, after all, Luca Giovanardi, and he'd never failed at a single thing once he put his mind to it...

# CHAPTER FOUR

'MY ASSISTANT BOOKED IT,' he explained with a rueful expression on his face, as though this were no big deal. 'I specified the presidential suite, which has multiple bedrooms. She clearly misheard and arranged the honeymoon suite instead.' Both pairs of eyes settled on the enormous king-size bed in the middle of the sumptuous bedroom. Olivia's heart stampeded through her body. Everything since the wedding had taken on a surreal quality, as though with the saying of their vows she'd somehow morphed into someone else entirely.

'I see.'

All she seemed capable of was thinking about kissing Luca. Her lips tingled with the remembered sensations of their wedding kiss, and every second that passed in the same room as him, with neither of them touching, was like a form of torture, a string pulling tighter and tighter until she thought it might snap. But to share a bed? Olivia had never *slept* with anyone in her life. Not in the sexual way, and not in the space-sharing way. It was literally beyond her comprehension to even *imagine* what that would be like.

'I'll sleep on the sofa,' she said with a pragmatic nod. 'I'm shorter than you—by a mile. It makes sense.'

His laugh was dismissive. 'No one need sleep on the sofa, *cara*.' Not just for show, then. The term of endearment rolled off his tongue with practised ease—and that was exactly what it was. Practised. Luca Giovanardi always had a woman in his life, he was simply using the term that came to mind fastest. It wasn't impossible that he'd forgotten her name, she thought with a bitter smile. 'We are going to have to share a bed once we return to Rome. We might as well start practising early.' At her continued scepticism, he lifted his palms placatingly. 'I'm quite capable of sticking to one side, and to making sure my hands do the same.' He turned, taking a step towards her, so their bodies were only separated by an inch. 'I presume you can make the same promise?'

Was he teasing her? 'Of course,' Olivia muttered, heat exploding in her veins. Their eyes met and an electrical current, fierce and obliterating, arced between them. Olivia couldn't look away, but in the periphery of her vision, the enormous, sumptuous bed sat as an invitation, beckoning her—them—to join it.

'Good.' He didn't move. Nor did she. The air around them thickened, holding them still, trapping them, and Olivia couldn't muster an ounce of energy to care.

She badly wished she had more experience with men—but when and how would she have found the opportunity? She dropped her gaze to his lips, wondering how they'd moved so well over her mouth, wondering how he had the skill to evoke such a response in her.

'Olivia.' The word was a gruff command, so she

frowned, forcing her eyes to abandon their exploration
of his mouth.

'Yes?'

'We agreed to a platonic relationship, but if you continue to stare at my mouth in this fashion, I'm going to
want to break that promise.'

'I'm not staring at your mouth,' she denied hotly,
forcing her eyes to meet his gaze instead.

'Yes, you are. I am a man of my word, but still a
man, nonetheless, with red blood thundering through
my veins. You are looking at my mouth as though you
can will it to kiss yours, and you were doing the same
thing in the elevator.'

'Was I?' Desire was so strong in her cells it left no
room for embarrassment, even though she knew she'd
feel it—in spades—later.

'Yes.'

'I'm sorry. I didn't mean—' But the words tapered
off, the lie failing, because he'd called her out, accu-
rately. It was exactly what she'd been thinking. A fur-
row crossed her brow. 'I just didn't expect—'

'No, nor did I.'

Her eyes flared wide, his confession surprising her.
'You didn't?'

'No.'

'When we kissed—'

He nodded.

'I didn't know it could be like that.' She lifted her
fingers to her lips, as though she could wipe away the
sensation. 'It was a charged moment. Our wedding, in
front of a priest, saying our vows. It was probably just

those factors that made the kiss seem so intense,' she mumbled. 'Right?'

'What else could it have been?' he asked, with a hint of mockery beneath the words.

She wished she knew. She had nowhere near enough experience to say with certainty.

He moved infinitesimally closer, his body swaying nearer to hers, so her eyes brushed closed as she surrendered to the moment completely. 'If it were not for our deal, I would suggest we test your theory,' he murmured. 'But that would be foolish.'

She hesitated, her eyes locking to his. He was right. Foolish. Stupid. Wrong. And yet… 'Surely, one kiss, on our wedding night, isn't such a big deal?'

His eyes flared and passion exploded between them. 'Are you asking me to kiss you again, Olivia?'

She wasn't capable of answering. Her lips parted and then she nodded, an uneven jerk of her head as she tried to reconcile what she wanted with what they'd agreed.

Luca moved closer, and her body ignited, burning white hot with a need to feel that same spark she'd experienced at their wedding. His fingers laced through her hair, dislodging it from the elegant wedding do she'd had styled, his body cleaved hard to hers before he claimed her mouth. It was only in that first instant that she realised how restrained he'd been in the church. That kiss had been passionate and consuming but nothing like this. Now, his mouth *ravaged* hers, his tongue tormenting, his lips mastering hers and disposing of any doubts, his body's proximity tantalising and insufficient. She wanted to feel him, to know him, to touch him, she wanted so much more than this alone.

The kiss stirred every bone in her body, sensuality she had no idea she possessed and was suddenly desperate to explore. He groaned into her mouth and pride exploded through Olivia, because he was every bit as lost to this as she was, as powerless to resist this passion as Olivia.

Her hands lifted to his jacket, pushing at it, sliding it from his shoulders and down to the floor and then her hands were forcing his shirt from his trousers, her fingertips connecting with the bare skin of his toned abdomen, warm and smooth, with a sharp electrical shock that pushed them apart. No, it didn't push them apart. Luca had stepped back as though burned, hands on hips, breath ragged.

'I think we have our answer,' he said, after a moment, the statement grim, as if it were the worst thing in the world that their experiment had failed. Olivia took her cue from him, but her veins were simmering, her mind at explosion point. She was a twenty-four-year-old virgin, she'd never explored this side of herself, never known it so much as existed, and suddenly desire was overtaking everything else. She blinked, turning away from him, needing space to process this, needing a chance to simmer down.

Wasn't a cold shower the legendary cure for frustrated desire?

She moved towards the bathroom with knees that were barely steady, closing herself in and sinking back against the door gratefully. After a moment, she met her reflection and wonderment stole through her. Passion was everywhere, from her swollen lips to dilated pupils, to cheeks that were flushed from the rapid flow of her blood in her veins. She stumbled forward and gripped the marble vanity, dipping her head forward and sucking in a sharp breath. Shower. Now.

She reached around to the back of her dress then groaned once more, this time with frustration. The gown had an intricate system of silk-covered buttons trailing down the back. The stylist had fastened her into it that morning and it hadn't occurred to Olivia to wonder how she'd get out of it again—nor had anyone offered advice, because the presumption had been made that Olivia would have her husband's help.

She tried several times to unfasten the buttons herself, attempted to push the gown over her head, and even briefly contemplated ripping it from her body—only the price tag was still emblazoned in her mind with an element of horror, the cost of the dress shocking to Olivia, who'd been robbing Peter to pay Paul for so long she couldn't imagine what it was like to have the kind of money to simply throw away on a dress like this, and no way would she do anything to damage said dress.

Balling up her courage, she opened the door, catching Luca unawares for several seconds, so she could observe him where he stood, now stripped down to his tuxedo trousers alone, feet bare, eyes trained on the view beyond the window. Flames licked through her. She'd *imagined* him naked more times than she could possibly admit—to herself or anyone—but seeing his bare torso was like a firework display right behind her eyes. She cleared her throat and he turned, as if coming from a long way away, his thoughts clearly distracted.

'I can't take off my dress,' she explained, mortification curling her toes.

'I see.' One corner of his lips lifted with self-deprecation. 'Another experiment?'

'No.' She'd learned her lesson. Hadn't she? 'Just a favour for a…friend,' she supplied awkwardly, because they weren't friends, they were strangers who'd just got married. The tangle she was in didn't escape Olivia, but remembering her destitution, her mother's situation, and most importantly the life Sienna deserved to live, propelled Olivia across to Luca with renewed determination. The ends of their marriage justified the means. She just had to keep a level head while waiting to divorce him. Only thirty sleeps to go… 'Definitely no more experimenting with kissing,' she said, for good measure.

'Turn around.' Oh, God. His voice was so sensual, his accent thick. She squeezed her eyes shut as she did exactly that, staring at the mirror opposite—except that was even worse, because the visage of Luca behind her was like catnip; she couldn't take her eyes away from the picture they made. She tried to focus on the most unsexy thoughts imaginable. She thought of the plumbing at Hughenwood House, she thought of the funeral they'd held for their nineteen-year-old cat, only two months ago, she thought of the day she'd had to leave school to transfer to the local comprehensive, but then Luca's fingers pressed to her back, finding the first delicate button, and all notions but the perfection of his touch evaporated from her mind. She bit down on her lower lip, to stem the tide of sensual need, but it did nothing, and the fact he was moving painstakingly slowly definitely didn't help matters. One button separated, and he moved on to the next, and Olivia held her breath, wanting it to be over at the same time she never wanted it to end. Once the third button was undone, the dress separated enough for her to feel the cool night air on her flesh, and then his warm breath, and goosebumps covered her skin. She was sure he'd noticed the telltale response, because his breath hissed out audibly from between clenched teeth.

'Cold?' he enquired, moving to the next button.

She shook her head. She was hot. Hotter than Hades, burning to a crisp. Their eyes met in the mirror and a tremble ran the length of her spine. She might not have any experience with men, but she recognised the emotion stirring in Luca's gaze, the heat of desire, because it was running rampant through her.

Whether he meant it or not, his body must have shifted, because his thighs brushed hers, and she had to catch a moan of her own. Her nipples strained against the lace of her delicate bra, painful and begging for touch. Surprise at her body's immediate response, at the strength of her reaction, had her lifting her arms, crossing them over her chest, as if to catch the dress as he unbuttoned it, when really she wanted to conceal the telltale response from him. She was too late though; when she lifted her face and looked to the mirror, his eyes were on her breasts, his cheeks slashed with dark colour, his shoulders shifting with the force of each breath.

Her stomach swooped to her feet and heat pooled

between her legs, a rush of need she'd never known before. So she wanted him to touch her nipples, yes, but, more vitally, she wanted him to reach between her legs and stroke her there until the flames were extinguished. But what about their agreement?

Fifth button, and the dress began to droop at her shoulders. Sixth, and the ruffled shoulder slipped down completely, revealing the top of her lace bra. Her first instinct was to hold on tighter, but some feminine knowledge reverberated through her, so instead she dropped her hands to her sides, her gaze holding a challenge when she met his in the mirror.

The dress fell low enough to reveal her bra, and her engorged, sensitive nipples. He cursed from behind her ear, unfastening another two buttons then dropping his own hands to his sides.

'That's enough.' His voice held a strained quality.

Was it? Olivia wasn't so sure.

'I presume you can manage the rest?'

She didn't want him to stop. She wanted to say to him that, actually, help with her bra would be very useful, starting with cupping her breasts then moving to unclasp it, but the sheer strength of her desire was terrifying to Olivia, so she nodded jerkily and stepped forward. Only she hadn't countered on the dress's length, as it had fallen down her body, and she almost stumbled, but Luca was there, catching her with one strong arm, steadying her, holding her for a second too long before dropping his arms to his sides once more and stepping back.

'We'll go for dinner when you're ready.' He turned

and strode towards the door, his voice and gait so normal that Olivia wondered if she'd completely imagined his responses to her, if perhaps she'd been imposing the strength of her needs on him. When he didn't turn to look back at her, she convinced herself that was the case—he walked away without a backward glance yet he was filling her mind, her soul, her thoughts and her needs. Thirty nights suddenly felt like a lifetime.

He dragged his eyes over the outfit with a glimmer of distaste and impatience. Having seen her half naked, and in the svelte wedding dress, he wasn't thrilled to have a return to the boxy, unflattering linen numbers, like the outfit she'd worn the night they'd met. But even with the average, oversized drab dress, there was no mistaking the natural beauty of Olivia. She shone like a diamond: stunning, elegant and irresistible.

He stood when she entered the room, noting that she barely met his eyes. Smart move, except her demure avoidance only made his desire increase ten-fold.

'Dinner,' he said with a sharp nod of his head, thinking that what they needed was to be surrounded by crowds, noise, bright lights.

'We don't have to eat out,' she offered. After all, this was a fake honeymoon for their fake marriage. Surely there were limits to how much play-acting he was willing to do?

'Yes, we do, and take photographs as evidence.'

'Right, of course.' He was very good at this, whereas Olivia had naively believed their marriage certificate would be enough to satisfy the terms of her father's will. Olivia moved to the glass doors that led to the balcony, rather than the door to their suite. The waters of Venice's grand canal glistened beneath her, the dusk light casting a shimmer over the surface, and the lights that had already come on in the buildings across the water gave the vista an almost magical look. 'Where shall we eat?'

'Do you have a preference?'

She wrinkled her nose as she tilted her face to his. 'I've never been to Venice.'

'No?'

She shook her head. 'In fact, I haven't been to Italy in a long time—fourteen years. But as a girl, I always loved it.'

'Where, in particular?'

'Florence. Rome.' She sighed, as memories tugged at her. It had been a different time of life. A better time, in some ways, and their occasional holiday abroad had been an escape from the doom and gloom and oppressive resentment that lived within the walls of Hughenwood.

'Did you buy other clothes, at Harrods?'

Her skin paled and he regretted having asked the question immediately. 'No. Why?' She looked down at the dress, and when she lifted her eyes to his face and he saw the shame lining her features, he could have kicked himself for being so insensitive.

'I know, my wardrobe isn't exactly…sophisticated. You're probably embarrassed to be seen with me.'

*Idiot.* He shook his head, moving towards her. 'No.' He pressed his finger to her chin, ignoring the blade of white heat that speared his side at the innocuous contact. 'I didn't mean that.' *Didn't you? What had you meant, then?* 'I intended for you to have new clothes because I presumed you'd like it. I gather your finances have been straitened in recent times, and that your wardrobe reflects that. The account was set up at Harrods for this purpose, not just for a wedding dress.'

'Oh, I see.' She swallowed, pulling free of his contact, looking beyond the windows, her delicate features concealing a storm of emotions he couldn't interpret. 'Shall we go?' The forced brightness in her tone made him want to eat his stupid question right back up, but instead, Luca nodded, gesturing towards the door.

Out in public was definitely better than here, alone. 'Yes. *Andiamo.*'

The hotel restaurant was beautiful, the food beyond compare, but instead Luca chose a small trattoria a five-minute speedboat ride away, and spent the entire trip trying to ignore the way Olivia's hair whipped her face and her hands flailed to catch it, tried to ignore the desire to reach out and help her, to offer to hold her hair for her, a fist wrapped around those silky blonde ends until the boat stopped and he could tilt her head to his, capturing her mouth once more...

Hell.

The trattoria was busy, just as he'd hoped, the lighting hardly what could be described as 'ambient'. The owner had run the same fluorescents for as long as Luca had been coming here, but the meals were exceptional, proper local cooking, hearty and plain. No fuss, no

Instagram-worthy presentation or indoor plants, just good, old-fashioned food, wine and service. As a result, the tourist trade largely bypassed the trattoria, leaving a swell of locals, so the voices that reached his ears were unmistakably Italian. But as they were led to their table, Luca realised the error of his ways. The restaurant was so crowded that there was anonymity in every corner.

'This is nice.' Olivia sounded surprised, and amusement crested inside Luca.

'It's quite ordinary actually. Hardly a romantic honeymoon destination.'

'But this isn't a real honeymoon,' she rushed to remind him. 'Romance definitely isn't necessary. Just a few photos.'

'Of course.' Had he seriously forgotten? Or just been playing along?

The waiter appeared, brandishing two laminated menus and a wine list. Luca scanned the drinks and flicked a gaze at Olivia, who was determinedly staring at the menu. He wished she wouldn't do that. It made him want to resort to underhanded techniques for attracting her attention, like brushing his feet against her ankles as he had at the restaurant, right after their wedding. He took a perverse pleasure out of watching her responses to him, out of seeing the way her cheeks darkened or her eyes exploded with sensual curiosity. But it was playing with fire, and surely he was smarter than that? 'Wine? Champagne?'

'Bubbles, yes. That Prosecco this afternoon was lovely.'

Luca didn't tell her that the bottle had cost almost

a thousand euros. He ordered another and handed the wine list back to the waiter, then gave the full force of his attention to his wife. The word shuddered through him like a sort of nightmare. But Olivia was nothing like Jayne, and their marriage was nothing like his first had been.

'Would you like help with the menu?'

She chewed on her lower lip and he wanted to reach across and wipe his thumb over her skin to stop the gesture—it was too sensual, too distracting. 'I should be able to read this better than I can. Even though mum's Italian, she rarely spoke her native language at home.'

'Why not?'

Because Dad didn't like it. She swallowed the acerbic response, reminding herself that their deal included not getting too personal. 'Just easier that way,' she said with a lift of her shoulders.

'Easier?'

'We lived in England,' she reminded him. 'We all spoke English.'

'I grew up bilingual despite the fact both my parents were Italian, and I was mostly raised in Italy.'

She dismissed him with a tight smile, but Luca didn't want to be dismissed. 'She didn't cook Italian food?'

'She didn't cook at all,' Olivia responded with a natural smile. 'We had staff for that, until…'

'Your father died?'

Turbulent emotions raged in her eyes. 'Yes.'

'And then what?'

Her eyes fluttered as she sought an answer. 'And then, my sister and I picked up the reins.'

'Of the household?'

'There was no one else to do it.'

'Your mother?'

Olivia laughed now, a bitter sound. 'My mother has many skills, but housework is not one of them.'

He frowned. 'You were, what, twelve years old?'

'Yes.'

'And your sister?'

'Eleven.'

'And at those tender ages, it was decided that you and she had more abilities around the house than your mother did?'

'You can't teach an old dog new tricks,' Olivia responded dryly, the words spoken as if by rote, leaving him in little doubt they'd been parroted to her often.

'And you juggled schoolwork as well?'

'Not particularly well,' Olivia said with obvious regret. 'My grades started to slip after Dad passed. I changed schools, so that didn't help—everything was new. But there was also a lot to do, which left little time for studying.'

'Or socialising,' he prompted thoughtfully.

She nodded her agreement.

'Anyway, that's ancient history.'

It was, quite clearly, designed to shut the conversation down.

'Have you eaten here before?'

'Whenever I'm in Venice.'

'Which is how often?'

'A few times a year.'

'Why?'

He lifted a brow.

'Do you have an office here?'

'No.'

'Then why Venice?'

'I like it.'

Her lips tugged to the side. 'I'm surprised you make time for leisure.'

'Are you?'

She considered him a long moment and then, as though she were forcing herself to go on, almost against her will, she spoke slowly, purposefully. 'I suppose the women you date expect a degree of attention.'

He relaxed back in his chair, despite the strange sense of unease stealing across him. Why did he want to obfuscate? To move conversation away from his previous lovers? The instinct caught him off guard and so he forced himself to confront it, by answering her question directly. 'Yes.'

She flicked a glance down at the menu, her features shifting into a mask of something he didn't understand. Uncertainty? Embarrassment? He narrowed his gaze, as though that might be able to help him. 'So you bring them here?'

His original instincts surged back, stronger, more determined. 'I can't remember.' He brushed her enquiry aside, even though he knew he'd never brought a woman here before. 'Let me help you with the menu.'

She nodded, a cool, crisp acknowledgement that pulled at something in his chest. He didn't *like* cool and crisp. Not when he'd seen her eyes storm-ravaged by desire. He scraped his chair back, coming to stand behind her, breathing in her sweet fragrance before he could stop himself. His gut rolled; he ground his teeth together. The first moment he'd seen her at that party in Rome, he'd imagined her naked. He'd fantasised about making her his. Why the hell had he thought he could simply switch that desire off? Because he lived for control—and the harder it was to get, the more rewarding success was. He *would* control this.

'Here, there is fried calamari.' He pointed to the menu, his arm inadvertently brushing her breasts as he reached across, and he heard the smallest of gasps escape her lips, so any idea of control ran completely from his mind. He leaned closer, his cheek almost pressed to hers, his arm deliberately close to her now. 'Rice balls stuffed with cheese, spinach and cheese pasta.' He paused, finger pointing to the next item. 'Scallops carpaccio. Do you like scallops?' He turned to face her, his lips almost brushing her cheeks, and he waited.

Sure enough, as though the same invisible, magnetic force were operating on Olivia, she turned towards him. They were so close, he could see every fleck of colour in her magnificent blue eyes; he could see desire in them too, even when they shuttered slightly, her eyes dropping to his lips in that disarming and distracting way she had.

*Kiss her.*

Temptation hummed in his body. He was only an inch or so away. It would be so easy to brush their lips—but how easy to pull apart? On the two occasions they'd kissed, it had taken a Herculean effort to stop what was happening between them.

'I have to tell you something,' she said quietly, the words just a whisper against his cheek.

'I'm listening.' He couldn't help himself. Luca lifted his thumb and brushed it over her lower lip, so her eyes closed on a wave of anguish, fierce need like a cyclone around them.

'Luca.' God, his name on her lips was its own aphrodisiac. Her voice was husky, as though they'd just made love, as though she'd screamed herself hoarse. He dropped his hand, letting it rest on her shoulder. *Stop this. Control it.*

But was there really any harm in a kiss? It wasn't as if they would be having sex. It wasn't as if they'd be falling in love. If anything, it might actually work to their advantage, bursting the tension that was building between them.

*Liar.*

'Olivia.' He deliberately layered her name with his own sensual needs, watching as the drawled intonation flushed her cheeks pink.

'This isn't—'

He didn't want to hear what this wasn't. He knew their marriage wasn't real, and he was glad for that, but that didn't mean the passion could be ignored. Perhaps there was a compromise? After all, they were two sensible, consenting adults.

But hadn't he set the ground rules here? Hadn't he been the one to insist they'd never be more than spouses on paper? Could there be new rules?

'I know what our marriage isn't,' he said gruffly, bringing his face closer to hers. 'But I no longer think it makes sense to continue ignoring what it is.'

Her lips parted, and panic flared in her eyes, so he

stayed where he was, thankfully with it enough to know that if they kissed now, it had to be her choice. He'd made it clear what he wanted. But would she be brave enough to admit what *she* wanted?

'I'm not ignoring that,' she whispered, her eyes like saucers as she leaned infinitesimally closer.

'Aren't you?' Her brows drew together.

She shook her head slightly, and with the movement, closed the distance the rest of the way. *Almost* the rest of the way, because her lips were still separated from his by a hair's breadth.

'But how—?'

'Do we really need to answer that?'

Her moan was the final straw. It was so quiet, only he could hear it, so sensual, he couldn't help imagining her in the throes of passion. Every cell in his body reverberated with fierce, undeniable need.

'Kiss me,' he commanded.

Another husky intake of breath.

'Now.'

Waiting was its own form of agony. He stayed where he was, even when he ached to claim her lips, to taste them, and this time he didn't want to stop, despite the fact they were in a busy restaurant.

'Our agreement—'

'We can make a new agreement.'

And then, thank God, she caved, mashing her mouth to his with all the urgency that was driving him crazy, moaning into his mouth now, so he swallowed the sound and ached for more. Her hands lifted up, catching his face, holding him there, as her tongue explored his mouth, as she took control of the kiss and he could do nothing but experience her greedy stake of ownership.

This was a terrible idea. He'd known he wouldn't want to stop what they were doing and he didn't. With every fibre of his being, he wanted to strip the clothes from her body and make her his, to hell with their agreement, their deal, their goddamned marriage of convenience. They could draw new boundaries, afterwards. They could do *anything*, after. For now, there was only this.

'Listen to me.' It was Olivia who broke the kiss this time, wrenching her lips away as if in desperate need of air, staring down at her lap. She withdrew her hands; they were shaking badly.

'Listen to me,' she said again, this time reaching for her Prosecco and taking a sip, as if that could erase the urgency of what they'd just shared.

He didn't—couldn't—speak, and so he waited, right where he was, body still close to hers, head bent, desire a tsunami in his veins.

'I've never done this before. I can't just—I don't know—what this feels like.'

He frowned, her words making no sense. He knew she'd never been married before. And he knew she'd never been to Venice before, nor to this restaurant. What was she trying to tell him?

'Are you trying to tell me you're a twenty-four-year-old virgin?' he joked, in an attempt to defuse the tension that was tightening her beautiful lips into a straight, flat line.

She pulled back from him as if he'd slapped her, cheeks glowing pink, eyes not meeting his. His own smile, already taut from the effort it took to dredge up past the storm of passion ravaging him, lost its will, and dropped from his face. He swore quietly, but they were close, so she heard it and flinched, took another sip of Prosecco then clasped the glass in her hands, at her lap.

'Yes.' It was so quiet he had to lean forward to hear the word, but by then he'd already guessed. He knew. He just didn't understand.

He jackknifed up, standing straight, staring out at the crowded restaurant without seeing anyone or anything. His mind was a whir of noise and movement, without the ability to comprehend.

'So when we kiss, I feel things, and I want things, but I have no idea how to—'

He lifted a hand, silencing her. He needed to get a grip on his own emotions. On the one hand, her revelation made him want to put a thousand acres of space between them, on another, it fascinated him, drawing him to her, making him want to teach her, to show her, to be her first.

He moved back to his seat, gripping the back of it, eyes on Olivia the whole time.

She was *so* beautiful. Literally, the sexiest, most stunning woman he'd seen in his life and, given his dating history, that was saying something. How was it possible she'd never been in a relationship before?

'You've never dated a guy?'

She stared at the table, shaking her head.

'You've never fooled around?'

Another head shake, more ignoring him, until she lifted her eyes, finally, pinning him to the spot. And there was cool and reserved Olivia once more—and for once, he was glad to see her. This was a conversation that called for level heads. He sat back down, assuming a relaxed pose he definitely didn't feel.

'Until our wedding, I'd never been kissed.'

He angled his face away, biting back the curse that filled his mouth.

'Why didn't you tell me this before we were married?'

'I didn't think it would be relevant. It's not supposed to be like this. I didn't even think we'd kiss at the wedding—my fault, that was naïve of me.'

'But you agreed to pose as my doting wife, for my grandmother's sake. Didn't you imagine we'd have to share some physical contact, at some point?'

Her eyes showed embarrassment and, inwardly, he winced, wishing he didn't sound so disbelieving.

'I don't know. I didn't—maybe. I guess I thought we might hold hands or something.'

'Hold hands,' he repeated incredulously. 'My God, Olivia, do you have any idea what I've been thinking about? What I thought about the minute I saw you?'

He ground his teeth together, trying to push away the memory of those thoughts, wishing his imagination weren't so damned vivid.

She shook her head, dropping it forward, shielding her face from his, so he wanted to reach across and lift her chin, to make her confront this head on.

But he couldn't.

There were some boundaries they could move. Incorporating a meaningless fling into their meaningless marriage-on-paper was one thing. But there was no way he was going to take her virginity. Not when sex would only ever be a physical act to him.

'I really don't,' she whispered softly. 'But I know what I've been thinking about…things I've never thought of before. My imagination has gone wild.'

'Don't tell me.' He compressed his lips, his jaw almost a perfect square. He didn't need to know that. There were other more pressing considerations. 'Tell me how this is possible.'

'Well, I simply forgot to have sex before,' she said with a tight smile, her joke falling flat, given that neither of them was in a laughing mood.

'You've never met someone who aroused your interest?'

She pleated her napkin over and over. The waiter appeared to take their order, and Luca could have cursed right in the man's face at the interruption. Instead, he rattled off a list of six dishes, hoping Olivia would like at least one of them, then waved his hand in an unmistakable gesture of dismissal.

'Go on,' he commanded.

She hesitated and he wondered if she was going to change subjects, or suggest they not talk about it. 'It's very complicated,' she said, eventually.

'We have time.'

Her lips twisted. 'It's not important. The details are—I can do a summation,' she said with a little shrug of her shoulders. 'My parents' marriage was a disaster. My mother and I don't have a straightforward relationship. She disapproved of men, dating, in fact, she basically disapproved of socialising, so Sienna and I had each other and pretty much no one else. Plus, I was running Hughenwood House from the time I was twelve years old. When would I have found the time to date? It's a miracle I managed to graduate high school.'

'So what? After that, you stayed home like some kind of modern-day Cinderella, with just your family and chores for company?'

'Don't mock me.'

'I'm not,' he said quickly, shaking his head. 'I'm only trying to understand.'

'I've been asked out before,' she admitted, with pink staining her cheeks. 'But my mother wouldn't have allowed me to accept. And I never liked the guys enough to fight with her about it.'

'And your sister?'

She hesitated, shaking her head. 'Sienna's life is her personal business. I'm not going to discuss it.'

'Fair enough.'

'So what do we do?' Her huge blue eyes blinked across at him, and the answer that sprang to mind was the exact answer he had to ignore.

'Do?' He reached for his own drink, draining it before replacing the glass on the tabletop, then leaning forward, pinning her with the intensity of his gaze. 'That's very simple, Olivia. We do exactly what we said we would at the outset. We remember the boundaries we drew, we remember what this marriage is, and we keep our hands—and mouths—to ourselves. *Va bene?*'

# CHAPTER FIVE

So much for being able to sleep in the same bed as Olivia without touching her. It was all he could think of. His whole body was on tenterhooks, wanting to reach out and touch her, wanting to feel her soft, supple skin, wanting to kiss her hollows, to taste her passion, wanting to make her his in every way.

He stared at the ornate ceiling, his pulse running wild in his system, as Olivia slept beside him. Thanks to the Prosecco, she'd fallen asleep as soon as her head hit the pillow, whereas Luca had ruminated on her revelation, on the fact she was completely innocent, until he was crazy with wanting.

But to sleep with a virgin…there was no way he could do it. She had no experience with men, with sex, with the euphoria that accompanied orgasms. How could they remain detached, as they needed to be, if they were sleeping together? He had to be able to walk away from this marriage in a month's time, and to do so guilt free—something he couldn't achieve if they complicated their arrangement with sex. And yet, for all that he'd wanted her before, knowing that she had no experience was an aphrodisiac he hadn't anticipated. He wanted to teach her. He wanted to show her body what she could feel, and he wanted to watch her as she felt her first orgasm, he wanted to go down on her until she could barely think, he wanted to lather her body in the shower then take her against the cold, wet tiles. He wanted…what he couldn't, wouldn't, have.

Ever since Jayne, he'd sworn off relationships. Sex was fine, anything more was where it got complicated. So? Couldn't this just be sex? A little voice pleaded with him, but he ignored it. They were trapped in the same house for the next month—there was no guarantee they could keep things casual. Particularly not given her lack of experience. He couldn't take the gamble that she'd be able to see sex as sex, and not start to want more. It was absolutely impossible.

Throwing off the covers, he stalked away from the bed, finally admitting defeat. He'd been wrong earlier. He couldn't lie with her and know he wouldn't touch. He was half afraid he'd reach for her in his sleep, without intending to, that he'd start kissing her without being aware of what he was doing, and that she'd kiss him back. Because, experienced or not, her body knew what to do, her body understood the chemistry that was flowing between them, and her body wanted to act on it.

Which was all the more reason he had to control this.

With one final look over his shoulder, regarding her sleeping frame with a surge of adrenaline, he left the room, opting instead for an uncomfortable, sleepless night on the sofa—where Olivia filled his dreams, if not his hands.

* * *

'What is this?'

Olivia stared in confusion, at first, and then horror, as a parade of not one, not two, but *six* hotel staff walked into their suite, each carrying armloads of clothing.

Luca nodded towards the master bedroom, and they filed in there, each returning with empty hands.

Olivia watched, bemused, confused, but also glad to have something to think about other than the confession she'd made the night before, other than the way she'd blurted out the fact she was a virgin. Certainly other than the way he'd immediately pulled away from her as though whatever he'd been thinking about a moment earlier was now a moot point.

Could she blame him for not wanting to sleep with a virgin? He was used to sophisticated, experienced women. What could Olivia offer him?

She watched as Luca tipped one of the staff, then pushed the door closed behind them, turning to face her, arms crossed.

'Luca?' It was then that she realised they'd barely spoken all day. He'd been working, she'd been pretending to read, anything to avoid the elephant in the room. How in the world was she going to get through the next month?

'You need new clothes.' He shrugged, as though it was nothing, when Olivia had seen the designer names emblazoned on the sides of the bags.

She groaned, shaking her head. 'I don't.'

'You do,' he insisted. 'We're going to have to attend events in Rome, we'll see my grandmother socially at some point. You cannot keep dressing as though you're a kindergartner.'

She flinched at his unwitting insult. He continued to stare at her, his eyes appraising.

'Was it your mother who insisted on this also?'

'On what?'

'Your clothes.'

Olivia looked down at her outfit—denim overalls and a pale yellow T-shirt—then lifted her shoulders softly.

'Partly,' she whispered, not meeting his eyes.

'Because she was jealous?'

'How did—?' She clamped a hand to her mouth. 'I don't know,' she said with a shake of her head. 'Let's not talk about my mother right now, please.'

'When she is at the root of so much of who you are?'

'I know, but...'

'Fine.' He lifted his hands in acceptance, trouble brewing in the dark depths of his eyes. 'Go and look at the outfits. We will have dinner in the restaurant tonight.'

She didn't need to have any experience to know she was being dismissed, but if there was any doubt, it evaporated as he turned away from her and strode towards the table he'd been using as a makeshift desk.

Fighting a dangerous urge to challenge him, she stalked out of the living room, into the bedroom, taking great pleasure in shutting the door as she went. Privacy. Oh, how she needed it!

It took almost an hour to remove everything from the bags. Stunning dresses, evening gowns, mini-dresses as well as casual clothes—designer jeans and jackets, simple blouses, but cut so they were the last word in flattering. She started with the bags on the left of the room, and worked to the right, so it was completely a coincidence that she left the lingerie to last. But as she opened a thick cardboard box, revealing a ribbon-wrapped, tissue-paper item inside, her heart did a funny little tremble.

It was unlike anything she'd ever seen before. Lacy knickers, ornate bras, and, my God, suspenders. She shoved them back in the box and stepped away, heat radiating through her whole body.

She couldn't wear them.

She couldn't wear half this stuff. It was too beautiful, too revealing, too…

But how could she resist?

Knowing that he'd chosen it for her? That he'd imagined her in it? As if that weren't temptation enough, there was a part of Olivia that had always loved pretty, feminine clothes, a part of her she'd been forced to hide, that she suddenly felt a compulsion to indulge.

Surrendering to temptation, she opened the lingerie again, withdrawing a particularly beautiful matching set, caramel and black silk. She kept an eye on the door as she changed, then glanced at her reflection, doing a double take at the woman who stared back at her.

And she *was* a woman. A flesh and blood, sensual woman. She took two steps towards her reflection, dragging her eyes over her body.

It was clear that he'd wanted her before she revealed the truth. Did he still want her?

Nothing had changed for Olivia.

She cast a glance over the bed, her eyes landing on one of the more outrageous dresses. It was a sure-fire way to get his attention…and suddenly that was what Olivia wanted most on earth. To hell with the consequences.

She slid the dress on—it hugged her like a second skin—then brushed her golden hair until it shone, pulling it over one shoulder. He'd bought her shoes too, and she slipped her feet into a pair with a red sole and a spiky black heel, pausing to admire the effect in the mirror. It was almost too much. The exact opposite of what she'd been raised to think she should be stared back at her, but Olivia fought the strong impulse to change into something less attention-grabbing.

You only lived once, right?

If he'd had any kind of heart condition, then Olivia's appearance would have tested it. She emerged from the bedroom like some kind of Venus, a transformation that completely took his breath away. He'd known she was beautiful—hell, she was stunning no matter what she wore—but when she was dressed like this, in heels that made her hips swagger, a dress that hid *nothing* from his appraising eyes, it was all he could do to stay in the kitchen with his hands by his sides.

'Will this do?'

He was drowning. *Would it do?* It would do for him to peel the dress right off her, not to take her out in public. He didn't want the rest of Venice to see her like this, he realised, even as, at the same time, he felt a purely masculine pride in the woman he'd married.

A muscle jerked in his jaw as he grappled with the contrasting emotions.

'Luca?' Her uncertainty confused him. Surely she knew how spectacular she was?

'You're perfect,' he growled, turning away from her on the pretext of grabbing a drink of water.

'There's something important I want to discuss at dinner.' Her cool voice was steady and calm—the exact opposite to how he felt. 'Do you think there'll be a private table at the restaurant?'

He dipped his head. Privacy was the devil—he had to avoid it. '*Forse.* Let's go.'

He didn't offer her his hand as they left, nor did he touch the small of her back to guide her towards the lift. In fact, he walked at least a metre away from her, and when the elevator doors pinged open he kept to his side of the small cube, mutinously staring ahead, refusing to look at her even when his eyes wanted to drink up the vision she made.

The restaurant was busy, filled with Venice's glitterati. Luca saw many people he knew, was recognised, heard the gossip, and also the change in tenor—the surprise at the woman on his arm. Was she being recognised? He doubted it. While her name might be well known, and well regarded, Olivia herself was somewhat of an anachronism. Unlike most people of her generation, she didn't have an enormous social-media footprint, or a paparazzi trail. It was further evidence, not that he needed it, that her life was every bit as confined as she'd indicated. That she'd been a virtual prisoner at Hughenwood House, a modern-day Cinderella, just as he'd charged the night before, left to do chores from dawn to dusk. Did that make him Prince Charming? Hardly. Nothing like it.

'This is perfect,' she said with satisfaction as the maître d' led them to a table at the front of the canal, set a little apart from the others. They were still visible, but their voices wouldn't carry, and that was foremost in Olivia's mind.

While he wanted to avoid being too close to her, Pietra had raised him with faultless manners, so he came to her chair and pulled it back, waiting for Olivia to settle before moving away swiftly, before he could do something stupid like brush his hands over her shoulders. But he did breathe her in, the same sweet, intoxicating fragrance wrapping around him, so he felt himself strain against his pants, as though he were some kind of inexperienced teenager, completely incapable of controlling his desire.

'You wanted to talk to me?' Please, let it be about something mundane and rudimentary. Let her bring up *anything* to take his mind off what he wanted them to share.

'When you agreed to marry me, we negotiated terms for our marriage that would suit us both.'

'I remember.'

'What if I want to change the terms?'

He sat very still. 'Which terms in particular?' But he knew what was coming. He braced for it, for the offer she was going to make, for the test that he was about to meet, no idea if he had the strength for it.

'The no sex thing.' She lifted her eyes to his, meeting his gaze with apparent calmness now. 'I want to lose my virginity, to you. Tonight.'

# CHAPTER SIX

HE DIDN'T REACT, but inwardly his cells were reverberating with exquisite anticipation. 'No.' He tried to put a stop to the conversation before it went any further. 'Absolutely not.'

'Hear me out,' she murmured softly. 'Nothing else between us needs to change. I know what you want from me, and you know what I need from you. In twenty-nine nights, we'll separate and, as soon as legally viable, apply for a divorce. I know you were worried that being married might make me develop feelings for you, but I promise, Luca, that's not going to happen.'

'How do you know?' he demanded bullishly.

'Another time, remind me to ask you about the string of broken hearts you've clearly left behind.'

He ground his teeth together. 'I leave women before their hearts can become involved. I'm very strict about it. That is the point.'

'Because of your divorce?'

'Because of my first marriage. Because I have no interest in repeating that mistake,' he contradicted flatly.

'Don't you get it?' She breathed out excitely. 'We're

on the same page with this stuff. Marriage—a genuine marriage—is my idea of torture, one I saw enacted every single day with my parents, and I would rather die before getting involved in that, for real. Believe me when I tell you that the only thing I want in life is my independence. Falling in love would jeopardise that—I'm not stupid.'

His eyes narrowed at the logic of her argument. He knew there were still risks, but her sincerity was obvious. It was easy for Luca to be persuaded by her words. And yet...

'You don't know you'll still feel that way after we've slept together.'

A single finely shaped brow quirked in cynical amusement. 'You think you're so good in bed I won't ever want to leave you?'

He laughed. 'I've never had any complaints.'

'Good,' she responded enthusiastically. 'That's what I want. I'm a twenty-four-year-old virgin, Luca. I want my first experience of sex to be out of this world. Can you give me that?'

'Olivia.' He fought her suggestion with every fibre of his being, even when he definitely didn't want to fight her. He wanted to scrape his chair back and throw her over his shoulder, drag her right back upstairs and bolt the door shut for at least the next forty-eight hours. How many times since meeting her had he had that fantasy? And now she was serving herself up to him...

'This would still be a business deal,' she said after a beat. 'We're both laying our cards on the table, explaining our expectations. I promise, I won't ask you for anything else.'

He balled his hands into fists where they rested on his knees and absent-mindedly wondered what he'd done in a past life to deserve the experience of a woman like Olivia Giovanardi *begging* him to make love to her.

Still, he clung to sanity and reason, even when the alternative was so appealing. 'You can't say that with certainty.'

'Yes, I can.'

'How do you know?'

She toyed with the linen napkin to her right, then fixed him with a direct stare. 'Because my father was a complete bastard to my mother. Because I saw him eviscerate and humiliate her every day of my life. Because I saw her beg him to love her, and he delighted in withholding that. It is complete anathema to me to give a man that kind of power. To love someone so completely you will tolerate that behaviour—' Out of nowhere, the sting of tears swelled in her throat and behind her eyes, so she tilted her face away, looking towards the Grand Canal while she composed herself.

The waiter arrived at the table to take their order—which Luca placed, handing the menus back then waiting quietly, braced in his chair, eyes tracing the delicate outline of her face in profile. Finally, when Olivia's emotions were under control, she turned back to face him.

'I will never love you, or anyone, and I will never ask you to love me. I promise.'

He felt the honesty of her confession, and it reached

right inside him, like a tentacle of ice. He'd never met anyone who'd spoken so calmly about love, and their aversion to it, but her words relaxed him, because it was exactly as Luca felt. Having loved once before, and then suffered through the devastation of that break-up, he had no intention of being so stupid ever again. Could he really trust this was a safe course of action?

'Why did your mother stay married to your father, if his actions were so terrible?'

Olivia's face blanched, in contrast to the fire in her eyes. 'Because she loved him.' The words were said with arctic disdain. 'We all did. It was only after his death that I began to see things with more perspective.'

'You were still just a girl. How were you to know that the way they lived wasn't normal?'

She pleated her napkin in her lap.

A strange sensation gripped Luca's gut, an unpleasant question formed in his mind and, at first, he resisted asking it. But he was Luca Giovanardi, afraid of nothing and no one, and he wanted all of the facts. 'Did he hit her?'

Olivia's eyes went round. She shook her head.

'Did he hit you?'

'No, no. He wasn't like that.' A tremulous smile tilted her lips for a brief moment before dropping away into a grimace. 'But I would still describe him, if I absolutely had to discuss him at all, as abusive. Financially abusive—he gave my mother an allowance while he lived, enough to maintain her to the physical standard he expected,' she said with withering disapproval, 'but not enough for anything more. She couldn't do anything without his permission—buy anything, travel any-where. She was his virtual prisoner.'

The original hatred he'd felt for the unknown Thomas Thornton-Rose grew. 'And when he died, she was still kept under his thumb, by the restrictive conditions of his will.'

'Yes.' Olivia's lips twisted. 'I don't think my mother knew how to react to that. We've all carried on just as we did when he was alive, the same dysfunctional household, the same attitudes, the same restrictions.'

'On you?'

Her eyes met his, and he could see the battle being waged behind her eyes. 'On Sienna and me, yes.'

'Such as?'

She pleated the napkin more furiously now, her fingers working overtime even as her face held a determinedly placid expression—an expression she fought hard to keep in place, he suspected. 'Our father was—'

She broke off when the waiter appeared, brandishing a glass of Prosecco and a glass of red wine for Luca. When they were alone again, he nodded once, urging her to continue.

She hesitated, and he stayed very still, aware that she was sharing something she didn't relish speaking about, but also impatient to understand what her life was like.

'He was strict. I think he was worried we'd turn out like her, so he did everything he could to discourage that. Where he saw similarities, he belittled them.'

'And are either of you like your mother?'

'I'm her spitting image,' Olivia murmured softly, not

meeting his eyes. 'If you were to see a photograph of her in her early twenties, you'd think it was me.'

'And so your father didn't approve.'

'He downplayed looks, generally, while at the same time expecting my mother to dress and look like a beauty queen at all times. It's so hard to explain. Someone like my father is very manipulative—a contradiction in many ways, and a total narcissist. That was his strength. We never knew where we stood with him, nor what would please him.'

She sipped her Prosecco then replaced the glass, running her finger over the condensation.

'For my twelfth birthday, I had a small party—just a few friends over to watch music videos, nothing particularly lavish. But I got dressed up. I did my hair and put on some of Mum's make-up. I'll never forget his reaction.'

She shivered, turning back towards the water, their vantage point affording an excellent view of the exquisite Basilica di Santa Maria della Salute. It shimmered gold, casting its reflection onto the Grand Canal.

'He was angry?'

'Coldly disapproving,' she corrected, 'but with an undertone of such venom, I've never forgotten it.' She pushed a smile to her lips, as if to change the subject. 'He didn't speak to me for days.'

'What about your sister?' He swerved the conversation sideways, instead, not ready to move on from the matter of her parents, but understanding Olivia needed a break from discussing herself and the ways in which she was parented.

'Sienna?'

'What were they like to her?'

'Sienna is—' Now her smile was genuine. 'She's the most darling person you'll ever meet. She's funny and kind, clumsy as anything, loyal to a fault. Have you ever met a person whose eyes literally sparkled? Sienna's like that. It's as though a thousand stars have been crushed into dust that's been poured into her eyes. She glows with kindness. I love her to bits, Luca.' The intensity in her eyes reached out and took hold of him. '*She's* why I had to do this. Oh, I want my mother to finally be free of my father's oppression, and I want her to have the security of a home, but it's Sienna who just deserves so much better. For all my parents made my life a living hell, it was ten times worse for her.'

'In what way?'

Olivia sipped her drink once more, searching for the right words. 'Sienna and I are total opposites. I'm very like my mother, in looks and emotions, I think. Where my mother and I understood what my father was like, and how to keep our heads low and avoid conflict, Sienna was like…a puppy dog, always bouncing around, looking for affection. It drove him crazy. He came down on her like a tonne of bricks, trying to mould her, to change her.' She winced, hating how it had felt to see that, hating that Sienna could never learn to just stay out of their father's way. 'And so my mother, trying to keep the peace, would be very hard on Sienna, unnecessarily so, criticising her for everything, even things beyond her control, like the colour of her hair or when she gained a little puppy fat. And I—' She swallowed, and now tears did moisten her eyes, so a strange lurching sensation took hold of Luca. 'I'm embarrassed to say it, but I used to be *glad* sometimes that it was Sienna who was in trouble, because when it was her, it couldn't be me.' She screwed up her face. 'I can't believe I told you that. I've never confided that to another soul. You must think I'm a terrible person.'

'You? No, *cara*. I think you're a by-product of your home life, and that you developed the skills that were necessary to get by.' He hesitated a moment, but the moment warranted honesty. 'I think you're very brave.'

She blinked rapidly, to clear her tears, but one escaped regardless, making its way down her cheek. Luca reached over, catching it before it could drop to the table, smudging it over her soft, pale skin, then kept his hand where it was a moment, holding her face, and her gaze.

'No one deserves to live like that.'

Her expression softened for a moment, and then it was as if Olivia visibly pulled a shawl around herself, a cloak of cool distance. 'Lots of people have it much worse. He was never physically aggressive, and we grew up living a very privileged life, as you've pointed out. Hughenwood House, for all it's somewhat run-down these days, is still a stunning country home, with an impressive history.'

She needed to project this image to him, and so he nodded as though he believed her, even when he heard the heartbreak behind her carefully delivered lines. He sat back in his seat, dropping his hands into his lap, watching her with the full force of his concentration.

'I take it this general family dysfunction explains why you're still a virgin?'

Her eyes widened, showing how unexpected the question was. 'Yes.'

He waited for her to continue, probing her eyes thoughtfully.

'You said dating wasn't approved of. Why not?'

'This is really very boring, isn't it?'

'No.'

A plea filled her gaze, and Luca understood it, but he held to his resolve. 'You are asking to modify our agreement. I need more information before I make a decision.'

'I—' She closed her eyes a moment, sucking in a deep breath, and her free hand trembled slightly as she reached for her Prosecco. 'I didn't understand why my mother was so adamant about this. After all, she was married young, and my father wasn't her first lover. How come I couldn't date? But I think—' She paused, wincing, so he waited, curious as to what she might say. 'My mother is a very vain person, Luca. She was always very beautiful, and then my father seemed to value only her looks, so that became what she focused on for a very long time.'

Luca's lips formed a grim line. 'And as you got older, and turned from a child to an adolescent to a stunning young woman, she became jealous of you.'

Olivia's eyes grew wide. He was sure he was right, but some delicate sense of loyalty seemed to prevent Olivia from agreeing with him, so he continued.

'This is why your wardrobe is as it is?'

Heat coloured her cheeks. She didn't respond.

'And she kept you from dating because to see men pay attention to you, and not her, would wound her vanity.'

Olivia pulled a face before looking away. He took her silence as all the confirmation he needed, and suddenly what he wanted, more than anything, was to erase every bit of pain and dejection Olivia had ever felt. What he wanted was to give her *everything* she wanted, to make up for all she'd been denied.

'Are you hungry?'

She frowned. 'I'm—not really, why?'

He stood, extending a hand to her. 'Then let's order room service. Later.'

His final word landed between them and her eyes widened as his meaning became clear. Later might as well have been 'after', and they both knew what that meant.

It was as though she'd forgotten how to walk, her legs were that unstable beneath her, her stomach in a thousand knots, her blood thundering through her fragile veins so she could hear rushing akin to a waterfall with every step she took. At the elevator, he pressed the button without looking at her, and when Olivia risked a glance at Luca she saw only an implacable, inscrutable face, his eyes hooded, his features set in a mask of determination. A thrill ran the length of her spine even as nerves seemed to be hammering her from the inside out.

This was really going to happen.

Delight and euphoria clipped through her. She fidgeted her hands in front of her waist as she stepped into the elevator, holding her breath as Luca came to stand beside her. The doors pinged halfway shut only to open once more as another couple stepped in, joining them. Olivia stepped back, her bottom touching the metal of the lift wall, and Luca mirrored her step, staying right beside her. As the elevator began to ascend, his hand brushed hers, and she startled as a thousand lightning bolts flashed across her skin. She glanced at his face to find him still looking straight ahead, but this time there was the hint of a smile on his lips and her heart stammered in her chest.

The lift opened and the other couple departed. Olivia's breath sounds filled the cabin. Her skin was flushed from anticipation, her insides all contorted. Her body was wracked with a thousand and one emotions, none of them easy to interpret.

A moment later the doors pinged open to their floor. 'After you.' His words were deep and throaty, throbbing with the same emotions that were rolling through Olivia. She couldn't look at him, and jelly seemed to have replaced her knee joints. At the end of the corridor, he pushed open the door to the honeymoon suite and this time, when Olivia crossed the threshold, she felt as though something fundamental had changed between them. There was an equality to their pairing, an honesty and openness that hadn't been there at first. Inside the suite, she turned to face him, slowly, her eyes round, her lips parted. She'd focused so much of her energy on convincing him that they should do this that she hadn't actually prepared for what that would entail. Nerves began to bounce through her.

Luca held her gaze as he removed his dinner jacket, placing it over the back of a nearby chair, before unfastening the top two buttons of his shirt. He then turned his attention to his sleeves, which he rolled up to just below the elbow, revealing tanned, toned forearms that were, even on their own, erotic enough to make her heart go full pelt.

She reached for the zip of her dress, but a short jerk of his head forestalled her. 'I'll do it.'

Her stomach swooped; her hands fell to her sides. 'If we do this,' he said, something impossible to interpret darkening his features.

'If?' she interrupted with soft incredulity.

He dipped his head in silent agreement. 'I need you to promise you understand the limitations.'

'Haven't we already covered that?'

He seemed to impale her with the force of his stare. 'It's important.'

She suppressed a smile, because he couldn't have spelled things out more clearly if he'd grabbed a white board and started writing it down.

'Just sex. No love. I got it.'

His eyes narrowed. 'When we sleep together, it's simply a biological urge. There's no true intimacy between us, no matter how we make it look to the outside world. When thirty days expire, we will walk away from one another. No regrets.'

A challenge tilted her face. 'That's exactly what I want, Luca. And it's twenty-eight days, now.'

His eyes narrowed. 'And if you start to feel differently, at any point, you promise you will tell me.'

'I won't feel differently. It's not possible. I won't feel anything.'

He seemed to consider that for a moment and, finally, nodded.

'So? Can we do this now?'

He laughed quietly at her eagerness. 'No.'

'No?' She balked at the rejection. 'What the heck do you mean, "no"?'

'You've been drinking.'

She gaped. 'A single glass of Prosecco.'

He moved closer to her, so close their bodies were brushing, his eyes hooked to hers, before reaching behind her and slowly, painstakingly slowly, easing down the zip of her dress. 'When…' The zip reached the line of her bra; she shivered as he crossed it. 'Not if,' he placated, when the zip had gone all the way. He moved his hands to the off-the-shoulder sleeves of her dress and dropped them, his palms brushing her arms. The dress fell from her breasts and she shivered, her strapless bra a flimsy piece of lace and wire. 'You will be completely sober.'

'I am.' She trembled as the dress pooled to the floor and she stood before him in only a bra and panties.

'Completely.' And yet, despite his words, he leaned forward and drew her lower lip between his teeth, so she arched her back, the contact searing and sensational.

'But I want—'

'You want to learn about sex,' he said, reaching behind her and unfastening the bra, dropping it to the carpeted floor, beside her dress. She stepped out of the fabric, stiletto heels still in place, underpants just a scrap of fabric that could barely contain her heat and need.

'I want to *experience* sex,' she corrected.

'Ah, my mistake.' His eyes showed a glimmer of amusement when they met hers. 'But there is so much to learn before you experience,' he said gently.

'Such as?' Pique and disappointment crested through her.

His hands cupped her breasts when she wasn't expecting it, so her eyes widened and her gasp was involuntary.

'Are you aware you can be brought to orgasm through nipple stimulation alone?'

Olivia found it impossible to answer, but her eyes contained a plea, so Luca laughed under his breath. 'Would you like me to show you?'

'Are you really going to make me beg?' She huffed.

'Yes,' he said simply, moving his mouth to the sensitive flesh just beneath her jaw. 'I'm going to make you beg over, and over, and over again. And you're going to love it.'

His mouth moved from her jaw to her decolletage, pressing kisses along her collarbone before he moved lower, his stubble abrasive on the sensitive flesh of her breasts, in a way that she adored. A moment later, his mouth clasped over one of her nipples and she cried out as a thousand shock waves rolled through her, amounting to a massive tsunami of need. The pleasure was intense. She'd never known anything like it. He rolled her nipple with his tongue, flicking it, then intermittently pressing his teeth down so there was a heady rush of pleasure and pain, a mix of feelings that were hot and completely absorbing. His hand toyed with her other nipple, tweaking it between his forefinger and thumb until she was moaning, panting, barely capable of breathing, much less speaking. He moved faster, then swapped his mouth from one breast to the other, the sensation of his fingers on her moist nipple bringing her close to an edge she couldn't see, an edge she'd never before approached.

'I—I feel—' But the words were lodged in her brain, impossible to locate. How did one describe a feeling they'd never known before? 'Luca, I'm— Oh, Luca!'

He moved faster, and as he plucked and tweaked he brought a hand behind her back, holding her close to him, pressing her womanhood to his rock-hard arousal, so through the flimsy fabric of her underwear she could feel the intensity of his need, and knew that it matched her own. His arousal pressed to her most sensitive cluster of nerves, promising pleasure and delights she'd never known before. Olivia was spiralling out of control, with nothing and no one to hold onto. Except there was Luca, strong, clever, Luca; she gripped his shirt as her world began to change, moving beyond what she'd ever known, becoming fierce and fiery. She held him as she fell apart, sounds of her pleasure filling the luxury suite; her own hips began to writhe, seeking more, needing more, as wave after wave of pleasure wracked her body, redefining her until she knew that the experience had turned her into something, someone, she didn't know any more.

He pulled his head up, his own eyes heavy with arousal as he looked at her, scanning her face as if to reassure himself.

'I'm fine,' she promised. 'Better than fine.' Her hands moved to his belt, unsteady fingers moving to release it, but he stilled her with his touch, taking a step back.

'No.'

'No?' She pouted, still trembling from her first orgasm. 'But I want more. I want to see.'

His eyes sparked with hers, surprise obvious. 'We have a month. There's no harm going slowly, to make sure you don't regret this.'

She ground her teeth together. 'I'm not going to.'

'A few more days to be sure won't hurt.'

'You think?'

His smile lacked humour. 'Not too much, anyway.' He reached forward, brushing his hand over her sex, so briefly, but so perfectly, she whimpered at the subtle contact. 'Please…'

'Tomorrow,' he said, but with firm insistence. 'Tomorrow I'll go down on you until you see stars. *Bene?*'

He deserved a gold medal. A whole goddamned cabinet full of them. He had never wanted to sleep with a woman more than he had Olivia. Every sound she'd made, every whimper, every arch of her back, every press of her womanhood against his arousal had threatened to bring out his not-so-inner caveman, to hell with chivalry. If she weren't a virgin, it would have been a different story. If she hadn't grown up in such a vile atmosphere, been undermined at every turn, made to hide her beauty, made to feel ashamed of it, if she were meeting him as his true equal in terms of experience and confidence, then he wouldn't have let a single glass of Prosecco stop him from possessing her in all the ways they both wanted. But Olivia had lived through hell and the last thing she needed was another man disrespecting her wishes.

But hadn't he just done that? A part of him—his libido, Luca suspected—argued back, just as fervently. She'd clearly articulated what she wanted, and he'd refused to give it to her. No, not refused. Delayed. Besides, he meant what he'd said. There was more to sex than the actual act. She deserved to feel and experience all the things most people did as teenagers, when their hormones were just coming into play and they were exploring and experimenting.

And as she felt, and learned, he would be in control at all times. He would have to be. This wouldn't be like a normal affair, with the sorts of women he usually bedded. He would have to be particularly careful to keep Olivia at arm's length emotionally, to pleasure her by night, but maintain their boundaries anywhere and everywhere else.

Out of nowhere, Jayne breathed into his mind, her beautiful face, her lying eyes, the way she'd looked at him when his father's crimes had been revealed, when Luca had discovered that his once billion-dollar fortune was now worth nothing. And that was how she'd made him feel, too. Like nothing. Nobody. And he'd loved her so damned much, it had felt as if she were stabbing him, or slowly strangling him, the pain spreading through him, only worsening when he discovered she'd had an affair—that she'd used Luca as a stepping stone to climb to what she perceived to be a better marriage, a wealthier husband. And now?

Luca had the last laugh, because he was one of the richest men in the world, and he wouldn't touch Jayne with a ten-foot bargepole. Her legacy had changed his life—he'd learned to keep all women at arm's length, and Olivia would be no different.

He bashed the pillow against the sofa, staring up at the ceiling with a hard-on that wouldn't quit, counting down the minutes until the morning, when her education could continue...

# CHAPTER SEVEN

OLIVIA STRETCHED IN the enormous bed with a feeling of contentment that brought a smile to her lips even before she could recall why she felt so darned good. She arched her back and ran her hands over her body, but as her fingertips collided with her nipples, and remembered sensations came screaming back to her, she sat bolt upright, staring across the room at the large mirror.

Heat flushed her body.

Had she really propositioned her husband for sex? And had he really made her feel so incredible with his hands and mouth, and her breasts? Bemused, she stared at her reflection, wondering how she'd never known her body could be capable of such pleasure. His promise hung heavy in the air, driving her feet from the bed. *'Tomorrow, I'll go down on you until you see stars.'*

She could barely contain her excitement as she ran a brush through her hair and cleaned her teeth, then contemplated pulling on something more modest than the cream silk negligee Luca had bought for her, before realising how absurd that would be considering what she had planned for their morning...

With a heart that was thumping in her chest, she drew open the door to the lounge and stepped out, hoping he'd still be on the sofa.

He wasn't. Luca was, to her chagrin, fully dressed, eating breakfast at the table with the spectacular view of the canal.

'Good morning.' His eyes lingered a little longer than was necessary on her face, scanning as if to see if she had any regrets.

She didn't, and so smiled with extra wattage, moving towards him slowly at first, a strange sense of nervousness that *he* might regret what she'd asked of him.

'Good morning,' she returned, husky-voiced, standing right in front of him.

Their eyes met and held, and electricity almost gave her a shock.

'How did you sleep?'

Really? He wanted to talk about sleep?

'Like a log,' she murmured.

'I'm glad.'

'You?' She arched a brow, unconsciously teasing him.

'I didn't.'

Her laugh was soft and spontaneous. 'No? Why ever not?'

He scowled at her before gesturing to the table, where an array of pastries and fruit was spread out. 'I think, even with your innocence, you know the answer to that. Have something to eat.'

'I'm not hungry.'

His body stiffened. 'No?'

She put a hand on his shoulder, drawing his gaze to her face. 'Not for breakfast.'

'You haven't changed your mind?'

She pulled a face. 'After your very effective demonstration last night? Not bloody likely.'

An arrogant smirk changed his features for the briefest moment and then he stood, towering over her. 'I haven't changed my mind either, Olivia. We take this slow.'

Oh, how she wanted to rail against that! How she wanted to scream that she was ready and to kindly stop telling her what to do and how she should feel, but even as she felt that surge of anger and frustration, she acknowledged the decency of his hesitation. She'd felt his arousal last night. She'd known he wanted her as badly as she did him, and yet he'd resisted. For her. To look after her. The realisation sent a strange wobble into her chest, and emotions of an entirely different sort threatened to overpower her so she tilted her jaw defiantly, employing all the skills she'd mastered in her life of concealing her thoughts and feelings from the outside world.

'So?' she challenged, eyes holding his.

'Ah, yes. I seem to remember I made you a promise last night.'

'Yes, you did.'

'Then I'd better make sure I don't break it. Are you ready?'

How could she ever be ready for such pleasure? How could she ever have prepared for the litany of sensations she'd experience as his mouth caressed her sex, his tongue alternately suckling and lashing, his stubble rough against her inner thighs, his kiss moving from firm and insistent to gentle and slow, until she was crying out, the torture of waiting causing sweat to bead on her brow as flames licked the soles of her feet and she wondered if anyone had ever had a heart attack from the intensity of this kind of passion? His hands held her thighs in place as his mouth drove her closer and closer to release, and as she began to soar into the heavens his hands cupped her breasts, tweaking her nipples as he had the night before, so shards of delight pierced her soul. His name spilled from her lips again and again, her nails scrambled to dig into the sheets first and then his shoulders, holding tight as she slipped off the edge of the world, into an abyss from which she wasn't sure she'd ever return.

Her breath tore into the room, rapidly at first, like a hurricane, and then slowing to a gale-force wind, until eventually she felt her pulse returning to something close to normal. He stood in the interim, turning his back on her, moving to the bathroom then returning a moment later, regarding her with an expression that gave nothing away.

'I'm starting to feel that this education is a little wanting,' she said, propping up on one elbow, uncaring, in that moment, for her nakedness.

'Oh? Is that a complaint?'

'Well…' she plucked at the sheet, heat spreading through her veins '…it does feel a little one sided.' Her eyes dropped, pointedly, to his trousers, which were still fastened, then returned to his face.

He stayed where he was, arms crossed over his broad chest. 'We have plenty of time.' He held out a hand, and she placed hers in it, so he could pull her to standing. 'Besides, we have plans this morning.'

'We do?'

He nodded slowly.

'What plans?'

'I thought we could tour Murano, seeing as you have not been to this part of Italy before. Their glass is in-comparable.'

Her heart stammered for a different reason now, his thoughtfulness wholly unexpected. This wasn't a real honeymoon, and yet he was acting as though it were, and there was a part of Olivia—a large part—that was happy because of it.

Except it was all make-believe; she had to remember that. This was all a ruse, and she had to play her part. 'I've always wanted to see Murano,' she murmured.

'Then get dressed.' But he didn't relinquish his grip on her hand; instead, he squeezed it more tightly. 'Be-fore I change my mind.'

'About that,' she said softly, allowing her own hand to brush his trousers, watching for his reaction. It didn't disappoint. His eyes lowered, his lips parting on a hiss of breath, and then he stepped backwards. 'Murano's been there for hundreds of years. Do you really think an extra hour will make any difference?'

'An hour?' He leaned closer, his eyes fighting with hers, his tone self-deprecating. 'Believe me, *cara*, if you

touch me, nothing will take close to an hour.' A frisson
of anticipation spread through her at the promise of his
words. 'I'll be waiting.' He released her hand and left
the room, with Olivia staring after him with a strange
mix of arousal, satisfaction and frustration.

Murano defied every single one of her expectations.
Brightly coloured buildings stood on either side of the
canal, and the sun shone as their boat cruised along the
water. Halfway, Luca asked that they stop, handing her
from the boat and gesturing to one of the buildings.

'This is one of the oldest glass galleries in Murano.
Come, see if anything takes your fancy.'

She walked beside him, happiness and contentment
lifting her soul. It only intensified when they stepped
inside the enormous ancient yet beautifully preserved
building.

'Glass has been manufactured on Murano since the
thirteenth century. The techniques haven't changed in
all that time.' He gestured to large timber doors that led
to a workshop. The area of creation was separate from
the gallery. A handful of tourists was ahead of them,
more entered behind, but as Olivia watched the work-
ers below, crafting unique, individual, ethereal pieces,
with Luca right by her side, she felt as though they were
the only two people on earth.

'They're so skilled,' she commented in awe as they
neared the end of the gallery, to a shop where various
pieces were displayed, their price tags conspicuously
absent.

'Yes. This is a family business. Each craftsman has

been trained by their parents, the skills passed down from father and mother to child.' He reached out, lifting a delicate glass. 'It's fascinating how just a few elements can combine to make something so unique.'

She blinked, strangely overcome by the experience, and even more so by Luca's apparent reverence for the ancient skill. She offered him a tight smile then moved away, needing a moment to compose herself.

Shelves lined with glasses, bowls and little trinkets—statues and decorations—clamoured for her attention, so she circled the store several times, scanning the objects with growing admiration. But each time, her eyes lingered on one in particular—a brightly coloured bird with large wings. It stood on a glass base. The whole thing was about the size of Olivia's hand, but every time she passed it she felt a tingling sensation in her fingertips, as though she simply had to touch it. On the third time she passed it, she finally gave in, stopping and admiring it from every angle first, before reaching out and gingerly lifting the piece.

Something locked into place in her chest. Her eyes met Luca's and flames with all the intensity of those the glass blowers worked with flared between them.

'You would like this?'

She lifted it once more, looking for the price. None was visible. 'It's very beautiful,' she said, non-committally.

He reached out, taking it from her, then caught her hand, guiding her towards the cash register, where an older woman was working at the computer.

'Ah, this is one of my favourites,' she exclaimed, eyeing Olivia and Luca with approval.

'My wife chose it.'

*My wife.* The words were said so naturally, but they sparked a thousand and one feelings inside Olivia, feelings that she couldn't fathom. There was panic, fear, a sharp need to say 'no', because being some man's 'wife' was something she had always, always loathed the idea of. And yet, in the midst of that, there was surprise and warmth, pleasure at being marked as Luca's. Her nerves tangled, making it impossible to understand herself or her feelings.

'My son crafted this piece. It is a *fenice.*'

Olivia turned to Luca, frowning. His eyes, when they met hers, were appraising. 'A phoenix.'

'Do you know the symbolism of the *fenice*?' the older woman asked as she carefully surrounded the bird in bubble wrap.

'Something about rising from the ashes?' Olivia suggested.

'Yes. In many cultures, the world over, it is seen as a symbolism of rebirth, of hope, of newness.' She taped the bird, then placed it into a brown paper bag. 'He will be safe with you.'

A shiver ran through Olivia at the perfection of having gravitated towards such an ornament. Here she was, taking steps to begin her own new life, and she had unconsciously chosen a symbol of regeneration.

Luca handed over his credit card, a matte black with a silver centurion in the centre, before the shopkeeper could announce the price. Olivia decided she would do better not to ask.

'Thank you,' she said as they emerged back onto the

sunlit street. They'd been in the glass factory for over an hour, and in that time the summer sun had warmed so it felt delightful against her bare arms.

They wandered the streets of Murano. The island was not big, and it did not take long, but as the temperature increased it was absolutely essential to stop and enjoy *gelati* from one of the street vendors. Olivia chose strawberry, and the sweetness filled her with a sense of completion.

'Thank you for this morning,' she said as she scraped the last of the *gelato* from the paper cup. 'I've actually really enjoyed our honeymoon.'

His short laugh sent tremors through her body. 'You are surprised?'

'Well, yes, frankly. Don't forget, when we married, I knew very little about you.'

For a moment, his smile dropped, and thunderclouds seemed to pass behind his eyes. 'Except what you read on the Internet.'

She frowned. That bothered him? 'That's right.'

'And still you chose to marry me?' he said as a joke, but she heard the caustic tension in his voice.

'I mean, I sort of had my arm up my back there,' she pointed out, then wished she hadn't when the mood changed completely. Oh, he still smiled at her, but she felt the change come over him, and couldn't quite pinpoint why.

'I thought we'd fly directly to Rome. Unless you have any objections?' he prompted as an afterthought.

The suggestion made her head spin. She was just starting to settle into her honeymoon and now he was

suggesting a change? Except, this wasn't really unexpected. He'd said their honeymoon would last for two
nights, and it had been that. It was time to go home
now. Not to a real home—at least, not for Olivia—but
to the place she'd live in for the rest of her very short,
very necessary marriage.

'Luca, may I ask you something?'

He regarded her from the back of the limousine with
a look that might have scared anyone else off, but Olivia
had lived with fear and intimidation all her life, and
Luca simply wasn't capable of causing her to feel either. He was nothing like her father. Nothing like she
feared all men might be.

'You don't have to answer,' she offered.

'Believe me, if I do not wish to, I won't.'

She *did* believe it. Luca wasn't capable of doing anything *but* calling the shots. She nodded her acceptance
of that, flicking her gaze to the window for a moment.
Rome whizzed past, the early afternoon light shimmering with that Mediterranean clarity. Ancient buildings
stood sentinel to their journey, grey and magnificent, so
Olivia wanted to stop the car and go and explore them
now, to trail her hands over each, one by one, until she
felt their secrets bury deep into her soul.

'Earlier today, you seemed annoyed to think I'd read
up on you.'

He was quiet for a long time. She turned to face him,
arching a brow.

'I'm sorry, was that a question?'

She could feel his impatience, and something else.

A hesitation born of an emotion she didn't understand. 'Yes. *Why* does that annoy you?'

'On the contrary, I think it's a wise precaution. You asked a virtual stranger to marry you. I'd think you stupid not to do a bit of research.'

'Sure, fine, but it still annoys you.'

He drummed his fingers into his knee, his eyes not leaving her face.

'You're not going to answer me, are you?'

He compressed his lips, and she felt a battle raging in his mind, a choice being made. Before she could determine who was the victor, the car drew to a halt. She could just make out a street sign, an old mosaic attached to the building at the corner. Via Giulia, it said. She didn't need to know anything about the street to know that it was expensive real estate. The buildings here were very old, beautifully maintained, with abundant greenery and splashes of colour bursting from gardens that were concealed by high walls.

He waited for her to step from the limousine, before gesturing to a dark wooden door, arched, nestled within a pale pink rendered wall.

'This is Palazzo Centro,' he said, pinning a series of numbers into a discreet electric pad. The door sprang open. He held it wide to allow Olivia to pass. Frustrated at having her question unanswered, she passed without looking at him, and was quickly overwhelmed by the sheer beauty of this place. She had expected something elegant, of course, but not rich with history like this. It felt as though it should have been a museum, and not a home.

'You live here?'

'When I'm in Rome, *sì*.'

'Which is how often?'

The garden was very old, if the size of the trees was any indication. A water feature was set against one wall, creating the delightful sound of rain falling, and in the centre there was a bird bath, with little balls of moss floating on top. A marble path cut through the garden, towards a front door that was timber, with gold detail.

'Most of the time. Perhaps three weeks out of four.'

'And the rest of the time?'

'Wherever I need to be.' He didn't need to push the door open. A housekeeper appeared, dressed in black, her hair worn in a low grey bun. 'Signora Marazzi, this is my wife, Signora Giovanardi.'

The housekeeper did a double take. 'Your wife?' she clarified in Italian.

Luca nodded. 'Please make her feel welcome when I am not home.'

*'Certo, certo.'* The housekeeper stared at Luca and then gave the full force of her attention to Olivia, who was, by now, feeling a little self-conscious. The housekeeper's scrutiny didn't help. 'But you are so beautiful.' She clapped her hands together. 'Like a Caravaggio figure with your porcelain skin and luminescent eyes.'

Olivia squirmed under the extravagant praise, a lifetime of criticism impossible to shake off.

Luca reached for her hand. 'We were married only two days ago and will want privacy. Would you see that the fridge is stocked before you leave, and ask the other staff to give us space?'

It seemed to call the housekeeper back to her duties. She blinked, smiling. '*Certo.* I will come back tomorrow afternoon, to see if *la signora* needs anything.'

Luca jerked his head by way of thanks, and Olivia watched the interaction with amusement.

'You know, that bordered on rude.'

He laughed. 'Believe me, Signora Marazzi will be almost as pleased as my grandmother that I've remarried— even if it does prove to be temporary.'

She ignored the tightening in her stomach as his words foreshadowed the end to their ruse.

He guided her through the entrance hall with its vaulted ceilings and chandeliers to a lounge room that was surprisingly modern.

'An electrical fire destroyed most of the house's interior and the owners could not afford the repair. I bought it for a steal, salvaged what I could, but, for the most part, a total reconstruction was required.'

'Oh, what a terrible shame,' she murmured. And yet, as she looked around the room, the juxtaposition of the ancient stone walls and modern interior had a sort of magical property, as though the house was bridging the gap between new and old. 'It's very striking,' she said sincerely.

'It works.'

'It reminds me of the *fenice*,' she said, with a small smile. 'A phoenix, risen from the ashes.'

He cocked a brow. 'I suppose you are right. I have not thought of it like this before.' His hands caught her hips, holding her still, his eyes probing, asking questions, wondering. She stared back, an open book.

'There are many things written about me on the Internet. It doesn't generally bother me. What strangers choose to opine about me or my family is more a reflection of them than me. And yet, the idea of *you* having read them, of you believing them, is strangely disconcerting.'

Her heart slammed into her ribs. 'I didn't say that I believe what I read.'

His lips formed a grimace. 'Some of them are true.'

'Such as you being a womaniser?'

He hesitated a moment before confirming that with a nod. Jealousy fired through her, fierce and debilitating. She pushed it aside.

'So? Do you think that matters to me? This isn't a real marriage, remember?'

'And if it were?'

She considered that. Would his philandering have had an impact on how she felt about him?

'It's not,' she dodged the question. 'As for your father, do you really think I'm in any position to hold the sins of one man against his child?'

Luca let his hands fall away, turning away from Olivia's penetrating gaze.

'And my first marriage?'

Olivia frowned. 'There was surprisingly very little about that,' she admitted, because she *had* looked. Curiosity had fired her fingers; she'd wanted to understand it—and him.

'No.'

'It wasn't amicable?'

He made a sound rich with disbelief. 'It was far from

it.' He turned to face her, speaking mechanically. 'My wife left me for someone she viewed to be far wealthier, far more powerful. I don't know how long it had been going on, but when my father went to prison, she walked out on our marriage. Jayne wasn't prepared to slum it with me.'

Olivia's lips parted with surprise, and anger. How could his first wife have been so callous? To leave him when he was already suffering so much because of his father?

'She didn't love you.' She answered her own question.

'No.' His lips formed a grim line. 'I came to that conclusion eventually, but it took a long time.' He seemed to rouse himself. 'Her husband did everything he could to rewrite their relationship, to avoid a scandal developing. I had no interest in dragging her name through the mud, so allowed the narrative to play out. There was very little tabloid interest, given the way it appeared on the surface.'

Sympathy softened her features. 'It must have been very hard for you—going through what you did with your father, and then Jayne.'

A muscle jerked in his jaw. 'But I had Nonna,' he said quietly. 'Without her, I cannot say with any certainty that I would have survived.'

But Luca didn't want to talk about his past. He never did, not with anyone, but he felt a particular distaste in discussing it with Olivia. He told himself it had nothing to do with making him look like a failure in her eyes, and everything to do with the vow he'd made himself, to keep her at a distance from him. There had to be some boundaries in their marriage.

But there were others they could disregard. Others they could tear down. Turning to face her, with eyes that glittered with dark speculation, he lifted a single finger, beckoning her towards him.

She dug her teeth into her lower lip as she moved, half gliding across the room, until she stood right in front of him.

Deliberately, with as little passion as he could display, he lifted his hands to her shirt, finding one of the buttons that lined the silken seam. Her eyes clung to his face as he flicked it apart, then moved to the next. Calm, in control, just as he promised himself he'd be with her.

'It's time for another lesson.'

He felt the shiver that sparked through her blood. 'I thought you'd never ask.'

# CHAPTER EIGHT

'YOU KNOW, TECHNICALLY that's a revision, not a lesson,' she pointed out, pushing up on one elbow when her breathing had returned to normal. He grinned from between her legs, before pulling himself up the bed, his body over hers, his arms braced on either side of her head as his full weight pressed her into the mattress.

'Complaining?'

'Not at all,' she assured him huskily. 'Just eager for advancement.'

'An A-plus student,' he murmured, nibbling her ear lobe. Olivia held him right where he was, his body so heavenly against hers, his proximity launching a kaleidoscope of butterflies in her abdomen. She could feel his arousal and yet she had no experience, no knowledge, and so, despite his obvious physical awareness of her, worry permeated her fog of pleasure, so her eyes flickered away from his, filled with uncertainty.

'What is it?'

She glanced back at him with a start. Was she so easy to read?

'Yes,' he responded to her unasked question. 'I can

tell when something is bothering you. Your face is very expressive.'

'I know.' She expelled a soft sigh. 'I've tried to change that.'

'It's your eyes. They give everything away.'

She grimaced. 'Perhaps a pair of very dark sunglasses,' she suggested thoughtfully.

'Or, you could tell me what's on your mind.'

'Well,' she pressed her palms flat to his chest. 'Actually, that would be you.'

Triumph shaped his features. 'I'm pleased to hear it.'

'Not in a good way.'

'I see.'

'I just…'

He waited, and when she didn't continue, prompted her gently. 'Yes?'

'Is there something wrong with me?' she blurted out, then pulled her hands from his chest purely to cover her face and the eyes he'd just said he could read like open books.

'Wrong with you? What the hell do you mean?'

'It's just, you seem to be able to touch me and kiss me and make me feel a thousand and one things, then walk away again. Don't you…*want* me?'

He swore in Italian, his eyes boring into hers. 'Look at me, Olivia. Look at my face. Do you not see the tension there? Do you not realise that it is taking every ounce of my willpower to take this slowly, to make your first time what it ought to be?'

Her heart stammered. 'But it's just sex,' she whispered.

'No, it is your *first time* having sex. After me, you may make love to whomever you want, and at whatever speed you want. With them, it will be "just sex". But with me, and for your first time, it is different. Special. Even when we have both agreed it means nothing, it means *something* because you have not done this before. If this were about what I wanted, and what I wanted only, I would have made love to you in the elevator in Positano.'

Her breath squeezed from her lungs. 'Seriously?'

'You think I didn't want you even then?'

He dropped his head, kissing her lips gently. 'You think I didn't want you the second I saw you at that damned party? I watched you and wanted you, even before I knew you were looking for me, *cara*.'

She lowered her gaze.

'So do not think for even one moment that I am simply walking away from you. I am torturing myself by waiting.'

'Torturing us both,' she promised throatily.

'And if I promise the wait will be worth it?'

'How long a wait?'

He laughed before moving his mouth to her breast. 'Not long.' He flicked her nipple lazily, sending arrows of pleasure barbing through her body.

'Do you realise I haven't even seen you naked?'

Heat slashed his cheeks with dark colour and then he pushed to standing, his eyes on hers the whole time. Their eyes locked as he moved his hands to his belt buckle and unfastened it, as he slid his trousers down, as her eyes saw his naked arousal for the first time. Olivia sat up a little straighter, fascinated, compelled, and utterly turned on.

'I—' She was at a loss for words. Helplessly, her eyes

drifted to his and stayed locked there as he finished undressing, then stood, stark naked, like an incredibly sculpted statue, a Roman deity, all muscled and mouth-watering. Her eyes flickered lower, across his broadly muscled chest, to his tapered waist, taut thighs, man-hood, and lower to his shapely calves. Her heart was in her throat when she dragged her gaze back to his face.

'And now you have seen me naked,' he growled, heat simmering in his eyes, pooling between them. She swallowed past a constricted throat then stood, match-ing his body language, slowly removing the last of her clothing, until she was also naked in this palatial bed-room with panoramic views over Rome.

The air around them crackled with a challenge, an invitation, and she felt Luca's tension as he decided what to do. Finally, he held out a hand to her. 'Come. Let me show you something.'

He led her from the bedroom, down the corridor, both as naked as the day they were born.

'What about Signora Marazzi?'

'What about her?'

'What if she sees—?'

'I suspect she left almost immediately.'

'I suppose she's used to your philandering habits.' Olivia giggled softly, wondering why the sound was oddly forced to her own ears.

He threw a glance over his shoulder. 'This way.'

She noticed he didn't respond to her statement. Well, so? What could he say? They both knew the lie of the land—he was a bachelor, through and through. Nothing about this was new for him, except the whole 'marriage' part, and even then, he'd been married before. Something rolled through her, something dark and fierce, surprising her. It was a mix of curiosity and something else, something fiercer, compelling her to understand about his first marriage, about his life before her, about the experiences that had shaped him. But that was none of her business. Per their agreement, she had no right to ask, and certainly, no expectation that he'd answer.

The hallway opened onto a landing and a narrow set of stairs. She followed behind his naked form, admiring the muscled firmness of his rear as he moved up two flights then pushed a modern steel door open. They burst onto a rooftop terrace, shielded from view by hedges that grew in large terracotta pots. At the centre of the paved terrace was a pool, submerged, and the most striking turquoise colour Olivia could imagine. The afternoon sun bounced off it tantalisingly, invitingly, so she glided towards it on autopilot.

'How stunning,' she murmured, not realising that Luca had followed. He placed his hands on her hips, drawing her back against him, so his arousal pressed between her buttocks. She closed her eyes on a rushed gasp, her pleasure only increasing when he brought one hand around to her breasts, lazily stroking her nipples before moving his mouth to the crook of her neck, whispering and tasting her there until she was moaning softly into the afternoon sun.

'Swim with me,' he suggested.

She wanted to do so much more than swim with him, but when he released her and dived into the water, she stood there, watching his lithe athleticism, spellbound by his masculine beauty, before she did the same, splashing into the water with a heady sense of euphoria. Her wedding ring glinted as she swam, catching her eye, the diamonds so clear and sparkling.

It was a sign of possession she'd always railed against, but on this day, in this minute, wearing this man's ring, Olivia couldn't say she minded, at all.

'That was incredibly delicious.' She dabbed her lips with the linen napkin, then placed it in her lap.

'Signora Marazzi is an exceptional cook,' he agreed.

'Does she make all your meals?'

'Or I eat out.' He shrugged.

'You never cook for yourself?'

'No. I never learned.'

'It's not rocket science.'

'Perhaps. But there's no need.'

'What about during your marriage? Don't tell me your wife was chained to the kitchen?'

'Hardly,' he drawled, without elaborating further. The same curiosity that had burst through Olivia earlier that day flooded her again.

She leaned forward. 'You don't have to answer if you don't want to.' It was a silly precursor to say—naturally Luca wouldn't do *anything* he didn't want to. 'When your wife left you, you went to live with your grandmother?'

'That is no secret,' he said, quietly though, warily, as though he was bracing for an even worse question.

'She wasn't affected by the bankruptcy?'

'He's her son.' Luca's voice was strained. She reached

over and pressed her hand to his. 'Of course, she was affected.'

'I meant in a financial sense.'

His smile held a rejection. 'My grandmother owns her own house, and her own business. When my father inherited from my grandfather, it was always on the basis that Nonna's assets would be held separate. There was no threat to her.'

'What a wise precaution that turned out to be.'

'My grandfather insisted. Nonna came from nothing, and he always joked that it was the only way he could be sure she really loved him. He made her a very wealthy woman even before he proposed, so he knew there was no financial incentive in her accepting the proposal.'

'He was a cynic?'

'Or a realist. He was worth a small fortune.'

'She obviously loved him.'

'She did. But even once they were married, her fortune was kept aside, all in her name, all her own. So when my father was charged, and everything he owned was taken away, Nonna lost nothing.'

'Except her son,' Olivia murmured sadly.

'And her good name,' he added. 'Thanks to my father, Giovanardi now means "mud" in Italian.'

Olivia winced. 'You don't deserve that.'

'Don't I?'

She pulled her lips to the side, shaking her head a little. 'Of course you don't. None of it was your fault.'

He placed his knife and fork on his plate, glaring at them. 'I wish things had turned out differently.'

'Do you speak to him?'

'No.'

'Your choice or his?'

'Mutual.'

'You haven't forgiven him?'

'Not really. And I know he'll never forgive me.'

'Why? What did you do that was so terrible?'

Luca's eyes met hers, almost as though he was challenging her to think as badly of him as he did himself. 'I caused it all, *cara*. It's my fault.'

'What are you talking about?'

'I discovered what he'd done. I couldn't fathom how he'd dug such a deep hole, and so I confronted him, hoping for a simple explanation. Only the one he gave made no sense. I could see there was never going to be a way to pay off all the investors. It was a Ponzi scheme, an enormous house of cards, ready to tumble at the slightest breeze.'

She grimaced. 'It must have been terrible for you to realise that.'

'He preyed on our friends, the parents of my school friends, men he'd known all his life. He was unscrupulous and greedy. When I went to the police, it was in the hopes some of the money could be recovered, but the scheme collapsed and everyone lost everything.'

'You most of all,' she said quietly.

He ran a hand through his hair. 'We were very wealthy, but it wasn't enough for him. He wanted more, always more.'

Olivia couldn't offer any words to comfort him, so she did the only thing she could, moving around the table and settling herself on his lap, arms hooked behind his neck.

'That isn't your fault.'

He met her eyes, and she saw the trauma in them, the regret, the fervent wish that things had been different. How she ached for him!

'Not your father's actions, nor your wife's betrayal. You didn't deserve any of it.'

He kept his gaze averted from hers, a muscle throbbing low in his squared jaw, so she lifted a finger to it, feeling his pulse, fascinated by the tightness there as he clenched his teeth together.

'How did you do all this?' She shifted the subject a little, waving a hand around her to the palatial lounge that opened onto the back garden. 'You rebuilt an empire from nothing.'

'Not nothing,' he corrected with a bitter smile. 'There was Nonna's business.'

'She handed it to you,' Olivia guessed.

'Yes.' His expression was defiant. 'She trusted me, and I desperately wanted to make her proud, to prove her right. I worked around the clock for two years, growing her small chain of accommodation into a global force of exclusive, boutique hotels, before branching out into transport logistics, and then airlines. It wasn't easy. None of the major banks in Italy would, initially, lend to me.' A cynical smile tilted his lips. 'Including Azzuri—the bank I plan to acquire.' The rejection had been one of many he'd experienced at the time, but it had cut him deep, representing what he'd thought to be the end of the road. The humiliation he'd felt, at having to go in there to beg, in the first instance, and having his proposal tossed out as though it were worthless junk. He'd never forgotten that humiliation.

'Even with your grandmother's wealth?' Olivia stroked his cheek gently.

'Even then.' Luca brought himself back to the present. 'Giovanardi means mud, remember?'

'What did you do?'

'Sold two of her hotels to raise capital.'

She shook her head. 'You must have been so scared.'

His lips twisted in a mocking smile. 'Angry, actually.'

She laughed softly. 'Yes, that too.'

'I hated the banks, all of them. And particularly Azzuri,' he was surprised to hear himself admit. 'It was when I expanded into new tech that things really improved. I was able to pay back my father's debts—every last one of them—and to create an empire my grandfather would have been proud of.'

She heard his drive and determination, and the dark forces that had compelled him to work so hard for so long, and felt a surge of pity. Would he ever feel that he'd done enough?

'Pietra must have been impressed.'

His smile was just a hint. 'Yes.' He lifted a hand to Olivia's cheek, tucking her hair behind her ear. 'She'd lost so much. My grandfather, then the family reputation, the business. I knew that I couldn't fail her.'

'You didn't.'

He dipped his head in acknowledgement. 'And yet,' he said quietly, 'it doesn't matter how much I am worth, or how much business succeeds, there is always a question hanging over my head. Did I cheat to get here? Am I like my father? Can people trust me? His shadow has dogged me my entire adult life.'

She shook her head a little. 'And yet, look at my father—a man whose ancient name earned him a seat at any table, who was thought of so highly, and yet, he was—as you said—a total jackass.' She leaned closer, her gaze intense. 'What does a name matter, Luca? It's the man that counts, the man you are, the deeds that you do. That's what people should care about.'

She ran her finger around his lips, tracing the outline there. 'And I think you are a good man, who's done great deeds. In fact, I think you're very noble.'

'Because I married you?' he prompted, his voice lightly teasing.

'Absolutely,' she responded in kind, only half joking, then sobered. 'You saved me. I mean that seriously.' Tears threatened so she forced a bright smile. Things were getting too serious between them, too intense. Neither of them wanted that. 'And because you paid back the money your father stole, when you didn't have to.'

'Not legally, but morally. Ethically.'

She brushed her lips over his. 'See? You're undoubtedly decent.'

He expelled a short sound of amusement. 'I don't think you'd say that if you knew the decidedly indecent thoughts I've been having about you.'

Pleasure warmed her. 'Tell me,' she invited, moving her bottom a little from side to side, watching as his eyes darkened with the unmistakable rush of desire. 'Or better yet…' She moved her mouth to his, kissing him gently at the corner. 'Show me,' she invited, pushing his shirt up his body, revealing his taut abdomen, her fingers brushing his wall of abdominals then discarding the shirt on the floor. He didn't fight her and she was so glad; she didn't realise *how* sure she'd been that he would fight her until he didn't and relief flooded her body. Relief, and a rush of desire.

She shifted on the seat, needing more purchase, more of him, so she lifted up and straddled him, allowing her head to drop to his chest, her tongue to tease his nipples, as he'd done to her on so many occasions. He shuddered beneath her touch, pleasure radiating through him, so power surged in her veins.

'Are you sure you want to do this?' he asked, and hope was an explosion in the centre of her chest.

'Do what?' she prompted with mock innocence, blinking her blue eyes at him.

He groaned, bringing his hands to cup her buttocks, drawing her right onto the hardness she could feel through his trousers. The smile dropped from her mouth as urgency overtook her.

'I'm sure,' she agreed. 'Did you think I'd change my mind?'

'I don't know.' His smile was taut. 'You only get one chance to lose your virginity.'

'Do you think I want to wait until I'm thirty?'

'I think you might want to wait until you meet someone you're in an actual relationship with.'

'We've discussed that.' She shook her head resolutely. 'I'm no more interested in an actual relationship than you are.' Saying those words felt good. Important. Because they also felt very wrong, and she couldn't understand why, but she needed to hold onto their agreement, the pledge they'd made to one another. 'I'm only after meaningless sex, remember?'

She moved back to kissing him, need propelling anything else from her mind. It was the same for Luca. Having held off for days despite the temptation, he felt, finally, as though he were about to be unleashed and his impatience knew no bounds. He undressed Olivia as quickly as he could, not wanting to move her from his lap but needing better access to lower her pants. God, if it weren't her first time, he'd have loved to make love to her right here, like this, with her on his lap at the dining table, God help him, it would be perfection. But not for her first time.

He stood, lifting her easily, wrapping her legs around his waist as he carried her through the house, up the stairs to his bedroom, his fingers kneading her buttocks.

'I can walk,' she said on a tremulous laugh, her voice brushing his throat.

'And then I would not get to hold you like this.'

His bedroom felt like a thousand miles away. Finally, he shouldered his way through the door and placed her on the bed, bringing his body over hers, not pausing to draw breath, just needing to kiss her properly now that he could. Her hands roamed his naked torso, feeling, touching, exploring, familiarising herself with him completely; he'd never known something as simple as touch to be so incendiary. He stepped out of his pants with urgency, needing to be naked and close to her, needing her with a fire-like intensity.

Her fingers glided down his arms, latching with his, so he held her arms at her sides as he kissed her, devouring her, passionately possessing her until he pushed her back onto the bed and they fell, a tangle of limbs, legs entwined and writhing as they sought the ultimate closeness. His need for her cracked through him, contorting him, so he had to focus to remember her innocence, to hold himself back, to stop from taking her as he wanted.

But at every step, Olivia met him as an equal, so that despite her innocence she was his match, her enthusiasm giving her confidence. But it was more than that. Holding back, waiting for this, exploring each other day after day, had built to a crescendo. They'd been engaged in a torturous form of foreplay for days and nights, desire building until it reached a zenith. Her touch drove him wild, driving all ability to think from his mind. She wrapped her legs around his waist, drawing him closer, and the tip of his arousal nudged between her legs, so he groaned, long and low, aching to push into her, to feel her muscles spasm around his hard length. But caution was ingrained in Luca, so even now, while incapable of stringing two words together, he knew enough to pull up and take a moment, to stare down at her, before reaching to his bedside table and removing a condom. His eyes latched to hers as he opened the packet, then slid it over his length—an act Olivia's own gaze devoured in a way that made desire spear him from the inside out. 'Do you have any idea what you're doing to me?'

'Me?' She purred.

He laughed gruffly. 'Oh, you know *exactly* how you make me feel.'

She reached up, grabbing him by the shoulders so she could pull him back on top of her. 'Maybe a fraction of how *you* make *me* feel?'

'Is that a fact?'

'I think it might be.'

'And what about this?' He pressed himself inside her, just enough for Olivia to gasp, her eyes widening, so confused wonder crossed her features.

'Are you okay?'

She nodded, her features tense.

'Breathe,' he said gently, lowering his mouth to hers, brushing their lips as he pushed into her completely, slowly at first, giving her time to adjust to the invasion of his arousal.

Olivia tensed as pain gripped her, unexpected, immediate, but searing, like a flash of lightning in the sky, and then it was gone, giving way to slight discomfort at first, and then a warm glow of pleasure as he began to move, his arousal so deep inside her that she felt a pleasure she'd never known possible. He kissed her in time to his movements and she scratched her fingers down his back as euphoria threatened to overtake everything else.

Only the sound of her rushing blood filled Olivia's ears. She would never have said pleasure could be excruciating but, to her, that was what it felt like, as each thrust of Luca's arousal seemed to bring her both pleasure and impatience all at once. Stars formed behind her eyelids and then, out of nowhere, she was bursting apart at the seams, pleasure no longer excruciating but almost too exquisite to bear. She rolled back her head and squeezed her eyes shut as she rode the wave of release, his name on her lips, filling the silence of the room, adding to the cacophony of her own body's pleasure.

He pushed up on one elbow, scanning her eyes as if seeking reassurance, and when Olivia's breath slowed, she smiled at him, wonder and joy in her features.

But it was only a temporary reprieve and then Luca was moving again, and now his possession was hard and fast, showing Olivia how gentle he'd been the first time, how deferential to her inexperience. Pleasure had built quickly, but it was nothing compared to this. As he thrust into her again, and again, hard and fast, a primal, animalistic need spread like wildfire, so she was pushing up and rolling over, needing to be on top, to take more of him, all of him.

He growled, a low, husky sound, as he grabbed her hips, holding her deep on his length for a moment, then letting go, so Olivia controlled the rhythm, bucking and rolling hard and fast at first then moaning softly as she slowed down. His hand brushed her sex, his fingers pressing her there until the combination of his possession and his touch was too much, and she was tumbling again, over the edge of reality, into a field of utter heaven. But this time, she wasn't alone. Luca lifted his hips, taking control once more, and then he was joining her, exploding as he said her name, then pulled her down towards him, kissing her as his body was wracked with his exploding pleasure, kissing her as both morphed into something beyond what they could recognise.

'So, that's sex, huh?' She pushed up a little, to see into his eyes. Pleasure still throbbed between her legs, and she was glad he stayed inside her; she wasn't ready to lose that intimacy yet.

'Pretty much,' he responded in kind, light-hearted, both somehow understanding that they needed to contrast the intensity of what they'd just shared with the casual nature of their relationship.

'Well, I'm not sure I see what all the fuss is about,' she said with obvious sarcasm, her body still trembling with the force of her release.

He laughed softly, caught her wrists then rolled them, pinning Olivia on her back beneath him, pulling out of her so she moaned, wanting him back more than anything. 'Then perhaps you need another demonstration?'

She batted her eyelids, pretending to consider it. 'That could be useful,' she said after a lengthy pause.

'Minx.' But he laughed for as long as he was able, before taking one of her nipples in his mouth and biting down on it, hard enough to make her moan. Olivia lifted her hips, surrendering to the hedonism of this, and in the back of her mind, in the small part of her brain capable of rational thought, she was aware of how fortunate she was. She'd married a man who was teaching her the pleasure her body was capable of feeling, and in a few weeks, they'd walk away from one another—no hard feelings. It was everything she hadn't known she'd wanted, until she'd married Luca Giovanardi.

# CHAPTER NINE

'Hang on. What are you wearing?'

He turned to face her, a sardonic look of enquiry on his face that made her simmer with desire. 'Brioni, I believe.'

'A suit? But whatever for?' After all, in the week since their first time together, Olivia and Luca had barely left bed, except to eat or swim, and even then they'd been naked.

'I have a meeting and I'm pretty sure, though not one hundred per cent, that nudity would be frowned upon.'

'A meeting? With other people?' She reached out a hand, drawing him to her, her eyes an invitation Luca couldn't resist.

'With the chairman of Azzuri Bank, in fact.'

Olivia tilted her head to the side, considering that. He'd only mentioned it briefly, but she hadn't forgotten the fierce look of determination that had gripped him as he'd referred to the bank that had refused to lend money to him when he'd been starting over in life. She knew what this meeting would mean for him.

'I've been out of the office way longer than intended,'

he continued, conversationally. Calm. In control. Just like always.

'I'll take that as a compliment.'

'As it was intended.' He pressed a kiss to the tip of her nose, aware that if he didn't pull away from her, he'd start undressing, adding a delay to his schedule he couldn't afford. 'You have no need to do anything so horrible as pull on clothing. In fact, I'd suggest you don't.'

A smile tipped her lips. 'Oh? What shall I do all day, then, Luca?'

'Lie naked in bed and wait for me.' He grabbed her hand, pressing it to her sex. 'Think of me. Miss me.'

Her heart stumbled and pleasure burst through her, but it was quickly followed by a surge of panic so fierce it took all her energy to conceal any display of it. Wait for him? Think of him? *Miss him?* What happened to the independence she was fiercely chasing? To never wanting to be like her mother, so stupidly loyal and in love she forgave Thomas anything and everything?

Olivia angled her face away on the pretence of scoping out the weather. 'It's sunny again today. I might go and explore. I fear clothes will be necessary for me, too.'

'My driver can take you anywhere,' he offered, after a slight pause.

'I'd prefer to walk.'

He lifted his shoulders in a shrug then straightened. She didn't fight his departure—she'd had a wake-up call and it had been a vital, timely reminder. Do *not* depend on him. Do *not* ask him for more.

'Suit yourself. Don't get lost.'

He moved to the door, all casual, breezy, non-committal, so she felt silly for having experienced a sense of panic. They were nothing like her parents. This was nothing like their marriage. Olivia would *never* be beholden to another person as Angelica had been Thomas.

And yet, a powerful need to underscore that drove through her, so she called to him, when he was almost out of the door. 'Only three weeks to go, Luca. Let's make the most of them.'

It was the affirmation she needed, words that were a balm to her soul, even when they pulled at something in her chest, leaving her scrambling, a little, to draw sufficient breath. Life after Luca loomed, and she no longer knew exactly what shape it would take.

It was precisely because he was thinking of Olivia almost constantly that Luca remained at his desk until after seven, that evening. He was getting close to securing the deal of the century. It wasn't final yet, but he finally had the support of the chairman of the Azzuri Bank. It had taken years of delicate negotiations, but he'd done it, and there was vindication in his success. Revenge, too. Because they kicked him while he was down, and he'd sworn he'd never forget it.

He hadn't.

And now the bank would be all his; he was sure of it.

It should have been all he could think of, the success of his day's meetings monopolising his thoughts, but instead, Luca found his mind wandering to Olivia, obsessing over his memories of her in his bed, of the way she'd looked when he'd left, so beautiful, so distracting.

While it was true that he had mountains of work to

catch up on after his spontaneous wedding, honeymoon
and protracted post-honeymoon holiday here in Rome,
and that his time was therefore very well spent in the
office, it was far more accurate that he was challenging himself to resist her. Or, proving to himself that,
after a week spent almost exclusively in bed, she had no
greater hold on him now than she had on the first day
they'd met. That was to say, she was a woman he found
desirable, that he enjoyed sleeping with, who he'd walk
away from without a backwards glance when the time
came. And the time would come—more surely than
in any previous tryst—because they'd agreed on that.
Three more weeks of Olivia, and then she'd be gone
from his life, just as they both wanted.

Having worked late, Luca had every expectation that
Olivia would be at home when he returned. He was so
sure of it that he'd already started fantasising about
how it would feel to pull her into his arms and strip
the clothes from her body, to kiss her until she was a
puddle of desire, begging him to make love to her. He
stormed into the palazzo, already hard, wanting her
with a strength that should have terrified him. But it
didn't, because this was simple and clear-cut—they both
knew what they needed from this relationship.

   Only, Olivia wasn't home, and the frustration that
gripped him was dark and intense. He stopped walking,
having inspected the house thoroughly, a frown on his
handsome face. He contemplated heating himself some
dinner, going for a solo swim, just as he would have in his
pre-Olivia life, but her parting words still rang in his ears.

*'Only three weeks to go, Luca. Let's make the most of them.'*

He reached into his pocket and drew out his cell phone, dialling her number then pressing the speakerphone button, so he could begin removing his work clothes as the phone rang. She answered on the fourth ring.

'Luca, hi.'

Her voice wrapped around him like tendrils from the deep sea, threatening to drag him under. He pressed his hand to the wall, emulating a nonchalant pose.

'Where are you?'

The sound of laughter filled the phone, distant and remote.

'Out at dinner.'

'With whom?'

'Myself.'

'Why?'

'You weren't home. I presumed you were busy, and I was hungry.'

'The freezer's full.'

'When in Rome, do as the Romans do. And I took that to mean, eat out,' she said, so he could just picture her slender shoulders shrugging with casual indifference. Hunger flicked through him.

'I haven't ordered yet. Why don't you join me?'

He jerked his head once in silent agreement. 'Text me the name of the restaurant. I'll see you soon.'

She might not know the city, but Olivia had exceptional taste. She'd opted for one of the most adored restaurants in Rome. Not the fanciest, nor the predilection of the glitterati, but a place where true Romans who loved good food, wine and conversation chose to eat. And because the owner Francesco understood the value of placing beautiful patrons in the windows, Olivia had been afforded a prominent table in the centre of the glass that framed the front of the venue.

Luca approached slowly, his eyes picking her from a distance, and, owing to the fact he was coming from across the street, he had several moments to observe her while she studied the menu, a small frown on her stunning face.

She wore a black dress, simple yet elegant, with cap sleeves and a neckline that was low enough to show the smallest hint of cleavage. The dress was fitted to her waist then flared a little, to just above her knees. Her blonde hair was left out, slightly curled, and she'd applied a coat of red lipstick, completing the look of femme fatale. She was beyond beautiful; she was exquisite, a completely unique woman who was impossible to ignore. Indeed, as he moved closer, he was aware of the table behind her—a group of four men on what looked to be a business dinner—casting lingering glances in her direction, appreciating her in a way that made Luca's blood boil.

But he stamped out that reaction before it could take hold.

He had no right envying her that kind of attention. Theirs was not a real marriage, and whatever they were sharing was a very temporary state of affairs. Sleeping together didn't equate to anything more serious—they both knew that—and he was glad. If anything, it was useful to observe her like this, to see her from outside the restaurant. The symbolism didn't escape him. A physical barrier stood between them, and in a few weeks that physical barrier would be a whole other country, and then, something more significant—a divorce. Soon, they'd be strangers, just memories to one another.

As that thought hardened in his mind and heart, she looked up, her eyes landing on him, widening, before a smile curved her perfect, pouting lips.

'Hello,' she mouthed.

His own grin was slow, and felt a little discordant, but she didn't appear to notice. With a graceful shift of her hand, she indicated the chair opposite, wordlessly inviting him inside, to join her. His gut tightened with something like anticipation and then he nodded, pushing into the restaurant. *Let's make the most of this.*

'*Buonasera,*' she greeted him as he approached her table.

He dipped towards her, pressing a kiss on her cheek, lingering there longer than necessary so he could breathe her in and placate nerve endings that were firing wildly, desperate for her, for more, for everything.

'*Ciao.*'

He slid into the seat opposite, grateful that the table was small and intimate, that their knees brushed and that neither shifted to break that connection. But why would they? They'd been far more intimate than that, and yet the small contact sent a thousand flares through his body.

'How was your day?'

He'd been floating on air after leaving the office, the

success of his meeting with the Azzuri chairman puffing out his chest. But there was a light behind Olivia's eyes, a thousand lights that made her whole face shimmer, that pushed his own thoughts of his day from his mind completely. 'Fine.' He brushed it aside as though it meant nothing. 'Yours?'

'Actually, it was pretty wonderful.'

His gut rolled. 'Oh?'

A waiter appeared to take their drinks order. Olivia met his gaze, smiled, and in halting Italian proceeded to order the bottle of Prosecco she enjoyed so much.

*'Bene, signorina.'* The waiter's eyes lit up.

Luca resisted the impulse to inform the waiter that Olivia was, in fact, a *signora*. What did it matter? She was his wife, they both knew it; nothing else mattered.

He focused his attention back on her face. 'You were saying?'

'My day.' She nodded, pleating her napkin into her lap, searching for the right words. 'I went sightseeing, and I had a revelation.' She paused, and before he could prompt her to continue, the over-zealous, over-attentive waiter appeared, brandishing the Prosecco for *'signorina'*, asking in slow Italian if she would like to taste the bottle. She turned to Luca, lost, and he shook his head, delighting in taking over the conversation.

Was he seriously jealous of a waiter she didn't even know?

He blamed his naturally possessive instincts. It wasn't Olivia he was asserting a claim over, so much as their temporary, meaningless relationship.

'The bottle will suffice,' he said in his native tongue. 'Leave it; I can pour.'

The waiter disappeared with a disgruntled expression.

'What did you say to him? He seemed cross.'

Luca flattened his lips. 'It's not important. You were saying something about a revelation?'

Her eyes chased the waiter with obvious sympathy, but then she blinked back to him, watching as Luca poured a generous measure of bubbles into her flute.

'I didn't go to university, you know. I couldn't have left home. Mum depended on me, and there was too much to do anyway. We couldn't afford any help, and the house was massive.' She pulled her lips to the side, her expression one of timelessness, as though she were back in the past. 'And somewhere along the way, I suppose I've lost sight of—'

The waiter reappeared, notepad in one hand, and a pen in the other.

Luca cursed under his breath. 'Bring us whatever the chef recommends,' he bit out curtly, then, as an afterthought, to Olivia, 'Is that okay?'

Olivia looked bemused. 'Yes. I'm sure that will be fine.' She turned a megawatt smile on the waiter, and, as a result, he left somewhat mollified compared to his previous retreat.

'You're cranky.'

'I've never known a waiter to interrupt so often.'

Her eyes widened with surprise. 'I'm fairly sure that's an ordinary amount, actually.'

'It doesn't matter. You were saying?'

'Yes.' She nodded slowly, then laughed. 'What exactly was I saying?'

'Somewhere along the way, you've lost sight of something.'

'Right.' She sipped her Prosecco, closing her eyes for a brief moment, to savour the ice-cold explosion of flavour. 'I have no idea who I am.' She delivered the words with complete calm, but there was a tempest in her pale blue eyes, so he knew what a momentous pronouncement that was. 'I don't even remember what I used to want to do with my life, before my father died and everything changed. I suppose the sorts of things every child fantasises about—to become a ballerina, an astronaut, prime minister.' She wrinkled her nose and, out of nowhere, he felt as if he'd been punched, hard. He leaned closer without realising it. 'But then, as a teenager, I never really developed any other goals. I suppose I knew it would be fruitless, that I'd never be free to pursue them. I didn't plan to go to university, I simply accepted that it wouldn't be my fate. And then today, I went to Il Vaticano, and as I toured the rooms, one by one, I remembered something I buried a long, long time ago.'

He leaned forward slightly. 'Which is?'

'I love art. As a child, I used to relish creating paintings, sculptures out of clay, craft from the garden. I adored the ancient paintings that adorned the walls of Hughenwood House, many of which we've had to lease to cover the running costs,' she said with a grimace of regret. 'But it wasn't until today that it occurred to me I could actually pursue art as a career. Or *any* kind of career. Once we divorce, I'll be free for the first time in my adult life. There'll be money to go towards the maintenance of the house, even to restore it to its former glory. I can take a flat in London and go to university, albeit as a mature age student. I can have a real life, Luca.'

His frown was instinctive. 'You do not need to wait until we are divorced—'

'I know,' she interrupted, taking another sip of her drink, her enthusiasm almost as effervescent as the drink. 'I was thinking that, too. And so I decided I'd go to the Vatican every day while you're at the office, and see every bit of art, taking notes on what I like and don't like, then expand to other galleries. I'm in one of the art hubs of the world—what a place to discover myself, and work out exactly what it is I want to do with my life.'

As she spoke, her cheeks grew pink and the sparkle in her eyes took on a stellar quality.

'You're right.' He reached for his own drink, holding the stem in his hands, watching as the bubbles fizzed.

'Anyway, the point is, I'm excited. It's like I'm just realising the horizons that are opening up for me, and it's all thanks to you.'

'Not thanks to me,' he said with a shake of his head.

'Without this marriage, none of it would be possible.'

His brow furrowed as he contemplated her father's will, the barbaric terms that had seen her penalised, infantilised, punished, for no reason other than her gender.

'A regrettable circumstance.'

She tilted her head to the side, studying him for a moment before a shy smile spread over her lips. 'I don't regret it though, Luca. I really don't.'

Strangely, nor did Luca.

# CHAPTER TEN

LUCA PICKED UP his phone with the totally foreign sensation that he was floating on air, calling Olivia without a moment's thought. She answered on the third ring.

'How's *il Papa* today?'

'I haven't seen him, yet,' she responded, quick as a whip. 'But if I do, I'll tell him you said hi.'

'Careful, he probably thinks I dance with the devil as much as the rest of Italy does.'

'Then I'll disabuse him of that mistaken belief, and tell him that you're actually a bit of a guardian angel.'

What was that grinding sensation in the pit of his stomach? 'Hardly,' he demurred, but a smile crossed his face.

'Are you home?' Her simple question took on a breathy quality.

'No.' He flicked a glance at his Montblanc watch. 'I'm calling to see if you can join me for a thing tonight.'

'A "thing"?' she repeated with obvious amusement.

'My offer for Azzuri Bank has been formally accepted by the board. The announcement went out this morning, and to celebrate the news, and encourage a smooth transition, the previous owners and I will be hosting a party this evening. It's going to be quite an event—high profile, lots of celebrities and, therefore, lots of paparazzi.'

'And it would be helpful for you to have a wife on hand?' she murmured. Was that strain in her voice? He wished he weren't so attuned to her, so aware of her every mood.

'Frankly, yes.'

She was quiet for a beat too long, but when she spoke, her voice was light-hearted enough. But was it sincere? Or forced, for his sake? 'Then of course I'll come. Where?'

'I'll pick you up from home.' He didn't give it a second thought, relief whooshing through him. 'Can you be ready by eight?'

The amusement crept back into her words. 'It's two o'clock. How long do you think I'll need?'

'About thirty-seven seconds,' he agreed. 'You could pull on a hessian sack and outshine anyone else in attendance.'

The throwaway remark seemed to spark something in Olivia though. 'Hmm, but there will be a heap of people, right?'

'About two hundred.'

She let out a low whistle. 'And you said celebrities?'

'*Sì*. Clients of the bank—old Italian money, celebrities, you know the sort.'

'So the dress code is—what?'

'Conservative black tie.'

'A ball gown?'

'A dress of some sort,' he responded. 'Ideally something that will not be too complicated to remove as soon as we are home again.'

Olivia was quiet, and he hated that he couldn't see her face, because he had no idea what that silence represented. She didn't laugh at his quip.

'Okay, I'll see you at eight.'

A Cinderella moment might have been a fantasy for many women but, for Olivia, the longer she spent being transformed into a society wife, the more ice flooded her veins, until eventually, a little before eight that night, she met her reflection with sheer trepidation. Look back at her from the full-length mirror in the bedroom was a younger version of her mother.

She'd turned into what she'd always run from, what she'd been made to run from. At first, she'd planned to do her own hair and make-up, but it wasn't as though she had much experience with either, so on a whim she'd asked Signora Marazzi to book her into a salon. The chic stylist assigned to her had spoken enough English to understand what Olivia had wanted, but somehow the instructions for 'understated' had still resulted in, frankly, a work of art. It was to the stylist's credit, not Olivia's, that her face was exquisitely made up. She wore barely any foundation—*'Because your skin is so glowing, we not want to cover it, eh?'* But her eyes had been made to look like a tiger's, with delicate eyeliner slashing out at the corner, and mascara applied liberally to her naturally long lashes, so she felt as though she were a film star from the sixties. A hint of bronzer on her cheeks, and cherry red on her lips, a complete diversion from her usual, natural colour. Her blonde hair had been styled into voluptuous curls and pinned over one shoulder, the perfect complement to the dress she wore—one of the gowns that he'd given her in Venice.

Their honeymoon hadn't been that long ago, and yet, she felt as though she were a different person. Luca was so new to her then, so unknown. So much had changed—between them, and within her. She was now an entirely different person, almost unrecognisable to herself.

When she'd tried on the gown—a silk slip dress that fell to the floor, with delicate ribbons for sleeves and a neckline that revealed just a hint of cleavage, in a colour that was silver, like wet sand in the moonlight—she had wondered if she'd ever wear it. It made a little too much of her assets, showing off her rounded breasts, her neat waist and gently swollen hips, her rounded bottom. She hadn't thought she'd *ever* want to draw attention to herself, the kind of attention a dress like this demanded. And she still didn't want attention. At least, not from the crowds, not from random strangers. But from her husband?

Heat took over the ice in her body as she imagined Luca's response to the dress. For him, this was worth it.

She slid her feet into heels, the red soles just visible as she walked, grabbed a clutch purse from her dressing table and checked it for the essentials—phone, credit card, lipstick—then made her way to the top of the stairs. Purely by happenstance, the front door opened as she reached the landing, so she had a moment to observe Luca without his knowledge. He'd changed at the office, into a jet-black tuxedo and snowy white shirt, a black bow tie at his neck. It was a completely appropriate outfit and yet his primal, raw energy made a mockery of the formality of his tuxedo. Even the suit couldn't hide the fact that he had a latent energy just waiting to be expelled. Her heart leaped in instant recognition, moving from its position in her chest and somehow taking up almost all the space within her body, so its rapid beating was all she was conscious of.

She placed her hand on the railing to steady herself, her wedding ring glinting in the evening light. She stared at it for a moment—for courage?—then began to move down the stairs.

Since when had her wedding ring become an object of strength? Initially she'd viewed it as a mark of possession, something she'd resented almost as much as the necessity of this marriage, and now she took comfort from it? Olivia didn't want to analyse that—she could barely acknowledge it to herself—as though she knew danger lurked somewhere behind the realisation, a danger she didn't want to face.

Luca placed his wallet and phone on the hall stand when a slight movement caught his eye and he turned, chasing it down before anticipating that it might be Olivia. One look at her and the world stopped spinning, all the breath in his body burst from him, and his eyes seemed incapable of leaving her.

She was—there was no way to describe her. 'Beautiful' was a word he'd used before, to describe other women at other times, so there was no way he could apply it to Olivia now, because she was more magnificent, breathtaking and overwhelmingly stunning than he'd ever known a woman could be. Her eyes held his as she moved down the stairs, and with each step she took it was as though an invisible cord formed between them, knotting, putting them together inexorably, unavoidably, until she reached the bottom of the stairs and then they were both moving, his strides long and determined to her elegant.

They stopped a few feet apart. *He* stopped, because he wanted to be able to see her properly, and she stopped because she hesitated. Her eyes clouded with something like uncertainty. As though she sought reassurance. Surely not. Olivia had to know that she was the most spectacular woman who'd ever walked the earth.

'What do you think?' she asked after a moment, her eyes almost pleading with him to reassure her.

A frown pulled at Luca's mouth. What was he missing? Her hand lifted, self-consciously running over her hair, and he remembered her disclosure about the time she'd applied make-up and done her hair, for her twelfth birthday party, and her mother had overreacted. She'd never dressed up again.

Not until now.

His gut twisted at his insensitivity, at the momentousness of this night, and he ached to reassure her and comfort her, but his own body was still in a sense of shock at the sight of Olivia, so it took him a few moments longer than he would have liked.

'I wasn't sure if it was appropriate.' She dug her teeth

into her perfect, bright red lower lip and every part of him tightened. He wanted to cancel the whole damned night. He wanted to throw her over his shoulder and take her back upstairs to bed, to strip the dress from her body and destroy her perfectly curled hair, to run his fingers through it until the curls were untidy and her make-up was smudged from passion. He wanted…but that was precisely the lack of control he wouldn't allow into this marriage. It was the reason he'd been forcing himself to stick to his regular work schedule, to limit their time together. It would be so easy to forget the terms of their marriage, to allow himself to want *more* of Olivia, and he would never put himself in that position again. He established the boundaries of his life. He relied on no one. He loved *no one.* Jayne had taught him well there, and it was a lesson he never intended to forget.

'You are perfect,' he said, the word coming to him out of nowhere. But it was the right way to describe her. He reached out, running the back of his hand over her hair. She swept her eyes shut, impossibly long lashes forming half-crescents against her cheeks.

'Not too much?'

'Perfect,' he said again.

'I wasn't sure.'

Her insecurity made him simultaneously sorry for her and furious on her behalf. How could a twenty-four-year-old woman be so unsure of herself? Her mother had failed Olivia completely. She'd been denied all opportunities to experiment socially and to explore herself, so that she might know who and what she was.

And yet, somehow, Olivia had come out of it as socially adept and fascinating as anyone he'd ever known. It was only her looks that made Olivia uncomfortable, as though by dressing to attract attention she was stepping into an unknown arena, one she'd prefer not to occupy.

'You will be the most beautiful woman in the room tonight.' *And every night*, he silently added.

Ambivalence flared inside Olivia. There was pleasure at his praise, his obvious admiration, but there was also a deep sense of guilt, as though she were betraying her mother. She offered a tight smile, then looked to the door. 'Should we go?'

His eyes held hers for a beat too long. '*Sì*. And we will stay only as long as is absolutely necessary.'

There was promise in those words and it fired heat deep within her, pushing everything else aside.

Olivia was aware of Luca on a cell-deep level in every minute that passed, from the moment they exited the house until they arrived at a restaurant across from the gold-lit Coliseum, the ancient stadium taking Olivia's breath away for a moment. She wasn't aware of the photographers standing in a roped-off area to the side of the doors—she was, briefly, not even fully aware of Luca, as she stood and gaped at the sight, surrounded by the hum of evening traffic, so stately and terrific, her heart trembling as she imagined the scenes of terror that had been played out, while simultaneously admiring the craftsmanship of creating such an epic space.

'Have you ever toured it?' His breath fanned her cheek, bringing her back to the moment with a rush.

She shook her head. 'We didn't have time when I came as a child.'

'And this week you have been far too busy with the Pope,' Luca teased, reaching down and weaving their fingers together. It was such a natural gesture, Olivia had to remind herself it was all completely for show.

'That's right. Though perhaps next week,' she said, and then, with a small frown furrowing her brows, 'Definitely before I leave Rome.'

It was like the setting of a stopwatch, or perhaps simply reminding them of the incessant ticking of time in the background of their lives.

They were halfway into this marriage of theirs. Two weeks down, two weeks to go. She glanced up at him but his expression gave nothing away.

Whatever she'd been about to say flew from her mind as a photographer's bulb flashed close by and instinctively Olivia flinched closer to Luca.

'Smile through it,' he advised, squeezing her hand as they began to walk towards the doors. Questions were flung at him as they went, in Italian, so she could only pick out certain words. Corporate. Purchase. Record-breaking. Scandal. Tradition. Outcry.

It was enough to draw her gaze to his face once more, but he was implacable, as though he hadn't heard a single question.

They moved through the doors, into a restaurant that was far more charming than Olivia had expected. The tables and chairs she imagined usually filled the restaurant had been removed, leaving only a tiled floor covered in the expensive shoes of Italy's wealthiest per-

sonalities. She recognised very few of those in attendance and was glad—there were none of the nerves one
might have felt when rubbing shoulders with celebrities
you knew and admired.

'The usual.' But his voice was gruff, sparking questions inside her.

'Is there a scandal because you've bought the bank?'

'They are alluding to the scandal of my past.'

'Your father's scandal?'

'Italian society has a long memory,' he said with
a smile that didn't reach his eyes. 'Let us find you a
drink.'

The first hour passed in a whir of introductions, and,
despite the fact Luca insisted on speaking English for
Olivia's benefit, conversation switched back and forth,
from Italian to English, at breakneck speed, so she
found it almost impossible to keep up. He didn't leave
her side, nor did he drop her hand, so despite the fact
she felt completely off the deep end, she was also en-
joying herself, the spectacle, the vibe, the noise, the joy
of life. It was the sort of event she'd never attended—
something she'd read about online or seen in movies,
but to actually attend, and with the star of the show, was
actually surprisingly fun. When the room was so full
she could barely move, he turned to her.

'I have to make a speech.' He pressed a kiss to the
soft flesh just beneath her ear, sending a thousand
sparks into her bloodstream. 'It will be in Italian, but
you'll get the gist. Excuse me.'

Olivia watched as he made his way through the
crowd, his dark head inches above most, his shoulders

broad, his stride somehow cutting through the gathering of people with ease.

At the front of the restaurant, a microphone had been set up, and even before Luca approached it, the crowd grew quiet.

When he spoke, it was as though Olivia were being pressed back against a wall. She saw him as he appeared to the rest of the world, as he'd appeared to her, the first time they'd met. He was no longer Luca, the man she'd come to know so well, but a powerful, self-made tycoon with more strength, arrogance and ambition than anyone that had ever lived. The crowd was completely captivated by him, the effect of his words inspiring laughter, then nods of agreement.

She was in awe.

'You are here with Luca?' The question was unwelcome, an intrusion on a private moment between Olivia and Luca—despite the fact hundreds of people surrounded them. She blinked away from him, annoyed, meeting the eyes of a beautiful dark-haired woman.

'Yes.' She smiled crisply then turned back to her husband.

'I wondered why I had not heard from him. Have you been together long?'

'Only a couple of weeks,' Olivia said, before remembering they were supposed to be playing the part of a happily married couple.

'Then I'm sure it's almost at an end. He never strays for long.'

Hairs on the back of Olivia's neck stood on end. 'Oh?' The other woman smiled banally, but her claws were out. Olivia felt them trying to find purchase in her back.

'He will get bored of you soon enough, and then he'll be back in my bed.'

Olivia's heart slammed into her ribs. This vile, beautiful woman was right. When their marriage ended, Luca would return to his normal life, and resume his normal activities, which, Olivia gathered, included this woman. It was the expectation Olivia had come into this marriage with, and nothing had changed to affect that. So why did her throat now feel filled with sawdust?

'Perhaps.' Olivia tilted her head to the side, affecting a look of nonchalance. If there was one thing she was glad of, it was that her upbringing had equipped her with all the skills to hide how she was feeling. To an onlooker, she appeared as zen as one could get. 'That's really up to Luca.'

The reply surprised the other woman, taking the wind out of her sails completely. She left without another word. But all of the enjoyment of the night had faded for Olivia, and she couldn't say precisely why. After all, nothing had changed. She'd married Luca knowing it was fake, and temporary. They had agreed to sleep together on the basis that sex wouldn't change the cold terms of their marriage. He would go back to his life, as it had been before her, and that shouldn't bother her. So why did it? Why did Olivia suddenly feel as though she were falling into the depths of the ocean? Why did it feel as though she were drowning?

'You are very quiet.'

Olivia blinked up at Luca, annoyed at herself for not

having been able to fool him into thinking everything was fine. After all, it was fine, wasn't it?

'Perhaps I'm tired,' she offered.

Luca's eyes skimmed the room. The crowd had thinned a little, but, at almost midnight, the party was still in full swing, the voices growing louder as the alcohol intake grew.

'We'll leave.'

'We don't have to,' she demurred with a shake of her head.

He leaned closer, breathing into her ear. 'I want to. We've stayed far longer than I intended. Let's go home.'

It was such a simple, oft-repeated phrase. It meant nothing. But when Luca referred to 'home', a hole formed right in the middle of Olivia's heart, because his wonderful property in the heart of Rome was not, and never would be, her home. That was in England, the dreaded Hughenwood House, and soon Olivia would have to return there. Not for long, but initially, to sort out their business affairs and launch herself into a new life. Uncertainty made her stomach off-kilter. It was the future she'd longed for, the future she'd fought damned hard for, even marrying a total stranger to achieve, so why did it stand before her like a pit of lava she was now obliged to cross?

# CHAPTER ELEVEN

'DID YOU ENJOY yourself last night?'

Olivia flipped her face on the pillows, eyeing Luca with a sardonic expression. 'Are you taking a victory lap, Signor Giovanardi?'

He frowned.

'I should have thought my enjoyment—on multiple occasions—was self-evident.'

He roared with laughter, lifting a hand and pressing it to his forehead. 'That is, naturally, very gratifying, but actually, I was asking about the party.'

'Oh.'

*He will get bored of you soon enough.*

She covered the glut of displeasure and the strange taste that filled her mouth with a steady smile. She hadn't been able to push the other woman from her mind, not for long, anyway.

'It was…fascinating.'

He grinned, lifting onto one elbow and regarding her thoughtfully. 'Fascinating? What exactly does this mean?'

'Oh, just unlike anything I've ever experienced.'

'Surely you've been to parties?'

She studied the ceiling, lost in thought. 'Not a lot, actually. As a teenager, a few casual things, but after that, not really.'

'You really have lived the life of a recluse.'

'Yes.'

'And after this?'

She turned to look at him, then wished she hadn't. Her heart clutched, echoing the worst indigestion she'd ever known. She'd been trying so hard not to think about 'after'. Why did he have to bring it up? 'What do you mean?'

'What will your life be like?'

She really didn't want to think about it. 'I don't know.' She inched closer, her body craving him despite the hours they'd spent exploring one another the night before. In the back of her brain, she imagined nights without Luca, and wondered how she'd cope, how her body would cope, without him.

'Is this normal?' She blurted the question out before she could second-guess the wisdom of asking him something so telling.

'Our life here?'

*Our life.* Pain sheared her chest. She blinked away, focusing beyond him. 'No, I mean…' She swallowed past a lump of embarrassment.

'*Si?*'

'Erm…sex. The way it is with us…is it always like this?'

He reached out, pressing a finger to her chin, drawing her gaze back to his face. 'No.'

Something shifted inside her. She bit down on her lower lip.

'At least, not in my experience.'

'How is it different?'

'Now who's taking a victory lap?'

'Is that what I'm doing?' she murmured. 'I wouldn't know. I have zero experience.'

'That's true.' He moved closer, so their hips met, his arousal pressing to her, and fierce heat flashed in her body.

*'He bores easily.'*

The question shaped in her mouth, but she found it almost impossible to ask. Shyness stole through her, even as they lay together, naked, far from strangers, so she couldn't simply ask him about the other woman, about what their relationship was. Or was it that Olivia didn't want to hear the answer? Was it that she couldn't bear to hear the answer? And if so, why was that? Where was the cold dispassion she'd been banking on? When was the last time she'd been with Luca and not felt as though a part of her were burning alive? And why did she suddenly want to grab hold of him with both hands and never let go?

Stricken, she could only stare at him, as her brain kept throwing questions at her, forcing her to face reality, to answer them, to acknowledge that what was supposed to be a straightforward marriage agreement was suddenly so much more complex.

A buzzing pierced the room, so Olivia glanced at Luca's bedside table first, where his phone sat with a dark screen, then over her shoulder to her own bedside table. Her sister's face filled the front of the device. She reached for it gratefully. Saved by the bell.

'It's Sienna,' she said crisply. 'If it were anyone else, I'd leave it…'

His eyes sparked as though filing away that piece of information, but Olivia was already rolling away, disappointment curdling inside of her at the distance between them.

'Hey, Sisi.'

'Libby! What the heck is going on?'

Familiarity was a new kind of warmth, running over Olivia, at the sound of her childhood nickname. 'What do you mean?'

'Are you actually engaged to Luca Giovanardi?'

Olivia sat upright, her eyes bolting to Luca's.

'Why do you ask?'

'Because it's in the papers. Mum's beside herself, which, I have to say, is actually kind of funny, but then, you did look ridiculously beautiful in the photos and you know she hates that.'

'What photos?'

'Have you not been online today?'

'No, I—' She glanced at the time and pulled a face. It was later than she'd realised. 'Haven't had a chance.'

'Well, there are enough gossip pieces about you and Luca Giovanardi to keep you busy a while. Speculation that you're engaged—even married.' Sienna's voice lowered to a hushed, earnest tone. 'I know about dad's stupid will, Libby. You really did it, didn't you?'

*What else could I have done?* She didn't ask it, because the answer was simple. Leave them living in destitution. Leave her mother paying the price of her father's cruelty for the rest of her life? Or worst of all, leave it to Sienna to get married before the deadline and improve their fortunes? None of those options were possible. This marriage was all Olivia could do, and yet she didn't resent it. She sure as hell didn't regret it.

'What else are the papers saying?'

'Let me see.' Olivia could imagine Sienna clicking open her iPad. 'There's a ton of pictures, all very nice. A bit of background on Luca, some scandal with his father a long time ago, his very, very varied dating past, including photos of—phwoar, did you know he used to date Elizabeth Mason?'

Olivia tried not to conjure images of the stunning American actress—and failed, so all she could see was Luca and Elizabeth, and what a beautiful pair they'd make. Jealousy gripped her, hard.

'There's a close-up of your hand—nice ring, by the way. And— Oh. This is a new article.'

Olivia tensed. 'What is it?'

'"In response to fierce speculation that one of Italy's most eligible bachelors has been removed from the market for good, Luca Giovanardi's grandmother Pietra has released a short statement confirming the marriage. 'My grandson has finally found happiness, and with a woman who is quite his perfect match. I am very pleased for them both.'"'

All the air whooshed out of Olivia.

'You *are* married?' Sienna squeaked. 'Tell me this isn't true?'

Olivia scrunched up her face, aware that Luca was watching her intently. 'It's true.'

'Oh, Libby. Darling, you didn't have to do this.'

'Didn't I?' She turned to face Luca and her heart jolted in her chest. *Didn't I?*

He reached out, putting his hand on her knee, a question in his eyes. She looked away. Questions were all she could feel now, questions about her choices, her feelings, and, most importantly, her desires. Because knowing their marriage was coming to an end felt like the slow dropping of an executioner's blade, and she desperately wanted to slow it, or to stop it altogether. She could barely breathe.

'No! This is for the money, isn't it? Oh, Libby. Why didn't you talk to me about this? We could have worked something out.'

Olivia compressed her lips. She'd shielded Sienna from the worst of their financial situation, protecting her sister from the truth of just how bad things had been for them, but the truth was they'd have been ruined if she hadn't gone through with this.

'Let's discuss it when I'm home.'

'And when will that be?'

'Two weeks. A little less.' Her heart splintered, her lungs burned.

'And will your *husband* be coming?' She layered the word with cynical disapproval and the bite of disapproval from kind-hearted Sienna hurt like hell—almost as much as the realisation that Luca wouldn't be joining her on that trip, or any other, once their brief arranged marriage was at an end.

'No. I'll come alone.' Her voice cracked a little. She swallowed to clear the hoarse feeling in her throat. 'I'll talk to you later, Sisi.'

She disconnected the call and pasted a determinedly bright smile on her face. 'Well, that went about as well as could be expected.'

'You didn't tell her about any of this?'

'No.'

'Why not?'

'Because I didn't think she would approve, and if anyone can talk me out of anything, it's my sister.'

Olivia placed the phone down and stared straight ahead, at the wall across the room.

'And were you right? Does she not approve?'

'It doesn't sound like it.' She pleated the sheet between her forefinger and thumb. 'Sienna is the kindest person you'll ever meet, but I've tried very hard to keep her from understanding the ins and outs of our family's financial predicament.'

'So you alone have borne this worry?'

Olivia tilted him a steady look. 'I'm the oldest.'

Disapproval marred his features. 'Your parents have failed you.'

She pulled a face. 'Look who's talking.'

'Perhaps that's why I can recognise the signs so easily.' He reached out, drawing her down to him then bringing his body over hers. 'You deserved so much better, Olivia.'

Their eyes met and understanding passed between them, a fierce sense of agreement, and then his head lowered, his mouth seeking hers, gently at first, as if to reassure her through his kiss, and then with urgency, passion overtaking them. Already naked, he simply pushed aside the sheet between them, and drove into her, so Olivia cried out with pleasure at his immediate, urgent possession, his arousal filling her, moving fast, deep, his rhythm demanding, explicit, exactly what she needed.

'It is not always like this,' he promised against her mouth, reminding her of their earlier conversation. 'I find I cannot get enough of you.'

Pleasure curled through her as his words mixed with the physical sensations he was arousing with such need, until she was incandescent with heat and fever, building to an unavoidable release, perfectly coinciding with his own explosion.

'I can't get enough of you either,' she admitted, when their breathing had slowed and he'd rolled onto his back, bringing her with him, so her head lay on his chest. His heart thumped heavily beneath her. *I can't get enough of you, but, eventually, this will have to be enough.* Their marriage would come to an end, and, while she was regretting that, there was a part of Olivia that was also glad. There was a danger here she hadn't appreciated at first, a danger of wanting so much more from Luca than she'd originally anticipated—and he was just the kind of man who would swallow her whole.

Olivia knew that love was a very dangerous force, and she'd always sworn she would avoid it, rather than turn into the kind of woman her mother had become, in the service of love. She just hadn't appreciated that love was a force all of its own, that it could chase after you when you had no intention of being caught, that it could bombard you and threaten to wrap around you unless you were ever, ever vigilant. And being vigilant while in the arms and bed of Luca Giovanardi was proving almost impossible.

Soon, it would be over, and she'd be able to breathe again. Wouldn't she?

'My grandmother has asked us to visit her for a night or two. Do you have any objections?'

Olivia met Luca's questioning gaze as she stepped out of the shower. He stood draped against the bathroom door jamb, his presence not an invasion so much as a sign of the intimacy she'd begun to accept as totally normal. In the back of her mind, a warning bell was almost constantly sounding, the small incursions something she knew she should fight back against. After all, she'd always sworn she'd maintain her independence and autonomy, but with Luca all her barriers were being eroded—and she didn't seem to mind. But there was no threat here. No danger. They knew when and how their relationship would end. She would never turn into her mother, no matter how much she surrendered to him, and this.

Ever-hungry, her gaze feasted upon his physique, her mouth drying as it always did when she allowed herself to drool.

'Olivia? Eyes up here.'

Guilt flushed her cheeks. 'Of course not. It's one of the main reasons we married.' She answered his question with a hint of embarrassment at having been caught out. But he laughed and prowled towards her, whipping the towel from her body.

'My turn.' He stepped back, and his own inspection

of her was so much slower, his gaze travelling from the tip of her head to her toes and back again, lingering on her curves, her most intimate body parts, until her breath was coming in pants.

'Luca.' The word burst from her.

'I know.' His eyes flashed with an emotion she didn't understand and then he drew her into his arms, kissing her soundly. A kiss was never enough, though. It was the flicking of a switch, the lighting of a torch that had to be burned down completely before it could be released. She kissed him back with full comprehension of that, her body cleaved to his, naked, hungry, yearning, as his hands reached behind her back and pressed her to him. She ground her hips to him, and heard the sharp expulsion of air, and then he was pulling apart, fire in his eyes as he glared down at her, heat in his cheeks.

He dropped to his knees and she groaned, because at first she thought he was ending what they shared, but then he separated her legs and brought his mouth to her sex, kissing her and whipping her into a frenzy, so she had to brace her palms on the marble counter, head tilted backwards, vaguely aware of what a wanton sight she must make—and not giving even half a damn. How could she care about anything but pleasure when there was pleasure such as this?

'Signora Giovanardi, thank you for coming.'

'My husband's message said it was important?'

The assistant nodded. 'Signor Giovanardi is just concluding a meeting and has asked you to wait in his office. This way, please.' The deference with which Olivia's assistants treated her brought a smile to Olivia's lips, but she was aware, all the time, of how temporary this was. When she wanted to savour every moment of their marriage, instead it was rushing towards its conclusion, seconds passing in a blur, days flicking by, so that she knew there was barely any time left.

She fell into step beside the receptionist, and, at the door to Luca's office, dredged up something like a smile. 'Thank you.'

'Would you like anything to drink? Tea? Coffee? Wine?'

Olivia suppressed a smile at the Italian indulgence for a lunchtime *aperitivo*. 'A mineral water would be lovely, thank you. It's warm out there today.'

'Indeed. Summers in Rome are unbearably humid.'

Olivia thought of the dark, dank hall at Hughenwood House, contrasting it to the sun-filled streets she'd traversed on the walk to Luca's office. 'I think it's lovely,' she murmured as the assistant left the room.

When she was alone, curiosity got the better of her, and she wandered towards his desk first, admiring the spotless work environment. No clutter, no personal effects, no photographs, just a laptop, and a Manilla folder with the word 'Singapore' on the side. She ran a finger over the top then eyed the boardroom table. Several more folders sat here. She moved to them out of idle curiosity and pulled up short when she saw her name on the side of one.

*THORNTON-ROSE*

Another folder, beside it.

*HUGHENWOOD HOUSE*

And another.

*PORTFOLIO*

Heart thumping, she was torn. It was abundantly obvious that these folders pertained to her, and her business, and yet she felt like a snoop to open them and look inside. Torn, she prevaricated and a moment later the door opened. She looked up, expecting to see his assistant, only to be met by the appearance of Luca, striding in with sheer, obvious impatience, his shirt unbuttoned at the collar, his hair tousled as though he'd been driving his fingers through it all morning.

He stopped short when their eyes met, a grim line on his lips before he changed direction and closed the distance. The door opened once more, and the receptionist followed with a tray—two coffees, a bottle of mineral water, and a plate of biscotti.

'Thank you,' Luca dismissed, without looking in his assistant's direction.

Once they were alone again, he lifted a coffee cup and extended it to Olivia. Their fingers brushed and sparks shot through her, sparks she might have imagined would have faded by now, but which had, instead, intensified, overtaking her completely. She took the coffee on autopilot, staring at the golden liquid a moment.

She hadn't wanted a coffee, but now that it was in her hands, she took a sip, relishing the strong, bitter flavour.

'You left a message for me to meet you here,' Olivia reminded him, wondering at the strange sense of hesitation—an emotion she hadn't felt a moment ago. But seeing the folders had unsettled her—it was as if her old life was slipping into the room with them, reminding her forcibly of why they'd married. It was a reminder she resented.

'Yes.' He looked awkward. Her heart went into overdrive. Was she here to discuss their marriage? They still had a little over a week left. Surely they didn't have to talk about the end just yet? She knew she was living in a fantasy land but Olivia wasn't ready to face the practicalities of leaving him—yet. When the time came, she would. She'd be strong, just as she had been at every other time in her life where strength was required, but for the moment she wanted to blot out the path ahead. Unless…what if he wanted to change the terms of their agreement? What if he wanted to extend things? Hope was an unstoppable force, exploding in her chest. She dug her fingernails into her palms, waiting, wishing, wondering…

'I'd like to discuss your finances,' he said with quiet control. 'Or rather, their ongoing management.'

Olivia could have been knocked over with a feather. 'Oh.' *Was that all?*

'I'm sorry to say, yet not surprised, I admit, that the lawyers handling your father's estate are as misogynistic as he evidently was. I was contacted earlier in the week and advised that I could collect this information on your behalf, now that we are legally married.'

'They've been ignoring my calls,' she said with a sigh.

'Bastards.'

'You're angry?'

'Aren't you?'

'Well, yes, of course.'

'I cannot see any God-given reason you should require your husband to collect your own financial documents,' he responded curtly, his anger obviously not directed at her.

Olivia's heart skipped a beat. His support was something she hadn't known she needed.

'I know financial independence is your goal and I'm sorry I've had to be involved in obtaining this information—however, these files contain everything you'll need to know about your family's business affairs. The money that is now yours, how it is invested, as well as other investments that will pass to you.'

Olivia blinked, her stomach twisting.

'There is also information pertaining to your sister's inheritance.'

'Thank you.'

His eyes narrowed, darkening. 'Don't thank me, Olivia. You should never have needed me, for any of this.'

Her heart swelled. 'But it's not your fault that I did. And I am grateful to you, Luca.'

His mood didn't improve and warmth spread through

her. It was a sign of his decency and loyalty that he was so incensed.

'Please, have a look.' He gestured to the files. 'I will be working over here, and am happy to answer any questions you have. Alternatively, I have the name of an excellent financial advisor, and can put you in touch. Just let me know.'

He nodded curtly, all business, so she wanted to start removing her clothing, piece by piece, to jolt him back to the intimacy they shared, the heat that exploded between them. And yet, how could she overlook this gesture? He was making everything as easy as possible for her. Right down to offering help without presuming she'd need it. He wasn't mansplaining things to her, but rather allowing her to find her own feet, waiting until she asked for assistance, but letting her know it would be freely given. It was the perfect gesture, and she was touched, right to the centre of her core; even, she feared, to the centre of her heart.

# CHAPTER TWELVE

'How come you didn't tell me?'

He paused, carrying her holdall over one shoulder as though it weighed nothing. 'Tell you what?'

Olivia wrinkled her nose. 'Well, that this place would be so—'

They looked around the entrance with its turquoise walls just visible behind dozens of paintings, each showing a different landscape or still life. The floor was large, marble tiles, and in the centre of the ceiling, a chandelier hung, ornate and—Olivia guessed—original to the history of the house. The exterior walls were a washed pink, and the garden was every bit as bright as the home suggested—exotic splashes of colour every which way.

'Extra? Over the top? Garish?'

'Perfect,' Olivia said on a sigh.

'I knew I liked you.' Nonna appeared from behind them, unseen and unannounced, her slender frame elegant in black trousers and a lemon-yellow blouse. Her hair was coiffed into a bun, high on her head, and a daisy pin that sparkled with, Olivia presumed, real diamonds gave the hairstyle some fun and glamour. 'Don't pay my grandson any attention. He's all about bland, modern aesthetic, whereas I prefer—' She swept a manicured hand around the entrance.

'Psychedelic vomit?' Luca drawled with a grin, so Olivia suspected this sort of sparring was the norm for them.

'Evidence of a life well lived.' Pietra winked at Olivia then embraced her, kissing both cheeks. 'I'm so happy you could join me. Come, I'll give you a tour.' She fixed Luca with a glare that was mock irritated. '*You* can put the bags in the room.'

He did a navy salute and Olivia couldn't help chuckling to herself as she was led away by Pietra. The entranceway was really just a hint of the bright, joyous décor throughout. Each room boasted a bright colour scheme, cheerful and somehow cohesive. Despite the fact there could be, in some rooms, blue walls and green curtains, there was always an element that drew it together, such as a sofa with matching cushions that picked up the colour scheme across the entire room, so it was far less chaotic and more harmoniously happy.

'It is a beautiful home.' Olivia sighed as they finished the tour on a balcony with black wrought iron and an abundance of red geraniums, which tumbled from their terracotta pots towards the pool below.

'Thank you. I am pleased you like it. In fact, may I make a confession?'

Olivia nodded slowly.

'I was nervous this morning.'

'Nervous?' Olivia's smile spread over her face. 'Whatever for?'

'That you might, perhaps, not like my home. That you might not want to come.' Nonna's eyes sailed across the countryside, fixing on Positano, sprawled beneath them. 'You see, Luca's all I have, and I couldn't bear it if you and I were anything other than friends. There is not so long left for me, and I want to enjoy the time I have—'

Emotions burst through Olivia, chief amongst them grief that none of this was real. Nonna was offering genuine friendship and Olivia knew it would never really come to pass. Her fake marriage was almost over. After this weekend, Olivia was quite sure she and Pietra would never see one another again. She blinked back a rush of tears and focused on saying what Nonna obviously needed to hear.

'I don't think my marriage would survive if I did anything to alienate you. I know how much you mean to Luca.' She couldn't acknowledge the older woman's reference to her mortality.

'And he to me.' Pietra reached out, tapping a hand on Olivia's. 'And you, *carina*. I never thought, after Jayne, that he would allow himself to love. It was such a bad time in his life, such a hard time for him all round, let alone dealing with her awful treatment. He pushed everyone away, even me, for a long time. I honestly believed I was going to lose him.'

Olivia regarded the older woman thoughtfully. 'Was it really so bad?'

'Oh, worse than you can even imagine. Every friend deserted him. My son swindled them all, you see. No, not every friend. There was one—Alejandro—who stuck by Luca. A man worth his weight in gold. But everyone else, including Jayne, turned their backs on him.' She waved a hand in the air, as if to dispel the recollection of such an unhappy time. 'And now, with you, he is happy. He is himself. Thank you.'

Olivia was overwhelmed—with emotions at the compliment, with guilt because it wasn't real, and then with sadness because she wanted, more than anything, for all of this to be true. The thought struck her like a lightning bolt, but it didn't come completely out of the blue. No, there had been precipitation and storm clouds building for days, suggesting that nothing was as it had first appeared, that everything had changed since their fateful wedding. There was also a jealousy—unmistakable now—for Luca's first wife. A woman he'd once loved, loved enough to have been destroyed by. Loved enough to have sworn off love and relationships evermore.

'And you are happy,' Nonna continued, then winced. 'Or you were, until I started to meddle.'

'Not meddle.' Olivia shook her head. 'I'm just… touched…that you have such faith in us.'

'Who that has seen you together could fail to have faith? And I must believe, you see, because soon I will be gone, and I do not want him to be alone.' Her voice cracked. 'Luca acts so tough, as though he doesn't need anyone, but when I look at my grandson, I still see the little boy I used to bounce on my knee. I want the best for him, *carina*.' Nonna's voice was a little wobbly and she pulled away with a determined effort to laugh. 'But enough of this. I am being too maudlin; Luca would not approve.' She straightened, making an obvious attempt to appear relaxed. 'You must go and explore the town while it is daylight.' She waved a hand towards the exceptional view of Positano. 'Dinner is served at six—I am afraid I eat unfashionably early these days; my medication makes me tired.' Before Olivia could offer a comment of condolence, Pietra pushed on, 'But it leaves you free to do something wonderful tonight, afterwards, no?'

Positano defied every single one of Olivia's expectations. It was prettier than a postcard, with the buildings carved into the cliff-face, a tumbling mix of colourful houses, terracotta roofs and the backdrop of greenery that grew beyond it. She walked beside Luca as he traced the well-worn path he'd traipsed as a child and teenager, pointing out interesting titbits as they went, until finally they began to descend, steep steps carrying them towards the beach and the busy main street that ran parallel to it. Cafes spilled out with tables and umbrellas playing host to a mix of elegant locals and happy, loud tourists. The boutiques boasted beautiful clothes and homewares, so Olivia scanned each with growing interest as they walked.

'Hungry?'

She only realised, as he asked the question, that she hadn't eaten all day. Never a big breakfaster, she'd woken with butterflies in her tummy at the prospect of travelling to Nonna's home, and the idea of remaining for an entire weekend. Of course, she shouldn't have worried, and now that she'd met Pietra again, the nerves had abated, and her hunger had returned.

'Actually, yes. Shall we grab something light? Nonna said dinner is served at six.'

He pulled a face so Olivia laughed softly. 'She also said that eating early leaves us free to do something wonderful after dinner...'

His expression relaxed immediately, speculation darkening his eyes. 'She's very clever.' He pulled Olivia against him, kissing her right there in the middle of the street, where tourists milled about them and the sun beat down, warm and golden.

Breathless, Olivia pulled away, something like hope trembling in her mind. This marriage was nothing like they'd planned for. 'Where do you suggest?'

'I know just the place.'

She smiled. 'Of course you do.'

In Positano, Luca was treated like royalty. He knew many of the shopkeepers, who came out to shake his hand as he passed, and each of the restaurant owners gestured towards tables, inviting them in, but he smiled, offered a kind word, a promise for 'next time', then continued onwards, until they arrived at a quaint trattoria— little more than a hole in the wall, with a green awning, a narrow door and six small tables set up inside. Each table had a round-based wine bottle with a candle in its top, the legs of wax running down towards the table.

'Gianni, *ciao*,' Luca greeted.

Olivia smiled through the introductions, tried to keep up with the Italian and then took the seat that was offered—affording a beautiful view, not of the beach, but of a small garden at the back of the restaurant, where a single bougainvillea had grown up to form a canopy of explosive purple flowers. Beneath it, there was a pot with a lemon tree, and as she watched a woman walked out, round and dimpled all over, wearing a dark blue apron, and plucked two lemons from the tree. When she turned around and saw Olivia watching, she winked, smiled so dimples dug into her rounded cheeks, then disappeared into a timber door with peeling red paint.

'Oh, Luca.' She turned to look at him, emotions welling in her chest. 'This is all so beautiful.'

He looked around, as though that had never really occurred to him. 'It's very traditional.'

'I love it.'

'I'm glad.'

The waiter appeared with some menus, and Luca explained the dishes to Olivia, translating the words and phrases directly.

'Tortellini—called this because they are like little cakes—torta—filled with cheese and spinach.' He moved his finger down the menu. 'Chicken with lemon and asparagus.'

She selected something light and sat back in her chair, watching him thoughtfully.

'Yes?' He lifted a thick, dark brow, continuing to study her.

Guilt flushed her face. 'What do you mean? I didn't say anything.'

'You have your "question" eyes in.'

'My "question" eyes?'

'How you look at me when something is on your mind. So? Out with it.'

She wanted to laugh, but also nerves were thickening her veins, making it hard to think straight. 'You—'

Gianni reappeared, brandishing two glasses of Prosecco, and two glasses of mineral water.

'Thank you,' she murmured.

When they were alone, Luca continued to stare at her, waiting, one brow cocked.

She flattened her lips. 'You don't have to answer this,' she said gently. 'I know we agreed that neither of us has to share our life story.'

'We did.' He inclined his head in silent agreement of that.

'Only, Pietra mentioned something about Jayne.'

He scowled. 'Did she?'

'Don't be cross with her.'

'I'm not. But I told you she meddles, no?'

'Yes, but only because she loves you so much.'

'And you have a question about my first wife?'

She knew him well enough to know he hated the idea of talking about her, but he stared straight at Olivia, holding her gaze. Fearless. Determined. In control.

'It's not really a question.' She furrowed her brow. 'Only...you must have loved her very much.'

He gripped the stem of his Prosecco flute until his knuckles glowed white. 'Why do you say that?'

'Am I wrong?'

He glared at her, and she knew he wanted to avoid the question, but this was Luca. He didn't shy away from difficult conversations. With a small exhalation of breath, he shifted in his seat, his pose a study in relaxation. Only Olivia could see beyond it, to the tension radiating from his frame.

'I was young and idealistic.'

'So you didn't love her?'

His nostrils flared. 'I would have died for her. I loved her with all that I was, Olivia. But I think, at that age, love felt like a rite of passage. I can't say that I would feel that way for her if we met now.'

Something like danger prickled along Olivia's spine. 'Or for anyone?'

He dipped his head in agreement, without hesitation, and it was that lack of pause that cut her to the quick. If he felt anything for her, she would have seen it then.

'And you believed she loved you?'

Cynicism curled his lips. *'Naturalmente.'* The word dripped with sarcasm. 'It never occurred to me that she was using me for money.'

Indignation flared in Olivia's gut. 'I can't imagine anyone fooling you.'

'I'm not the same man now that I was then.'

'Because of her?'

'Because of life.'

'But Jayne is the reason you've sworn off relationships.'

'I have relationships. You've seen the pictures on the Internet, remember?'

Pain lashed her heart. She forced herself to be brave. 'That's sex. I'm talking about emotion. I'm talking about connection.'

There was a storm raging in his eyes but he didn't look away. 'Sex is the only kind of relationship I'm interested in.'

'Doesn't that get lonely?'

His lips curled into an approximation of a smile, but it spread like ice through her veins. 'Are you lonely, *cara*?'

Beneath the table, his fingers sought her knee first, then higher, to her thigh, shifting the fabric of her skirt with ease so he could touch his skin to hers. She bit back a soft moan.

'What we have is just sex, and yet it suits us both perfectly, no?'

No. She wanted to scream her answer. She wanted to scream it at him as she punched his chest, but how could she? He hadn't said anything wrong. It was perfectly in line with what they'd agreed.

'And after this, you'll find someone else to have "just sex" with?'

It was like laying down a gauntlet, forcing them both to face a reality that Olivia personally wanted to hide from.

Her blood began to hammer inside her, and she could hardly breathe. She waited, and she waited, and agony invaded her every cell, until finally, he shrugged indolently. 'As, I imagine, will you.'

Olivia focused on the view beyond the window, doing everything she could not to react, not to recoil, when the truth was the idea of another man ever making love to her was like setting herself alight. She couldn't fathom it, and she knew, in that moment, that he was wrong. Luca Giovanardi would likely be the only man she ever slept with.

The water rippled against Olivia's breasts, the Lycra of her bathing suit turning an almost copper colour in the pale moonlight. Positano was a patchwork of lights beneath them, the view of the city and, beyond it, the ocean quite mesmerising. Luca came to rest beside her, standing easily against the pool's tiled bottom.

He cast her a smile and the moonlight met his face, bathing it in silver, so he was breathtakingly beautiful. It was an almost perfect moment. Almost, because Olivia couldn't blot out their conversation over lunch. She couldn't ignore the ease with which he faced the prospect of their separation, while she was aware, all the time, of the beating of a drum in the back of her mind, a constant, rhythmic motion, propelling her through time, almost against her will.

In less than a week, she'd leave Italy, and Luca. She had to. It was what they'd agreed. It was what he still wanted. *And what do you want?*

She wanted, with all her heart, to stay. It terrified Olivia to admit that to herself, but she wasn't an idiot. She knew what had been happening the last few weeks. Every look, every touch, every moment they shared had been drumming deep into her soul, making him a part of her in a way she'd sworn she'd never allow any man to be.

That was why she had to leave in a week.

Marriage to a man like Luca was too dangerous. He was too much—too easy to love, and she knew what love did. Her parents had shown her again and again. It was the most powerfully destructive force in the universe, capable of wreaking so much havoc and anger. She'd never allow that to happen to them. It would hurt like hell to leave Luca but at least she could leave while things were still great between them, and carry with her cherished memories of their time together. That was so much better than waiting for their love to turn to hate. She couldn't bear that.

'I came to live with my grandmother, after my divorce. I used to love this view.'

'Used to?'

'Still do,' he murmured, and her heart lurched in her chest.

'What was it like, living here?'

'It was exactly what I needed,' he said, after a beat, and she understood his hesitation—that he was contemplating pushing her to share what was on her mind. She was relieved he didn't.

'In what way?'

'Here, I was able to immerse myself in nature for a time, to strip everything away and focus on simply existing. I would walk to Positano almost every day, take out an old timber boat, catch fish that Pietra and I would eat for lunch, right here on this terrace. I would free dive for scallops, and swim through the caves at the edge of Positano. I walked until my skin burned from the sun, and until my legs were like jelly. I did everything I could to silence my brain, my thoughts, to blot out the real world.'

'What about your friends?'

A snarl curled the corner of his mouth. 'My father's actions affected almost everyone I knew.'

Anger pulsed in her veins. 'So they took it out on you?'

A muscle jerked in his jaw. 'Many lost their fortunes.'

'But you repaid them.'

He lifted his shoulders.

'Your grandmother mentioned one friend who stood by you. I can't remember—'

'Alejandro.'

'You're still friends?'

'More like brothers,' Luca agreed. 'He was the only one. I will always be grateful to him, for standing with me.' He turned away from her, his eyes roaming the horizon. She followed his gaze, the beauty stinging now. It was the last time she'd see it.

'Thank you for bringing me here.' Her voice was hoarse; she cleared her throat. 'I like your grandmother, a lot. I'm sorry I won't get to know her better.'

The air between them grew taut. She heard the unspoken implication of that sentence. The inevitable was coming.

'She would have liked to get to know you, too.'

'When will you tell her about our divorce?'

His features gave nothing away, but he turned towards her slowly, his eyes probing hers, as if to read something in her question, something she couldn't see or say.

'When I have to.'

'You'll continue the charade?'

He frowned. 'It's not exactly a charade.'

'You know what I mean. You'll pretend I'm still here, even when I'm back in England?'

'I simply won't tell her anything at all,' he corrected, then made an effort to soften his words. 'She'll be okay, *cara*. She is used to my short attention span with women.' His smile was barely a flicker of his lips, and the coldness of it turned her core to ice. Not because of Luca, but because of her father, and his supreme control of his emotions, because of the way he could turn on a dime.

He was wrong about Pietra. He clearly didn't understand how relieved the older woman was that Luca had, apparently, fallen in love. He didn't know what their marriage meant to her. The peace she would get on her deathbed, of believing that he was no longer such a determined loner.

Olivia shivered, despite the balmy warmth of the night. Everything about their surroundings was perfect, but she was cold to the core. 'I think I'll go inside, Luca. I'm tired.'

He watched her swim away, fighting a desire to follow her, to draw her back into the water or to follow her inside. They'd been spending too much time together, despite his best efforts to guard against that. She was putting space between them—and that was wise. The smartest thing to do was to go along with it. After all, in less than a week they'd be living different lives in different countries.

## CHAPTER THIRTEEN

As a child, Luca had never counted the sleeps until Christmas, or birthdays, or any life event, and yet he was aware, every minute of the day, of the nights remaining with Olivia, and he resented her that power, he resented their marriage for how easily it had become a part of him. For a man used to living alone, having Olivia at his side was strangely perfect.

Because she was undemanding.

Because she was temporary.

Because there was no risk that she would want more than he could give, that he might come to love her or she might come to love him. The black-and-white agreement they'd made offered protection, and in that protected space he'd come to *enjoy* her company.

His phone began to ring and he glared at it sharply. He wasn't in the mood for interruptions. He ignored it, standing up and striding to his windows, looking down on Rome.

Three more nights. And then what?

And then what? He berated himself angrily. And then, life would continue as it had before. She'd leave, he'd be alone, but he'd be fine—alone was a state he was perfectly used to.

\* \* \*

'I've let my assistant know you'll need to use the jet over the weekend.'

Midway through lifting a fork to her mouth, Olivia paused, replacing the bite in her bowl. 'Oh?'

'For your return to the UK. That was the date we agreed, yes?'

Her heart skittered around her chest cavity like an ice skater out of control. She focused on her plate extra hard, staring at the pasta dish until the noodles began to swirl before her eyes. *Don't cry. Don't emote. Don't express anything.* Suddenly she was eight years old again, caught between her father and her mother, in the midst of one of their terrible arguments. She tried to fade into the background then took in a deep breath and pushed a smile to her lips, forcing her eyes to meet his. 'Yes, that's right. But I don't need a jet. I booked a commercial flight ages ago, before we were even married.'

Was she imagining the way he expelled a rushed breath? Was it a sigh of relief? Or of something else?

'I see.' He took a drink of wine, then replaced the glass quietly on the table. 'You can cancel it.'

Her eyes widened. Hope danced.

'My jet is at your disposal.'

'That's completely unnecessary.'

He shrugged, nonchalant, unconcerned. Her throat felt as though it were lined with acid. 'As you wish.'

*I don't wish!* She blinked rapidly as she lifted some spaghetti to her mouth, silencing herself before she could make the protestation. This was best—for both of them. It was what they had agreed to, and she needed to go through with it.

* * *

Two nights to go. Luca was impatient and unsettled. He couldn't focus. He sat through meeting after meeting, glowering, so his staff assumed a permanently worried air—and he didn't notice. His mind was absorbed by another issue.

Olivia's departure.

A month had seemed like an interminable period of time when they'd first agreed to it. It was longer than he'd spent with any woman, since Jayne. He'd thought it would drag, and that he'd be glad to see her go, but he wasn't an idiot. He couldn't ignore the fact that he was looking forward to her departure in the same way a man might look forward to chopping off his own arm.

So, what to do?

He stood abruptly, and the meeting grew silent. He scanned the room, fixed his glance on his vice president and nodded. 'Take it from here.'

He needed to be alone; he needed to think.


Olivia packed carefully, each item she folded neatly reminding her of their honeymoon, when Luca had surprised her with bag after bag of couture—of a trip she'd had no expectations of, but that had quickly morphed into something way beyond her wildest dreams. In fact, that basically summed up their entire marriage. Nothing was what she'd expected, it had all been so much more.

She heard the closing of the downstairs door and her pulse went into overdrive.

Luca.

She continued folding, one dress after another, her

heart stammering in her chest, until she felt him behind her and turned slowly, a practised smile on her face. 'Hello. How was your day?'

She heard the stilted, formal question, so at odds with the relationship they'd developed, and winced.

He stood against the door jamb, casually reclined, as though he had not a care in the world, but there was something in his face, a mask of concentration, that made a mockery of his pose.

'Why are you packing? You don't leave for two nights.'

Two days. The words were like thunderclaps in her chest.

'I like to be organized,' she offered with a tight smile.

He said nothing for some time, simply watched her, and then, finally, his words broke the silence that was tightening the air in the room.

'I've been thinking.'

She continued with what she was doing, but her actions were stilted, because she was having to concentrate hard on such a simple task. Everything felt unnatural.

'Well, that's good, I suppose.' She aimed for levity, even when her cells were reverberating with a desperate need to know *what* he'd been thinking.

'When we agreed to get married, it was for a very specific purpose. Each of us benefited, and we made sure the marriage would work for us both—by having clear-cut rules in place.'

She arched a brow, her smile a quirk of her lips. 'I remember.' She cleared her throat, reaching for another dress. He pushed up off the door jamb, coming into the room, hands in pockets.

'When we agreed to sleep together, it was the same thing—we made an arrangement, we drew out the terms of what we were doing, to make sure we were on the same page.'

She nodded once, placing the dress in her suitcase, her fingers shaking a little.

'One of the terms was that our marriage would end after a month.'

She reached for a blouse. 'I'm familiar with what we agreed.' Her response was sharper than she'd intended.

His eyes narrowed. 'And what if we were to renegotiate the terms of our marriage?'

Her heart leaped without her consent. 'Which terms, in particular?'

'The term in which you leave.'

The world stopped spinning. She stared at Luca, trying not to react, trying not to feel, but her heart was exploding with something terrifyingly like joy.

'Hear me out.' He lifted a hand placatingly, perhaps misreading her expression. 'This marriage is obviously different—better—than either of us thought it would be. Why walk away from it after only a month?'

Her breath burned in her lungs.

'Why stay?' she asked instead, because she knew the answer she would give, but what was Luca's? Everything hung on his response. She stood there, waiting, and hating, because in that moment she became a child again, waiting for approval, waiting for more than it was possible to be given—by the man in front of her, at least. But Luca wasn't her father. What if she was wrong? What if?

'Because this works,' he said quickly, with no idea of how those words fell like the executioner's blade. 'We're good together, and a marriage like this—a marriage that's logical and sensible—suits us both.'

She bit down on her lower lip, rather than contradicting him.

'You saw your parents' disastrous marriage and swore it would never be for you. But what I'm offering is so different. I'm not suggesting we stay married because we're in love, nor because we're emotionally involved. I'm suggesting it because we're neither of those things. I like being around you, I like spending time together, I love sleeping with you. We make a good team. Isn't that worth staying for? Worth fighting for?'

Her heart was racing far too fast. A thousand things flashed into her mind, but she wasn't sure if she was brave enough to say them. He talked about fighting for their marriage, but she couldn't. She couldn't fight for what she'd never get—her mother had spent a lifetime doing that, fighting for the love of her husband, and it was withheld, cruelly, callously. Luca wouldn't ever intentionally hurt Olivia, but the effect would be the same regardless, because he'd never love her.

She stood straighter as the thought struck her like a lightning bolt, acceptance right behind. Of course, she loved him. The thought sank her like a lead balloon. She *loved* him. She loved her husband. Her eyes were as wide as saucers as she looked at him, shock reverberating through her.

'I know your experience with marriage was traumatic. The way your parents were with each other, the way your father treated your mother.' He moved closer to her and she flinched, because her heart was too raw for him to touch her. 'The love they shared turned to hate.' He lifted a hand to her cheek and her eyes swept shut, the contact sending shock waves through her body. 'That would never happen with us. A marriage that's built on respect and friendship, a partnership rather than a romance, protects us both.'

'But can't you hear how cold it is?'

His eyes flared. 'There is *nothing* cold between us.'

She bit down on her lip. 'I don't mean sex. I mean— emotionally. I don't want what you're describing.'

His eyes darkened. 'You don't want more of what we've shared this last month?'

Of course she did. She yearned for that.

'You don't want to depend on anyone,' he said gently. 'You want independence, at all costs. I'm not asking you to sacrifice that. I'm not asking you to share more of yourself than you're willing to share. That's why this works so well. Without love, we can be calm and dispassionate, we can meet each other's needs, we can be friends who see the world together, who live side by side. Hell, we can even share a family of our own one day, without any risk of getting hurt. Can't you see how right that is?'

No, it was all wrong. So much of what he was offering made her heart swell, because it was what she wanted—to see the world with him, to have a family with him, but without love? Even when she had seen the dark side of love, and was terrified by its power, she knew she couldn't stay with Luca, loving him as she did. It was better to leave, to nurse a broken heart, than to stay and yearn for what he'd never give.

'It's not what I want,' she whispered gently.

So gently he had to lean closer to hear her words properly.

'I have a life back in England, Luca.'

'Do you? Because it never sounds like much of a life, when you talk about it.'

Her eyes dipped between them. He was right; he knew her too well. She swallowed past a lump in her throat, and then his finger was lifting her chin, tilting her face to his.

'I have responsibilities.'

'So we'll go back for the weekend,' he said with a nonchalant shrug. 'It's a couple of hours in a plane.'

'No.' Now that she understood her feelings, she couldn't pretend any longer. The time they had left was going to be a minefield. She fidgeted her hands in front of her, then lifted one to his chest. 'We had a deal.'

Disbelief was etched in the lines of his face. 'And that deal originally included no sex. Then we realised we were attracted to one another and we changed the deal. Why can't we do that again?'

She dipped her head forward.

'Try it for three months. If this isn't working, we can both walk away then.'

But she wouldn't be able to walk away. If she was already finding the prospect to be a form of torture, how hard would it be in twelve weeks' time?

'I don't want to change our agreement.'

Something shifted in his features. Rejection? Her heart ached. She was hurting him. And he was hurting her. It was exactly what they'd sworn they wouldn't do.

'I see.'

'No, you don't,' she said with a small shake of her head.

He lifted a finger to her lips, silencing her. 'It's okay. It was just an idea, *cara*.'

She opened her mouth to explain, then slammed it shut. Just an idea. No big deal. He didn't care. It didn't matter. None of this did. When she left he'd replace her because, ultimately, she meant nothing to him. She was a convenient wife, just as she'd always been a convenient daughter, flying beneath the radar. Olivia's heart was on the line, Luca was simply trying to manoeuvre a beneficial relationship into lasting a bit longer. She'd said 'no', and now he was brushing it aside. 'Shall we eat out?'

She barely slept. Their strange conversation played over and over in her mind, tormenting her, making her doubt the wisdom of her response, so she wondered why she hadn't just accepted his suggestion. It would mean more time with him. Wasn't that what she wanted?

But at what cost?

Dawn light filtered into his room and, beside her, Luca woke, pushing out of bed and striding into the en suite bathroom. Olivia rolled over and pretended to sleep, pretended not to care that it was the first morning in weeks they hadn't made love. Her heart was splintering into a thousand little shards.

* * *

The house felt like a mausoleum suddenly. Olivia couldn't find peace, couldn't get comfortable. She didn't want to go out—she was too tired from a sleepless night—and she was finished packing. There was nothing left to occupy her, which left her mind with too much time to fret, to obsess, to panic.

Olivia caught a reflection of herself as she moved from one room to the next and stopped in her tracks. Her face was drawn, her lips turned downwards, her eyes dull, devoid of spark. She looked like her mother often had. Miserable.

Was this what heartache felt like? How had her mother lived with it for so many years?

And suddenly, Olivia knew she couldn't stay any longer. One more night sounded simple enough, but it would be a torment beyond what she could manage. She was turning into her mother, allowing herself to be hurt, and Olivia knew one thing: she wanted better than that. She pulled her phone from her back pocket and began arranging the logistics, bringing her flight forward and booking a car.

It felt surreal to coordinate this, and wrong to do so without Luca's knowledge, but wasn't her independence something she valued? They were two strangers, really, regardless of what had happened in the last month. She'd fought hard—not for their marriage in the end, but for her own life, for her independence—and now she could step into it and enjoy the fruits of her labour. She could go home and see Sisi, and know that her sister would never have to make the kind of pragmatic marriage Olivia had.

She told herself it was relief she was experiencing as the cab driver loaded her suitcase into the boot, the engine idling. She gave one last look at his exquisite home, then slid into the back seat of the car, dark glasses in place.

It was only once she'd checked in her suitcase at the buzzing Fiumicino airport that she dared to call Luca. She'd contemplated leaving a note at his house, but that had felt wrong. And she'd known she couldn't see him again, couldn't say what she needed to say face to face. It was cowardly, but self-preservation instincts were in overdrive.

He answered after one ring. 'Olivia.'

God, she would miss hearing him say her name. 'Luca.'

'How are you?'

She squeezed her eyes shut as tears filled her gaze. 'I'm fine,' she lied, shaking her head a little. 'Look, there was so much I didn't say last night, because I couldn't find the words at the time, and I was scared to admit what I wanted, when you were offering something so reasonable and sensible, something I might have jumped at, in another life.'

Each of his breaths was audible as he waited for her to continue.

'The thing is, the way my father treated my mother, it's just like you said—love turned to hate. They did love each other at one time, and they were happy, and then things went wrong, he never forgave her, and she was miserable. She's still miserable. There's nothing quite so awful as being married to someone you love, who doesn't love you back.' The words hung between them like little blades.

'But what I was offering cut that concern out of the equation.'

Her smile was bitter. 'For you, perhaps, but not for me.'

'I don't understand.'

'I know that.' Despite her efforts, a sob caught in her throat, punctuating the final word.

'Olivia, what is it? You're upset.'

'No.' She blinked around the terminal, the fluorescent light too bright, even with her dark sunglasses. A voice came over the speakers, muffled by static. She stood, pulling her handbag strap over her shoulder.

'Where are you?'

'I'm at the airport.' She sniffed.

'The airport? What the hell? Your flight's tomorrow.'

'I moved it forward.'

'Why?'

'What's the point in drawing this out? We want different things.'

'Because I asked you to stay another three months?'

'Because you asked me to stay *only* another three months.'

'To begin with,' he insisted, muffled noise in the background. 'You were the one who balked at the idea of a real marriage—'

'But that's not what you were offering.'

'You know what I mean—a lasting marriage, like we

have now, but ongoing. I thought three months would reassure you that there was an escape clause.'

'I don't want an escape clause.'

'Then why are you at the airport?'

She groaned, tilting her head back to stare at the ceiling. 'I realised something, last night. When you were offering a perfectly reasonable loveless relationship, a marriage founded, in fact, on the absence of love, I came to understand that it's the exact opposite of what I want. I love you, Luca. Somehow, I fell in love with you, despite having sworn I'd never love anyone. And if I stay here in Rome, with you, I'll start to hope you'll love me back, and the hoping will make me miserable, just like my mother was.'

'What did you just say?'

She moved towards the boarding gate, tears streaming down her cheeks now.

'My worst fear is being married to someone I love, who doesn't love me back. I know what that can do to a person, and I can't do it to myself—even for one more night. Now that I understand how I feel about you, I have no choice but to leave.'

'Olivia—'

'It's okay,' she interrupted. 'I've thought about this from every angle. I just wish I was brave enough to have said this to your face, so that you could see the genuine gratitude in my eyes when I thank you for what you did for me.'

He groaned almost inaudibly. 'Stay. Spend tonight with me.' His voice was deep and throaty. 'Come home.'

'But this isn't my home,' she said with finality. 'And

you're not really my husband. You never were. A marriage isn't a marriage without love, we both know that.' She waited for him to disagree, bracing for it, and then, after a long pause, shook her head. 'Goodbye, Luca.'

# CHAPTER FOURTEEN

'OH, COME ON,' she groaned, slapping her forehead as the announcement came over the PA.

'Owing to a technical issue with the landing wheel, Aster Airline flight 251 to London Heathrow has been delayed. We apologise for the inconvenience. Another update will be provided in thirty minutes. Thank you for your patience.'

Olivia ground her teeth together, scanning the departures board, hoping a different airline might be making the same trip to London, so she could book another seat, but there were no other flights for the next two hours.

Resigning herself to her fate, she strode towards the newsagent's, browsing magazines, looking for something, anything, to distract herself with. But a sense of claustrophobia was clawing at her. Having decided she wanted to leave Rome, that she needed to leave Rome, she found the delay completely unacceptable.

She chose two magazines at random, paid for them without looking at the covers, then found a seat apart from most of the crowd. Rather than reading the magazines, she stared out of the large, heavily tinted windows, at the concourse, watching as passengers disembarked planes directly onto the runway, from skinny staircases, walking in organised lines towards the building. Planes took off, others landed, but after thirty minutes another announcement was made: their plane would be delayed at least another hour.

It was tempting to go to the information desk and ask for more information, but the queue snaked halfway through their seating area, and the staff member there was already looking harried and stressed. Olivia had no interest in adding to her load.

She continued to watch the happenings of the airport, the piercing blue of Rome's sky making a mockery of her mood.

In her peripheral vision, she was aware of another traveller approaching and she bristled, wanting company like she wanted a hole in the head. She kept her gaze resolutely focused on the window, staring at the sky, actively discouraging any attempt at communication.

'Do you need a lift, *cara*?'

Her heart went into overdrive and her head turned towards him in complete shock, his voice jolting something inside her to life. She was too overcome to pretend calm. How grateful she was that her dark glasses were still in place!

'Luca! What are you doing here?'

'Did you think I would not move heaven and earth to finish our conversation?'

She stood up to meet his eyes, not liking the height disadvantage of her seated position.

'We did finish our conversation.'

'Too abruptly.'

'What else is there to say?'

He looked around, and in that moment she allowed herself the brief weakness of drinking him in, all suit-clad, six and a half feet of him. The power of his physique took her breath away, as it almost always did.

'More than I'd care to discuss here,' he said with a shake of his head, holding out his hand. 'Come with me.'

She looked at his hand as though it were a bundle of snakes.

'My jet is fuelled up. I'll fly you to London. We can speak on the way.'

Her lips parted. The offer of the flight was tempting—but to have her escape route shared with the very man she was running away from?

His eyes darkened as her hesitation became obvious.

'Fine,' he ground out. 'You can take the flight without me.' He lifted one finger to the air. 'On one condition.'

'Another deal?'

'Yes.'

'What is it?'

'Give me ten minutes first. To talk. Privately.'

Privately. A shiver ran down her spine, desire sparking in her belly. She looked away. 'Okay, that's fair enough.' Had she really thought she could avoid this? 'Where?'

But he took her hand, drawing her with him, away from the crowds, the disgruntled voices, and right back out of the terminal, towards a central concourse, and then across it. Neither of them spoke—not even when he gestured for her to enter a set of timber doors ahead of him.

A first-class lounge, so exclusive it wasn't even badged, awaited them. Luca was clearly known here by name. Here, it was easy to find a private corner—there were only half a dozen or so other travellers, and the room was enormous.

At a table in the distant corner, he pulled out a seat. She eyed it sceptically, nervously, then eased herself into it.

'Thank you.'

He took the seat opposite, and the table seemed to shrink about three sizes. She toyed with her hands in her lap, then forced herself to stop, to meet his gaze. To be strong enough to do this.

'What would you like to discuss?'

His laugh was a short, sharp sound, totally lacking amusement. 'What you said on the phone, for one.'

'Which part?'

His eyes narrowed. 'Which part do you think?'

She compressed her lips, the answer obvious. 'Why?'

'Olivia, you told me you *never* wanted to fall in love. When we agreed to this marriage—'

'I know that. I'm sorry.'

'You're sorry?'

'We had a deal. I broke it. I never meant to. I didn't *want* to love you.'

'How do you know it's love?'

She frowned, the question totally surprising her. 'How do I know the sky is blue or the earth is round?'

'Science?'

She smiled despite the heaviness in her heart. 'Fact. And this is fact. Not scientific, perhaps, but no less real.'

'Since when?'

Another question she hadn't expected. 'I can't say. Probably the moment you heard me out. I half expected you to get me thrown out of that party in Rome. That you didn't, that you listened and agreed to my crazy proposal, showed me what a decent guy you were. And every day since—'

'And every night?'

'Yes, every night.' She swallowed. 'But this isn't just about sex. I mean, that's a part of what I love, but it's so much more than that.'

He stood up, scraping his chair backwards, pacing towards the windows, gazing for a moment at the aeroplanes lined up on the tarmac, their tails forming a perfect line, then turning, staring at her as if pulling her apart piece by piece. 'The thing is, Olivia, I need to know that you know, beyond a shadow of a doubt. Because I thought I was in love, once, and I believed my wife loved me, but it was the worst mistake of my life. And yet, the impact of Jayne's breaking up with me is nothing compared to this.' He returned to the table, bracing his palms on the edge. 'With her, my pride was hurt. I was blindsided. But losing you—'

She held her breath, her features contorted by confusion.

'I can't have you say that you love me, if you are then

going to decide you don't. I can't let this be a real marriage, in every way, unless you promise me that's what you want. Don't you see, Olivia? I suggested a continuation of what we had because it was safe. What you're offering, what you're asking for, is filled with risks.'

'Yes.' She nodded, her heart soaring at what he was unintentionally revealing. Or was he? Her own feelings burned so brightly, she feared she'd lost the ability to comprehend his. 'I'm aware of that. Like the risk that you might not love me back. Or that your love for me might turn to hate, just as my father's did for my mother.'

'I know enough about love turning to hate. I had a masterclass in it with Jayne. But that doesn't mean I would ever hurt you. Not like your father hurt your mother.' His eyes probed hers. 'Ask yourself if I could ever be capable of the things he did, or if you could ever act as Jayne did. You know the answer to that.'

She bit back a sob.

'I love you because you're nothing like him,' she whispered, dipping her head forward. 'But that doesn't mean you won't hurt me. That you're not hurting me now.'

He crouched down in front of her face, reaching out and removing her glasses, placing them on the table softly. At the sight of her tear-reddened eyes, he cursed softly. 'I don't want you to go.'

'I know that.' Anguish tore through her. 'But I can't stay.'

'Even for love?'

'My loving you isn't enough. You know that.'

'What about the fact I love you, too? What about the fact I am terrified of what that means, but I'm here, saying it anyway, because I know one thing for certain—if I lose you, I will regret it for the rest of my life.'

Her lips parted in surprise.

He lifted up, curling a hand around her cheek. 'I didn't realise, until you called me an hour ago, and told me you loved me, that the reason I can't bear the thought of you leaving our marriage as agreed is because I don't want you to leave—ever.'

'You said that last night,' she groaned. 'But it's not enough to want me to stay. That's *not* love, it's convenience.'

He pressed a finger to her lips. 'I asked you to stay, not because I want to continue our convenient arrangement, but because I don't want to live without you. Because you have given meaning to my life, because you have made me smile again, *cara*, and because with you, not only do I feel complete, I *feel*, in here, after years of nothing.' He tapped a hand to his heart. 'Is there any part of you that wants to walk away from this?'

She squeezed her eyes shut, everything she'd ever known to be true in her life like an enormous impediment. 'No,' she whispered, finally. 'But I'm scared.'

'And I am terrified,' he countered. 'I thought I had been through the pits of hell when Jayne left me. I thought that was as bad as it got. But now, I imagine a life without you, I imagine you waking up and deciding you no longer want me in your life, and I know that it would be ten thousand times worse.'

She blinked, his passion obvious.

'Yet, I am kneeling here now, asking you to stay with me regardless because, whatever I fear, a life with you is worth the risk.'

Her throat was too thick with unshed tears for Olivia to speak coherently. A muffled sob escaped.

'I do not want you simply to stay,' he said, after a moment. 'I want you to marry me, for real. This time, in front of family, friends, the world. I want everyone to join in the celebration of our love, to witness our commitment, to understand that I am pledging myself to you, for the rest of my life. Love is a leap of faith, but what is the alternative, Olivia? To both run from our past, to keep ourselves closed off?' He lifted closer to her, so their mouths were separated by only an inch. 'To lose one another? This? For me to live each day without you, without what we share? Is there anything worse than that?'

Anguish tortured her, but it was pierced by hope and joy. She shook her head, tears rolling down her cheeks. 'There is nothing worse than losing you,' she confirmed.

'And so you never shall,' he promised. 'Olivia, the last time we discussed marrying, it was with very carefully worded conditions in place. Now, I ask you this: Will you marry me? With no condition, no caution, no limitation on our joy, our future? Marry me, stand beside me—your own person, as independent as you seek to be—but with my companionship, my love, and always, always, my support.'

A smile cracked her face. She closed the rest of the

distance between them, kissing him, and into the kiss, into his soul, she said the word 'yes', over and over and over again, because she felt it in every fibre of her being, every part of her own soul. She loved him, and always would. While it was true that love was a gamble, a leap of faith, the strength of their love had given them both wings to catch them, should they fall. She trusted Luca, and knew her heart to be safe with him—there was nothing she wanted more than to return to their life, as his wife, and to truly start living.

'Luca?'

'Mmm?'

'Let's go home.'

His eyes widened, the meaning of her statement not lost on him.

'*Sì, cara*. Let's go home.'

Luca loved his wife, and he loved her in a way that had expanded his soul, had expanded everything he knew about life. He'd learned that the fear he'd felt was actually excitement, that stepping into a life with Olivia gave him an adrenaline rush every day. A month after their airport reunion, they were married, and only one week later Olivia realised the reason for her changeable appetite and sudden aversion to cured meats and alcohol. A honeymoon baby, or close to, conceived during their first week together in Rome, when they had been making love and falling in love all at the same time. So that now, eight months after Olivia had told Luca she loved him, and he'd realised how he felt about her, he stared down at a little infant wrapped in pink, a new kind of love stealing through him, happiness making him feel as though he could take on the world.

'She is perfect, *cara*. How clever you are.'

'I think we can both take credit for her,' Olivia said with a smile, head pressed back against the crisp white hospital pillow. Luca had never loved her more.

'That is very kind of you.'

'Would you hand her to me?' Olivia asked, tired, but arms aching to once again hold their hours-old daughter.

'*Certo.*' He picked up their newborn, cradling her to his chest a moment before snuggling her into Olivia's arms, and watching as their baby nestled against her. Completion wrapped around him. Everything in his life was perfect.

The sound of wheels on linoleum woke Olivia, and a moment later Luca appeared, pushing Pietra into the hospital room. Three days after giving birth, and Olivia was feeling somewhat normal, except for breasts that suddenly felt so enormous she wasn't sure how she could stand without toppling over.

'Ah, Nonna.' Olivia smiled, pushing up to standing and wincing slightly.

'Stay, stay,' Pietra insisted, so much frailer than the last time they'd seen each other, but with eyes still sparkling with intelligence and wit, and a ready smile softening her slender face. Her continued wellness was, doctors kept saying, a 'miracle', but Olivia knew better. Pietra wasn't finished yet—from the moment she'd learned of Olivia's pregnancy, it had seemed to give her a new lease on life, a determination to stave off the ravages of her disease, or perhaps it was fate, being as kind to Pietra as it had been to Luca and Olivia, when it had delivered them into one another's arms. 'You do not need to get up.'

'I want to bring the baby to you,' Olivia demurred, love in her eyes as they met Luca's.

'Thank you,' he mouthed.

She moved to the plastic-sided crib and removed the swaddle, then lifted her daughter out. She placed her carefully in Pietra's arms, aware that Luca was there, waiting, ready to intervene if Pietra's strength failed her.

'She is so lovely.' A tear slid down Pietra's cheek. 'So much like you, Olivia.'

Olivia stroked their baby's head. 'I see a fair bit of Giovanardi in her as well.'

'Do you?' Pride touched Pietra's face.

'Oh, yes. She has your eyes.'

The baby grabbed Pietra's finger, curling her tiny fingers around its frail length.

'Does she have a name yet?'

'Actually, that is something we wanted to discuss with you,' Luca said, nodding, gently prompting Olivia to continue.

'We were wondering how you would feel about us calling her Pietra.'

Pietra's lips parted in surprise. 'I would be touched, of course. Are you sure?'

'It's the only name we considered,' Olivia promised. 'To us, she's already Pietra.'

* * *

'Luca, look!'

'What is it, *cara*?' On the eve of their tenth wedding anniversary, Luca emerged from the kitchen, apron tied around his waist, looking impossibly sexy. She loved him in myriad ways, but his determination to learn to cook for her and their children, and to be a present, hands-on father and husband, made her fall in love with him more and more each day.

'Look what I found!' She carried the item, wrapped carefully in bubble wrap, to Luca, triumph in her features.

'A toy? I don't know. What is it? The children's teeth?'

Olivia laughed, lifting a finger to her lips. 'You know the *fatina dei denti* takes those away.' She held the bubble wrap out to him. 'I was looking for my wedding dress, on a whim. Pietra was asking about it.'

'I am not surprised it was our daughter, rather than the twins.' He laughed with paternal indulgence.

'Rafaello and Fiero are busy with their soccer match, of course.' She rolled her eyes, because it seemed to be all their seven-year-old sons cared for at present. 'Anyway, I was looking in the box of wedding things, and found this.'

He peeled the tab of the sticky tape, casting his wife a rueful glance as she hopped from foot to foot, until eventually he revealed what was within: the Murano *fenice*. He looked from the bird to Olivia, shaking his head. 'I had quite forgotten about this.'

'Yes, me too. It's exquisite. Do you remember the day we chose him?'

'I do.'

'How did we ever forget?'

'Life,' he said with a warm smile. 'We have been busy living.'

Happiness spread through Olivia. 'Well, now I don't feel quite so bad. Where shall we put it?'

'Somewhere prominent,' Luca said, and then, as an afterthought, 'But far from the boys' football kicks.'

She laughed, sashaying through the living room, placing the bird atop the grand piano little Pietra was obsessed with playing each night.

'Perfect. And here it will stand to remind us that, from the ashes, good things really can rise,' Luca murmured, wrapping his arms around his wife, pressing his chin to her shoulder. They stared at the bird, content, and grateful, all at once.

'What time is Sienna arriving?'

Olivia glanced at her wristwatch. 'Their flight should land any minute.'

'Then I had better get back to the kitchen.' He kissed her cheek, then spun her in the circle of his arms, seeking her lips, never able to pass up an opportunity to taste his beloved wife.

'Are you sure you don't have any spare time?' she asked silkily, wrapping her arms behind his back, just as the twins burst into the room, speaking in rapid-fire Italian about alleged on-field grievances, so Olivia and Luca shared a glance of amusement and pulled slightly apart.

'Come into the kitchen and tell me about it, *terra-motti*,' Luca said, then, leaning closer and whispering, purely for Olivia's benefit, 'Tonight, *mi amore.* Tonight.'

It was a promise he intended to keep—for that night, and every night for the rest of their lives.

\* \* \* \* \*

*Fell in love with*
Vows on the Virgin's Terms?

*Don't forget to catch the next instalment in
The Cinderella Sisters duet!*

*In the meantime,
check out these other
Clare Connelly stories!*

Their Impossible Desert Match
An Heir Claimed by Christmas
Cinderella's Night in Venice
My Forbidden Royal Fling
Crowned for His Desert Twins

*Available now!*

# WE HOPE YOU ENJOYED
## THIS BOOK FROM

### 🅷 HARLEQUIN

# PRESENTS

*Escape to exotic locations where passion knows no bounds.*

Welcome to the glamorous lives of royals and billionaires, where passion knows no bounds. Be swept into a world of luxury, wealth and exotic locations.

**8 NEW BOOKS AVAILABLE EVERY MONTH!**

### #3981 FORBIDDEN NIGHTS IN BARCELONA
*The Cinderella Sisters*
by Clare Connelly

Set aflame by the touch of totally off-limits Alejandro Corderó, Sienna does the unthinkable and proposes they have a secret week of sensual surrender in Barcelona. But an awakening under the Spanish sun may prove seven nights won't be enough...

### #3982 SNOWBOUND IN HIS BILLION-DOLLAR BED
by Kali Anthony

Running from heartbreak and caught in a bitter snowstorm, Lucy's forced to seek shelter in reclusive Count Stefano's castle. Soon, she finds herself longing to unravel the truth behind his solitude and the searing heat promised in his bed...

### #3983 CLAIMING HIS VIRGIN PRINCESS
*Royal Scandals*
by Annie West

Hounded by the paparazzi after two failed engagements, Princess Isla of Altbourg escapes to Monaco. She'll finally let her hair down in private. Perhaps irresistible self-made Australian billionaire Noah Carson can help...?

### #3984 DESERT PRINCE'S DEFIANT BRIDE
by Julieanne Howells

A pretend engagement to Crown Prince Khaled wasn't part of Lily's plan to prove her brother's innocence, but the brooding sheikh is quite insistent. Their simmering chemistry makes playing his fiancée in public easy—and resisting temptation in private impossible!

---

**YOU CAN FIND MORE INFORMATION ON UPCOMING HARLEQUIN TITLES, FREE EXCERPTS AND MORE AT HARLEQUIN.COM.**

HPCNMRB0122A